In

by

Reviews

"Slaves of Men and Gods: Obroni Tales – Book One by Jacqueline Smith is an arresting, enlightening novel. It weaves urgent themes into its compelling plot and comes highly recommended by Chick Lit Café." Edith Emunah for Chick Lit Café Book Reviews

"In The Two Seeings, it was almost as if I was standing in the past and observing everything that was going on. The book was very thrilling and I enjoyed every aspect. The characters were well-developed and the storyline was compelling and enlightening. OnlineBookClub.org

Cast of Characters in/around the Maguire Family

Grandpa Harry Maguire b-1830 (Co. Fermanagh) 12-19yrs old during famine

d-August 1897 -67yrs & M-1853/**Grandma Mary nee Corsigan** b-1835

(Co. Fermanagh) 10-15yrs old at famine-d-1902-67yrs Mother & Father of...

Francis Maguire b -1861(Co. Fermanagh) - M-April 1885 –

Carter/Porter/Gatekeeper at Kirkston Mill

Uncle Bernard (Francis' eldest brother)-b 1854 (Co. Fermanagh-d- Greenock)

Uncle Harry (Francis' younger brother) b-1862 (Co. Fermanagh-d- Greenock)

(Francis' brothers in Ireland-**Seamus –b-1865 & Paddy-b-1871**

(Co. Fermanagh)

(Francis' sisters in Ireland: **Marg-b-1856-d.1865 /Catherine-b-1869/ Mary-b-1872** (Co. Fermanagh)

Aunt Rose Ann Watson-(Francis' elder sister) b-1857 (Co. Fermanagh-d.- Maldon, Massachusetts)

Aunt Rebecca Harman-(Francis' younger sister) b.1867 (Co. Fermanagh-d.- Boston, Massachusetts)

Rachel Scott –Francis' Cousin-M-

John Scott – Rachel's Husband (Alloa)

~

Matthew McInnley b- 1833 (Co. Monaghan)- d-(Glasgow)

Granny Annie (McInnley) **nee O'Connell** b-1835 (Co. Meath)

10-15yrs old during Famine, Glasgow

Mother & Father of...

Caitlin Maguire nee McInnley b-Jan 1861-(Glasgow), M-April 1885

(Caitlin's sisters- **Susan, Elizabeth & Margaret)** (Glasgow)

Bernie Maguire (F& C's 1st Son) b-January1886 (Glasgow)

Nora Maguire (F& C's 1st Daughter) b-Sep 1887 M - June 1919

Frank Maguire (F& C's 2nd Son) b- 1888 M-Jan 1915-Elizabeth Carberry (b-1885) (Glasgow)

Michael Maguire (F& C's 3rd Son) -b Sep 1890(Glasgow)

Caity Maguire (F& C's 2nd Daughter)-b-1893 M-1916-Jack Cameron (b-1892) (Glasgow)

Patrick Maguire (F& C's 4th Son) b-1896 - M-Feb 1923 Margaret O'Neill (b-1895) (Glasgow)

Jeannie Maguire (F& C's 3rd Daughter)-b-1898 (Glasgow)

Seamus Maguire (F& C's 5th Son) b-1899 M-1927-Anne McMahon (Glasgow/Paisley)

Mary Maguire (F& C's 4th Daughter) b. 1902-Ninth and

final child of Francis & Caitlin (Glasgow)

Paddy Maguire – Mary's cousin b- 1885 (Enniskillen, Fermanagh)

Therese Maguire b-1921(London)

~

Victor Simpson (Nora's husband) b-Mar 1892(Gorton, Lancashire)

John Murphy - Francis' Best Friend - Engineer (Glasgow)

Malky Murray – Francis' work mate - Carter (Glasgow)

Father O'Toole - Childhood Priest at St. Michaels' Apostolic Church (Nr. Ireland)

Father McNulty - Weddings & Victor's Confirmation; Priest at St. Michaels' Apostolic Church (Ireland)

Dr. Tom Paterson - Homeopath at Glasgow Homeopathic Hospital

Dr. Agnes Moore - Homeopath at Glasgow Homeopathic Hospital

Commander Walsh - Medical Officer at Cowden Hall Rehabilitation Centre

Pete Palmer- Mary's partner in Boston

~

CONTENTS

PRELUDE – Mary Maguire

The letter in Mary's hand shook with the tremble travelling through her body as it moved down her arms and shook again as a final jerk of her fingers propelled it to the floor. Seeing the name of the adoption agency Mary shook again as she realised it wouldn't have caused quite such a dramatic reaction to most other people but for her, it had been so long. She'd not forgotten, could never do so. But why hear now? Her breath was ragged on her shocked inhale making her cough, her breath coming fast and shallow as she stared down at it.

Maybe it wasn't that. After all, it could just be a request for a donation like most of these types of letters. She was getting carried away with herself, panicking for no good reason. She was thrown because how could they have found her? She hesitated to pick up the letter and then did so gingerly with the tips of her finger and thumb, holding it as far away from her body as possible while memories tumbled one over the other in her mind. Images of trains and faces, colours and places, and a rush of emotion pulsating in her belly as she quickly opened the nearest drawer and dropped in the letter before slamming it closed. She'd deal with it later, much later...donation or not. A deep exhale escaped her lips as she stumbled into her small sitting room and collapsed, still trembling into an armchair—then the remembering began.

~

It was like the same problem she had with her family. No sooner would she have sorted herself out and there they were. Try as she might to disappear them into the family drawer in her mind, at points over the years eventually one or other of her remaining sisters or brothers would write or call looking for her opinion or help or to give her some unwarranted, unwanted bit of advice or news; usually of the disturbing kind.

It hadn't always been like this. She was the baby of the family, or at least of those in her generation. Then again, apparently her brother, the eldest one - first born and usually most lauded, had been and gone before she was born and already aged thirty-one by then. So maybe there'd been more than one generation even just between her and her siblings. Bernie had not been forgotten. Having died in the First World War, his death was recorded at Arras in Belgium for posterity. But not just in Belgium, she reluctantly reminded herself, but also much closer to home on a stained-glass window in St Michael's Apostolic Chapel in Kirkston. Its very name made her shudder at the thought. Stale scents of incense and old man sweat wafted in from the past and she wrinkled her nose, sneezing it away before the memories sneakily surfaced. But yes, that village had been her beginning and went on to shape her future. Though some other, older family influences shaped her just as much, and had refused to stay in the past.

Her Granny O'Connell had early on confused everyone by reverting to her maiden name after her husband died, but then again that was mostly hearsay to Mary, having come at the tail-end of her own mother's lengthy reproductive surge.

God, how had she have managed having all those children so close together? It was beyond Mary, but as these things turn out, not beyond her older sister Nora, who'd had as many into the next generation and God only knew where they all were now.

~

Still, Mary had loved her Granny O'Connell. She remembered that visiting her was a bit of an adventure, especially as a child in those days. For Mary the journey was from Kirkston to Granny O'Connell's wee single-end in Tradeston, Glasgow using the horse buses, though that first time at the stop in Moorhead, wide-eyed, she'd watched the scary horses towering hugely above her. Nora had shaken her from her glaikit stare, pulling her up the steps into the carriage but not before she saw the horse dropping a big smelly plop on the cobbled street.

"Oooh yuck!" she exclaimed, holding her nose while giggling as other adults behind hurried her forward with a brisk push to sit next to Nora, who hissed "Eejit!" at her. The horse buses weren't around for many years longer after she first began staying with her Granny O'Connell. A couple of years later came the trams and a less bumpy ride.

They'd left home to travel that day after coming out of Mass. Their mammy had been a one for ensuring they got to the evening service at St. Michael's at least once a week as well as Mass on Sunday mornings. Then there was confession once a month too. At school round in Broad Street, they had prayers morning, noon and night. It was the same for everyone and she had actually enjoyed, or at least been quite affected by her Holy Communion service with the others in her class at school the year before, but who could say it wasn't to do with her mammy being ill at that time too.

She, like all the girls, had to wear a white tunic and veil while the boys wore white sashes with their smartest shirts and trousers. It seemed to her like a bairns' version of the adult weddings she occasionally glimpsed happening at the chapel; no scrambles at the bairns' version though.

She remembered being in the church downstairs in a small hall where they all waited to be called up to receive their first host from the priest. She was listening to the hymns being sung in the distance, especially the one, '*Faith of our Fathers*' when she felt a strange sensation of something alighting around her shoulders. In her belly, the feeling was like a deep presence and she had the urge to bend to her knees, but by that time she had to follow her classmates into the church to take their seats until called forward. Did that mean she'd received Jesus into her soul like in the prayer she'd said with her mammy that morning? What else could it mean and who could she have asked with her mammy sick in bed and not wanting to bother her?

A First Communion
My Jesus, I believe that You are present in the
Most Holy Sacrament. I love You above all things,
and I desire to receive You into my soul.
I believe it because you have said it and
I'm ready to give my life to maintain this truth.
Amen.

Waiting for them in front of the altar was Father O'Toole, who spoke Irish the same way her Granny O'Connell did. She didn't much like Father O'Toole with his smelly breath and fingers touching you all over whenever he got a chance, but her mammy wouldn't hear a word against him. She'd realised this after hearing her brother complaining and her mammy giving him into trouble for "Saying bad things about a priest. Do ye want to go to hell?" Was he getting special treatment too? She had a quick glance at him now, standing behind the priest waiting to do his duty as an altar boy for the service. Frank winked at her while his pal Sean had his head down engrossed in trying to undo the mangled chain of the incense burner. After the service the schoolchildren filed back downstairs to have a short Communion breakfast of a bread roll and a cup of milk.

Weeks before her Communion, Father O'Toole had told her to come to the chapel where she was to sit with him in the sacristy as he tested her Catechism. Always she had to start by answering his questions, the same ones they had to answer every day in religious instruction at school.

Who made you? God made me.

Why did God make you? God made me to know him, love him and serve him in this world, and to be happy with him forever in the next.

And it went on and on, but Mary thought the scariest bit, after many more questions and her sometimes hesitant answers, was the first part of the Apostles Creed:

Where is God? God is everywhere.

Does God know and see all things? God knows and sees all things, even our most secret thoughts.

Father O'Toole expected her to come to the chapel after school most days and she thought that was just so unfair. He wasn't asking any of the other children that she knew of, so she guessed he wasn't scaring them with his smelly hissing breath on their necks as he demanded that if she loved God, she should be very grateful for his attention. "Ye've been singled out of all your classmates to be given this special treatment," he'd said with a strange crooked smile. After he told her this she had, at first, felt very special and didn't want to share her secret with anyone, not even her best friend Kathleen at school. But mostly, because after stroking her in her dirty places and grasping her against his bony chest, she would tremble and shudder, especially when he'd warn her that God not only knows and sees, he hears all things too, "So ye'd best not be telling anyone or God will be fierce angry with ye and take away all your special treatment and leave ye to burn in hell, so."

She trembled with fear most of the time, her mammy getting annoyed with her for always dropping things and jumping with fright at the slightest touch. Each Sunday morning her belly cramped at the thought of going to Mass, but who could she tell? God would hear her. She'd be punished much worse than this if she did. After she made her Communion, it carried on for her coming Confirmation and after that was completed, he said, "Ye need me guidance so ye don't become a bad girl hanging around the fellahs at school. I'll look after ye in the flesh, like your own father would if he was still here and not already taken to heaven to be with God. Ye're very blessed to have me guidance, Mary."

"Thank you, Father," she'd say as she blessed herself and shakily genuflected under his creepy stare. She had thought to ask her Granny O'Connell on one of her monthly visits but as time went on Granny had become maudlin, spending more and more time talking about her days in the old country.

"*If we had no hope - for a cure, for the end of war, for being free of abuse, or for having food, warmth, clothing, and shelter - we would have no reason to go on. What you hope for doesn't matter, but rather the essence of hope itself.*"

Bernie Siegel

PART ONE

1845-1860

Chapter 1 - An Droc Shaol - Annie

As a woman might do in Ireland when under the influence of deep and absorbing grief, Annie O'Connell did now in Glasgow when she sat down. Locking her fingers into each other, she swayed backwards and forwards in silence. Talking again about *An Droc Shaol* -'The Bad Times' had set her mind racing with memories flooding in fast. Her granddaughters had just left to return home to their mammy in Kirkston. She tried to rest but her mind refused, taking her back again until she could remember standing outside her family's cottage. Though Co. Meath and much of Leinster were not quite so hard hit by the famine as in the west country, the house and yard had about them all the marks of recent decline. The thatch on the roof was becoming black, and in some places rotting and sinking. Everything had the sickly-sweet smell of decay. The yard itself was untidy and dirty, there being none of them left with the energy or inclination to clear or sweep.

The hedges were coming apart and walls breaking down as drystane by drystane fell to the ground and not returned to their place in the wall. Broken gates were lying about, or swinging on single hinges, no longer needed for the long-ago sold pigs. The whole air of the farm was disturbing to Annie as she looked at it, seeing it now from a stranger's view and couldn't avoid feeling shame over what had become a pointless struggle that they'd finally had to abandon. The chimneys, where the thatch had sunk down, stood up with the incrustations of lime round their bases. She could see that some of the corner bricks had fallen from the gable and the plaster was dropping from the walls and in several places, broken on the ground. The whitewash was becoming yellowed and blackening with growing mould, its smell adding to the odour of decay and neglect.

Earlier, herself and some other women and girls had been seen by those neighbours not

bedridden with the fever, at any hour of the day gathering weeds and herbs of all kinds to sustain

the meagre supplies left to them. She'd had a verbal scuffle that morning too before trudging home after procuring a few handfuls of young nettles, chicken-weed, sorrell, bug glass, and *casharraivan* roots (that would also be used for a tea or mashed in a poultice to help bring down swelling in bruises and sprains) to bring home as food. The busybody who'd been traipsing close behind her was soon pointedly demanding,

"Ye brazen jade, why are ye taking the *casharraivan* when ye've already got some chicken-weed in that there *ciseán?*"

"What, in the devil's name are ye drivin' at?" Annie snapped, while carrying on pulling from the patch of dandelions. The woman harrumphed and tutted and couldn't quiet herself.

"Many a poor stranger is lying in ditches, barns, and in outhouses without a living being to look to them, or reach them any single thing they want. And ye're takin as much as ye can while only being a colleen on her own."

"There's my mother, father, and three little ones to feed too." The woman flushed a little, the only colour in her pale cadaverous face.

"To be fair, I'm nothing but a born devil when the fit's on me. God bless you, a colleen machree and make you what you ought to be." She still watched though, waiting while Annie reluctantly pulled a last dandelion before she left the woman to finish off the patch. Carrying in her basket what she'd collected she headed for home, or to what used to feel like home.

Inside, the tables, chairs and general furniture of the house had once looked cared for but want of energy had descended in the event of all the illness and death. The months of poverty and hunger had undone the years of their previous efforts at home-keeping. The floor was beginning to break up into dips and gaps, the tables and chairs now sitting lopsided on the uneven ground. The dresser, though clean, had a cold and bare look. But worst of all, inside the chimney-brace where, in more prosperous times, they used to be able to keep sides of bacon preserved with salt arranged in rows; now showed nothing but dusty hooks on one side of the old salt-box. On the other side a stripped string of onions. With a little buttermilk in a jug, her family would be able to have her scavenging efforts with the few herbs she'd gathered.

What was left of the family consisted of her mother Mary O'Connell, and Annie, being the eldest daughter, who in the last few months Mary had seen lose her usual brightness, and the younger sisters and brother. All of them were scantily and poorly clothed in rags, and if that *slinkeen* had needed any more proof that poverty was among them, it was found in their heartbreakingly pale, emaciated features; in their careworn and depressed exhaustion, which slowed her family's movements to dead slow or stop. It was in the unusual dejection of her young sisters and brother, who, instead of being their usual cheerful and lively selves, now moped about without energy and sat drooping in corners or arguing over a space to warm themselves near the sparse fire.

They brightened for a moment when she described the scolding from that woman. Her mother, her eyes full of concern, asked, "Did ye get afeared of her?"

"Not of a vile *scuabán* like that, so. Before I let out the devil in me and told her the grass should grow at her door, she made her apologies and gave me a blessing, so I left off with the cursing." Annie could feel her fierce anger rising again at the injustice of the woman's accusation. Her mother said,

"Well, I'm glad of that. We've enough troubles without us women fighting and ending up pulling out each other's hair, so."

~

That whole summer had been a sunless and wet one. In fact, the ceaseless rain fell day after day, week after week and into the months, until the heart-breaking realisation arrived that any change for the better would now come too late. It seemed in those conditions that nothing was certain except famine, disease and death. The season was, of course, late and any crops that were ripe had a sickly look that spelled crop failure.

Most of the fields, which, in other autumns, would have been ripe and yellow, were now covered with a thin, backward crop. It looked unnaturally green, meaning maturity was out of the question. Low meadows were underwater, and since alluvial soils removed sediments and nutrients flowing in the adjacent water, the ravages of the floods were visible in layers of mud and gravel deposited over many of the wilted cornfields. The peat turf lay in soggy heaps, for there hadn't been enough sunshine to dry it properly for use. Because of this wetness in the firing, the appearance of the countryside was dreary and depressing. Owing to the difficulty with which it burned, or rather wasted away without light or heat, their view was of only masses of billowing black smoke that trailed slowly across the sky. In addition to the somber hue that the absence of the sun cast over everything, the smoke hanging like dark omens or as Annie's mammy muttered while blessing herself: "T'is *pisthroges* it is; damnable evil charms!"

In less smoky conditions corn lay cut but unharvested, scattered over fields waiting on an occasional ray of warm sunshine. Whole fields with richer soils, while waterlogged, were green

with the sprouting of destructive second growth. A morose stillness seemed to lay over everything. Groves and hedges were silent; even the birds had stopped singing and with so many people dying or leaving, the uncanny silence of absence was strange to bear. The earth seemed to mourn for those already fallen and for those still to fall. Much of the country was also under water with flooding from the overflow of rivers. While the low, monotonous hiss of bursting channels poured out, their bubbling murmur was a background to the eerie silence and the only other sound to be heard.

Chapter 2 - Roads to Nowhere - Annie

The failure of the potato crop, especially in its rotten blackness, as well as that of the grain, was not only the cause of hunger and distress but also of the sickness that soon arrived. They were forced to dig their potatoes before they were fit to eat and the consequences were disastrous. Annie, with mother Mary and their father John, had tried to lift as many potatoes from their five acres as they could but the crop putrefied overnight until it was only the stench that remained.

Annie was scared for herself and her family. She was scared of the hollows and dark shadows in her father's face, carved there from biting hunger.

"Wife, I'm away to look for some work. Sure, aren't they giving out tickets for the public works that, useless as they are, might get me a few pennies to buy some bread for us, so." Their father had then gone off to seek a ticket along with the other ravaged-by-hunger men of the nearby townlands, so as to not have to take their whole families into the workhouse. A couple of days in the first week he'd stumbled back with a heel or two of a loaf or a half bag of meal, drooping with failure; his skeletal frame aching from the heavy digging and lifting and breaking up of rocks to build roads that led nowhere. They hadn't heard from him in several weeks now and their mother was becoming fever-stricken. What was Annie to do? Her mother tossed and turned and Annie had to lean in to hear the whisper of her father's name on her mother's dry and split lips. She brought the mug close but her mother choked as she tried to gulp down the water. Heat emanated from her mother's body as the disease emptied her bowels, though the lack of sustenance available to expel made her give hoarse gasps at the cramping in her belly. Her cries became quieter and her tossing ceased as the first light of morning approached. Her racked body had nothing left to give. Instead, her life force had seeped away. Annie silently wept as she covered her mammy's face and turned to comfort her siblings.

Fever and sickness were beginning to appear in their neighbours too. The wetness of the summer and autumn had spoiled and tainted everyone's grain so much that the use of it changed the sickness caused by the unripe and blighted potatoes into a deathly epidemic. Cholera and typhus bloomed where the crops had not. This scourge and its effects, having started in the last few months, were seen carrying death and misery to every townland. The roads were becoming black with funerals and as people passed along from parish to parish, the death-bells were pealing in slow dismal tones. Each day was filled with more desolation and profound mourning that was for each family often repeated more than once. Annie's family was not immune from this grief of death and loss, since their mother had succumbed to the fever they were soon another of those families joining the line of black-clad funerals.

As they stood around their poor departed mother, Annie and her family looked marked with thin and haggard expressions from the destitute way they had been living. Skin that had been fair and glossy with better health was now pasty and drooping. The long bones of neighbours come to pay their respects were obvious in their sharp relief with their overlapping garments hanging loosely around feeble, wasted bodies. There was a dullness in everyone's eyes, which seemed to turn slowly in their sockets only with effort. It was hard at first to get the service started since everyone was distracted, most likely from the constant hunger that gnawed painfully in the belly and which, like a sense of guilt, took over their every thought and action day-to-day.

The ceremony consisted of Annie and her younger brother and sisters and a small number of neighbours and friends joining in with the prayer for the errors, frailties, and sins of the departed:

God our Father, in company with Christ,
Who died and now lives;
may they rejoice in Your kingdom,
where all our tears are wiped away.
Unite us together again in one family,
to sing Your praise forever and ever.
Amen

Annie cried quietly while grasping close her even quieter-than-usual younger siblings. Nevertheless, she felt it was a beautiful thing to see their miserable and half-famished friends and neighbours joining in the prayers and singing with weak and hoarse voices while shrunk and pinched with hunger. Especially since several of them laboured with the beginnings of illness, while others were still recovering and all sharing the grief of loss for one or more family members.

Chapter 3– Eviction - Annie

About half-a-mile from their cottage lived the greedy moneylender and local meal-monger, who

was canny for keeping back meal until the arrival of a hard year like the last few, when he'd sell it at extortionate prices. He dispensed it only at terms dictated by his own miserly spirit or, when he could stand it, the pitiful crying of those in need who were prepared to sell anything they had left.

Matt Murphy's house was filled with large chests and wooden hogsheads which, since they were never opened unless during a time of famine, had crevices musty with cobwebs. These

stretched precariously to the dresser itself, where they could be seen clinging to most of the shelves, webbed across neglected utensils that other families, when they had had some, used for food.

His enclosure beside the farmhouse in which crops were stored, was also known for having in it, throughout the year, sacks of oats or wheat or sometimes one or two large ricks of hay; all kept in the hope of a crop failure or a famine.

In a room next to the kitchen, Murphy had a beam, a pair of scales and a set of weights, all of which could have been doing with a visit from the authorities. He was seldom known to use metal weights; instead, he used round stones, which, since it skewed things in his favour, seemed to him a very beneficial way of doing business. Rogues like Murphy were probably the curse of half the townlands in the country, especially during seasons of distress and failure of crops like then.

People mulled around outside his place, silent and dejected or wasted, feeble, and sickly; sometimes in small groups of two or three. Other times a single individual was seen hurrying as if the life of some child or parent depended upon their arrival with the little meal they'd managed to barter with some last piece of land or a pig they'd hoped to keep to pay their rent with.

Then there was the magistrate who was also a middleman and found himself an interested agent in the operation of one of the worst and cruellest systems that cursed the country and its

people. A third party that stood between the head landlord and farmers.

In this system, the problem lay in the principle on which it rested, rather than in the individual who administered it. It held so many opportunities for abuse in the management of land and in payment for labour that it required much personal virtue and self-denial to be able to resist the fraud that it offered. Their middlemen landlord, had, like others before him and not only to them, whenever leases under which their property was held were near being expired, resorted to calling in the Royal Irish Constabulary to ensure removal of the family from his land and especially those who had made improvements to it. Then he could let it to other claimants at a higher rent in proportion to the improvements.

Annie suspected that Matt Murphy had taken full advantage of their situation after their father had disappeared and their mother died. In less than a week since their mother passed, the landlord came knocking and he was not alone. Several RIC officers on horseback and two on foot in their short black capes and hats, guns in hand, pushed their way inside the door when Annie had gone to answer their knock. The little ones had crawled deeper under their blanket and she could hear them whimpering at the gruff sound of the landlord's voice and their careless barging against the remaining odds and ends of furniture. She knew she couldn't stop them and while hurrying the children into their breeks, shirts and jackets, tried to bundle up anything she thought might help them outdoors: a lantern, a stone bottle, the last husk of bread. The RIC officer grasped her tightly by the arm and the children clung to her skirts as they were pushed roughly into the yard, having to watch as the fellahs dumped what was left of their possessions in a heap before a torch was put to them, quickly erupting into flames. Then the torch was thrown onto the thatch on the damp roof, where it sparked and smoked at first and Annie so hoped the damp and rain would fizzle it out. They sent another torch up onto the far side and it took light immediately. The heat of the fire, as welcome as it was in the bitter cold, made them have to step back farther and farther away from their home as its roof collapsed and their last hopes with it.

Annie with the little ones trailing behind her, made straight for Matt Murphy's place, for she knew he'd have something to do with this happening. Sure enough, the wide-eyed expression when he saw her and jouked behind his door was enough to confirm her suspicions. She pushed inside and his words stuttered and stumbled over each other in excuse and justification.

"T'wasn't till I knew yis'd be put out of your farm that I offered for it, and now you'll to be speakin ill of me everywhere, saying I bid for it over your heads—aye, an I'm not denyin it, but is that any reason that I'd not bid for a good farm, when I knew that yis'd be put out of it."

"May the crows have your carcass Murphy, ye disgustin gobshite. Me with the wee ones and nowhere to be takin them and their mammy just passed, so."

Chapter 4 - Wild Dogs - Annie

After that, passing through the fields sometimes they met small family groups like theirs bearing home on their shoulders with difficulty a coffin or two. People's features were gaunt, eyes wild and hollow and their gait feeble and tottering. Apart from the fever from starvation; in cholera, victims were cut down by a sudden stroke, which caused a shock both to the victim and the survivors. Its effects were so quick acting that it was dreaded.

In typhus, the approach was slow and gradual, so that all the effects of the illness reached the limits of human suffering after a full and painful time by having to endure the struggles only a long illness inflicts. Many perished and it wasn't unusual to meet other families accompanied by children, not knowing where they were going, or one or other of them having to lie down by the roadside. They were as well off as what was left of Annie's family became, if they succeeded in finding a sheaf of straw or broken branches, mud and leaves to build a 'scalp' under which to lay their aching heads and get out of the rain; though even if they did it was no surprise when some never rose again. For her, there was soon the pressure of dealing with the children's throbbing heads, moistening their parched and burning lips and hot rashes on their bellies. There were too, the long nights of listening to their cries from the racking pain, which day after day sounded like raging torture. Then the period of uncertainty when the balance of each of their short lives hung precariously. She continually sobbed in silence as they succumbed one by one and there was not a thing more, she could do to help each of them.

Plenty of temporary sheds were erected on or near the roadsides containing fever-stricken people who, like them, had no other home. When people died, it was common to also place the

coffin on the roadside with an empty plate on the lid, in hope that those who passed by might offer some aid or manage to give something for the sick and starving survivors. She had to leave her brother and sisters' bodies out in the elements within days of each other, having no money to even buy the use of a 'Trap coffin', which were made, as the name suggested, with a trap door in the bottom. The coffin was placed over the grave and the trap door opened to drop the body in. There was no money to get their bodies to the cemetery or even a container or plate for alms. Annie left each one of them there, with a few branches laid over them; stumbling on, feeling bereft and worried about the still occasional wandering dogs, as starved as people, that would worry or more at their little bodies.

Contrarily, she'd heard that there was a significant number of strong farmers, situated across the country with bursting granaries and immense enclosures beside farmhouses in which crops were stored, who, without quite coming under the title of misers or meal-mongers, were in the habit of keeping up their provisions in large quantities, because they could afford to do so, until, like Matt Murphy, a year of scarcity arrived when they drew on their stock precisely when famine and prices were both at their highest.

Annie, like other ordinary folk, became still more frustrated seeing the long lines of provision carts that met or intermingled with the funerals on public paths while on their way to neighbouring harbours for export. It seemed unbelievable that day after day ships laden with Irish cattle and foodstuffs, drawn from a population suffering from obvious hunger as well as with disease, were sailing from the ports, while other ships sailed back in weighted with their own provisions. These had been sent back through the reluctant charity of England, but were never enough since the English had already taken the largest share for themselves.

It was no surprise that famine riots became regular sights. Annie tried to stay clear, still in a state of grief, but her desperate hunger, like so many others, propelled her to follow the carts with the hope that something might drop off along the way. Several carts were attacked and robbed and she had to keep a keen eye out to both avoid injury and take advantage of any opportunity to gather stolen foodstuffs. The muted talk was that some farmers had also been visited and two or three misers obliged to become benevolent with bad grace. For the townspeople involved, any lingering traces of self-respect or sense of modesty was thrown to the winds. Under the terrible pressure of the destitution that they suffered, anything like shame was forgotten.

She watched scenes where wild crowds struggled for some charity; looking ragged, sickly, and wasted away to skin and bone. Their wildness also taking place at public soup kitchens and other places of relief. Annie saw them tearing as if at the remnants of some carcass like many hungry vultures, amid noise and screams. She was afeared at the sights and sounds on watching a timid girl, a modest mother of a family, then a decent farmer being goaded by their intense cravings of hunger as all sense of restraint was abandoned. While having to resort to fighting for a few mouthfuls of food, Annie never lost her sense of shame and cursed the god whose prayers she'd been fed by the priest and her mother. They were as much good as the empty grain sacks and meatless bones occasionally left strewn around for the dogs to pick at and fight over.

~

The dreadful typhus in all its deadly power was accompanied by a panic that invested it with terror. The moment fever was confirmed or even guessed to have visited a family, infected persons were avoided by their neighbours and friends as if they carried death about them, as they often did; so that its presence caused all sense of community and good-neighbourliness to be withdrawn. And so it happened with Annie. People knew of the children's demise, whatever its cause and this terrific scourge, unquestionably an epidemic, was considered to be dangerously and fatally contagious. No-one except nearest relatives, of whom she had none nearby anyway, and people with feelings of religious duty, had the courage to enter the houses of the sick or dead for the purpose of administering to the afflicted the care that they needed. Annie, having so far managed to survive free of fever, began to help nurse other people, so that she would have company and perhaps a bite or two of whatever each remnant of a family managed to gather.

Before he'd gone off to the public works, Annie's father had told her that since the introduction of the potato into Ireland, no year had ever passed that, even some remote place or other, had not been affected by the blight. The climate of Ireland was so unsettled, he'd said, and its soil so variable in quality and the potato so liable to injury from excess of either drought or moisture, that he had no hesitation in stating the startling fact of this annual famine as one he could personally vouch for. "Neither has an autumn passed without a complaint from those who feed solely on the new and unripe potato." Her mother at the time couldn't quite believe when he'd told them, "Ever since the year 1832, it's been known as the 'potato cholera.'"

"Is that what all those griping pains were, so?" her mother had asked, the explanation making the answer like an old piece of the puzzle fall into place. Annie sighed, remembering her mother's previously ruddy cheeks and full head of shiny red curls that had bounced on her shoulders when she laughed. The image of her father's strong jaw and proud nose was fading in her mind as she wondered where he was now, was he dead or alive? When Annie had to leave the bodies of her sisters and brother, she'd taken it upon herself to attempt finding her father or at least a clue to his disappearance and asked many people in passing, "Have you seen John O'Connell? Have you heard anything about where he might be?" In response, she mostly received sad shakes of the head until one day a fellah in rags, who looked vaguely familiar sat her down by the roadside.

"He's gone Annie. T'was a landfall at the side of the road we were building. He and a couple of other fellahs were right below where the rocks fell. He was gone in a moment. Too fast to have known what was happening or to have felt anything. T'was a mercy, colleen. And your mammy and the bairns, where are they?" It was Annie's turn to sadly shake her head before thanking the man and trudging on that little bit slower, her back bent that little bit lower.

It seemed to Annie that the whole country was in a state of dull but frantic upheaval, and the wild crowds, as they came and went in their melancholy, were worn down by the obvious widespread poverty and suffering. It was enough to fill her heart with fear as well as pity. People's cadaverous and emaciated bodies had something in them that seemed like the wild dogs, and the fire of hunger roared in their hollow eyes and though it was likely they only looked the part, she was still wary of getting too close to them on the road, some of them half-naked. Others led their children about or carried in their arms little living skeletons, wan and yellow, with grimaces of pain and suffering on their fleshless features. People were almost lost in their own garments if they had them. Some were, like her, without coats or jackets to protect them from the elements, having been forced to part with them for food.

The entire country seemed to be pouring out famished hordes trying to intercept meal-carts and provision vehicles of all kinds. Some on their way to market, or to the next seaport for shipment or to attack the granaries of contractors or meal mongers, and all who, having food in large quantities, refused to give it to the poor free or even at a cheap price. Carts and cars, often mostly the property of innocent people, were stopped on the highways and broken into. The food that they carried was boldly taken, and, in case of any resistance, those in charge of them were badly beaten. Mills were also attacked and pillaged, and in many instances, large quantities of flour and grain were not only carried off, but strewn about the streets and destroyed.

Annie saw people on the open highways and streets gobbling up the raw flour and oatmeal. She saw others, more fortunate, tearing and devouring bread with a fury. Brought on by the gluttony of starving people, sickness of various kinds happened: giddiness, retching, fainting-fits, convulsions, and, in some cases, death itself. She noticed too that some kept a greater restraint over their hunger and watched them hurrying home in all directions, loaded with the easiest-to-carry foodstuffs. Others told her, "We're going to try to get to the stock-farms across the country in the hope of being able to procure a portion of blood."

"How will you travel such distances, when you can hardly walk?"

"We'll try at the docks first. They might let us take some from the heifers and bullocks that are held there before being shipped to England." People were desperate for any nourishment to prevent themselves starving and perishing like the abandoned dogs.

Dogs weren't able to bark; those that had survived were nothing but ribs and skin. Both day and night, but at night especially, their hungry howling could be heard across the country, or mingling with the wailing that people did over those whom the typhus was sweeping away.

~

Annie startled awake in her chair, the echoes of howling dogs in her ears, as wiping drool from her chin she sighed deeply. Those days were long gone but she still felt her mammy and daddy around her; she still missed her sisters and brother. She would get herself to Mass early in the morning to light a candle and say a rosary. Both her and Michael had survived and made it here; but the fever got him still. He died in 1869, never quite getting over the damage done to his health during the years of the famine. Still, he had given her the gift of four daughters who had since grown up and found fellahs to make a life and children of their own with. Despite how hard things could be here in Glasgow; she was glad they'd never known the starvation the likes of *An Gorta Mor* in Ireland.

OVERTURE – Mary Maguire

Mary looked from her window onto the rain-slicked road and the individuals hurrying along the street below her. She was still a 'sousider', but it was a while since she'd lived in Kirkston where her immediate family had eventually settled after the years in Tradeston and Gorbals.

Her laboured breathing was gradually returning to what was normal for her. What a fright she'd given herself over a simple letter. It had taken her several tries just to make herself open that drawer. You'd think the thing would have jumped out and bit the hand off her the way she was behaving. Really, it was clear now she was always going to expect to hear something from someone, no matter her age. It had been an underlying tension all along, with bouts of denial and suppression lasting years at a time when she'd lived as if nothing had ever happened in the first place. Mary shivered as she undressed, getting ready for bed. The darkness closed in at late afternoon now as the year moved towards its end; the worst time when the chill winds of memory would creep in.

~

Carrying her one-year-old son on her hip, heavily pregnant Nora anxiously paced the floor. Mary sat cowed in the nearby armchair with tears dripping down her face; her shoulders clenched to her ears and unable to slide any deeper into the chair. All she really wanted was to curl up in a dark corner somewhere.

"Jesus, Mary and Joseph! How could you let this happen?! Sure, haven't we had enough to be dealing with these past few years?" On cue, little Wallace started to gripe and squirm.

"We'll have to arrange some way to sort this without anyone finding out, but after me and the bairn have a nap. Can you just get on with the tea, so?" Nora rarely gave into the expression of anger, but Mary knew when the shock wore off she'd best be ready. Nora gave an exhausted sigh after shushing the child and left, while still shaking her head in disbelief, to try settling them both for a sleep in the other room. Mary wiped her eyes with the hem of her shapeless housedress and trembled. It had been hard enough to tell her eldest sister, who still hadn't asked her how it had happened or who was responsible. No doubt Nora would be running off to Father McNulty, the local priest, for advice as soon as she was able, though she had reverted to type with her first thought to hide the fact of Mary's pregnancy. What in heaven's name would she say to the priest's inevitable look of extreme disappointment and the sound of his disapproval-drenched words anyway? As it was, later that day he made certain that she knew there would be no going to heaven for her. Not surprisingly, bible in hand, he had her on her knees, a rosary clicking all the while, praying to save her soul from the fires of hell.

"Yes Father, I understand but there wasn't much opportunity not to get in the family way. If you'd just take a minute, to let me explain..."

"Don't be talking back to Father McNulty, Mary. He's only trying to help." Nora butted in.

"Help. You call this help?" Mary snapped.

"That's very uncharitable Mary." The priest said. "The church only wants what's best for the baby and it's my duty to explain the spiritual consequences of such a fall from grace in the eyes of God. I'll leave you to your family and hope you pray fervently to save your own soul, though it may be too late for that." The front door closed with a bang as her brothers then filed in on the heels of the outgoing priest, looking more severe than even he had.

"What're ye all about Mary?" An inebriated Patrick demanded. Nora spoke for her when she clammed up at their fierce exclamations demanding to know who was responsible. Their lips thinned white with rage. Seamus was refastening his jacket to leave having not had time to remove it yet.

"Just tell us his name Mary." He was red in the face now, the vessels in his neck bulging.

"Yeah, we'll string the bastard up!" Patrick blustered and couldn't stop himself staggering backwards in his anger. He banged against the kitchen table, shaking the crockery that clattered together from the impact. Frank was the only one to say nothing so far and that was only because he was at home in Pollokshields and hadn't been told yet. Unlike Nora, Mary was no longer a devout Catholic, though she kept that as quiet as she could for fear of the further tongue-lashing she'd be subjected to. God hadn't been there for her when she really needed him, so what was the point now? She knew they would try to make her have the baby adopted if she didn't get rid of it. She thought that might be okay since she felt pretty terrified by the thought of bearing a child and really didn't want to be a mother just yet, especially under the circumstances of its conception. Nothing immaculate about it, quite the opposite in fact; there would definitely be no virgin birth here.

She'd since found another way to use her upbringing to make her feel wanted without too much religious devotion. The meetings she'd managed to attend in the Govanhill area of Glasgow had inspired her and she'd been made to feel that welcome. Govanhill was known locally, as 'Little Ireland' and she'd loved hearing so many folks' voices sounding just like her now long-departed Granny O'Connell.

Her throat closed and eyes filled again but she swallowed the tears down, sniffed and stood abruptly, making for the kitchen to peel potatoes in an effort to forestall yet another crying jag. She avoided thinking about it all by daydreaming over the sink about one of those trips over to Ireland that the folk at the centre had been talking about—that was if and when she'd be able to save up enough money. She was still working in the Moorhead Mill and would be for at least a couple of months more before things came to a head; though the thought of that made her tremble again causing the knife to slip from her hand, clattering on the wooden floor. She wished her other big sisters were here. She missed Jeannie the most since they'd been closest in age, though she'd died three years before. Nora was right about all the things they'd had to deal with these last few years. What had happened to Jeannie and Frank were just some of the heartbreaking, family-straining events.

"Life is not an easy matter...
You cannot live through it without falling into frustration and
cynicism unless you have before you a great idea which raises
you above personal
misery, above weakness, above all kinds of perfidy and
baseness."
Leon Trotsky

PART TWO
1861-1893

Chapter 6 – Maguire's Country - Francis

Francis knew his ancestor's blood still ran in his veins. It was hard to explain to John Murphy, his friend and best man when he and Caitlin got married in St. John's Chapel in Portugal Street, now at least five or six years ago. "Here I am, having crossed the water and sure aren't I getting involved in another tussle, so?" John listened as Francis tried to explain that his home across the Irish Sea was in Fermanagh. "There's an inland county in the province of Ulster in the north of Ireland, surrounded on all sides by beautiful mountains, so it is." The grand characteristic of the county was Lough Erne, formed as two lakes, which is likely where the county took its name - *Feor Magh Eanagh*, or 'Country of the Lakes.' "However it came by its name," he continued, "Fermanagh is connected by a deep winding strait on an island in the centre of which stands the county town of Enniskillen where the castle is. I'm sure I told ye that before, in fact, are we not supposed to be having your company next time we go to visit me mammy, so?"

"I'd love to, but I don't know about that Francis? It will depend on how the shillings are nearer the time, mate." Francis nodded as he continued with his story,

"Well, if you do make it you'll see that, like I told ye before, my family's townland is Enaghan where about a dozen farms are located. Aye, Ireland is known for its lush, green fields, so gets the nickname 'the Emerald Isle', but unless they've been, people don't realise that it also has huge areas of rugged, rocky landscape and is dotted with damp peat bogs in the midlands and west coast, where for years, fellahs have dug and cut it for fuel, so they have." He called to the barman for top-ups to their glasses and after taking a sip leant closer to John.

"Here's a secret you didn't know, I'll bet. The greater part of the county t'was for several centuries known by the name of 'Maguire's Country,'"

"Maguires, as in your family, really?" responded John sounding impressed.

"Aye, well as one of many distant descendants of that particular family, I can feel that territorial urge rising in me again." Francis was shaking his head in confusion at himself.

"Over a days work on a job that pays pennies in a city and country that isn't even your own!? It must be something to do with the arrival of the new kiddy in September. You can't be that serious." John, unlike Francis' spare, wiry build, was rotund though not quite jolly with it, rather, he was a more reserved, sardonic person. He was middle height, and strongly built. His legs didn't have the robustness of a countryman's, but were well suited to his body. His face had harsh features, which gave it character. His cheeks were fallen in, and the lines from his nose to his mouth were strongly marked. His eyes were clear and bright, and his chin forceful. His fingers, broad at the tips, and short, were those of a clever workman. His bonnet and blue turned-down collar were characteristic of the worker he was. He lived in a tenement in Govan, consisting of a room and kitchen. He hadn't yet married and though carrying a

many-generations-past Irish name, didn't follow events in
the old country. In fact, knew very little about it, other than
what his friend Francis told him. He was bred in Govan
town, and before becoming an apprentice in his works was a
message boy. When his time was served, he became a Union
man, and thought all the world of his District Delegates.
He was a very good workman who could turn his hand to
many things and make a job of them all. He was intelligent,
and had a clear perception of injustice and according to his
friends, was a reasonable man. He stood up for himself not
only against the common enemy, his employer, but also
against his comrades in allied trades if they invaded his
boundaries. He was gruff, intractable, and independent, and
his latent irritability took fire if his rights were infringed. Of
servility, he had not a trace.

John had a good sense of humour, all be it the sardonic
kind. He had a keen sense of ridicule, and feared nothing
so much as being made a butt of others' jokes. He had only
one best mate in Francis, but tended to go with the crowd
when it came to sports or politics but wasn't that sociable
or aimlessly talkative, not willingly telling of his breakfast
or his appetite or the love he'd carried for his best friend's
wife since not long before he'd been asked to be best man all
those years ago. He'd early on been unable to restrain himself
from making a play for Caitlin despite his belief he was a still
a loyal friend to Francis, except recently, since the rebuffed
advances he'd made long ago and the persistent longing he
nowadays secretly cradled inside, had him questioning
himself if loyalty was an accurate assessment of what had
made him hang around. He liked Francis but in truth, they'd

little in common beyond whisky. Francis wasn't a football fan like him, didn't read much, which John did; liking to learn new things and keep up with the news. Francis often seemed stuck wishing he was still living in Ireland, often going off on nostalgic sorties in his head, especially when in his cups like now, or railing against everything in comparison to his memories of Ireland, which was so far from how they'd probably be almost twenty years down the line.

If John was taken to task for his reserve, his answer would quite likely be, "Aye, man, but you lot talk aboot things I couldnae be bothered talkin aboot." Which helped deflect from his sometimes dour train of thought and any deeper queries about his unmarried state, mainly caused by his so far unrequited feelings for Caitlin. He could argue on abstract points, and quibble with tireless persistence. He had a liking for his football and the gaffer, and on the latter subject he would, at times, tend to break into cursing, "He's a cunt! Aye, that's just whit he is!" And so recently, Francis' worries about his job and the goings on in the railways gave them something new to share despite its potentially damaging outcome.

John had become a domesticated man due to living alone and he was a good hand at breakfast, which was just as well, for since porridge went out of fashion, his favourite was bacon and eggs. When spending the evening by the fire, he'd take a read of the papers. His drink wasn't beer, but whisky, a preference he shared with his friend Francis, who was at that moment, topping up their glasses once more.

"Well, I'm certainly worried about wee Michael's health, maybe it's that right enough, especially since he came along makes it four wee ones and very little money to keep everyone fed." Francis had previously been working as a carter, helping out driver Malky Murray, with the horse and cart doing deliveries around Glasgow city centre. He'd rented a wee room in Nelson Street when he got to Glasgow soon after arriving at Greenock Port from Ireland in 1880 with two of his brothers, Bernard and Harry. That was after the 'Phoenix Park Murders' in May the year before had sickened the lot of them.[i]

They and their other two brothers, Patrick and Seamus, had supported their father Harry Snr, to keep the farm working as best they could during the bad harvests and threats of eviction while the 'Land War' of the previous few years raged on. They thought the new changes and arrangements by Gladstone and Parnell were a step in the right direction. Where was the need for murdering people?

That wee room in Tradeston had been okay for himself and living there was how he'd met Caitlin, who'd lived in the next close. They had done that thing where both of them had been lost in thought or daydreaming instead of looking where they were going.

"Would ye watch where you're going mister? Ye near knocked me over there!" Caitlin wobbled before she regained her balance after the thump of the fellah opposite slamming into her.

"I'm fierce sorry for that! I was in a hurry, too much of one by the looks of things. Are ye alright?" Francis recognised the young woman with surprise. He'd admired her from his window above a few times and had wondered how best to get to meet her. He was sure she was the one but there were a couple of women up that close that looked like they were all from the same family. It was the long black shiny hair that caped her shoulders he remembered most, not to mention her still noticeable generous curves, visible despite her thick winter coat. He had to act quickly.

"Can I make it up to ye…what was your name? I'm Francis, from up this close here." He pointed over his shoulder with his thumb.

"Aye, I think I've seen ye afore just no quite as close as this, mind." She watched as Francis' face reddened. "I'm Caitlin. How were ye thinkin tae make it up tae me?"

"Sure, I could take ye for a walk down Glasgow Green some weekend if ye like?"

"Okay, I'll let ye know. I live one up to the left. Give us a chap and ye can meet my mammy while ye're there as well."

"See ye then." Francis said as he nodded emphatically and rushed on his way with a smile on his face. Caitlin watched his receding back while suppressing her own grin behind the collar of her coat before continuing into the close and up the stairs. Wait till she told her sisters! They'd all noticed this good-looking fellah recently moved in up the next close and wasn't she the lucky one. They'd be so jealous! Though Caitlin had been born in Glasgow, her mammy, an O'Connell, was Irish through and through, born in Co. Meath and moved to Glasgow a couple of years after the Great Famine ended in 1852. Caitlin and her sisters had been born a bit farther to the east-end of Glasgow in King Street but had lived in Nelson Street for some time since.

The sisters barely remembered their Da since Mathew McInnley had had an early death from the fever when Caitlin was just five years old, so their mammy had to work as a cleaner and they, when old enough, as machinists to keep themselves going.

Sure enough, Francis appeared at their door the next Sunday, luckily after they'd returned from Mass. Annie O'Connell welcomed him into their wee home where three of her daughters also lived, while the eldest Margaret, lived in Scotstoun with her husband James. It was a bit of a crush but they'd been muddling along in the two rooms over the years, negotiating with quarrels and quibbles to make the limited space work. After that, Francis was a regular visitor to the delight of the others and sometimes of chagrin to Caitlin. She was more delighted when they could be alone without her preening sisters in his room up the next close. Within the year, they were discussing marriage.

After him and Caitlin's wedding in the Gorbals, he'd moved in with her and her mammy and sisters, sleeping in the fold-down bed in the kitchen, to pool their shillings and until after the bairn came, when they knew as well as they could that their first-born Bernie (named after Francis' younger brother) would survive. Of course, in no time at all, it all became even more of a crush.

They lasted only a short year there before Francis convinced Caitlin to make the move to the countryside. It had to be better than them all being crammed into those two dingy rooms and

besides, his cousin Rachel was living in Alloa and working at Kilncraigs wool-spinning mill; an important source of work for the small town on the Hillfoots of the Ochils in Clackmannanshire.

He thought she might be a help to Caitlin. He'd hoped it would, at least, be a better life for the family and feel more like his beloved Ireland.

The town lay on the north bank of the River Forth, about six miles east of Stirling and two miles west of Clackmannan. Being near to the water was another bit of familiarity for him and he looked forward to seeing ships of up to 100ft long being built at Alloa harbour.[ii] Unfortunately, the railway lines didn't yet reach Glasgow, so they had to save up from the little Francis made from his final few runs as a carter to plan the move and make the journey.

~

They'd arrived tired out after covering the distance had taken two days, with needing to stop overnight in Bonnybridge. They'd hired a scotch cart to bring what few possessions they had with them and been glad of the dry, though cold and damp, weather. They were feeling jostled and jolted from the rough tracks all the way and Francis was now trying to lead the borrowed horse down the narrow, cobbled streets of the town. They slowly came down Mill Street on Shilling Hill past Springfield Woollen Mill and then into King Street where they'd rented a small room and kitchen next to cousin Rachel. Caitlin felt optimistic since the street name, King Street, was the same as where she'd been born in Glasgow.

Francis was happy she was happy. Bernie had started to whimper, though luckily up till then he'd remained sleeping for most of that day's journey.

"Wife, let me help you down and get you and the baba into the house, now." Before he'd helped Caitlin off the cart, his cousin Rachel and her husband Joseph, had come out onto the street. Rachel was a thin woman who appeared to hold herself tightly, offering only a brief unsmiling nod in Caitlin's direction and a quick pat on Francis's arm. Her husband was shorter in height and round-bellied to her straight-backed frame. Francis noticed his florid red nose: the tell-tale sign of a drinker. Not that Francis would ever say no to a dram himself, and in fact that was exactly what the husband invited him to do on shaking his hand, but Francis chanced his luck on asking for some help and just maybe have that whisky too.

"Sure, we'd get to that whisky quicker, so we could, if you could see your way to helping me unload some of these crates and boxes, fellah?" Francis turned to help Caitlin indoors with the child. "I'll be back out in a jiffy to get started with that lot," he said, while pointing his thumb over his shoulder indicating the overladen cart. He heard Rachel tut and sigh and it so reminded him of his mammy, who was a fierce woman unless you knew how to get on her good side. He'd have to be looking out for cousin Rachel's good side here, for it wasn't so obvious.

Inside the dark wee room, Caitlin managed to pull back the dirty stained fabric from the small window to let in a dull light and found a rickety chair in the kitchenette to rest a moment and feed young Bernie under her shawl. She suspected the drawn mouth of Rachel would pucker all the more should she be seen openly feeding the bairn till they were better acquainted. Francis drew a cup of water from a creaky gurgling tap that he had to run a few moments until it cleared, and brought it to Caitlin; kissing her and then baby Bernie's heads before going back outside to unload their meagre belongings.

Within a few months, Caitlin was pregnant again. They had tried really hard to make it work here in Alloa town. Francis had believed there would be work with unloading the many vessels docking at Alloa harbour, especially the thousands of tons of coal exported from there each year, and there was, but his chest became so congested with coal dust he increasingly had to take time off to recover. This caused tensions with Caitlin and Rachel. Caitlin felt worn down by her quickly occurring pregnancy, having to look after Bernie and Francis too and despite or because of the physical nearness, Rachel was coming knocking on their door on an almost daily basis, mostly to complain rather than help.

"What kind of man brings his family all the way from the city to lie in his bed all day instead of out working? And were ye not imbibing the whiskey again last night, so?"

"I'd just a hot toddy to help me chest, so I did. When that's sorted, I can get back to work can't I? Ye're not being very helpful Rachel. Is there not something that Caitlin could be using a hand with, so?" She tutted and swerved past Caitlin who entered the room at that moment with a bucket full of wet nappies.

"Rachel, could you...?" But she was gone, the click of the door closing the only thing she left behind. Caitlin shook her head in annoyance but she had heard the whiskey remark and, though she'd never say to Rachel, she was as worried and becoming resentful herself about Francis' drinking. Just these last few months as he got sicker, Francis was using up too much of their meagre income on his hot toddies and the effect on his mood and motivation was becoming quite noticeable while adding to her workload, but she felt heart sorry for him with his coughing and fevers and that drookit hangdog face he put on that she knew was about not being able to provide for them, especially since he'd initially been so excited about this move.

Rachel though, could definitely have been more help instead of making the situation feel worse. Yet another morning she arrived at their door.

"It's yourself, Rachel! What a surprise." Francis said in a deadpan voice. Caitlin couldn't prevent her immediate snigger that was followed by Rachel's usual tut and lift of her chin as she peered down her sharp nose and pushed her way into the room where Caitlin was feeding Bernie; which she didn't attempt to cover up. She'd given that up; wouldn't try to save that auld biddy from her pretend shock and preaching of disapproval. Caitlin thought it more likely jealousy since she hadn't produced any bairns of her own, yet still acted like she was mother of all wisdom when it came to bringing them up. How would she be able to stand it when the new bairn came?

"Away wae ye. I'm melted wae tiredness. I've been up since the crack of dawn at the mill and here yis are just getting out yer scratcher. How can ye expect tae get anywhere wae that attitude, so?"

"Well, yer not our mammy to be telling us how to live our lives, Rachel. I thought ye were going to help Caitlin wae the bairn, especially now she's another on the way." Caitlin's head shot up as he said this. He wasn't supposed to say anything just yet. Rachel's face twisted in contempt as she took a breath in, ready to give them yet another tongue-lashing. Caitlin rose, moving swiftly to hand the baby to Francis and crossing the small space put her arm around Rachel's shoulders, herding her firmly to the door just as she started up with, "Jesus, Mary and Joseph!"

"Ach, Rachel. I'm really hungry the day. Would ye have any of that soda bread that ye made afore? That'd go down a treat right now." Rachel's mouth clamped shut then contorted into a prideful grin.

"Well, I might have some left over but ye'd need tae help me make the next batch if ye'll be eating what's left of the last lot, so." Caitlin opened the door and pressed her arm against Rachel's back in encouragement.

"That'd be great and I'll give ye a hand tomorrow. Just have to feed myself up so's tae keep the milk coming in for feedin the bairn again later the day.' She grabbed her shawl, threw an eye roll in Francis's direction and went out the front door with Rachel. "I'll just come and get that bread the now, will I?" They'd got a tongue lashing anyway and not for the last time. Caitlin tried to keep the woman happy while resenting it all the same. You'd have thought she was their landlady the way she busy-bodied about the place. Tutting at Caitlin's cleaning, at her care of the bairn, of her husband

and at her husband when he had to be home from work with his chest the way it was. There was little in the way of real help, though she did look after Bernie now and then as Caitlin's pregnancy developed and it became difficult to carry or amuse him.

It all came to a head the night Nora was born. Caitlin had started going into labour the previous day. By noon the next day, the pain was becoming much stronger with each contraction. Waves of cramping squeezed her insides making Caitlin want to bend double and bear down but she held back and tried to rest between contractions; tried to prepare for the next one. "Rachel! Did you send for the doctor?" she called but there was no answer. "Rachel! Francis! Is anyone there?" Caitlin's voice was weak and her throat scratchy and soon the silent response to her shouts brought lonely tears to her eyes. Where was Rachel, she was supposed to be helping with the birth?

She began to feel scared as another contraction surged, the pain seeming to increase each time and there wasn't more than a minute or two between them. She felt exhausted, sweaty and her mouth and lips were dry. "Rachel!" She screamed as best she could but the baby kept pushing, in no mind to wait for the attentions of the absent Rachel. Caitlin groaned while no longer able to hold back from pushing. If only Francis were here to hold her hand. She became breathless and all of a sudden, the tension released, the baby sliding out in a rush onto the ruffled sheets. Well, having to wash those would serve Rachel right, since she hadn't been here to help Caitlin prepare by putting old towels and sheets below her to avoid so much mess. She carefully lifted the wee slip of a child, looking more like a skinned rat, its skin red raw-looking. Caitlin gently turned the child over into her arms. She was a girl! The hair was reddish and sticky and she crumpled up her face before letting out a loud cry. Caitlin burst into tears at the same time, exhausted and alone with her new daughter.

Neither Caitlin nor Francis could forgive Rachel after that. She'd promised, though obviously just to make herself feel like she was a good person.

Afterwards despite the obvious nearness beforehand of the imminence of the birth, when confronted she whined shamefacedly "I didn't know. How could I have known?!".

Caitlin did feel anger and doubt about Francis too, since he'd eventually turned up at home swaying in the door, crowing about the new baby and how he'd been wetting the its head in anticipation. He quickly looked shocked to find her lying across the bed bloody and soaked in sweat, her leeched pallor scaring him as he lifted the scrap of a child from her arms only to find the cord hadn't yet been cut. He quickly scalded a knife and did so before wrapping the child up in a sheet and placing her carefully in the drawer he removed from the chest for the purpose. He tried to make his wife more comfortable before sliding furtively into the next room when she fell asleep, feeling a hefty dose of guilt settle on his shoulders. He, with great difficulty, restrained the urge to break out that new bottle of whiskey. The scarily weakened and collapsed state of Caitlin had really shocked him but as the night wore on and the baby started up with the crying, he gave in, deciding there was no reason why he shouldn't have just one more drink to celebrate his first daughter's birth. Later, when recovered, Caitlin was neither convinced or happy about what she thought of as excuses that Francis gave for his late return,

"Where were you, Francis? I wis feart being here on ma ain."

"I was at work beforehand and hadn't you made an arrangement with Rachel to help ye?" There was no point going on about it with him, he was right. It had been Rachel who'd promised to help.

They lasted in Alloa for just another couple years, due as much to the chilly atmosphere between themselves and cousin Rachel as well as the fact that Francis' health wasn't improving that much. When Caitlin became pregnant again, they decided to move back to Glasgow so that she would have the support of her mammy and sisters. Nora was three and a half by the time they made the disappointing journey back.

Chapter 7 - The Great Scottish Rail Strike - Francis

Having been brought up on the farm in Fermanagh left a deep impression on Francis and he constantly felt the effects of living in the dirty, smoke-filled city on his lungs. His cough had become worse recently, no doubt as much due to the carting around the streets, though that coal-bagging in Alloa hadn't helped much either. He'd sounded out a job as a railway porter, hoping that would prove to be more regular and help with his chest since he'd be working inside the station. However, those draughty open platforms and coal smoke from the train engines soon put paid to that notion.

As he'd settled into the work at Central Station in Glasgow, Francis made more friends but not without having to get through the taunts and prejudice by other railway men about his Irishness. They were still being accused of taking work from Glaswegians and he had to learn to ignore the name calling. A little tipple helped now and then and overall, he enjoyed the work and liked to keep up with what was going on in other areas of the station despite his lowly status as a porter.

Eventually he became torn about what to do over the impending rail strike. Their third son and fourth child after Frank was Michael, who had only just been born in September past and was now quite ill. Caitlin was struggling with the wee fellah's sickness and Francis was feeling like he'd let his family down again. Nothing seemed to go right for them. They'd arrived back in Glasgow just a year ago bringing their first daughter Nora with them and had had another wee one, Francis Jnr (who they took to calling Frank to save confusion) soon after they were back in the city.

Francis had made sure after escaping the tyranny of Rachel, that they'd not go back to live with Caitlin's mammy who still had two of her other daughters, Susan and Mary, living there. She was a real trouper that one, but with bairns coming so quickly, there was sure to be even more overcrowding and cause for argy-bargyin. They managed to rent a couple of different places having needed to expand as their family grew, all further along from Nelson Street at South Coburg Street into the Gorbals, while still keeping them within walking distance from the bairns Granny O'Connell and Caitlin's unmarried sisters. They'd been who Caitlin had missed most when in Alloa. And a real help they sure were, wee Michael having been poorly since he was born.

Nevertheless, the work situation had seemed to offer necessary opportunities. Getting the job as a railway porter had been lucky and was what had kept them going this past year, especially since the doctor's fees for wee Michael were mounting up.

~

A few men were huddled in a corner of the station discussing their plans. They were talking about meetings that had been held in various railway centres in Scotland over the last two weeks in late November and early December. It was clear from their chat, Francis realised, that while the men in Glasgow and Edinburgh were in favour of a strike, those in the country districts had seemed less so. In one of the huddled groups was Billy Logan, a bit of a loudmouth Francis thought, but didn't say since plenty others seemed not to mind the shite that came out of his mouth. He'd been one of the eejits who'd needlessly pointed out his nationality.

"You there! Porter." On turning at the sound, he noticed the voice came from a man in company uniform, so he'd be a manager, an engineer or a driver.

"What can a be doing for ye, fellah?" The man hesitated for a moment, then asked one of those stupid questions with a stupid smirk.

"Are ye a Mick or a Paddy then?" Here we feckin go again, Francis thought.

"Neither, I'm a Francis. Is there something I can help ye with, so?" The man looked annoyed at his response but he wasn't much for caring about that.

"I just wondered if ye could give me a haun wae this box?"

"Sure, as long as no passengers need me and it won't take too long, I can so." And he helped the man as he quizzed him in an offended tone about how Francis'd managed to get the job as if he shouldn't have. Francis had to hold his tongue and the box he was carrying tightly lest he gave the man a tongue-lashing or crushed toes.

"But ye're daein a great job, aw the same. I'll put a word in for ye wae the high heid yins and let them know." That was Billy Logan, the big mouth. He was at it again now.

Being a relatively new incomer to the city as well as to the situation, Francis kept his own council and watched the manipulations with interest and a bit of alarm, since striking signalmen and engine drivers would put more than themselves out of work, whether in agreement or not. As Francis watched he saw his workmate Joe, glancing around while speaking, as if worried they'd be seen, though his height made that a certainty regardless of anything else. Even Billy Logan had to look up to Joe and didn't seem comfortable with that.

"The reasons are obvious, are they no? Work isnae as difficult in the country as it is in the towns and cities, and in the country, men live in wee groups scattered ower a bigger area." He looked down at the others to gauge their response seeing Conor pluck at his jacket sleeve while answering.

"Aye, a suppose they're more settled in their habits and no used tae gettin involved in company matters unless it affects them badly, it's true." Billy jammed his hands in his front pockets before adding his concerns.

"Well, it's about tae affect us aw badly. They cannae stay oot ae it while the restae us are fightin tae get the rotas sorted or for others tae have a decent length ae time tae work in a day rather

than knock oor pans in from exhaustion." The thud and clank and hiss of the nearby steam engines, as they got ready to leave the station, all but drowned out his agitated words. "We have tae get this strike underway as soon as possible." They all solemnly nodded in agreement before slapping each other on the back and moving off in different directions to resume their duties for the Glasgow and South Western

Railways and their own designated tasks to help make the strike happen.

At the meeting of the 14th of December, the Executive members stood at the front telling the workers that they didn't consider the number of notices they'd received justified a stoppage of work.

"How many notices of resignation have ye had?" A short stocky man querulously demanded.

"4,173 notices of resignation have been handed to the Executive so far. This figure is based on the Society of Railway Servants in Scotland membership of 9,000," he pompously declared.

"But that's nearly half and they hivnae all been counted yet." As he stood quickly in annoyance, Joe towered over Executive member Ian Duncan, leaning forward as Duncan faltered,

stepping back from Joe's intense stare.

"N...n..nevertheless, that number of notices shows that it's still only a minority in favour of a strike," he said, trying to sound convincing. The grumbling and under-the-breath cursing around the Albion Hall indicated a current feeling among the men that was clearly against the Executive.

"They're just trying to undermine our proposed strike action, that's all they're doing. I thought they were supposed tae be supporting us here, y'know just like we said before - aren't they supposed tae dae as they're tellt?" Conor loudly exclaimed. The men's mutterings of discontent finally found further expression through Billy Logan, who was sitting in the area at the back of the hall. Dressed in grubby work overalls, he stood and raising his voice to be heard by all said,

"A've been disappointed at the way this meeting's gaun. A came here prepared no tae start work again, or at all events no tae start efter Monday week." There was much applause at this comment. He went on: "What's proposed by the Executive is gaun backwards when we want tae go forwards. Cards like these we now haud are the same as what was sent to us twelve months ago. A dinnae intend tae sign this one and I know that a great many others are of similar thinking." He looked around him at the men gathered in the hall under a pall of tobacco smoke as he said this, seeing emphatic nods of agreement and decided to state his proposal.

"A move that an amendment, being that the report shouldnae be adopted, but that the men agree tae cease work a week from now." Loud and prolonged cheering rattled the walls of the hall as the men received the amendment with overwhelming enthusiasm. When the men calmed down a bit Billy continued, "A know that the proposal isnae according tae the law but in Glasgow, law or no; the proposal is tae give a week's notice on the 14th December for a strike on the 21st."

However, despite the men's urge to strike, the counterproposal of the Executive for delay was carried on the 14th December at several meetings around the country.[iii]

At the meeting held in Glasgow a week later on 21st December, the Executive announced again, that additional notices of resignation were still necessary, and that they would continue to

hold back from advising an immediate stoppage of work. Billy Logan was up in the gallery this time, where he could be seen and heard even easier. He could feel his and his fellow workers' contempt and frustration at the Executive's continual stalling. He stood and rapped on the gallery rail for attention and when all eyes turned in his direction, called out: "How much longer are ye's gonnae stall? I move that we DO NOT resume work!"

A member of the Executive tried to dampen obviously fraught tempers. "Billy, you seem to have rightly interpreted the general feeling, but it doesn't do to discuss legal points with men like railway servants, who know nothing about law, and, further, have no time to consider it." Many of the men just laughed at this comment but he wasn't finished yet. "If you're all resolved on this course, the directors of the railway companies might put you in jail." Billy came back with,

"If they did so, we would have something to aim for and then we'd be sure of our hours." The crowd responded with more laughter. Another railway servant in the hall gallery, who sat beside Billy raised himself to his feet with a loud grunt that betrayed his age, loudly stated:

"I'm no happy wae that report submitted by the committee. For at least ten years us men have had the same papers submitted tae us ower and ower and ower again." More laughter from the men at him slowly winding his arm in circle after circle. "I'm definitely in favour of an immediate strike. Breaking an agreement isnae a criminal offence, so we cannae be put in prison, and surely there's enough money in the society to pay the fine of any man who's charged." One of the men, his bunnet low over his face, forced himself to stutter out,

"I..I..If the..the.. amendment was carried, and an immediate strike wasn't successful, the Executive Committee would turn round and say, 'Oh! Y..y..you should have done as we wanted, and everything would have been fine.'" Billy stood up again to counter that argument.

"The fact is that the Executive are far too cautious. They've never made a real effort tae get the society brought into prominence by risking something tae win something. They've always wanted us tae go on and on with nae advantage or benefit to us workers."

The man in the bunnet, which he was now turning in his hands, was still nervous about the whole situation. "W...w...we could lose our jobs and the superannuation allowance that Mr. Walker put forward so often, and then there would be nothing left for us but the poorhouse."

Most laughed at this but some looked more concerned than before, muttering to their neighbours with questioning looks. A member of the committee said,

"It isn't the fault of the Executive that we've acted as we have. The remedy lies with you men. If you don't want a cautious Executive, you should elect men who aren't cautious." A rough voice from the crowd retorted:

"Aren't the Executive supposed to be here to do what they're bid? We're fed-up of the never-ending and useless go-between with Mr. Tait, the secretary, and the railway companies." To which there was much applause. Billy's proposal, this time, was unhesitatingly carried with scenes of noisy excitement by 660 votes to 81. The news was telegraphed to the other meetings held that afternoon in Edinburgh, Motherwell, Perth, and elsewhere, and the motion for an immediate strike without notice was carried by convincing majorities at all except one of the centres.

Francis almost wished he lived there. Probably a wee country town like Alloa without cousin Rachel and men happy to get on with their work. So that was Christmas cancelled then, though his own family weren't exactly full of Christmas cheer anyway and not likely to be for some time. The strike was only going to add to the gloom that already hung over them. With the occurrence of the strike, on the one hand, the men felt uncomfortable with their own position and on the other, were encouraged by the successful result of the decisive measures adopted by their fellow workers in the North of England. The section of men numerous enough to carry their point across at the meetings of the railway servants had decided not to return to their jobs. Francis thought that in so doing, this quite risky manoeuvre gave the strikers an immediate advantage, though Billy Logan's possible machinations notwithstanding; it was doubtful whether the sudden stoppage of labour without notice was deliberately adopted with the view to securing such an advantage. [iv]

Christmas was effectively cancelled for many families. The railway companies were completely taken by surprise. They had not made, perhaps couldn't have made, provision for the operation of the traffic without the work of the strikers. The result was total chaos for a time. The internal transport of the central, eastern, southern, and western districts of Scotland was for a day or two utterly paralysed. A reduced passenger train timetable was prepared for all the lines. From the 22nd December onwards, for at least four weeks, the depots of the companies were blocked with goods, and unmanned engines were rusting in their sheds. The Glasgow City Underground Railway was closed for circle trains from the beginning of the strike until 28th January, a period of five weeks. Rushed decision-making was precisely the widespread view that was unfairly taken of their action. There was little doubt the public didn't realise that the proposal to strike had been made in October, and two months had elapsed since then. The constant deferring of the moment of engagement had been more demoralising to the workers than a possible defeat. The men eager for a strike appeared to instinctively feel that unless they took decisive action at the critical hour on the 21st December, resolve would be undermined before the real struggle began. The decision, bold and irregular as it was, was successful in getting the support of the general body of the men.

Chapter 8 - 'Doon the Barras' - Francis

Francis went home that day more worried than ever. Sure, he was far from the only one affected, there'd be thousands left in a similar situation and not only railway servants. The lack of coal and the high prices charged by local dealers were causing the most difficulty for the poorer classes, whose hardships were intensified by the increase in the cost of fuel during the height of what became an unusually severe winter. Caitlin and Francis now had four children to feed, clothe and provide heating for and he decided to go look for carting work again with Malky until the strike was over, but kept up with the few railway fellahs that hadn't snubbed him because he was Irish. There were always some melters.

"Francis, what are we doing wrong? I'm really trying tae look after wee Michael, you know I am. You don't blame me do ye?" She sunk back down into the stale, sweat-imbued blankets. Her dark hair had lost its shine. Caitlin felt drained of energy, as if since the pregnancy with Michael and caring for him during his illness she'd deflated like a burst sweetie bag.

"We're not managing Caitlin. It's too much for you with the wee one ill and all four of them to look after the way you're feeling and with this strike going on. My mammy and da still have a few of my other brothers and sisters at home to help out and plenty of food on the farm to keep them all fed. Another wee one won't make that much difference." Caitlin didn't seem convinced. She looked over at her serious-faced five-year-old son, Bernie sitting beside his three-year-old little brother, Frank. His face looked wary as if he knew they were talking about him and a tiny frown creased his forehead. Little Nora, was just four years old and would soon be the eldest child at home, replacing Bernie. The children got along well enough, partly because Nora always wanted to please and didn't like standing up to others while Bernie just wanted to get on with sorting his stones or whatever his latest collection was and could get annoyed at Nora or Frank wanting to play or draw and maybe mess up his things. They had very different needs and interests, and maybe being on the farm might work for Bernie and Caitlin just might get a little more rest. Besides, her mammy was already claiming poor relief because of her bronchitis preventing her from working at her cleaning job, so she definitely couldn't help with money or looking after the bairns.

"You know Bernie likes his routines and having wee jobs to do, don't you, fellah?" Bernie nodded, watching carefully as his daddy continued trying to convince his mammy. "Helping on the farm would be perfect for him, never mind the clean air." Little Nora toddled over, concerned at the intense emotion in her dada's voice about her big brother going away.

"Dada no smile. Dada angry?" Francis pulled her onto his lap and held her lightly. He hugged her saying, "No, *achora*, dada's not angry," before he continued trying to cajole Caitlin. "You know he's been getting chesty and the weather isn't going to get any warmer for months especially with the coal shortage on top of that. Michael can have all your attention and Nora here, can at least help you out by playing with wee Frank. You'll be helping your mammy, *acushla,* won't you?" He tickled his daughter, eliciting giggles from her. After the wee ones were in bed, he felt it had been a happy sound to remember on a sad morning since Caitlin had eventually agreed to young Bernie going to Ireland. He took a relieved slug of whisky. He hadn't had a drink all day.

He knew she would miss her old-before-his-time little man awfully; he was such a sensible boy. Francis sent off a letter to his parents to get their agreement about dates so he could make arrangements to book their passage on the steamer. Paying for that would need finding something to pawn or a visit to his brothers down in the Port.

~

In the city and around the country, many public works were closed almost immediately because of lack of fuel.[v] The passenger traffic in the Christmas and New Year weeks was seriously affected. It was discussed in the newspapers that it was likely that around 100,000 people had an unwelcome extension to their Christmas holiday.

Day by day, during the strike, the men in the Glasgow district met at noon in the Albion Halls in College Street. The audience, until the Executive appeared at two o'clock each day, passed the time with songs and occasionally a dance or playing of musical instruments; keeping their spirits up as the days dragged into weeks. Francis would go along every couple of days to find out what the *craic* was. He was only a railway porter with no hope or expectation that even a 'successful' outcome would make much difference to his situation but liked the camaraderie that was more on show when everyone was together instead of under usual individual working conditions. It was also a chance to sound out a few of the fellahs with his new idea about how to make some money to keep his family going and maybe help out a few of the men and their families.

Francis had recently been 'Doon the Barras' as the locals described it, discovering that there were all sorts of interesting things. He got a bit of a fright when he saw his first-ever black man, who turned out to be blue-black skinned man who told the onlookers that he was an African chief named Bonsu. He was selling a product called Health Oil that he said was infused with snake venom and was being touted to help the aged and cure the lame. He also claimed that it was guaranteed to give relief from aches and pains. Francis wasn't about to try it himself though. It seemed near as dangerous as the fellah who looked like a gypsy, and performed his tricks after collecting bottles that he broke in a sack, then emptying the contents on the mat placed there for the purpose, before laying down on his back on top of them. He didn't even wear as much as a simmet. The fellah challenged anyone in the crowd surrounding him to stand on his chest; jump up and down with all their strength. One, not so slim, fellah rose to the challenge and was encouraged to not be so gentle when he seemed nervous and halting in his jumps. Each time he landed, the crowd gasped, expecting to hear the Gypsy cry out or see blood spurting from wounds he didn't seem able to avoid. When the Gypsy stood up the crowd gasped even louder, for there wasn't as much as a scratch in sight and you can be sure there were plenty onlookers turning him back to front to back, giving him a thorough going over, checking with disbelief his unbroken, bloodless skin. There was no understanding what he had seen and Francis shook his head in wonderment as he passed on to complete the business he had come to do.

After he'd pulled his attention away from the 'crazies' he was agog at the abundant variety of available goods, from cups and saucers to lamps and mattresses, tables and settles, old curtains and bed sheets. There were 'diamond' rings, christening robes and communion dresses with plenty of second-hand couture label clothes for those pretending not to be affected so much by daily poverty or the recent industrial action. Food-wise there were everyday staples like bags of oats and sugar and flour, not to mention things ready for eating such as mussels and whelks and roasting chestnuts straight from the trees in Glasgow Green. And there were cigarettes. While there, he got talking to a couple of fellahs whose ears perked up and eyes twinkled when he mentioned his possible use of the horse and cart. Sure, this last year he'd spent most of the time working in the station but with the recent closures because of the strike, he'd just the other day, called on Malky to find out if they could help each other out once again.

He remembered in the old days the pipes that used to be given away in their thousands by publicans, to be filled with a variety of tobacco products until mass produced packs of cigarettes originally from W.D & H.O Wills Tobacco Company in Bristol became much cheaper to buy and less of a fuss to smoke. What really needed to be in the hands of those thousands of striking men, he decided, were the many cheap, mass-produced cigarette brands that had begun appearing on the market some years before. If what the fellah at the Barras had suggested was true, and there were some 'forgotten' crates of Woodbine, Smith's Glasgow Mix, and Three Nuns brands he had access to, they were in line to make a few bob and help calm the ire of the strikers at the same time.

As Francis was looking around the hall for familiar faces, the chairman announced the next striking entertainer. "Mr John Smith, engine-driver, Polmadie - for a song," and everyone began singing along while Francis found a seat. Later, after announcing another volunteer, a welcome surprise happened with the next act.

"Ayr station, Jack Scott - singing 'Afton Water.'" Jack was a well-dressed, powerfully built man who sang with unexpected sweetness. As he listened Francis found himself feeling melancholic and craving a tipple remembering the family *craic* in the Enaghan farmhouse kitchen, everyone together singing all the old songs. He was looking forward to the soon-to-occur trip with young Bernie to smell again the earthy aroma of cut peat, its woody smoke curling from the cottage chimney and the healthy tang of the farm animals.

Sometimes when he visited the Hall, a brakesman with an innocent face and ungainly air would sing a rollicking topical song, in which incidents from the strike were set to very rude verse. But it was all very orderly and full of good humour. The audience was easy about tolerating lapses in memory, and the music as a rule was energetic rather than melodic. Francis noticed Billy and moved seats to have a word with him about the cigarettes he had arranged with

Malky, the carter, to pick up. Being a loud mouth, Billy was sure to let plenty of the men know on his behalf. Billy nodded eagerly at the promise of a couple of free packs for the favour.

Reports were also being read daily from the districts, describing situations from the point of view of the men there. Statements were read from telegrams: "Motherwell—All out here, stand firm; sure to win." But Francis knew the real work of the strikers was done at night and in the early morning. And he knew those men would be keen to have their 'forever friends' between their fingers for company on those long stretches standing about night and day.

Picketing, especially at the beginning, was a serious factor in the railway struggle. Through the secretary, Mr. Tait's 'plan of campaign', pickets were dispatched directly from the meeting to St. Rollox, Polmadie, and other places in the Glasgow districts. Similar parties went to Motherwell and elsewhere to pass on information and bring more men out. The picketing of the first Sunday was the greatest success of the strike. The enthusiasm of the men who had actually been engaged in the movement caught on and men at all the centres joined them in droves.

After the heat of the first moments of action was over, and during the six weeks of the struggle, it became a dreary business. Pickets from the body of the strikers were paid out of the strike funds but there were many volunteers besides who joined the paid pickets and spent time with them in the dark time between eleven o'clock at night and five or six in the morning. Hopefully they'd all be puffing away, whether it was on the hillsides of the Lothians tramping from cabin to cabin across the moors, on the road at Polmadie or watching the Caledonian Railway Depot gate all night in snow and that cold east wind.

The pickets were organised in relieving parties. They carried copies of the Conspiracy Act in their pockets, just in case of being harried by the police. The men were urgently warned against "intimidation" by the captains of their pickets but a serious encounter did take place between steelworkers who had volunteered to picket and the police at Polmadie, in which several people were injured. One of the other guardsmen had been over at Polmadie to report back on the goings on there and rushed back into the halls exclaiming,

"Ye should see they steelworkers fighting back wae the polis who went in heavy-haunded like they always dae. But, man, did the pickets no give them a great run for their money."

"What were the casualties?" The foreman's expression was serious.

"Well, after the steel workers got attacked by the polis, they moved the wounded ones tae the side then picked up whatever they could find and made a run at the polis, knocking off their bunnets tae give them as good a hammering as they'd got. There was blood everywhere! There must have been at least ten or twenty injured on each side. It was a bit much but ye canny fault they steelworkers for their support, that's for sure." The foreman looked even more worried as he shook his head and took notes on what the guardsman was reporting.

A real testing-point came on Monday, 5th January, when the public works would usually have re-opened. The goods traffic had to be dealt with or the industry paralysed. The chief incident, and one which affected a large group of related industries, was the lack of coal. Stocks in Glasgow were becoming exhausted, and though considerable quantities were carted from local pits to the benefit of their owners, who sold their output at enhanced prices, steam coal for ships' use or exportation was almost unavailable. Steel works, engineering works, shipbuilding yards, and cotton mills closed their doors, and many more thousands of workers were thrown out of employment.

Meanwhile, the impossibility of dispatching coal accumulating at the pitheads forced the coal masters to stop working, and in the mining districts thousands of miners became idle. Some were for the time, supported by their trade unions.

The daily newspapers were, with a couple of exceptions, opposed to the action of the rail workers and opinion was mostly against the strikers. The prevailing feeling was one that by

striking without notice the men had embarrassed the railway companies and endangered public safety. Yet there was an undercurrent, which found expression at public meetings of tens of thousands in Glasgow and Edinburgh that the grievances of the railway men would somehow have to be remedied. It took six weeks of more or less misery for their demands to be settled and each railway company did it in their own time and way with, to Francis' relief, Glasgow rail workers eventually returning first.

Chapter 9 - Michael's passing - Caitlin

Caitlin was becoming thinner as her grief seemed to intensify and lines had begun to etch crevices of sorrow into her face. For months after the strike was over, she had nursed little Michael, the son she had named after her daddy. At first, he just seemed to keep falling asleep when feeding or becoming too tired to eat. Then he seemed sicklier and lost his appetite. Soon his short-lived baby fat thinned away and he just would not; could not gain weight again.

In the summer of '91 his breathing became laboured or would rise and fall so fast that he was becoming short of breath as if he'd been running a mile, no matter that all he did was try to eat. He never quite got on his knees to crawl or feet to walk since just attempting to sit up tired him out so much. It broke her heart some mornings to see him struggle to lift his head. Once the sharp cough developed, the congestion in his lungs made breathing, therefore resting, even harder. Fever with sweating arrived and his wee face became hot and flushed. His body seemed to be either overheating or cooling down too quickly as he alternatively became cold and clammy.

"Francis, don't you think he's getting better?" Hearing the plea in Caitlin's voice, Francis peered over her worried shoulder.

"Sure, he seems to have put some weight back on. But the wee fellah, he's still not himself, so." The weight he had appeared to gain had surprised Caitlin.

"That's come back on even quicker than he lost it, but how's that when he disnae seem tae eat much more than before?" When the doctor next came to give Michael another examination, he simply shook his head afterwards, sighed and remarked, "It's the Dropsy. He hasn't much longer, Mr and Mrs Maguire."

Caitlin took a quick inbreath as shock thumped her in the chest then expelled only a quiet, "No." as her eyes filled and Francis pulled her to him. But they knew Michael was dying and from then on could only watch as their baby's legs, ankles, eyelids, face, and belly, visibly swelled so out of proportion that Caitlin feared he would burst. He cried and cried when able and there was nothing they could do to help relieve his pain and discomfort. They tried their best to keep the other children away from what they could of Michael's distorted and disturbing appearance but they could not muffle his plaintive cries. In November that year, he eventually passed away and the undertaker soon came to take the swollen body of their baby to the funeral parlour. Nora was heartbroken and kept asking for him.

"Where's Micky, mammy?" It took all Caitlin's patience to not scream at her..."He's gone! He's DEAD!" Nora'd loved having another wee brother to coo over but while he'd been ill, she'd had to be constantly checked to be careful and to try not to touch him on the rare moments she was allowed a glimpse. This often ended in tantrums that were even more frequent now. Bernie was very quiet and tried to help his mammy in that little-big man way he had and spent a lot of time with wee Frank, both playing at the back of the room in subdued voices. A few days later after a very brief service with the priest saying a few words, the tiny coffin was gently let down into the grave by Francis and John Murphy who was his usual attentive self when it came to Caitlin. Francis turned in on himself for a few weeks after and when she pushed him to come back out he reacted fiercely.

"Leave it alone Caitlin. I've more on my mind than just our Michael, so!"

"Like what, Francis? What could be more important than that?"

"If ye have to know, it reminds of when my eldest sister Margaret, died. Brings up all those dark thoughts." He couldn't stifle the wrenching sob that burst through his clenched teeth or the disobedient tears that lined his eyelids before insolently dripping to his chin.

"Holy Mother of Jesus! Don't these things ever leave ye, so? I was only six and she was nine. One of those damn fevers from decades ago." His head dropped to his chest as he dashed away the wetness from his face.

"Aye, I ken whit ye mean. Ma daddy passed wae a fever as well, when I was only five tae." She reached for his hand and this time he didn't pull away when she said, "Aye, but the grief disnae go away just cause ye want it tae, Francis. Maybe it just goes tae sleep. And now wae wee Michael's passing it's woken it up about your sister and ma daddy again." Her own tears started up and she'd to brace herself to not flinch from Francis' embrace. She, herself was not feeling particularly receptive to Francis or John's ministrations. Nevertheless, they tried to comfort each other while each was smarting from the rawness; from the sting of death.

"Can I get ye anything Caitlin? Is there anything I can do to help? Ye know ye only need tae ask, hen." John asked again as he leaned over the bed, where she was resting that afternoon a few days after the funeral. Caitlin shook her head, turning her face from him, eventually feigning sleep. She felt more harried by the pity than anything else, which soon turned to irritation when she began to feel as if she was being smothered between Francis and John's solicitude.,

"Will ye's just leave me alone?" she'd snap and only then they'd back off. In truth, Caitlin had lost any enthusiasm for even getting out of bed and more than ever, appreciated her mammy and sisters making time to help her now that she was buckling under, not just the load of care for her living bairns, but the weight of grief for Michael.

Francis, by necessity, within a few weeks was eventually back working at the train station, having been able to get his railway porter job back at the end of January when the passenger trains started running properly again. That was a boon, since there'd been a drop in cigarette sales since the strike broke and he had had less access to fewer men. He'd done alright by that time and despite his return to work at the station, if possible, he wanted to keep on with the fag sales. He'd yet to explain to Caitlin how they'd managed these past few months but knew from the quizzical looks that passed across her face periodically that she was dying to ask him. Until or unless she asked him outright, he was loathe to have to face the barrage of Catholic guilt he expected to be heaped on him for admitting to doing something 'illegal'. That day he was saved by her mammy climbing the stairs with the sisters and rapping on the door just at the very moment he was sure she was about to confront him. She managed to sit up before calling him over to the recess bed, "Francis, I've been meaning to ask ye...Damn! Who's that now?"

"You settle yourself, *acushla*. I'll get the door." He let out a long-relieved breath. "Mammy O'Connell, Susan and Mary! Just in time, I'm away to work," he overly enthused in a higher than usual voice. Granny O'Connell narrowed her eyes at him as they moved past each other. He was out the front door and she moved into the kitchen to see her daughter still languishing in her pit.

"Will ye not get up and sit over here while I get this dinner on, so? It's been a month since we buried the bairn, *achora*. Time to start living again for the wee ones still here and those still to come?"

"Mammy, what are ye doing here? Aren't ye bad with the bronchitis? And can ye not be talking about more bairns just yet. I'm exhausted with all that it takes out of ye tae make, love, rear and bury them just the now."

"Well, another can help ease the fierce pain of loss, so."

There was a basting pot over the fire and from it came the delicious smell of stew. Her mammy had spent the last hour chopping vegetables and had brought that wee bit of beef to add.

Her elder sister Mary decided to feed and dress the children early and the younger one Susan, started to make some headway with the sheets. A red-headed beauty, she'd never shied away from the trekking to the steamie on

Gorbals Main Street. The bairns' old pram frame always came in handy for the trip there and back with piles of sheets. She decided to take Nora with her for the company and the craic. She thought her such a sweet, polite wee girl who easily made friends with other kids. Wee Frank who stayed by his mammy, was a lively, cheery wee boy who had been getting into all sorts of trouble before he could even walk, mostly because he loved to explore beyond the limits he was allowed. At age three he was getting his determination up, but could usually be distracted from a tantrum with a game like 'hide and seek', but Susan just wasn't able to manage him, Nora and the sheets. Mary looked after wee Frank, while Caitlin, still pale and wan and grieving for Michael and missing Bernie, couldn't stop thinking about how the children's father had described his and Bernie's journey to Ireland a few weeks before. She did though; appear to liven up when the stew started bubbling away and its savoury aroma drifted into the back room.

Chapter 10 - Over the Water - Francis

The rain was lashing down as Francis grasped onto his eldest son Bernie with one hand and the luggage with the other, while they rushed to get to Central Station via the Clydeside. He had eventually managed to pay for his return and Bernie's single passage. The increase in rail passengers trying to catch up on lost business or visits to family after the strike, had come at a good time for Francis and put less pressure on him to pawn any more of their belongings; as had the extra income from the sale of cigarettes. Railway porters were usually forbidden to accept gratuities, but it was a common enough custom to get tuppence, or if lucky, a sixpence for transferring the luggage from the cab to the train or vice versa. The railway company's issuing discounted Circular Tickets, available for rail, coach and steamer had also made things easier.

He struggled with the constant poverty that made him feel so inadequate when it came to looking after his family. Each day was a trial to get to the evening feeling he'd done his best. He tried not to let it get him down and escape into the bottle, as was his habit, and he mostly succeeded, but his cigarette smoking was heavier, affecting his dicky chest as a result and those stolen fags were just another thing to make him feel the guilt weighing him down. At least he'd felt a burgeoning sense of pride at, despite being moderate, the extra income had definitely given the family finances a welcome boost, but he had no idea how much longer it would last. He'd recently heard rumours about the police asking difficult questions and had himself sometimes felt as if he was being watched. Any checking he'd done gave him no indication of who or what. The unpredictable financial state of affairs was also why he'd suggested the idea of taking Bernie to Fermanagh. One less mouth for them to feed, at least for now, and a better start for his son, though it broke his heart at the thought of leaving him behind when he'd be returning, but in that moment, he pushed it to the back of his mind.

Had he not met and fallen for Caitlin, it's unlikely Francis would have remained in the city. It had been a big shock to him at first compared to country farm living and had taken some time to come to acceptance, but he'd never get used to it. Despite being glad to be out from under Rachel's Old Testament judgements, it was a real shame Alloa hadn't worked out.

As they hurried over the Broomielaw Bridge across the River Clyde bypassing the quay for the 'Derry' boat since they wanted to stop in Greenock, he repeated to Bernie what he himself had been told: that the name Broomielaw was associated with the wharves but took their name from the street that ran behind them, where traffic flowed to and from the quaysides. Looking west along the Broomielaw from the junction with Oswald Street, despite the sheets of rain, they could see the street was nevertheless, busy with horse-drawn merchant traffic. The carts were heavily laden and Bernie ogled at the huge Clydesdale horses pulling them. Francis commented to his son, "It must be hard work for the horses to haul those loads over the cobblestones. See how bumpy they are, so?" Bernie nodded as he looked nervously at an overladen cart with a mighty mare at the front, charging towards them through the rain. Francis mused to himself how much easier a job they'd have if it was lighter cigarette cartons. He knew, from what Malky had told him that some time before, tobacco was sent directly to Scotland by American merchants. In fact, the city's early fortunes depended on them and therefore that of the African slave trade that he knew little about. As the bonded warehouses on the banks of the Clyde quietly filled up with huge tubs of the crop, work began on converting it into a range of smoking products: snuff, cigars and shag for pipe smoking before the invention of the machine that rolled them individually. However, some casks were still imported by Imperial to supply all of Britain, and some of those still arriving in Glasgow could, as it turned out, be finagled away for private sale.

A cart passing on the left side of the road belonged to the United Cooperative Baking Society Ltd., famous for its biscuits, not that he had spare coins to try them himself, but some of which would've been packed in the containers loaded on the back and destined for the steamers and their ports of call, like Francis and Bernie. On their right were several businesses including a café, shaded by a dripping awning and offering ice cream on warmer sunny days. Next door was a restaurant and then the Argyle Vaults bar. Francis was tempted by the pub but they had a train then the steamer to catch and his brothers would be waiting for them when they stopped at the new pier at Greenock for their first port of call.

Though they were barely visible through the curtain of rain, Francis pointed out to Bernie five of the bridges that spanned the Clyde. Francis could see that Bernie was trying to look interested but the heavy rain made it hard to appreciate anything except somewhere to shelter from the deluge, so they hurried on up Oswald Street to Central station.

The train journey would take up to an hour to Greenock then at least ten hours on the steamer to Belfast after that, but before then they would stop off to visit with his brothers and Bernie's uncles. The station was busy from workers piling off trains to get to their work in the city centre. They had to push through the crowds of men and he waved in response when a few of his fellow railway porters called out on spotting him. They finally boarded their also busy train, which like all the engines waiting at platforms was puffing out steam as its engines fired up. They found and settled in a third-class carriage. Bernie was excited to be on the train for the first time and his eyes gleamed as he peered out the window at the other steam locomotives and at all the people coming and going and the guards blowing whistles and people calling for porters or exclaiming greetings and screeching goodbyes as trains pulled into and out of the station. By the time they were three-quarters into the journey Bernie, his excitement having subsided, now looked despondent as he stared at his feet, kicking his heels repeatedly off the chair. "Stop that kicking, now!"

"Sorry Da. W..w..when will I see mammy again?" he demanded. Francis gulped. What was he to say? He didn't know the answer but in the space between hearing the question and responding he made up his mind, "I think we can say summertime, perhaps. That's not too long and you've a lot of work to be helping out with on the farm before then. Granda will keep you busy with the calves, the hay and the pigs."

"Will the pigs bite me Da?" he said with wide eyes.

"Ach no, bouchaleen! They're a bit smelly but they're quite friendly. You'll be grand, son. I'll be after calling you Farmer Bernie, in no time at all." This time Bernie's mouth twitched into a smile. "I'll be the best farmer, da!"

"That you will for sure, boyo. You'll be a grand helper to your uncles and aunties. Sure, ye've your granny to look after an all. She's the one whose good side ye need to keep on, so. She's fierce good at the cooking and will keep any fellah that's hard-working well-fed." Francis rustled in one of their bags and pulled out a heel of bread for his son to chew on until breakfast on the steamer after they left Greenock. They made good pace and it was Francis who was feeling excited this time as they pulled into Greenock station. He hadn't seen his older brother Harry, for a number of years and as he approached, he could see how time had quietly ravaged his previous good looks. He must be close to about forty Francis reckoned, but looked at least ten years older and it wasn't long before the cause was obvious. Francis noticed his washed-out pallor and the flecks of blood on the cloth Harry was using as a hankerchy while coughing. They clasped hands and pulled in to briefly hug.

"What are ye about fellah? Bernard couldn't get away. He's still grafting as a navvy in yon shipyard but he says to tell yis he's sorry he won't get to meet the wee fellah here and he'll catch up with his other big brother again, so." Bernard was younger than Francis by only a year to the five- or six-years' difference between him and Harry. All be it, they'd been close but too competitive to be around each other long term, it hadn't stopped him naming his first-born son after him. Harry though, had been the one they both looked up to and eventually followed to Scotland.

Young Bernie was huddled behind his legs, the shyness in him making him want to hide. Francis pulled him forward to greet his Uncle Harry, and then they all walked together to a nearby bench for a brief conversation before they'd to board the steamer. Francis heard the most recent news about their own father's ailing health but was reported to still be determined to bully his wife and daughters into running around after him. Francis wondered how his youngest brothers Seamus and Patrick had coped with their brute of a father without the elder ones to divert or diffuse the anger. It had been the only thing that had given him cause to hesitate about sending wee Bernie to the farm. It was too late to back out now; he just hoped his father had mellowed with age. God, he was weak, just as his father had always said. He was glad Caitlin knew nothing of his father except what he'd selectively told her. His mother would no doubt be the buffer she'd always been. She was a match for oul Harry and no mistake.

Looking over the pier, they could see the daytime paddle steamer '*Adela*' was readying to pull away from her berth, her two beige funnels belching smoke and the water rushing as the paddles gained speed and the water gurgled and roared. Once they'd hurried up the gangplank and while they travelled they managed to find a corner out of the wind and rain to sit out the long journey while looking forward to breakfast soon and dinner much later on, when going up Belfast Lough.

INTERLUDE – Mary Maguire

She could smell the sweet scent of birch smoke as the light faded, while firing the whin or gorse (also known as 'The Beltane Tanel') on the hill slopes as darkness fell on the evening of 'May Day.' It was a common practice among the young people of Kirkston and well within the memory of many of the older villagers. No doubt a few of them could still recall similar merry evenings spent on the braes between Rilloch Glen and the locale of the "kissing tree," romping round the bonfires as Mary and her friends did on these occasions to welcome in summer time. This relic of the ancient Celtic festival of Beltane, celebrated by the Druids for this season of the year, made goose bumps rise on her arms as she tripped on the damp grass that chilled her ankles, under her now-dragging skirt. When the sacred fires were kindled with the new light, this custom was, when Mary was old enough and allowed to participate, a way to encounter any fellahs for could-be husband prospects. As her and her friends, male and female, got older, the romping around the fire later became fumbling in the firelight and they soon moved closer to the 'kissing tree' for more intimate clinches. Some had been more memorable than others. Some she'd prefer to keep buried and some she wished had never happened at all.

'Gathering the Yarrow' was another ritual carried out even less these days by the girls in Kirkston on May Day evening. They hoped the fates would acquiesce to providing the appearance of their future partner in life, all be it in dreams or visions. To work, it had to be done just as the sun went down. Having culled the plant, whose buds were yet to bloom into its usual tiny white flowers that Mary likened to flattened daisies, she could smell a strong liquorice-like aroma with a sweet flavour, though her nose wrinkled at its tinge of bitterness. She took it home and placed it under her pillow where the strong aroma remained, its reputed influence expected to evoke the required dream. Just before she fell asleep, she slowly repeated the age-old rhyme: "*Yarrow, fair yarrow! I hope before this time to-morrow/ That you will show me / Who my true love shall be;/ The colour of his hair/ The clothes that he will wear/ And the words that he'll say/ When he comes to court me in May.*" Mary had tried it a few years in a row but didn't ever remember a dream of her could-be husband. Each year on waking, she felt the bite of disappointment at the absence of a vision to encourage her romantic quest, and grabbing the still liquorice-scented dried herb, disposed of it as soon as possible. That didn't prevent her exploring other ways and means of furthering her plans, until as the years passed on she left those childish pleas behind.

~

The Kirkston cottage had three rooms with the hall joining the kitchen and the bedrooms. At the rear, there was a small scullery about four feet square with a china sink and barely enough room for a small cupboard. The scullery adjoined the main living room that had a 'hole-in-the-wall' double bed with a heavy curtain. Her mammy hated the surprise and chill of draughts, of which there were many. The bed was only a few feet from the blackened Victorian cast-iron range. They all knew to avoid their mammy if the fire inside was ever let go out. This was her main appliance for cooking and water heating. Bathing took place in the scullery sink until they were all big enough to become stuck, then each of them graduated to the tin bath on the kitchen floor, which was kept hanging on a nail in the hall. A large square table dominated the kitchen, which was used for everything from food preparation to lessons. It was covered in wax cloth with a pattern of entwined roses. Their main furniture consisted of one armchair, a folding 'bed chair', and a couple of dining chairs.

The hall, which allowed passage to the girls' bedroom, contained a large wardrobe, a wooden coalbunker, an electricity meter and the big tin bath. The hall or 'lobby' was also wide enough to have a clothes pulley on the ceiling and suffered badly from damp, making the clothes take forever to dry then retaining that musty smell. Caitlin could be overheard muttering curses under her breath while nailing up the wallpaper to stop it collapsing over the coalbunker. Mary could still remember Henry, their coalman, coming up the path with a sack of coal on his back and tipping it into the bunker causing a huge cloud of coal-dust that permeated the whole place; leaving them coughing and tasting coal dust for a while afterwards and her mammy cursing again; this time about the state of her washing.

The bedrooms were the poshest part of the cottage with their bay-type sash windows looking out over the street. One had another hole-in-the-wall bed and appeared slightly bigger than the kitchen because there was no large table taking up space. In the main room, there was an armchair and a settee, all second-hand, with a few small tables with plant pots on them. The focus of the room was a very old melodeon (pedal-organ) which had been passed on by a friend of her mammy, which Patrick learned to play after some excruciating years of the rest of them having to put up with his practice. Prominent in the girls' bedroom was the Singer sewing machine. Over time Caity became a dressmaker of quality. She had trained with all the major tailors and dressmakers she could find before her first child was born. Eventually she was in high demand locally and then in Paisley for her skills in everything from alterations to complete wedding outfits. She'd bought her machine new in 1917 with her savings from working in the mill after having such, as she thought, a terrible dress to be married in. Her making and altering clothes continued even after her marriage to Jack and so her kids were always the better turned out.

Before and after Seamus had figured out how to build a radio from a young age, they all played cards mostly for fun, with games like snap and 21's then trumps and rummy and very occasionally after a scramble they would gamble with money or use some matches if they hadn't. It was pawnees and banker and three card brag. But when older, the brothers included all sorts of more serious gambling activities. Placing bets on the horses and dogs at the weekends would often get them deeper in debt. Although gambling on these were common, it broke the law, just like gambling on football did.

So, the bookies runner would visit the street and in a back lane with lookouts placed to keep the 'edgie' for the police, would produce his sheet so that the waiting punters could each pick a horse.

From 1922, the BBC had begun broadcasting and in Scotland it took till a year later in 1923, before they could tune in. As the 1920s drew to a close, the number of broadcasting stations had begun to increase rapidly. Valve and vacuum tube production rose and accordingly the costs fell. Despite these advances, just like Seamus, many crystal set enthusiasts remained and the crystal radio continued to be built and used by quite a few families, maintaining the popularity of radio for many years to come. In the kitchen they had a 'cat's whisker' or crystal radio set built by Seamus that employed no amplification, though he'd discovered that a reasonable signal could be had by using an external wire antenna. Crystal sets and kit radios which were available to buy, were popular since people could assemble them, but they often made at least some components themselves. Theirs showed the coil, the cat's whisker detector and a switch, for band switching; along with the tuning capacitor control. A popular approach to enclosing the crystal sets was to use a wooden box with a cover which meant the crystal set/cat's whisker radio could be closed to prevent damage or any accidental change of the dials and settings. Seamus had banged one together from an old vegetable crate and then, if there were enough coins in the meter, it played as a background to their card games.

As a result of so many tuning in, lots of wire antennas could be seen sticking out of the back of houses in the village and around the rest of the country, allowing everyone to enjoy, among other offerings that initially filled the airwaves, news supplied by an agency, music, drama and 'talks', even if for only a few hours a day. It was a great day for Seamus when they acquired a tube radio since he was much abler to amplify the reception to listen to his favourite shows.

Depending on the family funds, the sisters tried to occasionally visit the Glen Hall, which was only a ten-minute walk from their home, to watch British Pathe newsreels of the war. After the war ended, most of the family could go to the Pavilion in Moorhead, where they revelled in silent films and documentary reels about different locations in Scotland.

~

The village seemed a grand place to Mary as a young girl. She rarely went out alone. There was always a sister or brother to keep an eye on her. Playing hide and seek with her school friends was a favourite and if you were 'het' you weren't allowed to peek. Mary would close her eyes and count to ten before running to catch them all, then when she'd grab Kathleen, who was not happy about being 'het', the game started over again with first caught, 'het' the next time. 'Kick the can' was similar. They looked for the players just the same and if you were caught you had to wait until the can was kicked, then you'd run away again.

All the girls played hopscotch on drawn out beds on the pavements; hopping and skipping and using their legs to push or kick the peever stone because they were only allowed to use their feet to hop into the numbered boxes chalked on the street.

"Hey, what're ye doin? Ye're not allowed tae push." Mary brushed the chalk from her skirt as she lifted herself from the ground while Kathleen quickly hopped with a sly grin to get to the top of the hopscotch grid first. Then there were games of playing at ropes while singing their songs, but they had to take a turn to caw when they got it wrong.

Even when she started school at St. Michael's primary, Jeannie would accompany her, not always happily; being three years older and feeling that she was too grown-up a young lady to be bothered with a whiny wee sister who couldn't walk fast enough for her liking. Other days Jeannie was burdened with having to go the messages for their neighbour next door on the terrace, which she said was even worse than taking Mary to school. With a cigarette dangling from her mouth, her hair in curlers and her hands on her hips, Mrs. Montgomery gave her some money wrapped in a note. Jeannie complained that her stained baby-doll nightie looked out of place on the old woman, saying to her sisters,

"She looks more like a bag of bones with her pale skinny face and wonky lipstick spread *around* her lips." Jeannie's lip curled in disgust and she shuddered when mentioning Mrs. Montgomery's wrinkled stockings that failed to hide her veined corned beef legs at the front door.

Jeannie and Mary would walk to school along Main Street past the Co-operative, whose window always displayed tantalisingly bright-coloured boxes of, when pointed out, what were actually boring household goods like

Lifebuoy and Sunshine soaps, Co-op Tea leaves, Dolly Blue to whiten clothes and grate polish. There was a dairy at Auldhouse too with its big slabs of golden-yellow butter or Bluebell Margarine where the assistant carved out pats with her wooden paddle. She would chase them with it if she caught her and Jeannie skulking by the door staring at other customers or coveting the sweeties in their big glass jars deliberately stored on the highest shelf. A thing they all regularly fought over was the cream at the top of the glass bottles of milk delivered to everyone's front doorstep by the dairy in a horse-drawn cart.

While her brothers were busy playing cops and robbers, she loved it when Jeannie and her played shops in the garden or in the fields, copying the tottie man who would come round selling fruit and veg; delivering it to their door. There were carrots, turnips, Brussel sprouts and new Ayrshire potatoes. For fruit, he sold Fyffes bananas and oranges and pears, attracting the wifies out onto the front step to make their choice. When playing shops, they'd set out their stalls on flat boulders or pieces of wood they found in the garden as the counter to put up their 'scales', alongside a moneybox for a till. Using an old spoon, they would dig the soil; a pile of dirt as mince or clods for potatoes to make their game. They'd fill boxes and tins and paper pokes. They used berries for pretend fruit, grass for leeks or lettuce and any worms that came up with the dirt were meat or fish. The next best thing to use instead of coins was glass. Each piece of glass had a value for trading. Clear glass was common and considered the lowest grade for small coins; coloured glass from bottles that once held whiskey was valued more and next in line came porcelain from a shattered plate or cup, and terracotta earthenware from perhaps a broken jug. The fish van always came round on a Fridays, since the seller was canny about the Catholic tradition of having it for tea only on that day, but it wasn't as much fun to play at.

The parish priest, Father O'Toole, made his weekly rounds visiting the sick, the elderly and those who missed mass the previous week too and she'd pray to God he'd go past their door, but he never missed a chance of a cup of tea and biscuit if they were being offered. Mary always hid in the bedroom when he came to the cottage, to many questioning looks each time that she, for some reason, managed not to have to explain, though Jeannie pestered her often with "What's up with you. You could at least say hello for mammy's sake"

"I see him at Mass tae say hello, don't I? He gives me the creeps, so just leave me alone, okay!" Jeannie wasn't convinced but knew her wee sister would have a 'maddy' if she kept asking her about it. She'd noticed Mary was always wanting to go the long way to school so's to not have to pass the chapel but would quickly forget about it when she saw her pals further along the street; dashing off to catch up and leaving Mary struggling to follow.

On the First Sunday in May, the chapels were packed since the Roman Catholic church hijacked this, linking it with the 'Visitation' and called 'Candlemas'. It was based on another Celtic festival 'Imbolc', that celebrated May 1st as the most important day of the year and the end of winter, halfway between spring equinox and summer solstice when the festival of Beltane was held. It was thought to divide the year in half, between the light and the dark. Symbolic fire was one of the main rituals of the festival, helping to celebrate the return of life and fertility to the world. But in Kirkston, the 'Beltane Tannel' was the preferred way of celebrating the surviving remnants of ancient dances around living trees as part of spring rites to ensure fertility.

At Easter after Mass, a whole crowd of them would run up to the braes where sheep and cows grazed, noses to the grass until startled by the noisy children. They all went further up the hills to roll down boiled eggs, covered in flowers and bunnies and all sorts of fancy designs painted on their shells.

Mary had moaned the face of Jeannie so they wouldn't have to pass the chapel when on their walk to school and instead, go down the back way on High Street to get to the school building. She thought that sometimes Jeannie was just the best big sister ever, though she knew she'd somehow make her pay later for the privilege. Since her so-called favouritism by the priest from when in primary three, she shuddered if they even got close enough to be seen from the other side of Main Street. Mary would imagine Father O'Toole staring at her, trying to scare her into coming inside the church. Even the thought of just his eyes on her always made her shudder and she'd hurry away.

*"You have to go through the falling down in order to learn to walk. It helps to know
that you can survive it. That's an education in itself."* **Carol Burnett**

PART THREE
1893-1910

Chapter 11 - Old Feuds - Caitlin

Caitlin had eventually been able to get herself up and about though she never stopped thinking about Michael; he was a bruise in her heart and a blot in her mind that she had to shy away from to keep functioning. With Bernie, she'd managed a visit to see him over at the farm in Fermanagh and he'd seemed to be happy enough, although distant with her.

"Hello Bernie, love." He'd grown so much already. It had been more than six months since their last visit and she was missing so much of his growing. Bernie's cheeks flushed a little and she had to cajole a brief hug from him. "Have you been working hard on the farm?" He nodded distractedly then his face brightened and when she looked behind to find out why, saw Francis come through the cottage door, ducking his head to miss the lintel.

"Da!" Bernie rushed at his father who struggled to grab him while holding bags and baby Seamus. Jeannie was holding onto Caitlin's skirts and Nora held Patrick's hand as she followed behind Francis coming in the door. Granny was busying about the low-ceilinged kitchen preparing the ham hock and had a couple of the sisters peeling potatoes and chopping cabbage for their dinner. Bernie took father and his barely-known little brothers out to see the pigs while Caitlin got their bags into the back bedroom with its two beds for the lot of them, much the same as at home. Its whitewashed walls were showing a bit of black mould in the corners but Granny had lit a fire to take the chill off the air and the girls claimed the bed they'd sleep on by jumping up at once to bounce on the mattress.

"Lassies, granny will give ye's a red bum for that! Stop your nonsense!" They giggled excitedly but tried to refrain from further bouncing. Caitlin felt disappointed that Bernie hadn't been happier to see her. She missed him so much when in Glasgow, but he was a child who'd been taken away from his home, parents and siblings at a moment's notice, it was unfair of her to expect more. Grandpa Harry sat at the top of the scrubbed wooden table at which they sat around to watch Francis' remaining brothers demolish the Colcannon mash and ham with gravy. It was delicious when the rest got to eating theirs. The silence emanating from Grandpa Harry's scowl was enough to keep them all subdued but soon Granny Maguire broke it.

"So, Francis, how's your work at the railway station since all that stramash before, fellah?"

"Ach, mammy that's all done with now and it's not so different. It didn't affect me so much before or after except for the loss of work when everything was closed down. I'm getting on with things and still looking to get out the city as soon as we can." His father cleared his throat.

"Wife, get me some more praties!" he demanded then turned while pointing his fork at Francis. "Told ye that boyo, told ye ye'd regret pissin off tae Scotland and abandoning us here at the farm. If ye weren't so weak we'd see ye back again here in time tae help with the harvest." Francis' face clouded over and the anger behind the scowl broke through as he stood abruptly, knocking back his chair and spluttering through his tatties. He thumped his fist on the table and the dishes jumped.

"Ye just cannae leave it, not for five minutes, can ye."

"Watch your tone boyo. Don't be playing the eejit with me who's been here looking out for your son."

"Your grandson!" Francis fired back at his father. Young Bernie, Patrick and Frank had just re-entered for their dinner and immediately became wide-eyed with the raised voices. Jeannie started to cry and pulled her skirt over her head, hiding from the whole lot of them. Nora moved closer to put her arm round her wee sister. Caitlin patted and tried to reassure them as she went round the table tugging at each of them to follow her to the bedroom. She was stopped short when young Bernie pulled away and scarpered to his usual room with Francis' younger brothers, his uncles. She was hurt, appealing to him. "Bernie, come in with your brothers and sisters, please." He pretended not to hear her and shuffled behind the men as they also exited the kitchen leaving Harry senior and Francis staring at each other across the table.

"Jesus, Mary and Joseph! You're both scaring the childer!" exclaimed Granny Maguire as she and her daughters started clearing the table of potential missiles, loading them into the deep Belfast sink out of reach of their hands. Francis stomped out the front door, forgetting to duck and cursing after clipping his head on the lintel, then pulling out his flask and baccy to calm himself. Grandpa Harry pushed away from the table.

"Wife! Get me some poteen. That's your favourite son for ye. An embarrassment; a melter is what he is."

They gathered their things together the next morning to make their way home to Glasgow later that day. Both Caitlin and Francis tried to spend some time with young Bernie but there was an air of deep sadness in their attempts to make the best of the inadequate ending to what had become a cruelly short visit. Granny Maguire wrote afterwards to discourage any more visits, saying how much it had upset Bernie all over again when they'd left in such a hurry.

~

For some time after Michael had passed, every time Francis moved towards her, arms outstretched, Caitlin shied away, dodging past him before he could enfold her.

"Are we grand Caitlin or have I got on your nerves over something ye're not telling me about?" There was raised-eyebrow-hurt on his face that she struggled to pacify.

"Sorry Francis, I'm just feeling so knackered, darlin. It's takin me a while tae recover from all that wae Michael's birth and death." Inexplicably, she felt herself averse to mostly any touch and especially the business of baby-making. She didn't want him to feel her shiver of revulsion; hoped he could see her as how she felt: the very picture of an exhausted housewife. Her skin looked sallow, her body felt bloated and she seemed to sweat embarrassingly freely. She couldn't stand either stuffy rooms or cold air. Due to a constant ache, she walked around holding her back like a strange bird with half-extended wings that had forgotten how to flap. If it wasn't her back it was congestive headaches, and that dragged-down feeling. She often felt so worn out with the cares of home and children that she wanted only to lie down and rest, often her very eyelids drooping from weakness. She would lash out at the children too and at times, despite Francis's attempts to help all he could, she felt extremely irritable with him no matter what he did right or wrong. When he moved towards her again it felt as if she had to hold tightly to something to keep from screaming.

"Please darlin, I haven't the energy for getting frisky wae ye. I need some time."

In her run-down condition, she felt stupid, dull and forgetful, unable to hold a conversation with even the milkman, never mind trying to explain how she felt to her husband. From her behaviour, she appeared to her own mammy and sisters like a rebellious dissatisfied woman desperate to abandon her husband and children.

"He's been great wae ye, colleen. Why're ye so off wae him. I've seen ye flinch when he comes near ye. Ye should be glad of the attention after all this time." Her mammy was wringing her hands and tutting before lifting one of the toddlers as he began to whine. Her youngest sister Susan in particular wasn't impressed since she hadn't met anyone she'd like to marry yet, but lived ever in hope.

"Aye she doesn't know when she's lucky, dae ye Caitlin? Always need to feel ye're better than everybody else."

Despite her aversion, little Caity, her name-sake, had arrived in October '93 and was a fiery blessing. It did though, take some additional time for Caitlin herself to recover again and the same burdened state reared its head again. "Dae ye's no understand? I've just given birth again and my body wants a rest. I'm no sure I've anything left tae give anyone right now, never mind Francis." Her lips trembled on trying to holding back tears. She also felt unusually protective and fussed over this baby's health. She wasn't the most affectionate of mothers at the best of times, though with the other children it was better now because they were older and a little less needy, more independent, but maybe because of what had happened to Michael it had stirred up some guilt. Francis had been really trying too but was feeling frustrated at his wife's sometimes excessive anxiety,

"Ye said ye needed a rest, let Susan take her out for a breath of fresh air," he'd implore.

"Aye, come on Caity, ye cannae keep her holed up in here wae the fire smoke and cooking smells all day. That'd be worse for her, d'ye no think so?" They despaired trying to calm her when she seemed loathe to let the bairn out of her sight.

All in all, they had an okay life despite that they, like most families were often living four, six or even eight to a room, so that the acceptance was as much down to the fact that their neighbours were all in the same boat. In those early years in the Gorbals, she remembered the folk up the close were always helping one another, even when it was her turn for gathering the back green clothes poles. Many a time she'd also noticed that the close had been washed with utmost pride including the white clay border on either side, after wee Senga from downstairs had been on her hands and knees with soap and water and elbow grease, scrubbing away while Caitlin was dealing with her bairns. She was let off easy, for it was an unwritten rule that missing your turn, could be considered by some as a hanging offence. There was usually a number of women from the close all giving a hand by taking turns to clean the toilet and the stairs.

Funny the things she remembered now that she hadn't realised had made it feel like home at the time, like the regularity of the 'Leerie' who would come to light the gas up the close before going round the streets at dusk with his lamplighter pole over his shoulder, at one end a hook for opening the glass door of the lamp, and adjacent to it a naked flame for putting to the gas mantle; so-called due to the way it hung like a cloak above the flame. The leeries, of course, had their problems, particularly with mischievous boys who used to taunt them, knowing that the lamplighter, burdened with his ladder and pole, couldn't chase them. So, it was a favourite game in many city streets, the lads waiting for the lamplighter to light the lamps in one street, shinning up the lamp-posts to blow the lights out, then shouting to the leerie from a safe distance about what they'd done.

Wee Seamus sometimes got away from Nora to chase after the bigger boys just as it was turning dark and the Leerie was lighting the street lamps. She'd have left him playing in the puddles with plenty other wee ones while she was playing 'tig 'at the close wall with her pals or cawing and jumping in with the old washing rope; their games being played to the singing of rhyming songs. Then the hunt would be on with her other pals to go and find the mischievous group of under-fives making a bid to be part of the big boys' gang and freedom from being under the eyes of big sisters, maws and aunties leaning out of the windows.

One thing she didn't remember with fondness was that in the close, everyone upstairs had to share one old toilet on the landing, which was cold in the night with only wee squares of old newspaper for wiping. It could be a nightmare to keep clean with so many having to make use of it. One of the neighbours used to always burn a candle in the toilet to cover the smells. Like most, they kept a chamber pot under their beds for themselves and the bairns to use through the night, especially on particularly cold evenings.

At the steamie it felt like a great community spirit among the women, which was appreciated all the more since most of them saw no-one else but their children or husbands, day in and day out. They each booked their stall at the steamie well in advance and had their own favourite cubicle. They'd all separate their washings ready to boil, nappies and colours and dungarees, armed with a washboard and carbolic soap. There was a clothes-horse about ten hands high that had wheels, going to and fro to let hot air circulate, if they paid their tanner. They'd wring out the washing into pails then hang it over the clotheshorse rails, then roll it back into the wall so the washing was dried much quicker than at home.

The Corporation Burial Ground in Gorbals Main Street opposite the steamie was one of the district's few green spaces. It was great for the bairns to play in, with some children leap-frogging over the tombstones while the women were inside scrubbing and mangling the sheets and clothes. Living near to the baths and steamie also meant the company of other women was a constant and they could become either as close as sisters or a catty as enemies. Marcie

Corcoran was the worst. She seemed to have it in for the McInnley women.

"They're a murder of crows, so they are. I saw that Susan wan flirtin wae ma man, so a did." The woman Maggie, at her side, leaned away from the foul breath emanating from Marcie's black and decaying teeth as she dripped her poison in as many ears as she could get close to. They knew it was she who was spreading lies about them but it was always the question whether to ignore or confront her. For the most part they ignored her, as did most of the other women. The general consensus was that not a word that came out of her rotten mouth was to be trusted.

Their little patron saint, Patrick, arrived on 17th March three years later and by that time, they had to move a few closes down to number 60, since there were four bairns again to make room for. People often wondered where everyone slept with having only two rooms. The answer was simple - anywhere they could fit in, and in winter there was just an extra blanket or two and stone jugs with hot water in them to warm their feet. St Patrick's day was always celebrated and especially so that year. Old pals and family came along like Paddy the Coalman, Jimmy the fiddler, old uncle Kieran and more. The fiddle and accordion came out and the mouth organ too, and other old instruments, no doubt found in some jumble sale. Bottles of Bushmills Whisky too of course. Wee boxes of shamrock were sent over from Ireland still damp and a sprig would be put in their glass of whisky, a toast called 'drowning the shamrock' was said and then drunk. (The children, not just Francis, who was in his element, had a wee hot toddy for the occasion, which was known as a cure-all for every wee sniffle) They sang some lively songs and some sad ones, bringing tears to everyone's eyes. They all had their whisky glasses topped up once more and stories of the old days started the rounds, including the one about the Banshee, a fairy spirit who howled when a family member died, usually by screaming, wailing, shrieking, or keening and an eerie light was often seen. This was the time for the bairns to hide behind the bed recess curtains and Caitlin to feel the pain of Michael's memory and her own keening time.

They tried, despite the Maguire grandparents' warnings against it, to visit Ireland at least once a year. Absent Bernie was eleven years old now and not missed any less, though it was easier sometimes for both parents to not think overly much about him. As Nora and Frank were the only siblings who'd known him, his place in the family was often overlooked because rarely mentioned except when it became time for the trip to Ireland.

On their return, depending on the family's finances, Caitlin would take them all down to the Caledonian Tailors to rig them out for the next year with second-hand wellies, sloppy joes, trousers or skirts, a new coat (maybe only once, mind you and then handed down each year, which was the case for each item of clothing or pair of shoes, if they lasted long enough.) but sometimes they had to make do with the second hand clothes given to them by the poor relief or the amateur running up on a neighbour or Caity's old Singer, of shapeless tunics made from the fabric also given by the parish poor law. The wellies were worn all winter and in summer they could just be rolled down below their knees. When the boots were just about worn out, they had to fit in pieces of cardboard to keep the wet out. Caitlin worried that they'd be pointed out as poor because of the red ring that ran round the kids' legs just below the knee from the wellies rubbing, except theirs were definitely not the only red-ringed calves in the street. If either of them was short on clothes for the bairns, it helped that her and her sisters could pass various articles of clothing between them.

Even though they were hard up, they still managed an occasional day trip to Rothesay during the summer months. The kids got so excited and so did Caitlin. It was a blast of freedom from the overcrowded dark grey streets and rundown houses with their odour of damp, smoke, fried food and poverty.

"Mammy, mammy! Look at the smoke from the big chimney!" Nora shouted.

"They're called 'funnels' love," she gently corrected. The Broomielaw quay was crowded with many people having the same urge to vacate the city even for just a couple of hours. Caitlin and the children who could, were loaded up with blankets and lunch pails and bottles of tea while hanging onto their hats as the nippy breeze tried to steal them into the sky. "Keep hold of your brother and sisters' hands. Don't get lost now! Don't go near the edge, the water's deep there! We'll get on the steamer soon." Caitlin was feeling a bit frantic trying to herd the four wee ones and keep her balance with her once again fast-growing belly.

~

The year after Francis' brother Bernard arrived at their door was one of their most difficult years they'd had since Michael died. Right at the beginning of the year in January, Francis was laid off work with bronchitis, which hit them hard. High unemployment in the area meant that the Scotia Theatre on Stockwell Street was operating a soup kitchen during the day to provide some food to local residents. When things became really bad, he would take the young ones there, bundled up against the cold as best Caitlin could. Nevertheless, he soon had to swallow his pride and claim Poor Relief. He was greatly troubled with the situation. He hadn't planned for this. The arrangement with Malky had come to an end due to the death of his horse and not enough cash to buy another, despite what they'd made so far. Francis also thought Malky was scared. "Can't we put together tae buy another horse; even a pony would do?"

"Away wae ye. I'm no the rag and bone man trying tae gaither junk for a sweetie. I'll just have tae wait till I've saved enough for a motor van, even a second hand one." Francis immediately had an image of the local bedraggled Rag and Bone man belting out "ANY OLD IRON?!" then ringing his bell. He was a Glasgow version of the pied piper as kids queued up to feed the horse or pony with sugar cubes or hand him broken household items or sheets and trousers and dresses and bones. The bones collected from mammies and daddies left over after being picked clean and boiled for soup would be handed over to him, then he'd sell them on to be then boiled down again to create glue or fertilizer. The rags would be sold to rag merchants, who paid the rag and bone man by the weight and quality of the rags they collected.

There was a class system even for rags: woollens then cottons then canvas bags. He offered lollipops to kids, before he threw their treasures, his rags; on the back of the cart then starting up with his call and the bell when entering the next street with a trail of ragless kids following behind. Francis shook his head to dispel the image and tried once more to convince Malky.

"But how're ye gonnae save up if ye've no horse tae be transporting goods, Malky? That disnae make any sense tae me, so." Malky avoided his eye but refused to budge, reminding him that the police had been nosing around. He had to admit that much and give up his efforts, angry that it was possible some, in his opinion, jealous bastard, had grassed on them. He'd thought they would've got on their feet again properly with the extra ciggie money but with each new baby, it had dribbled away like water down the toilet. It meant he had to steel himself for the visit from the Parish Inspector for fear of the family having to go into the workhouse.

"Come away in, sir." The tall bespectacled man had to stoop on entering the front door. Francis had managed to delay having his usual dram or two that he'd usually have had even by this time at midday. He didn't want the Inspector smelling the whiskey on his breath. These officials could be cruel in their judgements on a fellah. They didn't seem to care how hard things were to deal with so he lit yet another fag.

"Good afternoon Mr. Maguire." Francis nodded and indicated a place for the man to sit near the range in the kitchen. The kids were in the other room trying to be quiet with Caitlin having to frequently shush them as they became impatient with their enforced inactivity.

"Shall we get started? I just need to go over a few details to properly assess just what you need for your family. So first tell me about how long you've been living here and what the rent is."

"Didn't I give this information to the fellah yesterday?" Already Francis was feeling the humiliation rising and his face heated up. His wheezing was audible while being made to repeat the information again.

"Yes, you did Mr. Maguire but I'm duty bound to go over all the previous details and gather any additional necessary information so that your claim can be processed as quickly as possible." Francis gave a curt nod and proceeded to share the details required at not much more than a mumble, his head lowered the whole time. The man spent the next hour asking him to repeat often about Francis' parents in Fermanagh, his religion, previous job, where Caitlin and he'd been married and all details of the children's birth places, year born and why he was requesting poor relief.

"'Tis my bronchitis, like I said to your man yesterday." He wheezed again as he handed the Assistant Inspector the certificate he'd received from the medical officer the previous day after having to submit to an examination up at Eglinton Street health service. Just as the inspector got to the end of his sheet, young Caity ran from the other room knocking the papers from his knee, sending them to the floor. Francis caught her by the arm and pulled her to him.

"Come here to me, acushla." He lifted her onto his knee.

"Dada, Caity hungry. Caity want to play now."

"Could you control your daughter sir? Loss of the information may mean having to repeat the process all over again." Francis glowered at the man.

"I have her sir. The bairns are just bored not being able to run about. 'Tis such a small space as it is, never mind having to stay still for so long." Francis' breathing was becoming more laboured.

"Nevertheless, sir. We cannot complete our business if the child is not under control. A sharp smack might help if she won't do as she's told." Francis' face rushed red once more as he spluttered out his indignation.

"My daughter is in no need of a smack, sir and I'd thank you not to give your advice so freely. I can look after my family without your help, so." Caitlin was wide-eyed and shaking her head in the bedroom doorway.

"Shall I just rip up your application then sir, since; all of a sudden you can do without my help." Francis gulped and glanced towards the door seeing Caitlin's expression of dismay.

"Sure, I only meant I don't appreciate your slapping suggestion sir. You can clearly see my health is affected and stopping me getting back to work to feed my family. That's the only help I'll be needing at the moment, thank you very much." The assistant inspector smirked into his collar and signed the sheet as he had been trying to do before Caity had barrelled into the room. He slowly stood, unfurling to his full height and his eyes gave a condescending sweep around the room, resting briefly on Caitlin and the other children watching in a huddle from the bedroom door.

"Well, I'll see what I can do in the circumstances. You should hear from us in a matter of days if you've been successful in your application." His long legs got him to the door in no more than three strides. Francis couldn't close it quick enough and then immediately lit another fag before going to dig out the bottle of whiskey from under their bed. Caitlin turned from him in disgust, herding the children back in front of the meagre fire.

Because they didn't hear in days as the inspector had indicated, Francis and Caitlin spent the time worrying that they'd been refused. Having a large family always led to shortages of money they were constantly having to improvise. Their fire was usually spitting out smoke from its filthy flue, polluting the air inside and out and along with everyone else's, regularly creating smog outdoors and dirty clothes indoors. The fire was used like a second bin too. If it could burn, in it went. Even potato peelings out of the sink were heaped on the fire; the skins becoming baked. They had what was called a 'back to back', an open range in matted black and not only did it heat the place, it gave hot water to wash and also had space for the cooking pots on top of the fire. They tried to stock up on coal briquettes, this, when you put them in the fire, would then reduce the amount of coal they had to burn. The other trick when there was only dross left was to shovel it into damp newspaper, making a parcel so that it would burn longer. When they ran out of briquettes and coal then it was time for the reserve. After that, any old shoes had usually been kept as a last resort. It was all right with the canvas and leather ones but the rubber-soled ones stank the place out, but burning them kept them warm. Black-leading the fire-range every month became Frank's job, since in Bernie's absence at age eight he was the eldest boy. Because money was often short, they also made sure to send Frank down to the bakery to wait for the return of the baker's van in order to buy the leftover bread at a cheaper price.

It took until the second week of February for them to receive the ten shillings they were from then on allocated each week until Francis' health improved enough for him to get back to work. Caitlin tried to hold onto or spend as much as she could on food and essentials before Francis could, in her opinion, waste it on buying whiskey. She'd already given him a tongue-lashing for almost losing their claim and she really didn't know what to do for the best about his worsening drinking habit.

Nora was the eldest child at home being nine years old by then and had been helper for her mother with any new babies, who were all from then on, delivered in the hole-in-the-wall bed. She wanted everybody to be happy but felt very unhappy herself when her Da did that staggering about and slurring his words thing. She felt even worse when he'd spent the relief money before her mammy had been to the shops and there was no food to eat those days. Nora went quiet and shuffled around trying to find ways to please her mammy then, but mammy was too upset and angry with their Da. Crying under the covers, she'd pray to Jesus to show her how to do that loaves and fishes trick she'd heard about at Sunday school.

However, she also regularly had friction with Caity then and in later years. Caity was much more demanding of attention or she'd tantrum about not getting it, especially from her father. Nora would always remember that and hearing the snap of the mousetraps at night while her mother sat sewing, close to the fire adjacent to the kitchen sink and the small window above that looked out over the back court and the middens.

The middens were magnets during the day. Be it hide and seek or kick the can or running away from the bogey man, or her, Frankie and Caity would climb on the midden bins then jump on top to dreep down the six foot drop off the dyke. Just for badness the bigger boys thought it was fun to set light to the middens and watch them burn, and everyone had to put up with stink of putrid smoke from the burning of rotten vegetables and other unmentionables. One of the favourite pastimes the kids had was filthy and smelly and ran the risk of being dubbed a 'midgie-raker', but none of that stopped them searching in the middens for a 'lucky'. They'd hunt through all the bins in every backyard for hours, as long as they weren't spotted from the window by mammies and daddies. Sometimes they would strike it rich with a broken toy or an old lipstick. Other times they'd play daredevil games like 'follow the leader' on jumps with names like the Duke and the Royal, or the Devil's leap and the wall of death. Long after leaving the Gorbals, Nora's face still warmed when she remembered her midgie-raking days and she could still smell that awful stench of rotting vegetables, dead cats and cheap perfume.

Her Granny O'Connell and aunties were still living along the road, but bairns called every female neighbour 'auntie'. They all looked out for them but there were good and bad sides to that. It meant they always had to duck and dive out of sight of them hanging out their back windows. They were notorious for never missing a trick and terrifying any number of kids who thought they'd managed to elude their beady eyes and the promise of a leathering until at the last moment hearing the screech of their name and then the slow march of dread after hearing: "GET UP THAT STAIR RIGHT NOW!"

Chapter 12 – Brothers – Francis/ Bernard

At the end of the summer, they had that unexpected visit from the kids' uncle and Francis' younger brother, Bernard. With money being so short they hadn't been able to organise their usual trip across the sea that year and Francis wondered at his younger brother's appearance, immediately fearing the worst for their brother Harry.

Bernard was tall and muscled from his navvy work labouring in the shipyards. His clothes were a tad raggedy and he wore a beard of reddish-gold with a ponytail at the back.

"No! It's Da that's died not Harry, though he's not in the best of health either, so." Francis stepped back awkwardly. He wasn't sure how he felt but it had definitely caused a place in his heart to quickly empty. He felt as if his body was draining, feeling it travel from his head to his feet. "Are ye alright fellah? Ye've gone very pale there?" Bernard grasped him by the shoulder, clamping him to his broad chest, the difference in height now even more noticeable. Francis felt his eyes fill and struggled out of Bernard's grip.

"I'm grand." The words fell out like a hoarse grumble before he turned into the house, Bernard following him. He quickly packed a small bag and gave an abrupt explanatiokissing Caitlin and the children goodbye then left within half an hour of his younger but taller brother's arrival. He felt already removed, already his father was even more in his past with just the final necessities to complete. The

stronger feeling was his unreasonable irritation about
Bernard's rude health. He felt unreasonably irritated by the
fact he'd grown taller than him and definitely felt irritated
by his brother's handsome looks; all feelings which he
considered not to be in the least unreasonable at all. The
green-eyed one was raising its head and it wasn't a
leprechaun, though the spirit of that roguish trickster who
can't be trusted and will deceive whenever possible, could
well have been responsible for the self-contempt and
hostility towards his brother that he was struggling to
contain. Bernard was watching him from the side, as that
critical glare he'd been glad not have had to put up with the
last few years, landed on him now.

"Ara Francis, what the devil are ye being so crotchety for,
so? Is it about Da? I thought ye'd be happy about that. He
wasn't your favourite fellah, now was he?"

"No, it's not that, though I wasn't expecting this to
happen so soon; wasn't expecting you to be giving me news
like that and I wasn't expecting this crevice of emptiness to
open up." Bernard shook his head.

"Bayjesus, you're such a torn-faced eejit sometimes
Frankie. We should be having a dram to celebrate before we
have to pretend grief in front of mammy, who ye haven't even
asked about yet."

"And I definitely wasn't expecting you to be all grown up
into a working fellah and me having to be looking up at ye to
see ye eye to eye and being told off like I'm a *bouchaleen* for
not
     askin after my mammy. Who's the big brother here, ya
lanky gobshite?" Bernard saw the smile breaking reluctantly

on his big brother's face and punched him on the arm a good one. Francis's

face looked a bit shocked and right there on the pavement outside the close at South Coburg Street he punched Bernard back but not on the arm. He clipped his jaw before Bernard dodged the full punch. Then they set-to like they hadn't since being on the farm years before; laughing and cursing and grunting in pain when a good one landed. Caitlin and a couple of other neighbours stuck their heads out their dirty windows above at the noise of the brothers wrestling, which was a version of what was likely to be heard on a Saturday night but definitely not on a Sunday afternoon. For most of the fellahs that was usually sleeping off the hangover time.

"Whit ye daein Francis? Have we no enough troubles without you and your numpty brother having the polis called on yis? Away and catch that train afore ye miss it. Ye know there isnae many on a Sunday and ye'll miss the boat if ye miss that train." The brothers reluctantly ended their fracas and after wiping the blood from dripping noses, they shook hands then stepped on towards the station wearing foolish grins. The tension had dissipated for now but that would change not long after they got home to Fermanagh.

~

The 1845 - 52 famine had attacked the farming underclass. Many died of starvation or, hunger-ravaged, of typhus epidemics against which they had no resistance. Others emigrated - one quarter of the Fermanagh population disappeared between 1841 and 1851. Some, having no other choice, fled the countryside to the town workhouses. Francis' thoughts vividly returned to their country and county's past on travelling from the steamer port to Derry then onto Fermanagh. Just short of 50 years later, he wondered how much different things actually were today. There hadn't been another big famine, or rather the English hadn't stolen so much of their food, due to changes in how the land was cared for. Despite their longstanding differences, his late father, who had lived through the famine as a young man, had described to them what that had meant for farmers of the next generation, which should in that case have been him and the two brothers he'd come to Scotland with. Harry Snr had explained that from the time of the famine, farmers came to understand that they would be the only reliable guardians of their future, and looked for freedom in a series of land reforms. He'd said advantages of the Land League and the land reforms of the 1880s were sometimes underestimated. The concessions of the 'three f's' - fair rent, free sale and fixity of tenure and compulsory land purchase at the turn of the century eventually shaped the social values of people in Fermanagh and elsewhere more than any other political event. From then on, farming communities owning the land were like the backbone of rural Fermanagh.

There were thirteen farms or smallholdings in and around Enaghan and they'd learned to support each other as best they could during the bad times. Most farmers kept some cattle, grew cereals - wheat, oats and barley - flax and the ubiquitous potato but they began to concentrate increasingly on livestock. Great numbers of milk cows were kept across the county, and large quantities of butter were made and brought up to the neighbouring markets, mostly for the merchants in Belfast and Newry. Luckily their farm wasn't in the mountain districts, since much of the land there was cultivated with only the single-sided spade or the old heavy wooden plough. In theirs and other parts of Ulster, the use of the improved double-sided spade, the iron plough and light angular harrow became universal, as well as that of all other new and improved implements when they could be afforded.

Francis wondered about the muffled sobs that he could hear as the light spoke-wheeled cart pulled up to the farmyard behind the byre. All around the farm was quiet on that soft day but for the low keening they could hear coming from the cottage. The brothers looked at each other with some alarm, the falling rain around them misty to the point of invisibility yet still wet to the touch. There was a hazy sort of cloud, but the temperature wasn't too cold and the drizzle seemed to linger in suspended animation as the notes of grief hit a high before plunging lower to sound like that soul was being torn from the depths. Francis bounded from the cart with Bernard following. "It must be our mammy!"

They both flew into the kitchen, remembering to duck under the lintel as they did so. All around the table were Francis' first sight of young Bernie in some time, looking like he'd stretched and was pale in the face, his hair every which way and their younger brothers Seamus and Patrick beside a sombre-looking Harry. Sisters Rebecca and her squad of childer, Kathleen and Mary were openly crying with hankerchies at the ready. He noticed Rosie wasn't there. She was next oldest after Harry, and who'd decided to start a new life in America some ten years before and had never returned. No-one expected her to, but she was still especially missed at times like these and the pall of death reminded him of the American wake they'd had before she left, as was done for all those who chose to emigrate for they may, like Rose, never return to Ireland again.

"Where's mammy?" Francis asked while looking around and starting to make his way towards the bedroom he remembered as that of his parents. His younger sister Rebecca halted him with a sharp "Wait!" He looked at her, puzzled as she shook her head, her dark curly hair bouncing with each shake. "Let her be - it's taken the last few days of her being too quiet. Now she's realising he really won't wake up."

"Is she still in there with him?" asked Bernard.

"Ara boyo, of course and it's as well yis made it here today for the oul yin must be buried as soon as we can. The priest's waiting for us to give him the word for the morning service," Seamus commented. Harry was trying to suppress his constant coughing, practically stuffing his rag into his mouth to mute the sound and staunch the escaping flecks of blood, in fear the rest of the family would notice how bad is illness was. Francis bent close whispering urgently in his elder brother's ear. "What are ye about Harry? Ye shouldnae be here wae that consumption. Ye'll infect the lot ae us an yir no well enough for this." Harry shook his head fiercely, replying,

"Feck off Francis and see to our mammy." Francis gave an exasperated sigh before addressing his other siblings, nieces, nephews and his son who was staring at him eagerly awaiting his attention. He crossed to his son's side, kneeling down to give him a hug, the boy's arms immediately grabbing on with a fierceness that surprised Francis as he detected the tremble emanating from Bernie and pulled back to look at him but Bernie wouldn't let go, holding fast. Francis encircled the boy with his arms and instinctively made to lift him but quickly realised, the now 11-year old boy, was way too old for that, letting go after the brief hug and a tousle of his hair. Despite his age, Bernie still reluctantly let go of his Da. Francis stood again looking around once more.

"Where's all his friends? Wouldn't they be wanting to mind the body for the wake?" Francis was confused since he'd expected the place to be full of neighbouring friends and farmers; especially their wives, who'd traditionally be supporting the wife, his mammy at this time and cooking up a storm so's no-one would be refused a bite to eat. Though he had as likely fallen out with any number of them with the temper he had on him. As he looked around, he noticed then that there were dishes and pots on the sideboards and a collection of half-empty poteen and Jameson's whisky bottles, they'd been already. Francis could hear the now muted sounds of grief from the back bedroom and his brother Bernard's belly grumbling with hunger. "Ye'd best crack open some of those pots, so. Bernard here's destroyed by the journey and we've both a fierce hunger on us." The sisters rushed to take advantage of the distraction and do as asked by their brother and the sounds became that of clinking cutlery and clattering plates. It was as if that keening had paralysed them and their base appetites, their living desires and their ordinary hunger had broken the spell.

The commotion also brought from the bedroom the diminutive figure of their greatly aged, to Francis' eyes, mother; her eyes reddened and face drawn as she sat with them to eat, or at least take a few miniscule bites to keep their concerned exclamations to a minimum.

The family and neighbours congregated for the final night of the wake with more sobs and jokes ensuing for the next few hours. There were plenty shouts of Sláinte! Sláinte, which was literally translated as 'health' and in their keen declarations everyone seemed to be desperately trying to ward off the inevitable, to which his father had already succumbed. There was also a might of slagging going on and a person was wary of getting up for a piss to be heckled with the likes of, "Look at the walk on it!" or "Stop acting the maggot!" for those getting carried away with their consumption of poteen, or Francis even heard, "That one suffers from a double-dose of original sin," when they were making their usual kind of judgements on a woman suspected of sneaking outside to meet with a fellah.[vi]

Francis woozily staggered over to his father's coffin in the back room and stared at the waxwork-like mask of his face, lined and creviced and marking his full sixty-seven years. It no longer looked human although Francis struggled to remember when he'd ever acted like one. He stroked a hesitant finger across his father's powdered forehead leaving an empty line that his Aunty Noreen noticed immediately.

She didn't castigate him however, she simply gave him a sorrowful look remarking,

"'Tis only a stepmother would blame you. Don't worry yourself. There's no need to feel badly about a small mistake like that. Your touch was out of love and respect for your father, such a grand man." He tried not to choke on his immediate urge to disagree with this overblown, patently untrue sentimentality instead he just silently shook his head, leaving his father behind for the last time.

Next day at noon, after a guilty farewell with a beseeching Bernie, a tremble on his son's lips and again the clasping arms having to be pried from around his neck, Francis and his two brothers left soon after the burial and will-reading to travel back to Derry for the late afternoon steamer to Glasgow. They were quiet most of the way and only commented briefly on the unsurprising outcome that meant the farm would pass to younger brother Patrick; any claims they might have had being denied to them for leaving the farm to come to Scotland. Their only other exchanges were some concerned remarks about their mother's health.

"I think she'll be better when all this furore settles and be relieved she doesn't have to deal with the oul bastard anymore."

"Ara, but didn't you hear the grief coming out of her? I couldn't believe it after the way he's treated her all these years." They all slid into silence then until they reached Port Glasgow and then swapped brief embraces and promises to meet up again soon before Francis had to run for the last train back to Central Station.

It wasn't more than a year before Bernard came once more to Francis and Caitlin's door to give the news about Harry's passing. It was tuberculosis after all. No surprise of course and it did make Francis wonder if any other members of the family had been infected. He supposed Harry's wife Agnes and their two children would perhaps have been most at risk. He couldn't not venture down to Greenock for the wake and funeral. Another rain-sodden grey and depressing affair contributing to the depletion of his family.

Chapter 13 – Help to Heal - Caitlin

Caitlin continued, with degrees of difficulty, to individually deliver each of her last three children into the world and it was close to a miracle that eight of the nine she'd carried, had so far survived. That number of children in working-class families wasn't very unusual in those days, especially for followers of the Roman Catholic faith. They still lived in the Gorbals then, though their rooms became increasingly more crowded and claustrophobic. They all had to share this life not just with other Scots and Irish but there was a substantial community of Russian Jews and even some folk from Lithuania. All having been more at risk of poverty and danger, in some cases in fear for their lives, in their own countries than there in Glasgow.

Caitlin most of all was feeling the strongest effect of that much close living. These days she castigated herself for not feeling able to experience love as excitement and enjoyment or as a

natural and necessary blessing; which most of her friends, when she could stand their company, sometimes described as their kind of experience. For her it was just like a responsibility, which often came to feel more of a burden. Though the burden of poverty was a shared weight, like it or not.

The most difficult aspect for her was how to express love towards her children. Wee Jeannie and Seamus came in quick succession in '98 and '99, adding to the ensuing exhaustion that made demands for her affection that the bairns expected, in fact needed, very difficult. The older boys were generally expected to grow up to be stoic men with family duties; not offering or receiving loving responses, especially as they became older.

That children had to attend school between the ages of five and thirteen would have been a blessing for Caitlin, except there were very few Catholic schools. She tried to show concern by providing instruction, assuming the role of teacher for letters and counting. She'd learned some letters from their doctor; a kindly man who'd from then on began to help them out with medicines over the years, and not just the usual ones. He told her his name was Doctor James Paterson, and that he practiced as a homeopathic doctor and Caitlin, always having been interested in unusual takes on the world, quizzed him about the difference from other doctors. He told her that he had studied medicine at Glasgow University and went on to become the Dispensary Physician at Glasgow Homeopathic Hospital and the Scottish Homeopathic Hospital for Children.[vii] But, this was after initially solely practicing the conventional medicine of the day, that included practices such as bloodletting, purging and the widespread use of crude doses of mercury, arsenic and lead.

"I felt, in my, at that time, limited experience, that it left a lot to be desired and, in many cases, we seemed to be doing more harm than good. Then, not long after my graduation from the University, after listening to an early lecture by Dr. Robert Gibson Miller, who'd been a previous physician at the Glasgow Public Homeopathic Dispensary some ten years before, I became excited when he described cases taken and cured by none other than the illustrious James Tyler Kent" [viii] Dr. Paterson stopped speaking for a moment as if remembering something and a wry grin appeared on his face,

"You know there is another interesting link between Scotland and Homeopathy via a separate materia medica." [ix] Caitlin was trying to keep up with all the big words and new ideas in his interesting but somewhat mystifying monologue but Doctor Paterson failed to notice as his flow of words continued about how it heralded the principle, 'like cures like', that became the basis for an approach to medicine called 'homeopathy.' "But, never mind that, where was I? Ah, yes. We were following the eminent Dr Robert Gibson Miller." Caitlin blinked and gulped as he kept going and she tried to pacify the toddlers around her feet as he talked.

"He travelled from Scotland to study with Kent in St. Louis in America in 1884 and then brought the beginnings of Kentian Homeopathy back to Britain, in particular, to Scotland."

This lecture had so inspired Paterson, now based at Sauchiehall Street where the dispensary had been moved to, that he further studied the system, learning from Gibson Miller how and when best to use either low or high potencies, guided by the principles of individuality and the minimum dose. But Caitlin was quite lost and her brain was starting to fizz and she had to excuse herself that day by reason of needing to get the children home. If only it was just a pretext rather than a life sentence. Her journey home with the children, much as she did love them, wasn't the most uplifting way she could think of to pass yet another day, going back to cleaning and caring for them and her often inebriated husband. Next time she was able to get away to see him the doctor continued, just as men always seemed to do, that is, grab the attention for themselves first, as if there hadn't been several weeks and a whole lot of drudgery for her since their last conversation.

He gave Caitlin a fair introduction to his reasons for using his smattering of wee white pills, telling her, "Homeopaths strive for insight in order to match the drug for a particular sick patient. We need to gaze through a maze of symptoms, parts, and disease labels; forever looking deeper."

"Disease labels?" Caitlin managed to jump in to ask this time.

"Yes, the usual terms we hear, like measles, tuberculosis etc. We must always be interested in the whole patient: body, mind and spirit, not just to the names given to the effects."

"I suppose that's true. After all, the only one who can really tell what the matter is, is the person, isn't it?"

The doctor was based in the city centre and she so wished she'd known him years before when Michael had been ill. Just maybe his kind of treatment might have made a difference to the outcome. She came to realise what he'd meant about the body, mind and spirit part, since when he'd eventually stopped lecturing her and spent the time, what turned out to be quite a long time, to find out what was wrong with her, the questions covered every part of her body from head to toe, stopping off at food and drink, women's problems, sweating and of course, how she *felt* about any and everything. It had been so unusual for anyone to ask her such questions that she struggled to find the words to describe many of the sensations and even harder were naming her emotions, beyond the huge reservoir of guilt for having desires other than what the church expected of her.

"But why use so little medicine? How can it be enough to help someone get better?" She'd queried. He gave a low chuckle.

"No offence to you, Mrs. Maguire. It is a common question and based on another fundamental principle in the homeopathic system known as using the minimum dose."[x] Her thoughts were thrown into disarray at the amount of knowledge and experience he must have to be able to make prescriptions for his patients.

"You sound like a very learned man Doctor. We'll see if your wee pills manage tae lift this weight it feels like I'm carrying. I really do hope it helps. Thank you for seeing me and are ye sure a shilling is enough? Not that I'm rich or anything but it sounds like a lot of work ye're havin tae dae." He handed her a small packet in exchange for the silver coin she put in his open palm.

"Please do not concern yourself Mrs. Maguire. That will be more than sufficient. Put one dose of this medicine under your tongue tonight. Please be sure to write down how it affects you

to inform me of at our next consultation, yes? How is the writing coming along anyway? Are you managing alright?"

"Yes, thank-you doctor. I'm sharing what you teach me with the older children, since I haven't managed to find a proper school and I don't think Francis would approve of what's available locally. I'll let you know if I'm having any problems. That reminds me, I must buy a newspaper on the way home to practice my reading. Good afternoon, Doctor."

Caitlin included the girls in the practice of reading and writing too. Why shouldn't they learn something else that could help enhance the quality of their lives? Being daughters and knowing the expectations of a man's world, when old enough, there was still a place for the usual sewing and cooking, laundry and other household duties to learn to manage. Much to Francis' chagrin she also encouraged the boys to learn to darn their socks and what was involved in keeping their clothes clean, especially having so few. By encouraging the children's independence, she felt that it helped her and them. At the very least, their home was, despite the lack of space, filled with the children's ever-changing pictures after she'd managed with difficulty to get Francis to spend a little on chalk and boards rather than whisky, which helped them all to keep practicing their letters which they would, after writing practice, become fun with drawing. It had also encouraged her to try some drawing and sketching of her own. Mostly she drew the children in their few still moments, usually when sleeping. There were the occasional times one or other of them might be engrossed in their games and she would try a quick sketch. She wasn't happy with many of them and glad of the slate and chalk that could be easily erased with a quick wipe but as time went on, she found a few pennies to buy some paper and pencils for this one thing of her own that helped her forget the weight of poverty and drudgery for even just the time it took to draw or sketch.

As a wife Caitlin however, had no easy outlet for her lack of love; no natural expression. She just couldn't make it develop into encouraging words or affectionate cuddles. It wasn't absent, but the expression of her love felt benumbed and difficult to express. So, she fell back on duty and gave in to Francis' demands for sexual relations, for not only was it her duty as a wife but her duty to God to bring children into the world. Even when at the end of her reserves, her sense of duty kept her going until, at times she gradually began to resent, what felt like, her incarceration; a prison of responsibility and the feeling that she was struggling against the ties that bound her. That feeling produced some dark times. Her wretchedness seemed, at those times, to project gloom; a darkness around herself like a whirlpool of discontent. The remedy *Sepia,* which Doctor Paterson prescribed for her was like a magic pill, it gradually lightened her sense of heaviness and soothed that bitter resentment, changing her attitude so drastically that she began encouraging the advances firstly of Francis and then, sometime later, of a long-time admirer.

~

When Doctor James Paterson first practised, he used to visit patients on his bicycle no matter the weather and one night was said to have even walked five miles to visit a seriously ill child with pneumonia. He'd been on that bicycle the first time she met him. In fact, he became the second important man in her life that she'd met in collision when, like Francis, he nearly knocked her over, the only difference this time was by with what means: a bicycle.

"Jaysus! Dae ye need tae be going so fast?!" Caitlin struggled to gain purchase as his bike clipped her in passing, knocking her off balance.

"I'm so sorry, dearest lady! Are you alright? I get a little carried away on my flying machine." He chuckled while his face reddened and she couldn't help but laugh with him. They ended up in an involved conversation where he told her he was a doctor and the reason for his hurry. Before he sped away to his patient, he arranged with her to meet for tea in a few days and Caitlin felt a long-forgotten frisson of excitement that there might be a new person with new activities and ideas in her life. She never attempted or wanted to be any kind of intellectual but missed discussing new ideas and activities she may sometime get to undertake.

When they eventually met up properly, he'd told her that he'd wanted to become a doctor because as a small boy he'd always been interested in natural history and living things. Whenever he visited any art galleries in Glasgow, he missed the pictures and went to see the skeletons, animals and birds. It was also well known that he hated draughts, so he told her he'd regularly received many Christmas presents of bed socks, window wedges or something concerned with keeping him warm. She agreed with him over her own difficulties in keeping warm. Much, in her case, with several episodes during her many pregnancies of blood loss contributing to her seemingly ever-present chills.

Caitlin remembered meeting him later in the homeopathic dispensary on a bitter cold winter's day and when he asked her what kind of day it was, she replied 'Terrible!' He said,

'Bottom of the class. Bottom of the class. This is an '*Aconite*' day!" She was puzzled by his response, not yet knowing the remedies well enough. He was a bit of, what would be called an eccentric, but those little pills he'd prescribed definitely made all the difference to Caitlin's indifference and later Francis' bronchitis.

Francis was pretty sceptical at first, but only until Caitlin began to initiate lovemaking whenever an opportunity arose, though initially he'd been a bit shocked. Where had that come from? He couldn't believe his luck, but then his wheezing gave him pause. Caitlin tried to explain about the kind of treatment the doctor offered and Francis agreed to give it a try. Why not, he wouldn't be charged much and there was nothing else on offer, except Caitlin of course, which he wasn't presently in any condition to accept, no matter the desire.

"You're holding your chest Francis, why's that?" Francis looked down to see that he was in fact, holding his hand against his chest. He looked back at the doctor, puzzled.

"Sure, I don't know. To keep it warm; for a bit of comfort? I'd really just like to be at home lying down and not moving at all, so."

"Ah, how does moving affect you then?"

"I start coughing a bit more." *Bryonia* was what Doctor Paterson ended up prescribing for him and not for the last time. Its effects helped Francis recover a bit sooner and stay well longer so that he had managed to return to work at the railway a bit sooner than expected. When he later suffered intermittent bouts of bronchitis from both the coal smoke and the cold environment while working on the platforms as a porter, a situation he couldn't change and which according to the doctor was called a 'maintaining cause', the Bryonia in winter time was a regular medicine for him. A bonus was its positive effect on his levels of irritability. He also no longer suffered from Caitlin's sometime disappointing indifference, which hadn't helped. Now he sought ways to calm and melt her back into being his beloved wife. He too, wasn't the best at demonstrations and declarations of love but he attempted in his own way to be committed to his family and all it entailed and hoped his efforts showed his love. When it came to supporting the children, he was more of a rule-maker. He preferred that they were encouraged to respond to discipline rather than indulgence, though Caitlin like him, took no nonsense either. With so many children appearing regularly how else could they manage them all without some rules?

Chapter 14 - The Plague - Caitlin

A disease had been brought into Glasgow, then a major port, by an infected rat on board a ship or so it was originally believed. Nevertheless, Glasgow was subsequently declared a plague-infected port in late August, 1900. For sure, there was no shortage of rats in Glasgow, but how many were now infected and in turn infecting all their neighbours? A few men were standing congregating on the corner watching the hurrying officials, getting in the way, ignoring their shouts. "Away back tae yir hooses. Can ye no see, ye'll be makin things worse staunin there, passing the miasma tae even mair folk!" But they were engrossed in their serious deliberations.

"Was there no the Plague in them foreign countries where they Indians came fae? Didn't Mr. Bogan work as a docker on the ships gaun there?"

"Aye, a bet he brought the disease hame wae him."

"Naw, he only worked on ships that sailed aroon Britain. Couldnae hae been that."

"Mrs. Bogan worked in the salt market wae aw they stinkin fish. Since she died first it couldae just as easy been her, d'ye no think so?" This wasn't confirmed by the men going up and down their streets or mentioned in the papers.

Caitlin had worried greatly when the news and incidence spread quickly around the neighbourhood. She tried to keep the children at home as much as possible. The streets were rapidly emptying of all those clusters of children playing in the gutters. The Maguires lived at number sixty and after they heard about young Catherine Mackie, a

14-year-old across the road at number 57 South Coburg Street, who'd worked as a cigarette packer and died in the third week of August, Caitlin was scared even to look out of her window, despite Francis not feeling able to miss work due to their present dire straits. Then at the end of the month at number 6, a fifteen-year-old lad was taken to the hospital on London Road with the same illness. In September, two weeks later, four people from the Mackie family across the street followed the lass at number 57, being taken to Belvidere Hospital. Caitlin watched from her window with horror as her neighbours and their children were stretchered away by attendants swathed in masks and protective overalls. Only two returned having recovered. As morbid and frightening as the situation felt, Caitlin had an urge to draw those stretchered souls, to somehow capture these crucial, and for some, tragic moments. She'd started using small charcoal pieces from the grate and the darkness of the coal lent a solemn atmosphere to those sketches. An older lass of twenty years old, Mary Mackie, the other married daughter, and Robert, her brother, even younger at age twelve, didn't make it home. Across the whole area, it seemed to have started up the top at Rose Street and made its way towards them, but surprisingly the Hutcheson's Grammar School at the back of their street didn't close.

Thanks to its slum housing and the subsequent rats, due to the large numbers of people living on top of each other, Glasgow in 1900 was still a haven for various nasty diseases. It was in August that year that this new kind of 'fever' in the Gorbals had the city medical experts scratching their heads in confusion. The wife and granddaughter of Hugh

Bogan, a docker, died on August 3rd from what was initially believed to be gastroenteritis and zymotic enteritis, but soon, other people in the neighbourhood also began contracting and dying from a serious illness.

As in the first case, various different causes were given in the newspapers but reports were sparse, as if the authorities were trying to keep it all quiet. However, the medical people were not convinced about the current explanations; something else was wrong. Finally, in late August, a doctor at Belvedere Infectious Diseases Hospital diagnosed the miasma as Bubonic Plague. An extensive trapping and extermination campaign was undertaken, which included the examination of 236 rats from the Gorbals and over 100 from other parts of the city, but they found no evidence of plague in the rat population at any time during the outbreak. This led them to conclude that plague must have spread directly between humans through clothing among other means, and possibly by fleas, since some victims had been noticed to have several flea bites, a fact that had been initially ignored. They did eventually discover a trail of victims leading from a rag shop

The Sanitary Authorities were then very quick to act. Fumigation of infected homes with liquid sulfur dioxide and disinfection with a formalin solution commenced while the windows were removed in Florence and Rose streets where the deaths had begun. They took furniture and bedding, some of which was destroyed. Men were then going around with chloride of lime (chlorine powder) and carbolic solution, after calls to disinfect all the trams, all the ferries, even all the coins in people's pockets in case they should carry some kind of contagion. They were up and down the closes wearing face coverings, trying to track the spread of the Plague on the streets below Caitlin and Francis' window, looking for anyone who might have had the slightest contact with the Bogan family.

The authorities did use this clear out to try improving the previous terrible state of the areas' health.[xi] Some of the later victims of the outbreak had nursed Mrs. Bogan or been to the wakes held for her and her granddaughter. Wakes for the dead had always been very popular, particularly in the Irish communities of the Gorbals but the church weren't happy with that or the idea of cremation of bodies.

It began quietly. Sadie Mackie and others paid their respects to the recently deceased lying in an open coffin in the main room of the house. There were, she could see, a few total strangers who had turned up just for the alcoholic refreshment. It was what happened when free drinks were being handed out to visitors for the passing, as was usual at wakes. As the night wore on, a party atmosphere descended, people were singing and enjoying themselves, while children played among them. Over a hundred people must have been at Mrs. Bogan's wake during the day and into the night.

The authorities had a time of it discovering who all the attendees were but kept looking until they found each one, since they decided it was they who had spread the Plague. Those hundred people rounded up from Mrs. Bogan's wake were quarantined in a "reception house" so they could be monitored.

The staff in the hospitals and reception houses were inoculated but the locals refused the vaccine and from then on wakes were prohibited. Everyone's house was evacuated of all family members and every room fumigated; all clothing and bedding was disinfected or destroyed. Isolated people had to have two examinations per day and could go to work and socialise, which didn't go down too well when another building opened for isolating women and children in Tollcross who were confined to the house and kept behind a fence if taking air outside. When people left after their ten-day isolation, they had trouble with neighbours not letting them back into their homes. There were petitions and meetings objecting to many of the restrictions and the freedoms allowed those affected, including those employees suspended from their jobs until given a certificate saying they were free of the disease before being allowed to return.

Caitlin became petrified that any of her own children or Francis would become infected or die, rushing to her mammy's rooms along at Nelson Street. "I'm sorry mammy. I couldn't think of anywhere else. They said the fumigation would only be overnight, and then we'll be back along the road.

"Did ye bring something for the bairns to eat. I've only some 'goodie' to give them."

"I did mammy, but they love that bread wae milk and sugar. They always talk about it after they've been here." She'd left the children there and made her way to the West-end to speak with Doctor Paterson. He asked if she'd noticed or any of her family had complained of the common signs and symptoms, which he'd said included: fever and chills, extreme weakness, abdominal pain, diarrhoea and vomiting or bleeding from the mouth, nose or rectum, or under the skin or shock.

Caitlin gladly answered not but asked about the dreaded appearance of the development of swollen and tender lymph nodes called buboes.

"Ah, from the Greek 'bubon', meaning groin, where they're often found." Dr Paterson explained.

"Do they buboe things burst?" she wondered aloud.

"Well, a victim's buboes can swell so much they burst through the surface of the skin, most often around the fifth day after infection.

"Do they smell?"

"In the case of bubonic plague, the buboes are red at first but later turn a dark purple, or black, which is what gave the 'Black Death' its name. Sometimes the buboes burst of their own

accord and a foul-smelling, black liquid oozes from the open boils, but this is a sign that the victim might recover."

"And is it painful?"

"You see, buboes associated with the bubonic plague are commonly found in the armpits, upper femoral, groin, and neck region. Symptoms also include things like heavy breathing,

continuous vomiting of blood, aching limbs, coughing, and extreme pain caused by the decay or decomposition of the skin while the person is still alive."

"Those poor people, and some of them my near neighbours too. It sounds horrible, and happening to children as well. Can you give us anything to stop us catching it, Doctor?"

"Well, you know homeopathy usually treats symptoms that are present and there is also the possibility of a diagnosis of pneumonic or septicaemic plague for some but I could try to find the *genus epidemicus* if I can get enough information on those who have succumbed; not necessarily those who have died. I will send a message with the most appropriate remedies I can find after making my enquiries. Please do not travel again or be in close contact with anyone too often. I will be in touch as soon as possible." He noticed the puzzled expression on her face as he said this.

"What is it?"

"It's just that epidemicus genie thing. What's that when it's at hame?"

"It's an "epidemic simillimum", so a medicine that can produce similar effects to the epidemic. [xii] Often one medicine is identified and indicated more than the others-that one would be considered the genus epidemicus."

"Aye, okay then. I see whit ye mean, I think."

"Well, since we homeopaths work with the law of, 'like treats like'; it's a bit like 'the hair of the dog' kind of idea."

"Och aye, I see now, like when the men are hungover on a Sunday morning and insist that only another drink will help." Really, living with Francis, she knew about it more than she'd like to admit.

The family had stayed, all squashed together, at her mother's while their rooms in South Coburg Street were fumigated and given the all clear. It was the cleanest the area and streets had ever been and likely ever would be again. A messenger from Doctor Paterson had arrived a day or two after Caitlin had visited the dispensary with a small package of *Phosphorus* tablets to be given immediately to all her family members and another of *Baptisia* to hold onto with instructions to send someone to have the Doctor attend in case of any important changes. He'd reassured by indicating not to worry, since homeopathy had an excellent historical reputation for curing people in epidemics.[xiii]

Because an unusually high number of secondary plague infections was clearly occurring between members of the same households, it suggested that body lice or human fleas were probably to blame.

Francis had stayed well away from the wakes he'd heard about several streets further east, up towards Rose Street and then the chapel stopped the neighbours from having any at all, so that people wouldn't be spreading the disease further into the city. It was an especially sad time for the Mackies, not even being able to say a proper goodbye to their deceased family members. By the time the deaths had seemed to slow down, the Maguire family had luckily survived unscathed, but Francis became all the more determined to get his family out of Glasgow as soon as possible.

Overall, there were thirty-eight cases and sixteen deaths. An official cause for the source of the outbreak never appeared. The ban on wakes, an Irish tradition, and one of the original beliefs that the outbreak originated from an infected rat brought into Glasgow on a ship from overseas, fed into the negativity already held towards Irish immigrants and some sailors. This also meant that during the period of the plague outbreak some ships coming from Glasgow to ports around the world were held to be investigated before being allowed to dock.

It was the human way to blame out of fear, those deemed foreigners or incomers for any deadly disease that hit society because of their so-called 'unclean ways'. Unfortunately, this further resulted in an increase of the usual prejudices towards Irish families, garnering support among folk that the Plague's source originated and was spread by these groups.

A few months later on 22nd January 1901, Queen Victoria died of a cerebral haemorrhage while staying on the Isle of Wight after sixty-three years on the throne. However, she had long ago lost the affection of the people of Ireland after her government's lack of response to the Great Hunger in 1845, so Granny O'Connell was celebrating and Francis was mostly indifferent to the adulation and outpourings of grief from many across Britain. The rest of their families followed suit, despite pressure from royal family supporters at work, adding to the hostility they'd experienced during the plague.

Chapter 15 - International Exhibition - Caitlin

In May 1901, the Glasgow International Exhibition opened in Kelvingrove Park. Caitlin was determined she would visit. She'd been saving up a penny here and there in the last year to take along her eldest daughter Nora, as a special treat but ended up taking Caity too. Caitlin had watched Nora appear to observe the world through her shy and reserved nature, and who tended to heaviness in her blocky body and a harbinger of serious moods. Caitlin felt some guilt about that while being intrigued enough to want to sketch that glowering visage. Their decision to send Bernie, their eldest son, to Fermanagh to be looked after by his Maguire grandparents had left Nora as the actual eldest child with all the responsibilities that come with that in a large family. As a child, Nora was often well-behaved, responsible, obedient and extra co-operative, in order to avoid rejection by either of her parents. Susan, Caitlin's younger sister had pointed this out to her one day. They'd been in the room with the cooking-range, sorting out the dirty laundry for the weekly visit to the steamie.

"Mammy, should I sort out the socks intae pairs for you?" Nora's serious face looked so eager.

"No, hen, they'll be fine the way they are."

"But mammy, they're easier tae find if they go thegether, aren't they?" Susan nudged Cait to turn from the bundles of smelly clothes and watch her daughter stubbornly rake among the mound of washing to find each half of any pair of holey knitted socks with an anxious expression on her face.

"Nora, will ye look at this mess ye're makin, hen? I said they were fine. Dinnae fash yersel ower it." Susan nudged her sister again as Nora's face fell in disappointment.

"Thanks love, wae all they holes you'll be hard pushed to make even wan pair, won't ye?" Caitlin smiled as she gently pushed her daughter on top of the mound. Nora flailed in surprise as she flumped down, then her younger sisters Cait and Jeannie jumped in with the boys trying to get on top of them. Susan started to tickle Frank, Patrick and wee Seamus and they all collapsed and rolled on the dirty washing laughing so much they had to start sorting it out all over again. Nora cracked a giggle or two but Caitlin could sense her sensitivity to disapproval, her fear that she wouldn't be able to please her mother. She craved her father's approval even more. Nora doted on her father who could be equally serious and who was certainly seen by his neighbours as a pillar of family responsibility, at least on the days he wasn't drunk. At those times Caitlin watched as Nora tried her best to avoid him becoming crabbit and angry with her because that seemed to frighten her, so she made sure to try keeping him happy

"Hello Da, can I make ye a cup of tea?" was usual as soon as Francis had put a foot through the door. "Do you want me to comb your hair or tickle your feet?" might be heard after dinner was done. This slavish manipulation often annoyed Caitlin, but then she saw the tense smile break into a wonderful grin that transformed her daughter's often-pale face, at times the skin seeming thin as a fragile veil that inspired capturing on paper that transformation from the glower to the smile.

She held her tongue now and let the child please as she would, especially since she could be so gentle and kind with the little ones, which was such a great help. The other side of this quality was her bringing home stray flea-ridden kittens because of that sensitivity to responding to hurt or sick animals. With the plague not long in the past, she implored Nora to realise the potential danger. Responding to making friends with the local kids her own age though, seemed to take longer due to Nora's apparent lack of confidence and shyness. Caitlin was worried she might become a 'loner', but her sister Susan reminded her how friendly she was at other times with the other kids when at the washhouse with her.

"Ach, she's grand wae the other bairns as far as I've seen. Whit ye worryin aboot? She's a few wee pals she gets on wae doon at the steamie."

"Thanks Sue, I forgot aboot that, no being with yous so much."

Recently, Caitlin had noticed Nora's difficulty in saying 'sorry' or admitting mistakes and maybe she needed another blether with Susan, since as she grew older there was a worry this could become a pattern of withdrawal and defense or a tendency to get into arguments and quarrels with the fixed idea that she was always 'right'. Some recent squabbles she'd been involved in were testament to that potential entrenchment.

"That's mine! Why are you always touching my things, Caity? It's not like I have that many."

"They're not yours. Mammy got them for me, not you! You always get the most and the best just because you're older. It's not fair!"

"No wonder. You're such a baby. Always crying to mammy or da. Can't even fight your own battles, can you?" At that point, Caitlin swiftly intervened but ended up supporting her younger daughter's claim since it was true, she had bought them for her. Consequently, Nora immediately withdrew, a grimace marring her attempt at a conciliatory smile. Caitlin didn't want the emotional barriers she seemed to be building to intensify Nora's feeling of isolation. Her sensitivity made her prey to easy offence and being vulnerable to any criticism, deserved or not. It revealed her conviction that perceived insults and injuries, no matter how small were meant to hurt. She seemed able neither to forget, nor forgive. Sometimes she had that 'don't touch me' attitude with Francis and Caitlin, which just made her feelings of unworthiness worsen. The formerly affectionate and well-behaved little girl was becoming moody and unhappy, which ended up with her pushing away their love and security with abruptness and irritability, that she nevertheless seemed to crave more than anything.

~

The Fair was such an unusual and historical entertainment with the exhibitions, shows, stalls and businesses, that she hoped it would fuel her curiosity for some time. She also wanted to show Nora especially that there was more to the world, to life; than just household duties and looking after children, which despite her young age, she'd already had too much experience of. Caitlin loved events, happenings that were out of the ordinary and since she'd been prescribed that medicine from the homeopathic doctor last year, she felt much more like her old self and looking for new intrigues. The main new intrigue was with an old acquaintance. Francis' best man, of all people. It had been that surge she'd experienced initially around Francis after her previous avoidance tactics over her lack of feeling; her lack of desire. He'd been well pleased except he then became less able to take her up on it due to his worsening lung problems. That left Caitlin feeling frustrated and when John next came a calling the spark she'd long tried to suppress was easily lit again in her present state.

"How are ye John? We've no seen ye for a while. Where've ye been hiding?" Caitlin laid her hand on his arm and squeezed gently while stroking it with a lingering look. John was a bit taken aback by Caitlin's enthusiasm. He'd not seen her so bright in a while and it gave him a flutter in his belly. "I..I'm awright, hen. I can see ye're feelin better the day. Ye've done your hair an all haven't ye?"

"Ye noticed!" she said smiling and patting down a few stray strands as she checked with a quick glance that the children and Francis were out of earshot. "Come away in. Are ye over tae see Francis?"

"Aye, I wondered how he wis daein wae the bronchitis, an that." She was still gazing at him and he was unsure what all the attention meant. Francis was in the next room and as much as he'd love to encourage her, previously in years past she'd made it clear she wasn't interested in his advances, so what had changed? She took his arm again and encouraged him into the kitchen proper, busying herself with making tea while he went ben to the other room to see how his oldest and closest friend was coping with another bout of bronchitis. He was snoring and wheezing away though, so John edged away from the bed. When he sat down at the table, he had the two smallest children trying to climb onto his knee.

"Sorry, he's sleeping John and a didnae want tae wake him. His sleep's been that bad wae the wheezing. Disnae sleep for long, but his fever's down a bit the day. If ye can wait a wee while, he might wake again soon?" She smiled at him again while nodding her head, as if hoping he'd say yes.

"Well, I'll finish this tea ye made me an see if he wakes by then, otherwise I'll come back anither day, aye?" Caitlin leant towards him and he quickly pulled back thinking she had been going to kiss him, but she startled a bit at his haste then lifted Patrick onto her shoulder, with a slight smile at his reaction and sat on the opposite chair blowing her own milky tea to cool it before offering some to the bairn. Francis hadn't woken by the time John's tea was finished and as she saw him to the door slipped a crunched-up slip of paper into his hand. Again, he jerked at her touch but grabbed tight onto the scrap of paper as Caitlin smiled at him before she closed the door at his back. He'd couldn't help wondering what that was all about-didn't want to get his hopes up.

Caitlin, feeling the stirrings of excitement at the thought of him reading her note, soon wondered why she hadn't thought to do this before. But quickly she knew why. Not because of any sense of guilt but because the babies came so quickly and increasingly it took so long for her to recover, the last thing on her mind was relations with the other sex. It really hadn't just been being with Francis she'd had that distaste about marital relations with; it was her own previously wearied and burdened state that had put her off. Any guilt about her revitalised ardour being directed at John was definitely there, but mild in the face of her desire. Self-expression, unique or mundane had always been a desire rarely satisfied in her life and now the strength of desire seemed to be lining up to propel her into an all-be-it potentially reckless situation. She trembled at this realisation; trembled with anticipation and hope that John wasn't going to be faint-hearted about what he'd previously made clear, what he definitely desired. But had it taken her too long?

Her other motivation was her concern for the girls. Any form of change and novel environments were what being young was all about. Since she had always liked pushing the boundaries of what was considered normal, she didn't mind when the children wanted to try out interesting new activities. She also had enough loyalty and stability to provide a strong foundation for her family, and with Francis being such a traditionalist they helped balance out each other's influence between them, despite the occasional parental conflict. Caitlin simply didn't feel the need to be bound by traditional family or gender roles, and would've been happier with her freedom but the love, no matter how difficult she found it at times to express, for her husband and the compulsion by the church and inability to control the arrival of children meant she just had to find some freedom within the unavoidable confines of her life. Despite the release the remedy had given her, she knew the everyday drudgery of looking after all the children would eventually soon weigh her down once more. Her drawing and sketching gave her some small relief but she supposed the thought of the unrelenting housework and care of the children was where the desire for the relationship with John had come from; something to raise her spirits once in a while to keep on going.

She'd always had a variety of friends and acquaintances despite her circumstances and sought to teach her children to be open-minded and curious about people from all walks of life, particularly in light of the repeated prejudice they'd experienced being of Irish descent and brought up in the Roman Catholic faith. Caitlin also tried to encourage their ability to think deeply and come up with creative ways to sort out their problems. Francis, despite his misgivings, had praised her for being a great role model for looking towards the future rather than becoming stuck in the present or the past, which he could be guilty of. Her and Francis' main trial as parents had always been about learning to open up to their children emotionally. Caitlin tended to be more comfortable with intellectual thought than with feelings, so she'd always had to work at being tender and nurturing; had to resist the urge to withdraw from her children when they'd been needy or upset.

She wondered how much she was prepared to sacrifice over what she was hoping to initiate with John Murphy. That he seemed to be less of a drinker was a positive because for all the chest difficulties had reduced their relations, Francis' drinking wasn't helping.

She'd given John the details of when and where to meet her while at the International Exhibition but was unsure how to do this while Nora was with her, then remembered with a leap in her heart, her decision about taking Caity too, which meant she could slip away easier and Nora would still have company; even if Caity definitely wouldn't have been Nora's first choice of companion.

~

The International Exhibition opened in Glasgow on May 2nd 1901, with one of the main festivities being in celebration of the 450th anniversary of its famous University (est. 1451). All the shops and stores along the route had closed that day and crowds of people poured out along the ceremonial route, like a wide ribbon encircling rows of volunteers and schoolboys who formed the boy's brigade. The children were made up of several schools, with every pupil wearing a cap and a white belt and carrying a gun. Both the volunteers and the schoolboys had their own orchestras so that music was blaring uninterrupted along the entire route. Many people attending the exhibition were wearing black and the iron railings across the city were also painted black as a mark of respect to the recently deceased Queen. The procession was attended by officials, City Council members, the Mayor and several Scottish Lords - all wearing their finery, among which the robes of the Councillors, consisting of long gowns with ermine capes, stood out.

The Duke and Duchess of Fife had been greeted at the railway station. As soon as the Duchess alighted from the train carriage, she was reported to have been met by a little girl who presented her with a huge bouquet of flowers almost as big as she was. Then everyone was led to the waiting ceremonial carriages, drawn by horses harnessed in single file, and then proceeded along the decorated streets towards the exhibition.

The exhibition ceremony would have had a royal opening, but King Edward VII and the Royal Family were still in half-mourning after the death of Queen Victoria in January. According to the papers, the ceremony itself was open only to invitees and was held in a large round formal hall and consisted of an address being read out and then its text being presented to the Duchess in a golden casket as 'a memento', the Duke's responding speech and finally declaring the exhibition open on behalf of the King. Every attendee was said to have risen to follow the Ducal couple to the art department housed in the newly built Kelvingrove Art Gallery, whose grand opening was deliberately planned as part of the Exhibition. The royal couple stopped before the locked gallery entrance. A key was reported as having been brought to the Duchess on a gold cushion, with which she unlocked the door and the exhibition and the gallery, was officially declared open.

From their place in the excited waving crowd outside, Caitlin, Nora and Caity feeling squashed up with so many folks all wanting to see the royals, watched the Duke,

Duchess and the participants return to their carriages then being taken on a ceremonial tour of the exhibition before they disappeared, apparently to the City Hall in George Square for a formal banquet.

At three o'clock, the entrance doors were flung open for the ordinary mortals like them, then thousands of Glaswegians poured in en masse. People shoved and pinched and kicked while trying to get to the front of the queue for the ticket booth first, all semblance of decorum having disappeared with the royal couple. When the three of them made it in with a few scratches and Caity whimpering in fear, Caitlin quickly opened her drawstring purse to pay the admission of one shilling for her as an adult and two at sixpence each for the under 14's. The thrupenny official guide was added to that, one of which they'd splurged on for a keepsake, though Caitlin knew already whether John came today or not, that she'd be returning. It would be open until November and there was no way a single day trip would allow her to appreciate all there was on offer. Once inside, the Exhibition turned out to be very beautiful and based on their first impressions, very informative. Most women donned grey, blue or brown attire though those forgetting the old Scots adage: "Ne'er cast a cloot till May is oot!" were optimistic in their beautiful pink, yellow or lilac summer dresses with wide-brimmed hats, a few even sporting matching parasols settled on their shoulder, she supposed, to reduce the effects of the summer sunshine on their delicate skins. She laughed a little to herself at that, as she kept an eye out for the expected rainfall from the steel grey clouds gathering above.

She tried not to, but couldn't help comparing their own clean but washed-out house dresses to all the finery around them and she could see in Nora's eyes that look of wishing she could hide; saw her dropping her head and curling her shoulders in towards her body and felt the same, but for the fact her attempt at shrinking was more about not being able to provide something just that bit nicer for Nora. She was at that age when things like how she looked; how she measured up to other people, was becoming a concern. The men, or rather 'gentlemen', were in suits, boaters and even top hats. No boiler suits and tammies here, she thought, though there was no shortage of boys in bunnets. Both her daughters were wide-eyed in wonder at the sight of all the people and attractions; their eyes shining with excitement. "Let's walk towards the river and find a seat to have look at the program before deciding what to see next, lassies, eh?" Caitlin put her arm around the shoulders of both of her daughters and pulled them briefly to her before Nora began to resist and called to her younger sister,

"Come on Caity, I'll race you to the river, come on!" before pulling away and lifting her skirts clear, making a dash towards the shade of the trees overhanging the riverside as Caity yelped then chased after her.

The tall monumental buildings had a more restrained, not boisterous fairground, style despite its title of 'world fair'. There was a mass of greenery around with the River Kelvin winding its way through the entire exhibition. The river featured a gondola imported from Venice and two singing gondoliers, who according to the papers, quickly became known as Signors Hokey and Pokey by the irreverent Glaswegian crowds who they heard calling to them as they rowed the gondolas with their charges up and down the river dressed in white blousons and black caps. They, all three of them, gaped at the swarthy-skinned men lending their arms ever so politely to help customers onto the gondolas for a sail down the river.

To Caitlin's joy and to where she'd return as many times as possible in the next few months, its centrepiece was the new Art Gallery and Museum that had appropriately become the Palace of Fine Arts, which included work by the 'Glasgow Boys' who were by now acknowledged as internationally important artists; among them Glasgow's own Charles Rennie Mackintosh, whose perspective drawing of the Daily Record Building in Renfield Lane drawn and signed by him, was exhibited in the Architecture hall. Caitlin was impressed by his penmanship and skill conveying the unusual design he'd created for this modern yet functional building. Charles Rennie Mackintosh had also designed a stall for the Glasgow School of Art and one, among other trade stalls, displaying ladies' underwear for Pettigrew and Stephens, which afforded the lassies some red-faced merriment.

It was mentioned in the newspaper that Mackintosh had missed out on the design commissions for the exhibition pavilions, which were awarded to James Miller. Miller had won the open competition with his design for the exhibition's main building, the temporary Eastern Palace. It looked Oriental, blended with a kind of Spanish style, and topped with a grand dome lit up by a beautiful electric-torch-wielding golden angel of light and exhorted many a gasp as folk looked to the heavens to see the angel captured in flying pose at the very top of the dome.

There were also separate buildings for industrial and machinery displays, concert halls, foreign pavilions, as well as many minor buildings covering subjects such as agriculture, heating and lighting.

Russia had their own displays with Tsar Nicholas II said to have personally paid out £30,000 to fund his country's "Russian village" of seven buildings (four of them being magnificent pavilions). There was a model farm complete with working dairy, windmill, a Grand concert hall with seating for more than 3,000, and a new sports ground at Gilmorehill with a four-lap cement cycle track, cinder pedestrian course, football pitch and stand accommodation for 25,000 spectators. Here, concerts took place, while numerous sporting events, including a football tournament in which Rangers beat Celtic in the final to gain permanent possession of the cup.

There was a switchback railway and a water chute, both of which were very busy that first day, to which after gawking at the gondolas, they'd been carried by the electrified tram system to and from the gates. Caity became very vocal, after being briefly quieted by fear, when she saw the chute and harped on at Caitlin and Nora until she got her way to watch, not participate. It would not be the done thing for the young ladies to be donning bathing suits, which they did not, in fact, possess anyway, in the middle of the park of an afternoon. They were instead, given permission to have a ride on the switchback train.

Nora added to Caity's already smarting collection of pinches while Caitlin saw the advantage being presented to her when she realised, she would be able to leave them to trundle round on the railway. She gave them a few extra coins for a mineral when they would, as she directed them; make their way to Jenkins café in case she couldn't find them right away. As the girls waited to be admitted to the switchback railway area, Caitlin made her way to the Ireland Pavilion which was made up of several traditional thatched roof cottages which were so like that which Francis' parents had lived in in Enaghan, that she trembled at the thought that Granny Maguire would step round the corner any moment. She gasped as a hand landed heavily on her shoulder.

"Agh!" Caitlin's head whipped round, feeling the tingle of warm breath on her ear and neck.

"It's only me." John said in a low whisper.

"What, why are ye whispering? It's so loud around here I doubt anyone would hear unless they were right beside us." Caitlin gave him a warm smile and slipped her hand into his, leading him in the door of the nearest cottage. He reluctantly followed, reluctant only because just at that moment he had a flash of Francis lying in his bed wheezing.

"Come on! We can talk inside." Caitlin said before noticing that there was a small exhibition of Irish lace and moved towards it to have a look and get away from the door. The small card accompanying the first piece once again made her heart stutter and her breath catch, it read: *In the small hamlet of Bellanaleck, in the County of Fermanagh, in north central Ireland, the wonder and history of hand-made antique*

Irish lace is celebrated daily, of which this is a delicate, intricate, painstakingly created and timeless example.

Caitlin glanced quickly around again but her view was blocked both by John at her back and the milling crowds in front of her. She was just getting anxious with all these reminders of Francis' home but she made a mental note to mention this to him by way of an alibi. Jesus, she was thinking like a criminal already and she hadn't even done anything yet, well not very much. They moved on past other similar exhibits which she had to admit were beautifully made and ranged from Irish crochet lace, Carrickmacross lace, Limerick lace, Youghal lace to Inishmacsaint needle lace, according to their adjacent cards.

"Caitlin, what are we doing here. It's all very interesting and 'history in the making' if ye like that kind of thing, but why are *we* here?" She watched as John wrung his hands and gave her a pleading look. He was right, she'd deflected his advances for years and here she was, out of the blue, demanding his attention without, as yet, a word of explanation.

"I'm sorry John, it is unfair of me but..." she took a deep breath, and without being able to look him in the eyes, said "I...I was wondering if ye were still interested in me, you know the way ye used tae be? I'm sounding very bold and not at all ladylike but I've been thinkin a lot about what I might have missed with ye and..."

"Yes."

"...Yes?"

"Yes, I'm still interested in ye. Yes, I've never stopped being interested in ye and yes, when and where can we find somewhere to be alone so that I can show ye how interested I am?" His voice had dropped an octave, but his sheepish smile and flushed face couldn't hide the spark of joy in his eyes as they instinctively moved closer together but they were about themselves enough to go no further though both their chests moved quicker and their breathing became louder. When he grasped her hand, goose bumps erupted all over Caitlin's skin. She shivered a little and he welcomed the opportunity to put his arm around her shoulders and draw her a few inches closer while saying, loudly enough to be heard, "I think you're getting a chill Mrs. Maguire. I think a visit to Miss Cranston's tearoom might be the better choice at the moment, don't you, my dear?" They made their way towards Miss Cranston's Teahouse but before they reached the steps leading up to the tearoom, Caity, with Nora trailing behind, ran towards them.

"Mammy where have ye been. We were looking for ye." Caitlin felt her face grow hot and dipped her head, thinking fast.

"I was just coming to get you at Jenkins when I bumped into Uncle John. Isn't that a lovely surprise?" When she looked up, she could see the mild shock on John's face and the suspicion in Nora's eyes as she caught up to join them.

"Hello Uncle John, what're you doing here?"

"I was just coming along to visit the Irish Pavilions. Yer da has been trying tae get me tae come ower the water to Ireland for so long and I've never made it yet. This is the next best thing, I'd wager. Have ye seen them yet" He turned and pointed back the way they'd come at the squat buildings with sheep milling around munching on the nearby grass.

"Oh, that looks like Granny Maguire's cottage, doesn't it Nora?" said Caitlin but Nora wasn't so easily distracted.

"That's a bit of a coincidence that you're here the same day as us, Uncle John.

"Well, I'm not the only one am I? It's the first day of the Fair, there's thousands of us here today."

"It's an exhibition, not a fair." Nora rebuked him. Caitlin tutted at her eldest daughter's unusual disrespect.

"Let's go to Jenkins and get that refreshment. I'd love a cup of tea. Would you like to join us, John?"

"No, I'd better be off. There's a few other halls and exhibits I'd like to see before I need to get home. I'll be up to visit yer da soon girls. You have a lovely day now." With that, John gave them a wave as he purposefully strode in the opposite direction. Caitlin discreetly let out her breath.

There were numerous restaurants and cafes apart from Miss Cranston's which looked divine but those patrons in their top hats and tails had seemed a bit off-putting with her in her dowdy dress, despite it being her best one. Other establishments included the Royal Bungalow Restaurant and even higher-class Grosvenor near the Concert Hall, and the Grand Avenue Buffet. Jenkins & Company ran a lower-class, more affordable restaurant and tea-room where Caitlin treated the girls to a mineral while she had a welcome cup of tea and a scone. They made their way to the Mackintosh designed Ladies underwear stall; Caity giggling at the strange and exposing sight of the frilly items and Nora's face glowing red in embarrassment. "Mammy, I'm black-affronted you'd want tae bring us here!".

Then they visited their final exhibit that day, the Dido umbrella stand, stocked by Mr. George McCulloch, the proprietor of the "Dido" stores in Argyle Street in the city centre. The process of manufacturing was done at the stand. From a large choice of plain and fancy sticks a visitor could make a selection, and have the stick made into an umbrella from any of the covering materials available, but it was a sunny day and they'd managed with just their hats, though the fabric patterns had been appealing. Besides, they had their official guide as a souvenir. Caitlin rolled it up to put away in her drawstring bag before they stepped on through the homeward-bound crowds towards the stop for the tram to the Nelson Street terminus and perhaps a quick visit to Granny O'Connell before going home.

The girls were full of excited stories for at least a week but the novelty eventually faded since Caitlin gave no promises or made any offers to return with them anytime soon. When the Central Station hotel was closed, she did though worry about the rumours of a return of the plague in the city centre, especially suspect when there were so many world-wide visitors for the exhibition, but nothing was mentioned in the newspapers and she got on with planning her meetings with John.

That brief closeness had lent an exciting frisson to her daily life in anticipation of what might happen the next time and just how soon that would be. She was sketching more and craving not just John but the joy of the new circumstances was inspiring images to draw in charcoal and pencils though she had a desire to use more colour these days after seeing some of the masterworks at the art gallery.

Would Francis notice if she splurged a little bit on paints? He had always seemed happy to splurge on whisky, so why shouldn't she, she wasn't harming anyone, not even herself. Her mammy was keen-eyed and never missed a trick, sometimes catching her gazing in distracted thought (about John, of course) startling her in the middle of losing track of whatever she was cooking. "*Acushla*, you don't seem yourself, so. I can't say you're as down as ye were a few months ago, quite the opposite. Has something happened, colleen?"

"Naw mammy, I'm just feeling a bit better after the medicine Doctor Paterson gave me. Ye should have a wee chat wae him yersel. I'm sure he'd give ye something for that cough of yours." Her mammy looked unconvinced. She knew when she was being fobbed off but decided not to pursue it. She'd find out soon enough.

It was to the International Exhibition Caitlin went again and not for the last time. On this occasion she went alone, saying she had to see Doctor Paterson at the Dispensary in Sauchiehall Street, but stayed on the tram to the west-end instead. Caitlin recognised that just like in Ireland, India or Africa; everywhere the English imposed a civilisation that had as its goal comfort rather than spiritual needs, the gains of culture and progress were only enjoyed by the minority, the rich landlords who immediately became anglicised. All of the benefits were bought for the dear price of concentrating the land ownership in the hands of a handful of lords, bought by the tears of many thousands of families driven away from lands where their forefathers had lived, and bought by providing the rest of the population with miserable land plots and back-breaking industrial work only sufficient for meagre sustenance. She knew this was why Francis had very little enthusiasm for paying money to see the exhibition. For her, despite the nations' costs she wanted to partake of some of those benefits, for like it or not, it was the future and she could learn; her children could learn ways of getting from underneath the slag heap of society; could have a future of some quality and keep the best of before.

A brief visit from John to see Francis at home after their first encounter at the exhibition, had allowed them to once again pass a note with today's meeting place. At John's suggestion, after that they began meeting at his house in Govan.

Chapter 16 - Ibrox Disaster - John

Francis' mother had passed away in Fermanagh four months before. That wake and funeral was an intense time for all remaining family members. Already gone were his father, his sister Margaret, both his brothers Bernie and Harry but Seamus and Patrick and sister Mary who was looking after Bernie junior, and their families, whom he and Caitlin joined with their own. Their last child, another daughter, Mary, was born in the spring of 1902. Just four weeks before her birth, tragedy struck further into Govan on fifth April 1902[xiv]. The final match of the football season's British Home Championship between Scotland and England kicked off at 3:30pm at Ibrox Park. Francis had thought to go but changed his mind at the last minute. Afterwards John Murphy, the dedicated football supporter of the two friends, *had* gone to watch the game, coming by to let them know what had happened. He was unhurt but looked pale and visibly shaken.

John told them that the incident happened around thirty minutes into the first half of the match, when the back of the newly built, filled beyond capacity, West Tribune Stand collapsed. The estimated attendance figures for the match was a crowd of more than 68,000, half of whom were in that West Tribune Stand.

"It was when Bobby Templeton gained possession of the ball the crowd began stamping, swaying and surging forwards. All I could see were men jumping, screaming as Bobby made for the England goal across the field, and suddenly there was a gap, a space in the crowd that wasn't there before. Then police were running and people were shouting and screaming with looks of complete shock on their faces." In the stand itself just before the collapse, John had heard a gangly fellah wrapped in a jacket and scarf exclaim,

"Whoa, did ye hear that?" No one else seemed to have heard the cracking sound and now he could see the stand swaying. Watching from the end of the other stand John could see movement but thought it was just with the fans being so excited, then there was a shout. "Hey, this isnae safe. It's gonnae fall!" Just at that moment, the sound of the wooden stand cracking couldn't be missed even under the raucous shouting from the many thousands of fans around them, as the swaying became seriously scary. Men looked alarmingly at each other as the stand began to collapse beneath their feet. They each made a grab for the next man and the next and the next but it was to no avail as hundreds of supporters still fell the forty-foot drop to the ground below. The fellah in the scarf landed with a sickening crack as his head hit the concrete before others also landed hard on top of him or could be seen colliding with the steel girders creating blood-spouting injuries for those who were fighting for their breath under the weight of hundreds of bodies below.

"There was so much screaming and shouting and gasps of fear!" John said, shocked disbelief in his voice. "You could hear yelps of pain and moaning from all those with injuries like broken limbs and cracked skulls." He shook his head and dashed away tears that ran down his cheeks as he told Francis and Caitlin "I could see some spectators were suspended in the air until they could be rescued, having become entangled in the steel beams during their fall. God! All those people hitting the ground and the steel girders as they fell, it was awful!" Caitlin and Francis looked white–faced themselves as they got him a blanket and a warm sugary cup of tea, for his sudden shivering shock.

The scenes John had described were later said in the papers to have directly caused the majority of fatal injuries that occurred. Requisitioned horse-drawn carriages and taxis carrying up to thirty people at a time to the Western Infirmary, took the injured and deceased. John, along with other unharmed bystanders, couldn't get over the horror of what they'd witnessed. Those who first reached the ground alive must then have been dying from suffocation. They reckoned at least two to three hundred people had fallen through the hole. The Herald wrote that rescuers arriving first were met by, "a scene of indescribable horror and confusion ... a mass of mangled and bleeding humanity; the victims piled one above the other." The players had no idea of the extent of the carnage. The Herald reported one of them saying,

"When we saw the ambulance men at work we knew that something serious had happened. We were told to retire to the dressing rooms. I shall never forget the scenes inside. Dead bodies and groaning men were lying on the seats where only a short time ago the Scottish players had stripped. Even some of the players' clothing was requisitioned for bandages."

An investigation afterwards found that seventeen wooden joints had given way, causing a hole about twenty yards long to open up in the stand. Heavy rainfall the previous night was also said to have contributed to the stand collapsing. In total, twenty-five people died and five hundred and seventeen were reported as injured. The final victim, Peter Patterson, died three weeks after the disaster on May fifteenth just five days after Mary was born.

A final child and their first in the new century. Francis felt their hoped-for positive omen was undermined by the horror of that national disaster, but a new job offer, soon came that promised the life he had long craved for himself and his family. After talking to one of his workmates he was told of an opportunity in a village further south, outside the Glasgow city boundaries. It would be beyond the thick smoke that belched from the many factories and mills making the air foul to breathe, coupled with the lack of indoor and outdoor plumbing, which had been insufferable to him and deadly to many others. In the Renfrewshire countryside, they would have a new beginning.

Despite the relatively recent birth, Caitlin had an opportunity to comfort John over the lingering effects of the disaster when Francis was back at work in the station and her sister Susan took the children to the park to give her a rest. She'd boarded a tram up the road to Govan.

John was still pale and thin-faced with shock several weeks after the disaster and Caitlin handed him an *Arnica* tablet to put under his tongue and a sip of water. Then she led him from the clutter of the cooking area and the dying embers of the range into his bedroom. She undressed him slowly, despite her excitement, removing his overalls that stank of the sour sweat of fear and the oil from his trade. She murmured, "It's alright John. Ye're gonnae be okay, ma love."

And he let out a sigh as his lips met hers and they began moving together slowly at first and then as John grasped her closer and tighter their movements became frantic and John seemed to want to get closer and deeper in desperation, holding on like his life depended on it. She gasped a bit at the force of it since she wasn't quite healed from the birth. At his climax the bubble of shock burst and John pulled away, burrowing into a corner sobbing with deep rasps catching in his throat as he still resisted the unstoppable flood of tears. She held him from behind as he shook for five minutes and until gradually his sobs subsided.

"I'm sorry, hen. What was that ye gave me? It's made me no quite the man you'd be expecting. None of the suave love-making of those top-hatted gents at the exhibition, instead it's me just making a right exhibition of masel. I'm nothing but a big jessie."

"Och, John, ye're more of a man tae be letting out all that horror ye've been carrying around these past weeks in yer heid. It's how the homeopathic medicines work. Won't let ye hide it away pretending it's no affectin ye. Yer colour's come back now."

"Aye, am aw red an blotchy like a bairn greetin for its maw." Caitlin wrapped her arms round his big broad shoulders as John wiped his face on the sheet and returned her hug. They lay quiet for a few minutes before Caitlin started to become restless. Too soon feeling the hurry of needing to get dressed so she could make her way home in case her sister was wondering where she'd got to, not to mention the damp patches spreading across her chest as her milk came in for Mary's next feed.

"A hate this scurryin about Caitlin. All this duckin an divin."

"John, please don't start. I'm trying ma best, ye know a cannae leave Francis wae his health and all these bairns, especially now since wee Mary's arrived." Caitlin was surprised. He'd never said anything before; was usually very accepting of the way things had had to be.

"Well... I know but it has tae be said an now am saying it. I'm no happy Caitlin. Ye know a love ye and don't know how much longer a can dae this. Blame yer wee pill for not keeping it tae masel for a change."

Caitlin was not as shocked at herself as she might have been. She'd long deserved something of her own, not something that had to be shared with her husband or her bairns; just for her and the drawing on its own wasn't enough. She'd loved the sense of excitement, the relaxation and sensuality in her body rather than her previously constricted, wound-up trudging about to get through another exhausting day of fetching and carrying, cleaning and cooking. She blamed the exhibition happening last year for getting her started. It had reminded her there was more to life than just drudgery, that she'd had a life of her own, however briefly, before having children. As it turned out it wouldn't be too long before there was no more need for any ducking and diving.

Chapter 17 - Move to Kirkston - Francis

Like Francis, people were attracted to the area of Kirkston by opportunities to work in the mills and factories where they could earn higher wages than they'd be able to as general workers. And though there was smoke from the mill chimneys, it was so open and with so few inhabitants compared to their previously cramped living conditions in the tenements, that you could still breathe fresh air. The hills around were a great reminder to him of the many hills and mountains in Fermanagh, like his favourite, Cuilcagh for one.

However, life was still hard for most people both at work and at home. Similar to Francis, they would labour for twelve hours a day in a six or seven-day working week. There was a 'half-timer school' for children built at Crofthead, though he hoped not to have his children working in the mill at all if he could help it, though Caitlin appreciated the choice of education being provided.

The long working hours and a life of poverty for most meant that social activities were limited. Social interaction for men often revolved around inns and public houses, where alcohol was sold at cheap prices. However, it was also a place to gather, to exchange news and gossip and many clubs and societies had their origins in the village pub. The Auldhouse Bar with its barrels behind the counter, sawdust on the floor, and the smell of fermented liquor in the air was a balm to Francis.

This public house, like the few in Kirkston and particularly in Glasgow city, were purely shops for upright drinking; for the courts, in the interests of the young, had succeeded in making them places in which no man, from the fatigue of standing, would linger long. However, Francis often hadn't the stamina for any of that standing about on a regular basis. His face was new around the village (a very Presbyterian one at that) and he was a Catholic to boot, so felt the guilt of more drinking, never mind the scorn heaped on his religion by birth, so chatting overlong to another fellah wasn't really an option. He hadn't been so keen on the queries and quips while working in Central Station, about whether he was a 'Billy' (King William of Orange) or a 'Dan' (Daniel O'Connell); did he kick with the left or the right foot? A saying that had become lost in translation if ever he heard one. Coming from farming stock the use of spades for that endeavour and later industries, (like building those damn roads to nowhere during 'the great starvation' as he liked to call it) and that his and Caitlin's mammies and daddies had grown up through, made him and many others in Ulster well acquainted with the two-sided spades and their footrests compared to single-sided ones, which continued to be used in the rural areas in south and west of Ireland and consequently, more often associated with the predominantly Catholic population there.[xv] As a result, they were accused of digging with the 'wrong' or left foot and so was born the question about which foot did he kick with; claiming from that to be able to decide your religious views.

In his experience, the public houses here and in Glasgow were crowded, dour places, to which he often only came in for refuge from the rain. After a while, the standing grew wearisome, and the frozen stare of the barmen at his elbow made him feel unwelcome if he did not drink up and have another, then another again, and once more, and so on till the clock struck eleven, and the only direction then would be home. He could not, much as he might like, without offending accepted conventions established among regular folk, take Caitlin into a public-house. To say his wife waited for him on the pavement (which she'd never even consider doing in the first place) would be worse than no excuse at all. The finger of scorn would rise and the sarcastic dubbing, for which his mates were famous, and he'd never hear the end of it. 'A merrit man, God help him, a merrit man.' Therefore, his wife remained at home while he followed his own life. A situation that had recently become the norm and worried him some. Not that he shouldn't, more like she shouldn't and she was; that is, following her own life. She was mad about that daft International Exhibition. He'd lost count of the number of times and the amount of money she'd spent up in the West-end at shows and exhibits and presentations. If he wanted to see Irish Lace he'd go visit his mammy.

He had at times fallen in with men he was acquainted with from the railway, sharing in the round of drinks that was happening; to then withdraw without returning the favour would make him subject to the judgement of being 'a sponge'. Nevertheless, the men by favouring the practice of 'standing a round of drinks', had made it into their club, and it worked together with overcrowded tenement houses, to make family life an impossible thing as the husbands stood another and another round.

The factories and mills around Kirkston and Paisley required a higher number of workers and this was creating a demand for housing. Works owners were building blocks of housing, sometimes called 'Lands', which they would rent to their workers. These usually consisted of rows of single or two-storey buildings divided into separate dwellings. In Kirkston, new communities grew up at Crofthead, the Brig, Wylies Land and Low Banks. At first his own family's accommodation had been cramped and basic with large families like theirs inhabiting only two rooms much as in the Gorbals except for less overcrowding, but his new employment as the Crofthead Mill gatekeeper at least meant he didn't have to suffer breathing in the coal smoke from belching steam engines or stand out on the cold platforms.

The gatehouse was a small brick building on the Low Road with two metal gates at the entrance. Each mill worker had a small metal disk known as a 'check', which was about two inches in diameter with a number on it. On the wall was a large board where on arrival, each worker lifted off their number and dropped the disc into a metal box for the purposes of checking attendance, absenteeism and lateness. For latecomers, he had to mark them as 'quartered' meaning they would have fifteen minutes docked from their pay, which made him and the others working in gatehouse not very popular at times. Most of them, as if wee bouchaleens, best enjoyed blowing the steam-operated mill horn to warn workers about changes of shifts.

Bouts of bronchitis had continued to plague Francis over the years and unfortunately, their escape from the city turned out to be too late for him. Within a month after the family made their move to Kirkston, Francis started to see flecks of blood in his sputum when he coughed. He had already been experiencing unusual fatigue, occasional fevers and night sweats. Then he'd begun to lose weight, his clothes becoming looser as the months went on. His cough, which had been recurring for some years, became persistent and dry and kept him awake at night; leaving him with a headache the next day. Caitlin and the children often commented on his bad temper and snappishness and the beneficial effects of the remedies supplied by Doctor Paterson seemed to have a shorter and shorter duration.

Bernie having died from TB in 1898 not much more than a year after their father had passed, at the time, had sparked Francis' interest in the new discovery of X-rays which were being used to examine people's insides, including their lungs.[xvi] People had been getting very excited about it and you could even experience the wonders of X-rays if you attended a local fair or carnival, where enterprising carnies would show you your own skeleton, for a price.

In 1902, because of the medical demand and due to information regarding the risks and dangers of un-shielded radiation spreading quickly, within a short amount of time Doctor McIntyre opened a larger purpose-built unit, where x-rays were predominantly used in the medical field as a diagnostic tool and staff who operated them knew how to protect themselves. Francis was encouraged to have one taken by Doctor Paterson, who made him an appointment.

The results were not encouraging and his own diagnosis of T.B. was much in the apparent family tradition. He had by that time, just a few months to live.

Already his work as one of the Crofthead mill's gatekeepers was becoming more difficult by then. Caitlin had just given birth to their fourth daughter Mary at the beginning of May. Her hands were more than full with the children, who now numbered seven (eight including Bernie who was still in Fermanagh with his grandmother), and all of them squeezed into that two room house in Crofthead. He suspected that all those years living in Tradeston and Gorbals with large families living in each small accommodation with the soot and dirt and dampness on top of each other had made them even more likely to develop diseases like TB and spread it among themselves. He'd heard of a number of TB-related deaths of people he'd lived beside down there. As cramped as they'd been, at the time, he'd thought himself and his family lucky they or he, in particular, never had had to experience 'the penny line' where a fellah would be hung up on what was basically a washing line. For a penny, this held the sleeper up overnight by the oxters until the line was untied the following morning. This unfortunately, (at least for the lodgers, not the line owner) had to be created due to lack of beds in the overcrowded lodging houses down at the Tron and Briggait, close to Paddy's Market, which was named after all the Irish like himself and his brothers who'd arrived decades before, setting up stalls to sell old clothes in order to feed themselves and their growing families.

The only possible advantage to ever being in that area was the Britannia Music Hall, whose audience could comprise of up to 1500 people crammed into the small auditorium four times a day, squeezing up together on the rough wooden benches that served as seating for those who could afford it.[xvii] Those who couldn't had to stand at the sides and back of the hall. They all came to be entertained, have a laugh and escape from their difficult lives.

In Britannia Music Hall, the turns could find themselves pelted with Shipyard rivets, nails, rancid turnips and horse manure, while urine might rain down on them from the balcony. However, if the turn appealed to Britannia's audience, they might be rewarded with thunderous applause and foot stamping instead. Francis had dared to see a show with a daft comedian just the once and never returned.

As he drifted in and out of consciousness, he was remembering his childhood in Enaghan with the mountains that surrounded them and the gentle lapping of the Lough. Then his early days in Glasgow floated through his mind more and more as his strength failed. Sometimes he felt an urge to hold wee Mary, but it was bad enough they were sometimes in the same house, never mind him wanting to snuggle up with the little one. That the children had been taken away to avoid contagion made, despite his attempts to dampen them down, his eyes fill at times. He'd only just managed to get his family into a better situation out of the city and now he wouldn't get to enjoy it with them. At least it would be a better life for them even if he wouldn't be around any longer. The coughing was becoming incessant and the amount of blood alarming. Fever raged through his emaciated body until his weary, but still beautiful Caitlin, constantly sat with him; feeding him the occasional sip of water and holding his hand until he passed, which he did with a last ragged breath, aged just 41 years old on 16th October 1902, only five months after his ninth child Mary, was born.

Chapter 18 - The Comet & Kirkston Mill Strike - Nora

Since Nora's mammy had only just given birth to wee Mary a few months before her da's passing, Nora's help was needed a lot with her and the younger ones. Frank was fourteen now and had had to become the man of the house and like her, started looking for work. They had still heard nothing from Bernie at this point, who was, as far as they knew, still on the farm in Enaghan. He hadn't made it home for their da's funeral. He'd been gone so long that it was hard to relate to him being part of the family except as if like their other distant cousins, not their brother. Caity her sister, was nine, Patrick six, Jeannie four years old and Seamus was three and together a huge handful for their mammy on her own. Nora was destroyed by her da's death and had spent many nights and days when she could get away from the house and children, weeping buckets that was no help to anyone; especially her mammy who went to her bed and didn't get up for weeks and weeks. Frank, as young as he was, kept them all going with his serious taking on of the man-of-the-house roll; sometimes seriously funny in his imitations of their da, other times she felt heart sorry for the lost look she saw crossing his face in unguarded moments. And she could hear snuffles at night and not only from the wee ones

After a few years of the drudgery of life at home, she was champing at the bit to go out to work but the males had priority for that and Frank managed to get some work as an apprentice moulderer at the factory nearby. They desperately needed the money.

~

It took another seven years before Nora got her wish to start work in the mill. Many of the up to 1500 workers, comprised of girls travelling to it by train from Glasgow, Pollokshaws, and Moorhead. Nora was in her early twenties by then and it had taken a few years after her brothers and sisters were no longer babies, her mammy settled in the missing of her man leaving her bed and eventually needing less help, before she could think of applying. Caity at fifteen and Jeannie twelve, were now also old enough to help more when needed. It had taken some time for her mammy to get over their Da's death. To Nora, her only happy times seemed to have been when she was fit enough to draw those sketches of hers, or when Uncle John was around, which after her dada went, was a lot more often. It made Nora angry since it was like what she had suspected all those years ago turned out to be true. How could her mammy have done that to their da when he'd always tried his best for them all? It became difficult for Nora when John was around. She would leave the room when he came in and she knew from the look on her mammy's face it hurt her but she hadn't cared about hurting her da, had she?

Because of Nora's eventual employment at the mill, they had been recently allocated one of the relatively new-built workers' cottages on Threadmill Street quite soon after six months of showing herself to be a steady, reliable worker with a clear need for housing. Caity was seventeen and Jeannie thirteen years-old now with Frank at twenty still working as an Iron moulderer while Patrick and Seamus were twelve and nine respectively.

The cottage had three rooms and the boys and girls together in one each, had separate rooms in which to sleep. Their mammy slept in the fold-down bed in the kitchen where the back-to-back cooking-range was and had kept Mary in beside her until she was a toddler. Their mammy used to talk about the two halves of the family of children as the big yins: Bernie, Nora, Frank and Caity and since there was a gap of three years before the next baby, the wee yins: Jeannie, Patrick, Seamus, and Mary. Their mammy's health had never been that great, what with having only short periods of time between each pregnancy to try regaining her strength and their constant dips into poverty over the years when their da Francis, having to stop work every once in a while, to recover from his recurrent bouts of bronchitis, had taken their toll.

She never really managed to get back to full health and in early March 1909 Caitlin's health deteriorated rapidly. Death took her while all the children stood or sat around her weeping as she lay in that fold-down bed that hadn't been folded up again since the start of the new year. Nora was bereft. It had been her and her mammy like two halves of a tug 'o' war team since her da had died those seven years past; pushing and pulling for and against the trials of poverty and illness as the wee yins grew. Now it was like half of her was missing and while feeling that sense of amputation, she thought, no wonder her mammy had struggled all the more after her dada's death. How had she managed to function every day after their seventeen years of marriage together?

Before the death of their mammy, the biggest event of that period was the return of Bernie. Her mammy was delighted at this and couldn't do enough for him, or at least as much as she was able to in the short time before her illness took her. Bernie was now a 23-year-old young man, surprisingly very much in the mould of their Da. Looked like him, sounded like him and was, despite his young age, as old-fashioned like him in attitude. Within a month or so of returning, he managed to get work with Shanks in Moorhead which helped out with the family's finances, but younger brother Frank still decided to follow up on his mother's claim of the past years for outdoor poor relief that she'd kept going when needed after their Da's death.

Bernie, despite his close to twenty-year absence, chose to strip and replace the sheets, making use of the fold-up, not in a shared bed, after their mammy's wake and funeral; effectively keeping some distance between himself and his brothers as he took up his place at the head of the family. No-one objected openly, glad to have some certainty when they had so recently inherited the title of 'orphans' but soon after, his brothers, especially Frank, started to undermine him; at first in small ways. The worst one happened when after Bernie had made an order with the grocery van Frank cancelled it, leaving the family with no food for a few days.

"What did ye do that for, ye eejit? Mammy's not well and the wee yins need fed and now you've left us all wae nothing till they can deliver again?" Bernie was leaning into

Frank's face; spittle escaping from his thinly held angry lips and landing on Frank's face, further heightening the rage already apparent in his brother's bulging eyes.

"Why dae ye think? I'm the wan that orders the deliveries, not you!" He stabbed his pointed finger into Bernie's chest. Bernie stepped back with the force and shock of Frank's assault.

"That was really responsible then. We must make sure you cancel the next one too and hasten the death of my mammy."

"All of a sudden, she's *your* mammy after twenty years hiding in Ireland, eh? You're a melter Bernie."

"What does that make you then? A snivelling wee rat who cannae take somebody helping them, is all."

"Help? We can do without your help. We managed before ye came back, we can manage after ye feck off back tae Ireland an aw." He threw a punch that Bernie checked by grabbing Frank's fist and twisting his arm. They grappled and wrestled each other around the room, breaking whatever lay on sideboard, table and everywhere else. Caitlin went into a coughing fit and Mary started to scream when the two of them fell close by her. The screams jolted them both out of their clinch and Frank stormed into the front garden and out the gate, heading for the hills towards Rilloch Glen. A shame-faced Bernie went quickly to his mother and helped her sit up before running the tap for a cup of water. She was breathing heavily and both her and Mary were shaking with fear at the outburst of violence. Once he'd calmed them down and before the shops closed, he made his way to the new 'chippy' for an expensive family meal, grumbling that they shouldn't have needed it in the first place.

Bernie worked hard at the job he'd managed to procure at Shanks. The origins of the family-run Shanks & Co Ltd began when John Shanks opened a plumber's shop in Moorhead, entering the sanitary engineering business at a time when the link between cholera and typhus as water borne diseases became known. He soon began manufacturing brass fittings for the piped water and sewage systems just being introduced and by 1866, he'd opened a brass foundry, the Tubal Works, operating in Foundry Brae Lane, leading from the Main Street. The name referred to Tubal Cain; according to legend, the first blacksmith.

Bernie was one labourer among up to a thousand workmen in the factory and Victoria Pottery, helping to load the firing oven for making clay tubing. The company were well thought of in the sanitation industry and had won several gold medals at previous trade exhibitions, which Bernie came to feel unusually proud of and territorial about. His own sense of drift and uncertainty after the loss of his Granny Maguire who'd replaced his mother, along with his home and company of his uncles and aunts who'd been more like brothers and sisters on the Enaghan farm and the recent death of Caitlin, whom he'd hardly known, were working on him all the while. The job, despite his lowly status there and so different from farm work, at least gave him a reason to get up in the morning. He believed in working hard and he also, despite their doubts, believed in looking after his family, especially after his mother had eventually passed away in March that year.

~

The coming event of 1910 was what had long been common knowledge: that astronomers had foretold that that year was to witness the return to the skies of Halley's historic comet.[xviii] But while this expectancy was anticipated especially at astronomical observatories, another and more brilliant and altogether unexpected member of the Cometary family, known as Comet 1910a was suddenly announced in the papers as having been observed from Cape Town, SA. Following very shortly on this came the further announcement that it had been detected from the Observatory at Paisley. By the month of January, the wanderer was to be seen from many different stations and in due time, on the 29th of that month, as darkness came down, it became a very brilliant and conspicuous naked eye object in the western sky at Kirkston, presenting a beautiful and fascinating yet marvellous and awe-inspiring appearance, with a clear nuclear head and great fan-shaped tail spread out over a wide extent of sky. Nora and her sisters and brothers stared agog at the sight and prayed fervently to Our Lady and all the saints they could bring to mind.

"Jesus, Mary and Joseph! Would ye look at that?" Nora exclaimed with wide-eyes and hands clasped in prayer mode. Caity and Jeannie were hugging Mary to them and the boys were messing around as if this wasn't the portentous event it appeared to be, though the note of hysteria in their quips and jibes didn't go unnoticed.

"Definitely another virgin birth on the way, I'd say," remarked Frank as he smirked towards his brothers.

"It's the three not so wise men got lost. They should have been here weeks ago." Seamus joined in with a chuckle.

"T'is faulty navigation on that star's part. Messing up God's plans, for sure." The new man of the house, Bernie commented.

Nora was huffing and puffing but little Mary beat her to it. "You're all going to hell for making jokes about baby Jesus." But they chuckled on, nonchalant about their fate in the fires of hell.

They were out on the hills with many other villagers watching the celestial show. But what did this significant event so soon after Christmas really herald?

A few short months after this when Halley's comet itself appeared, the nation was startled by the announcement that the King, Edward VII, was seriously ill, so seriously that the earliest bulletin foreshadowed the imminence of his death, an event happening so suddenly that it was said to have given pause, not only to Britain, but around the whole world. According to the connections, accurate or not, made by many people; on May 6th, 1910, Halley's comet approached Earth and killed King Edward VII. No one could definitively say how it had, but many believed it certainly did. And that apparently, wasn't its only offense. Everyone involved in the strike at the mill who saw the comet appear, which it did on and off for months, had only to search the sky to find verification: a glowing dot brighter than most stars, though not nearly as bright as the moon. Soon its tail was visible, that dread tail that was said to be able to snuff out all life on earth, if the story proved true. Some of the women gasped at the sight of it. "What if it smashes right into the earth, and that terrible tail suffocates everyone without mercy?" Janet cried.

And there was even more apocalyptic tales surrounding the return of Halley's comet, named for astronomer Edmond Halley, who calculated that the celestial body would appear on average every 76 years. At the peak of the frenzy, in the first three weeks of May 1910, entire communities refused to work in field or mill, and gathered in shivering terrified thousands to await the heaven-sent holocaust. The women causing the uproar at the mill were subject to taunts about their apparently ill-timed call for strike action during this event. "Is it the work of God or the Devil, you lassies are up tae?" an old-timer shouted at Nora and Janet on their way back from their last shift.

A cruel prankster in the city, launched a homemade fire balloon from the roof of a tenement into a crowded street. When the balloon exploded, five hundred fright-maddened people trampled one another in a hysterical effort to escape.

From the rising of the stars, it hung there. Its unfamiliarity made it easy for the eye to glimpse, but it was very dim and distant, and there was nothing but a faint luminosity about the edge to suggest the tail to the naked eye. Late night returning Whit-week travellers peered at it from railway carriage windows and joked about the length of its tail. As the last thunder of the guns welcoming the new King George V died away in pre-dawn darkness, the comet was seen by hundreds of dock workers to glow at head and tail. Work stopped immediately. The population paraded the streets, wailing with fear and predicting dire events and dread of a war that would shake the world during George V's reign, if the world survived that long.

Other scientists dismissed the claim of danger as nonsense, but the prediction still sparked a minor panic. Before the comet passed by without incident that spring, many people sealed up their homes to keep out the fumes, stocked up on gas masks, and went to churches to pray for salvation.

Since the comet had approached in January of that year, with the spreading of information about imminent danger, some people had begun to sell all their worldly possessions in order to take advantage of the short time remaining[xix]. Others risked death by alcohol overdose rather than gas intoxication. Some caulked their windows in a fruitless attempt to prevent the poisonous gas from entering their homes. In some cities and towns, even in Kirkston, others took refuge in churches, the doors of which remained open during May 1910. In this atmosphere, charlatans seized the opportunity to sell anti-comet pills, based on sugar and quinine, or even an anti-Halley's comet elixir which the more gullible among them bought from street vendors.

In many places it was reported by the clergy that Halley's Comet did more in one week for the church than all the masses and church meetings in a decade. Never before had so many new members got so much religious fervour at any one time.

Most newspapers by now featured the comet on page one. They gave daily accounts of its speed (1,678 miles a minute), its distance from the earth (only a few million miles) and the local

time it was expected to make contact with the earth. Nora and Janet worried that the other cop winders would think it was a bad omen for how the strike would turn out. After all their hard work and marching and sacrifice and the chance of losing their jobs, it would be too much to fail under this ominous sign.

The following day after the earth was said to pass through its tail, to add to the confusion, the comet produced a broad spectrum of light across the face of the sun at high noon. A lunar eclipse on May 24th enabled thousands to witness the breath-taking beauty of the comet against a dark sky. By May 26th, the comet had even regained its lost tail. Comet parties, which had stopped for lack of heavenly support, became popular again. By mid-June 1910, when it passed from ordinary human eyesight, Halley's Comet was already being forgotten. The women at the Mill were having their own party claiming the Comet's appearance, at least for them, had been a very good omen after all.

~

What at first was only a small dispute affecting a single section of the work concerned, developed so quickly that in just three weeks, it had brought about a general strike involving at least 1500 employees, and possibly many more people; throwing idle all the workers in H. F. & J. Alexander & Co.'s large thread mills, which were part of The English

Sewing Cotton Co. Limited. There had never been a history of class struggle between the mill owners and workers in Kirkston until this period of unrest among these mill workers.[xx] It was down to a dispute between the women of the cop-winding department and the mill managers, over a reduction in rates of pay due to changes to the speed of the machinery, while all this was happening amidst fearful exclamations about the prevailing comet above.

Despite having felt she needed to keep herself to herself since her mother's death in March of the previous year, Nora realised that she wanted to be involved in the demonstrations. It had been difficult for her as the eldest girl in the family and for a time she despaired that she might be landed with the mammy role forever. She loved her brothers and sisters but it just wouldn't have been fair if it all fell to her again! Bernie arriving back had been a surprise and somewhat of a relief to her, since he very quickly assumed the role of eldest. Frank hadn't felt quite the same relief, having been the man of the family since their da had passed eight years before.

Subsequently, there'd been a few stand-offs between them since. For now, there was fragile peace of a kind, but she wasn't sure how long they would all be able to walk on eggshells around them both. This discord at the mill, despite her aversion to conflict, was a welcome distraction from both the lingering grief for her mammy and the latent aggression between her head-butting brothers.

She agreed with the objections being made about what was being considered by some, just a natural development in the work herself and the other cop winders did on a daily basis. The changes being introduced in the speed regulations of the machinery used in cop-winding in the Mill had been proposed and would make certain alterations in the prices paid for their work. This didn't meet with the approval of any of the women she worked with but Janet, in particular, was loud about it.

"I'm no standing for that. We'll be oot o' pocket and workin longer tae make up our usual wages! Why should we? They urnae daein that tae the mens' conditions ur they?" Her voice carried along the rows of the Arunco Package Winding machines. A few young women turned their heads at the strident note in Janet's voice. Nora saw some disapproving looks on their faces but also excitement in the eyes of others. They'd agreed to give the new process and new prices three days' trial, but each of the women seemed to have discovered that the change would seriously reduce their wages, and they decided that under the circumstances it was impossible to go on with the changes. They tried to make an appeal to the management when they realised the changes were not working for them but their pleas failed to affect any encouraging alteration to their grievance.

"We cannae keep daein this sir. It will make us the poorer." Janet declared while her

reddening face threatened louder and angrier scenes as they stood outside the manager's office.

"Aye, we've plenty bairns tae feed and families tae support." Nora chimed in to try getting the manager's sympathy but the round-bellied bespectacled man closed his eyes and shook his head to fend off her entreaty.

"How can we dae that if we're sae tired oot wae tryin tae keep up wae the speed of the machines that are cutting oor wages?" At Margaret, the round-faced matron of the girls, comment the managers frowned and again repeated 'no' as they walked away leaving Janet and Nora fuming and the others mumbling less than complimentary comments about their employers.

Eventually, with Nora's help, Janet gathered the most supportive ones among the workforce of machinists with roles including spindle and cop winders, spindle wrappers, slicers and material handlers. Those not involved around the mill from that section were quick to give differing and not always supportive opinions on their plight, but most involved were only from the assembly winding area and obviously more inclined to agree.

This first process known as cheese or cop winding, involved winding the cops received from the skip store onto wooden centres called 'cheeses', which were then put on the Arunco machines for the next process. After that the cops were placed on the spindles and run through tensions, to stop the yarn from snarling, then through pins and up over pulleys and wound round the 'cheeses' ready to start production. It could involve two or more cops being wound onto one 'cheese' depending on whether the machinist was allocated 2, 3, or 4 ply.

They thought that their refusal to work on that first process would make it difficult for the rest of the mill to continue production and give them a distinct advantage, but at first, for a short time, it seemed to have little or no effect on the other parts of the mill, which appeared to go on much as if nothing had happened. The one hundred and twenty women decided to stop work, and accordingly, on Monday, 16th May, 1910, a strike was declared in the cop-winding department and they left the mill in one body. At the outset of the movement the girls on strike had no connection with any Union, and were quite disorganised. But the representatives of The National Federation of Women Workers, early began to champion their cause, and meetings were held in the Glen Halls, under the guidance of Kate McLean and Esther Dick, of the National Federation of Women Workers (NFWW), at which large numbers of the workers, both those on strike and those not on strike, joined the Union. These women also ensured that wages were paid from union funds to tide the mill women over during the strike.

The meetings, when at first held in the Glen Halls, were of quite an orderly character. But, from the crowds that attended them, made up largely of outsiders, the halls became much too small for their numbers, and the meetings were eventually held outside on the football field. Here the crowd became still greater, and as the different speakers, each with his or her own axe to grind, harangued the assembled mass, excitement ran high, and, as a matter of precaution, a considerable number of police were drafted into the town.

At this stage several interviews took place between the management and the Federation

leaders, when an effort was made, by compromise on the part of the girls, to come to an understanding on the points in dispute. It was hoped, as the result of these consultations, that a possible basis of agreement had been reached. The attitude assumed by the directors, in determining that they would deal only with their workers and recognise no outsiders, aggravated the difficulty of negotiation, more especially as this was a mere arbitrary resolution on their part, the principle having already been conceded in the earlier stages of the dispute, by the management having admitted the Federation agents into several interviews.

But a telegram on the 25th May dashed hopes of any early settlement—contrarily, the directors wishing to deal only with their workers and not with outsiders incensed the crowd. By then 1,700 women and some men were embroiled in the dispute. In a hostile display of defiance, strikers smashed mill windows and personally targeted managers. With much indignation among the workers, following the announcement, and after a meeting held with their leaders, in the dinner meal hour, on Monday, 6th June, all hands, male and female, that were still in the mill, failed to resume work that afternoon; with the result that the gates were closed until further notice. The excitement which, up till this crisis, had been of a moderate character, immediately assumed quite a different aspect, and suddenly, became not only demonstrative but even aggressive, when manager, foremen, and all who were thought to be in any way against the strikers, came in for some rough treatment.

Mass demonstrations were arranged and led by Kate McLean and Esther Dick of NFWW. The support and numbers in attendance were so great that it became a cause of concern for the local police. On June 8th there was a march of 5,000 people complete with pipers, singing and banner-waving, including a large group of male trade unionists from Glasgow, who rallied behind a large demonstration banner that proclaimed: 'WE WANT JUSTICE, FAIR CONDITIONS AND A LIVING WAGE'.

After one of the meetings, held in the vicinity of the mill, many of the windows were smashed, not by the women workers, but by strangers and thoughtless lads who'd followed in their procession when the meeting broke up.

On the evening of Friday, 10th June, also with banners flying and headed by a piper, a

procession, mostly of women workers, began the long march of ten miles from Kirkston to

Pollokshields, through Moorhead, where they were joined by workers resident there. The object of the march was to have a demonstration in front of the manager's house; but there had been rain during the day and the roads were soft, soon becoming slippery due to the tramping of so many feet. As the evening set in, much fatigue and distress from heat and exhaustion was experienced by the women long before they reached the end of journey. It was, therefore, a matter of general satisfaction that, by the middle of June, it appeared that better feelings were beginning to gain ground, and that both parties were prepared to submit the matters in dispute to the Labour Department of the Board of Trade, who had been requested to assist, and consented to act. In due time a meeting was arranged on 16th June under the auspices of this Board, taking place in St. Enoch's Station Hotel in Glasgow city centre, and attended by a deputation selected from among the aggrieved cop-winders.

Nora and Janet were among the group chosen to represent the mill workers of their own cop winding section. They willingly and in Janet's case, vociferously, contributed to the discussions. This time though, Nora spoke up first. She'd been disturbed by the unfairness of it all on her and the women in their section and despite the excitement of the rallies and the attention they got from everyone, she hated the idea of everyone falling out. "It just isn't fair to, out of the blue, drop this expectation on us. We work hard and we don't want to keep this disagreement going on and on."

Janet snorted at her words and Nora glared at her hoping to shrivel her friend's tongue, but to no avail, she mouthed off as usual. "We're no standin for it an that's that. Ye can see we've got everyone's support so there's only wan thing you high heid yins can dae tae sort things. Give us a rise to make up for the loss wae the speedin up of the machine's or keep yer Mill shut." The managers tutted in disapproval at Janet's aggressive ultimatum but were soothed by the experienced parleying of Katie and Esther who kept the talks on track.

After full consideration and discussion, terms of agreement were come to, as - subject to the body of strikers approving of the doings of their deputation—would terminate the strike. With their intervention, which guaranteed an increase in wages, the strike ended on 17th of June and the women accepted work being resumed at the mill on the following Monday. Happily, the terms of settlement were considered satisfactory, and approved of at a meeting, held on the return of the deputation from Glasgow on the same evening, amidst much joy and cheering there seemed to be a general sense of gladness that the strife was past.

The dispute was regarded as a watershed, for when the previously unorganised 'mill girls' struck and joined the NFWW they broke with over half a century of paternalism. Buoyed by their success the mill girls marched to nearby Paisley behind another banner bearing the words:

'KIRKSTON EXPECTS THE PAISLEY GIRLS TO JOIN THE UNION.' But they and the NFWW met with little success, and while the NFWW attempted to establish a branch in Paisley the following month, the turnout was so small the meeting was abandoned. The Kirkston workers, the NFWW, and their political supporters were all perceived as 'unconnected' and from 'outside Paisley' which helped explain their failure.

The mill was opened again, and work resumed on Monday, 20th June, five weeks after the beginning of the strike. Nora fervently hoped the result of the agreement arrived at would lead to better and friendlier feelings between them all and inspire a desire for each to be satisfied by a real sense of justice in the future. In that case, the cop-winders strike would not have been in vain. She walked taller after it was all over. She had come to know many more people since supporting the dispute with the mill management and as for winning—they were treated like royalty by male and female workers all over the mill. But not by everyone. There was always a few jealous so and so's.

2nd MOVEMENT (Slow & Extended) – Mary Maguire

1911 brought the death of Granny O'Connell. Another passing perpetrated yet again by pneumonia. She had outlived two of her daughters and was now much missed by the surviving Margaret and Susan. Grandchildren Nora, Mary, Caity, Patrick, Francis and Seamus made sure to attend the modest funeral along with her other grandchildren. It was a rainy day, dull steel clouds weighting the sky. Mary would always after feel that dull weight of the vacuum left by her granny's death.

After those last playful, childlike times, Mary remembered from the end of the war onwards, as being overly populated with babies. Not hers, she was too young for that, or so she'd thought and in Scotland, for the previous few years she'd felt at first only annoyed, then angry at the British government's increasing attempts at controlling the behaviour of the population, particularly that of women. This had resulted in much more surveillance conducted by the Ministry of Pensions, which soldiers' wives like her sisters; widows, lone mothers, and young working-class women like herself and her friends had to contend with. Also parish councils, charity organisations, the newspapers, and working-class men all seemed to have opinions on the conduct of women. This was because of what those making the judgements described as women's 'khaki fever' and was also related to the idea that leaving or returning soldiers, uncertain of their futures, would engage in sex without marriage, therefore all the restraints appeared to be about preventing babies being born out of wedlock.

Of course, no-one seemed to mind or attempted to judge the behaviour of the men, rather, these fears were translated into the establishment of women's patrols across Britain. The Scotsman newspaper called the patrols "an organized chaperone system" to avert the development of "loose and dissolute habits". To this end, the Defense of the Realm Act was used to regulate women's behaviour. An example that made her particularly furious was when she'd heard that up in Fife, there was a military curfew which forbade women from leaving their homes after 10pm at night.

For someone of Mary's bullish nature, who hated to be told what to do and when; this was destined to do nothing but provoke the opposite response, especially in light of the recent beginnings of the War of Independence in Ireland, when again the British government was attempting to stop people deciding their own future in their own country.

The family were at a loss with the announcement on 16th April, 1912, of the news of the sinking of the Titanic. The Guardian, her recently preferred paper, reported that the maiden voyage of the White Star liner Titanic, the largest ship ever launched, had ended in disaster. In the house there was an initial panic. Nora running around like a chicken that'd lost its head. "How can we find out if anyone we know is on it?"

"Yeah, but why would they be?"

"But they might, ye never know? Scores of folk are always sailing off from Ireland to America and Canada."

"What, do ye know anyone who could afford the £7 a ticket they were asking to sail on that monster of a ship."

The Guardian News/1912/April 16th

"The Titanic started her trip from Southampton for New York on Wednesday. Late on Sunday night she struck an iceberg off the Grand Banks of Newfoundland. By wireless telegraphy she sent out signals of distress, and several liners were near enough to catch and respond to the call. Conflicting news, alarming and reassuring, was current yesterday. Even after midnight it was said all the passengers were safe. All reports, of course, depended on wireless telegrams over great distances. Late last night the White Star officials in New York announced that a message had been received stating that the Titanic sank at 2.20 yesterday morning after all her passengers and crew had been transferred to another vessel. Later they admitted that many lives had been lost. An unofficial message from Cape Race, Newfoundland, stated that only 675 have been saved out of 2,200 to 2,400 persons on board. This was in some degree confirmed later by White Star officials in Liverpool, who said they were afraid the report was likely to prove true. Assuming that only 675 of the passengers and crew have been saved, and taking the smallest estimate of the number of people on board, the disaster is one of the most awful in the history of navigation, for at least 1,500 lives have been lost.

"The main hope that remains is that the Virginian or Parisian may have picked up more of the passengers and crew than those saved by the Carpathia. As to this there is no news at the time of writing. A list of the first-class passengers (who are reported from New York to have been all saved) appears on page 6.

In a White Star statement in New York, 9.35pm. Mr. Franklin said, "I was confident to-day when I made the statement that the Titanic was unsinkable that the steamship was safe and that there would be no loss of life. The first definite news to the contrary came in the message this evening from Captain Haddock".

~

In 1914, the Maguire sisters danced around the room at the news. They'd been following the exploits of several suffragettes since 1912 when they saw a newspaper cutting from 'Votes for Women', 20 Sep 1912 with an article entitled 'Scots Wha Hae', which described Edith Johnston's offence (smashing glass at the Wallace monument) and her trial, and gave the text of her letter complaining about the condition of the police cell at Stirling and about her fight for privileges at Perth Prison.

On July 24th, 1913, suffragettes Ethel Moorhead and Dorothea Chalmers Smith were arrested during an attempt to set fire to an unoccupied mansion house at 6 Park Gardens, Glasgow, and taken to Duke Street Prison. Moorhead, who used a number of aliases, gave her name as 'Margaret Morrison' and used her shoe to smash three cell windows, knocking the prison governor's hat off his head when he refused to remove it despite being in the presence of a lady. Moorhead wrote a letter to the prison commissioners claiming that she and the suffragette prisoners were not being treated as political prisoners, so both women went on hunger strike. Ethel Moorhead was released on bail and Dorothea Smith was released under, what was better known as 'The Cat and Mouse Act'[xxi], at the end of July 1913 with a return date of 5th August 1913, for which she did not return.

The case came to trial on 15th October 1913. Both women were sentenced to eight months' imprisonment and found themselves back in Duke Street Prison, going on hunger strike again. They were both released on temporary discharge in October 1913 following a medical officer's report saying that Ethel Moorhead was extremely feeble and Dorothea Smith very weak. Both women failed to return before the expiry of their license. Amidst rumours that Dorothea was pregnant, she was ordered to be kept under police surveillance in her home, though she later escaped. Moorhead was recaptured in Peebles the following February and sent to prison in Edinburgh.

After two visits to Margaret Morrison while held as an untried prisoner, the Medical Officer's report on her general mental state said, "I'm of opinion that the visits have done her no good and recommend that no others should be admitted in the meantime." The commissioner agreed with him and appeared shocked at what he described as Miss Morrison, turning from a lamb to a lion, breaking eight panes of glass after giving her word that she wouldn't break or destroy anything.

The sisters thought these women's actions inspiring and very brave but with most being single and from more affluent families, they could afford to risk going to jail, something the older sisters couldn't do.

Helen Crawfurd Anderson was imprisoned in Duke Street Prison in March 1914 after breaking two windows of the Army Recruiting Office in Gallowgate, as a protest against the arrest two days previously of Mrs. Pankhurst. Helen was sentenced to ten days in prison but went on hunger strike and was released after eight days, again under the 'Cat & Mouse' Act 1913.She was then rearrested and returned to prison and after a second hunger strike, again released in a very weak physical condition. Members of the Women's Social and Political Union gathered at the prison gates and picketed the prison day and night during her incarceration. Mary and Jeannie went along to the prison gates on Duke street several times to lend their support. Nora couldn't take any time off work and Caity had her children to care for. These events carried on for some time until all the suffragettes were eventually freed and still no less defiant for their pains. It all did eventually pay off but not for some years yet and before then, war arrived.

~

Mary had started at the Mill in the middle of the war in 1916, joining Nora and Jeannie there until her big sister Jeannie's death in 1918 and then Nora's wedding to Victor in 1919, when Nora would have to give up work. It was easier for Mary in some ways with her sisters there. She could have a laugh with Jeannie but who as expected, only put up with her for short periods of time and stuck mostly to her own friends, but did deign to, at least, show her the ropes before introducing Mary to some of the other women. With Nora, it was harder having to live up to her eldest sister's reputation for being an instigator in the strike of six years before and who was now an unpaid supervisor, but took it no less seriously for that. The benefits of being out and about and meeting new people, men and women, was one of the best aspects of her new-found independence. It helped build her confidence. There was quite severe rationing, and apart from having to now contribute to the household costs, there was a limited choice of what she could spend her little extra money on.

When she wasn't working at the mill she seemed to spend her time going from Kirkston to Paisley to Pollokshields helping out, and although Caity and Frank's wife Lizzie, having given up work outside the home as was the custom, had main responsibility for their children but they never refused any offers of help.

At night, Mary did sometimes manage, with the help of a few sixpences kept from her pay, to go to dance halls, cafes or even the cinema on the odd occasion with Jeannie but mostly with her friends. One particular friend who'd gone on to work at the mill with her was Kathleen Jamieson, a girl she'd been at primary school with who was a great friend still, and who she often went on these excursions with. They'd also been able to try the new fashions and makeup, even swapping clothes and other items to make them feel like they had more than they actually did. She didn't yet though, despite all their years as friends so far, trust Kathleen with her new-found interest in Cumann na mBan. If she couldn't even tell her sisters, telling Kathleen was definitely out of the question.

There, women were looked on as equals to the men, but did they get to fight? Her burgeoning anger at the injustice of the major differences in how women and men were treated had become like a weight of molten lava in her belly and she'd noticed her levels of tolerance were dropping quickly. Like at the mill, despite it being predominantly women working there, the attitude, the presumption of men got her hackles up...well men like Robert, when he'd come to tell her that her break was up, "Mary, hen. Is it no time ye were back at the cop-winding?" Mary had been a bit gobsmacked when he spoke to her and had to gulp down a more unladylike reply before responding.

"What's it to you Robert? Are ye looking tae try for a promotion or what?

"Naw, it's just that the supervisor was saying..."

"The supervisor? So why does that concern you? You tryin tae curry favour or something? I'm sure if the supervisor's got something tae say tae me she can dae it herself, naw?" Robert was wide-eyed by now wondering what he'd done wrong.

"I wis just sayin..."

"Well, just don't, okay?" She turned her back to him and carried on her previous conversation with the other women workers who were tutting and shaking their heads at Robert's temerity. He went red in the face and stomped off across the canteen.

She'd liked being part of her sisters' weddings and had sometimes dreamed of her own nuptials, but the glamour and fantasy of it all felt like just that, a fantasy. She'd been fourteen when Caity got married to Jack between Christmas and the New Year, right in the middle of the war. None too flouncy gowns, even if Caity and Jack could've afforded it, and because of the time of year; but they weren't the only ones choosing to wed then. In Scotland, it seemed to be a peak period for marriage around the end of December because closely followed by the New Year's day holiday. A popular rhyme among young women for the best month to marry mentioned December too: "*When December snow falls fast, marry and true love will last."* Many girls dreamed of their own such lasting love.

Her older brothers Bernie, Patrick and Seamus had not been keen to join up when the announcement about the start of war in early August 1914 was made. It was the British Empire's war and they still carried the family bias in favour of their Irish heritage. Seamus was only

seventeen when conscription came in 1916 but he was determined not to be the only one left at home with the women. At fourteen Mary could feel in the pregnant silences of the adults all around and the sobs behind closed doors, that something serious was happening.

The war occurring did make for some hasty but not always cheery celebrations. With

weddings it could be the last time a couple might see each other if the groom was heading off to or re-joining the army.

Mary was delighted about her role as flower girl at Frank and Lizzie's wedding. Had the war not been on and more money available for a bigger celebration, all the older sisters would have been bride's maids. At the time it made her feel kind of happy about the war. She did, though feel a bit jittery about walking down the aisle, especially beside Mark, Lizzie's younger brother. He was a year older than her with a very handsome face, his hair brilliantined to one side and the look of the smart shirt and waistcoat he wore. She tried not to blush when he smiled or spoke to her and really hoped her hand wouldn't sweat holding onto the flowers, just in case he had to take it after handing over the rings to her big brother and she to his big sister.

After the service, kids in the street outside the chapel were going mad while they watched, eyes riveted as Lizzie's dad reached into his pocket for a handful of change to chuck their way. Mary watched as all the kids pushed and shoved to be strategically placed. She remembered that where you stood was always a gamble when the money that started the scramble appeared. Then it was all thrown up to the sky. Tanners, ha'pennies, pennies and thrupenny bits falling and flying through the air, everyone trying to catch as much as they could all at once. They squealed as they pushed and shoved each other even harder, chasing the coins that were rolling around, some going down the gutter where the last few pennies plonked out of sight. She knew that after the stramash they would stop to count all their cash and examine any resulting cut and grazed knees.

Except for the annual Gala Day, she was too old for things she used to copy her brothers

doing with peashooters and slings and their potato guns. They all played at dodgy with the tanner

ball or died as soldiers in 'dead man's fall'. All the boys and girls played together at rounders on the chalked-out base. Then playing in the holes of the drain covers; a game she would play with her school pals for a penny or for marbles. If they didn't have any marbles, they dug three holes a few feet apart and chucked their pennies to see who'd start up and down and then up again. The first to complete would win the game. They used to give each other coaxies and play at tig or long for another scramble or wait until Halloween, from the Scottish shortening of All-Hallows Eve, that had its roots in the Celtic festival of Samhain. At that time of year, they would go out guising, from the original belief that, by disguising themselves and dressing up as witches and ghosts with a bedsheet, they would blend in with any wandering spirits and remain safe from harm.

And they'd have to put on a show performing tricks or songs, so they'd be given gifts in the form of apples and oranges, monkey nuts, sweeties and money, to help ward off evil. At school they'd bring in neeps (turnips) to carve scary faces into them, creating lanterns that would scare off ghouls wandering in the witching hour. They dooked for apples without using their hands, but could try biting or dropping in a fork to spear one. Her mammy used to make scones on the griddle then hang them up covered in treacle on a string, so that any guisers had to try taking a bite, again without using their hands.

Now her thoughts were about other exciting possibilities after the wedding was finished. She thought Mark would come looking for her at Auldhouse and want to take her up to Rilloch Glen. She shivered at the thought of him mentioning 'the kissing tree'. What would she do if he did? She wouldn't be able to tell anyone, though maybe Jeannie, as long as she swore not to say anything to Nora, because she'd have her up to confession at St. Michael's chapel in a moment. Or she might get out the nail brush and soap to make her scrub out her mouth. What would get scrubbed if they ever found out what Mark actually did to her later and it was much more than kissing.

It mostly seemed, very unromantically, to Mary, that the whole escapade of marriage was very banal or despite her lingering romantic leanings, a bit of a set-up. The couples, at least in

Kirkston, went to the St. Michael's RC chapel where the priest (gladly, no longer Father O'Toole) married them if they'd had the banns read three Sundays in a row, so that it would be considered

'regular'. The papers talked of many 'irregular' marriages happening during those years, where there was no priest or minister, just a couple of witnesses. Which was, in fact, the way it used to be done but with the whole village at the 'Paying or Penny Weddings' joining wholeheartedly in the revelries of celebration, not just a boring witnessing with two people. In Caity and Jack's case, due to the war and subsequent food shortages, there was no wedding breakfast or gathering together other than back to their own house for steak pie in the kitchen with just the family around and a wee dram or two for the adults. Nora had kept that melodeon organ that still took up too much space in the main room and Patrick was persuaded to play for the couple and provide a wee dance or two. A few friends gave them a jug of cream or a twist of sugar. They thought themselves very lucky when they were also gifted a pair of hand towels.

'Separation Allowances' for husbands in active service, which after their marriages became their situation, were said to be given to help wives manage while the men were fighting, but the price was control over their sexual and social conduct as a condition of eligibility. Why would they mind if they were 'good wives'? Negative judgements about working-class women, no matter their situation, ensured that the benefit system was framed in a way that also even tried to guarantee the 'good behaviour'' of widows of servicemen who received war pensions. Reading these reports in the newspapers continued, when she could dispel her fantasizing, to put Mary off marriage for herself. It was that thing about control in all the attempts at what was called 'help'. Any 'help' was clearly an excuse to keep women in line.

For Nora it hadn't been that much different, except that not being married to an active soldier during the war had saved her from the military rules for women's conduct about financial support. The war was over when she got married but only by a year and things were still tight with food supplies. Caity had moved in with her in-laws after marrying Jack but Victor, Nora's new husband, did the opposite and came to stay in Threadmill Street with them, since he was from England and didn't have family up here, or so he said.

Mary hadn't felt so sure about Victor. She was 18 by then and much more of a womanly shape with curves instead of straight lines up and down though with a tendency since that unmentionable time, to freeze when any male person touched her and Victor was one of the first men, besides the teasing from her brothers, to notice the changes. He was a very persuasive man; yes, handsome and Nora of course, had been besotted ever since Patrick had introduced them after the war when Victor came up to visit and decided to stay, not just in Scotland, but right in Kirkston at Crofthead, close to the mill and where she'd been told their family used to live. Mary had sometimes wondered at how easily he'd slipped into the bosom of their family.

Before Patrick introduced his army mate from England, Nora had definitely been getting melancholic about the lack of available men since so many hadn't returned from the war or, like their brother Frank, had still been recovering from his experiences. She was already thirty-one when her and Victor's wedding took place and if nothing else, at least it was in the summer months and a bit more pleasant for that.

Victor was a dark-haired wiry kind of person, naturally charming, which made him much sought after by many more women than Nora and therefore, suspect to most parents, not to mention Mary. He seemed a hard-working fellah employed as a butcher down in Crofthead and going on about his 'growler butty' - or meat pie in a 'barm' that he tried to get his boss at the butchers to sell to the workers at Kirkston Mill. He claimed to have been smitten as soon as he saw Nora, yet they seemed to some, a mismatched or perhaps complementary couple; he was slim and energetic, she heavier-built and someone who took her time over everything from walking to thinking to making a decision. Victor was always on the move; even his speech was faster than the Scots around him and it took a while, with his Mancunian accent, for most to properly understand him.

That spring of 1919, before Nora's wedding, Mary had become caught up in several situations with fellahs, one of whom was a lad from the mill at what would be her very last Beltane Tanel and the one she regretted for the rest of her life.

The Witch Burn flowed from two sources, one in Dumgrain Moor and joined the other branch, which rose in the moorland south of Knockglass farm. The united streams continued as far as the Witch Burn, and crossed under a bridge on Uplaw Road. She'd arranged to meet Tom at the 'kissing tree'. She was tramping along beside the now flowing tortuous channel, wondering what she was doing, where the banks of the river consisted of several high terraces, which the waters had scooped out in the course of long ages in the dark. The burn plunged over a shelving rock forming a waterfall, into the meadowland below and she, heart in her mouth, had to carefully watch her footing. An electrical storm had been brewing as she'd made her way up the glen, sparking flashes of lightning while the weather was still dry. It was now about ten p.m. The night had become very stormy, and intensely dark. The whole sky, except along the eastern horizon, which showed a faint streak of light, was filled with dense clouds. The wind blew in great gusts from the north-west, across the high land of the moor, with occasional sharp showers of small hail; and at intervals broad sheets of lightning, accompanied by an audible, soft fluffy sound, passed sluggishly from the masses of cloud in the west to those in the east. The road through Greenfield moor dipped into a slight hollow where the moorland stream passed under the bridge at Witch Burn. Scarcely had there been time for her to realise the conditions before a phosphorescent blue light engulfed her. She had evidently entered an electric stratum, as her eyebrows immediately began to emit a faint crackling sound and her hair twitched and seemed to shimmer with luminosity. On getting beyond the bridge, under which the water was running, the phenomena entirely disappeared. It was evident that the atmosphere at this place was highly charged with witches' magic or that the electrically-laden clouds were so low as to cause their electricity to combine with that of the earth; and that the points of her hair had become the medium of making it visible. Her breath became ragged as she inhaled sharply, her heart thumping in her chest, making her wobble and have to grasp at damp grasses and nearby prickly gorse bushes to keep her balance.

His journey usually made on horseback, her 'uncle', John Murphy, had been in the habit of coming to Kirkston to see her mother regularly before she died. Since evening had generally set in before he left to return home, so great was his dread of being caught by the witches at that place after dark, he always asked her brothers to accompany him as far as the Witch Burn in Greenfield moor. Patrick had remarked in the past that, "Nearing the burn, he'd come over all suspicious and watchful, checking behind, to the sides. He was jumpy and as a bag of kittens squirming to get away, but when safely past that uncanny spot he became cheerful, and bid us 'good-bye' in great spirits." No doubt, her brothers considered his caution commendable, their own safety being assured by their number on the way back, despite their own protests about not believing in magic or witches.

Mary wished she'd brought someone to accompany herself too, but that was the thing about secrets, they locked you out of the ability to ask for help. The need to not get caught left her vulnerable on many levels, like this one to witches' curses and magic and the threat of personal injury. Where was Tom anyway? The picturesque and romantic ravine she was heading for was situated on the southern slope of a range of hills, nearly opposite the village of

Kirkston. Both its banks were finely wooded with well-grown trees, and it had been celebrated in song as the home of the crawflower, anemone, and primrose. The glen was a comparatively short one, and consisted of upper and lower glens. In times of drought, when the burn water was low, many potholes could be seen in the bed of the stream. In some places they had been worn into one another, giving rise to many fantastic shapes, which had been forever, in one way or another, associated with "The Witch of Rilloch Glen." The smoother parts between the holes were her 'floor,' and her 'hearth'; while the cavities, according to their shape and depth, were her 'cradle,' her 'water-stoups,' and her 'grave'.

From Rilloch Glen across Fereneze Braes to Paisley there was, and had always been a footpath, or right-of-way. The "Kissing Tree," which was well studded with nails, stood on the crest of the hill by the side of this walk, connected with which tradition had it that the boy who succeeded in driving a nail into its gnarled trunk at the first blow was entitled to claim the kissing fee.

She was mulling over this story that had been around for years and had been acted out by her and her friends with boys from school many a time as children in a playful, harmless way. It was a game to them but the stormy weather and strikes of lightning amid the darkness and downpour gave it a much less than playful atmosphere now. A hand landed abruptly on her shoulder and she attempted to swivel round to see who the presence lurking behind her was but was quickly grabbed around the waist, her arms pinned to her sides and pushed forward against the tree. She tried to cry out but her words were swept away by the wind. She screamed as her undergarments were torn from her, letting the bitterly cold rain and wind whip against her bare legs and exposed body before the ramming began. Again, she screamed into the thunder and her face was painfully pressed further into the tree. The nails studded there dug into her skin as she struggled to free herself from the assault but he kept on pushing his sex into her, the dryness of sudden entry burning a path all the way inside her to thump and bruise, to pummel her like a punishment she didn't know had been decided that she deserved.

After what seemed an interminable length of time she was let go and carelessly discarded, her body dropped and left slumping at the base of the tree. She instinctively curled into the shock of a question mark; sobbing and shaking for a cold and fearful stretch of time until glints of daylight began filtering the sky. The attack had left her bruised inside and out and the trip home was more than awkward as she slowly stumbled her way back from the glen, down the hill and into the village, hoping upon hope that due to the early hour, she'd not come across any neighbours. This was one of only two uncursed moments of that bewitched walk of shame. To her knowledge, no-one saw her stumble and close to collapse, enter the gate of the cottage in her destroyed state. Her sisters Nora and Jeannie provided the second moment when they didn't see or hear her crawl into bed that morning and for the most part life went on uncomprehending for the family.

Apart from dealing with the loss of Jeannie and her eldest brother Harry, who, with Jeannie, she afterwards so wished she'd had the courage to share with her big sister - her other sisters, including Caity, and one of her older brothers Frank, by 1921 already had been coping with the arrival of six wee ones between them. The government (and the priest) would be glad to hear, all within the 'sanctity' of regular marriage, of course.

"It is not the function of the government to keep the citizen from falling into error; it is the function of the citizen to keep the government from falling into error." **Robert Jackson**

PART FOUR
1911-1921

Chapter 19 - Wedding Bells and War - Frank

Frank was trying to waylay his soon-to-be wife's anxiety about where they would hold their wedding. "Lizzie, I'm sure we can organise it at your church since we'll be living in that area afterwards. It's for the best."

"But don't all your family's weddings and important celebrations happen at St. Michael the Apostle's? It seems like it's some kind of a family tradition." Lizzie bit her lower lip after saying this. She actually really wanted to have the ceremony at St Margaret's in Pollokshields where her parents had wed decades before.

"But this is our wedding; your wedding. It's up to you where we have it."

Lizzie's face split into a huge grin as she crossed the floor to hug her soon-to-be-husband. Then she stepped back, her lip chewing recommencing. Frank looked surprised. "What is it?"

"Nothing." But she had gone quiet and glanced at the floor. Frank moved in closer and lifted her chin.

"Come on. Tell me." He noticed a glimmer of tears in her eyes before one rolled down her cheek. Lizzie had promised she wouldn't do this but telling herself that didn't change the reality of their situation.

"W..w..wherever we choose we'll have a lovely day, then a few more lovely days or even months, th..th..then you'll eventually have to sign up and leave and I might never see you again."

Tears began pouring down both her cheeks now and hiccupping sobs slipped out as she leant her head on his shoulder. He pulled her into a hug to stop her seeing his own burgeoning tears. There wasn't much he could say while wanting to speak but knowing it would be useless to do so and confusing for them both if he did. She was right. He'd put off making the decision to fight for the country, to join the army by signing the papers but eventually he'd be forced by fellow workers and other villagers and finally the British government's conscription to do it and be given his date to leave for training in England. He comforted her silently as best he could then they both wiped each other's faces and kept their chins up next day, going ahead to arrange having the banns read at St. Margaret's. It truly was the very least he could offer her, the love of his life, his soulmate. As soon as possible the ceremony, at which Mary got to be a flower girl, happened along with the members of the Maguire family, mostly all of Frank's sisters and brothers, Lizzie's parents, younger brother Mark, (the pageboy) and older sister Helen, attending too.

The year started well with the wedding, despite being in Pollokshields, and the house on Threadmill Street became ever quieter with Frank now having set up home with Lizzie. With the brothers still working and not yet having to join up, they tried to keep their heads down. They felt that their loyalties still lay with the old country and the treatment of past and present family and with the British Empire's continued hold on Ireland kept them reluctant to lend their support.

Later in 1915 just after Mary's thirteenth birthday, there was general excitement about the big rent strikes in Glasgow, which went on for months, lasting until September of the same year. Nora followed the story in the newspapers and read it with Caity when she came over, minus her previous bruises, for some company bringing her bairns for a visit since her Jack had signed up for the army before conscription. "Don't ask," she'd say when her brothers tried to challenge this decision but it was obvious, Jack wasn't Irish, didn't care about what was happening over the Irish Sea; cared more about doing his duty for King and country. It was the same response when anyone queried her blue or greenish contusions that she tried to hide with her long hair. Right now, the other sisters and women in Kirkston were just glad their rent was tied up with their jobs at the mill and not decided arbitrarily like all those tenants' homes in Glasgow.

Nora read aloud from the Herald that, "...*as demand for war workers in the industrial areas around Glasgow increases, the demand for housing has rocketed, as has the rents that landlords are charging. However, many homes are said to be of a poor standard and in dire need of repair. Increases in rent, as well as the rising price of food means that those at home are struggling financially. This has led to huge protests.*"

"Yous and anyone else in Mill properties are the lucky ones here. I canny see Alexander & Co. trying anything like that on, not after the 1910 strike over much smaller concerns."

"Emm, excuse me. I don't think it was that small a concern. There, thousands came out for us too and it was our working conditions and wages affected - really quite important concerns, you know!"

"Alright, don't be so defensive. I wasn't trying to offend you. I was trying to say you've probably prevented the Company from even thinking about doing something like that. It was a compliment, ye moody eejit!"

In February 1915, local Govan women had formed the Glasgow Women's Housing Association to resist any rent rises. In May 1915, the first rent strike began and soon about 25,000 tenants in Glasgow had joined in. The campaign was effectively organised by women who used propaganda and meetings to get their message across. Like in the Kirkston Mill strike a few years earlier, the radicalisation of the women inspired male factory workers who began to strike for wage increases, putting the government under pressure. The government responded with the Rent Restriction Act, which froze rent at 1914 levels unless improvements had been made to the property. The strikers' demands were met and wartime production was maintained without disruption.

~

A year later Bernie, Frank and Patrick had joined the silent group of some fifty or sixty other fellahs who were waiting in an anteroom. There they stood, staring morbidly at each other. There was nothing to be said; comradeship disappeared in the solemnity of the moment. Occasionally an old joke was passed among the groups, but the laughter sounded forced and hollow. Most of the men made brave attempts to hide their thoughts of home and family. What little talk was rough, inclined to bravado, punctuated by laughter that rang strangely out of place, like laughter in a morgue.

Abruptly the door opened, and they were herded into a darkened room. An officer in uniform was rustling through a mass of blue and yellow papers with an inkwell and Bible standing before him on the table. A hooded light cast weird shadows over them while they stood about and waited. For a time, the officer's attention was focused on the papers while barking out hoarse, unintelligible orders to a pale fellah who dashed in and out of the room. Suddenly, so suddenly that many of them jumped, he stood up, and raised the Bible over his head, holding it aloft as he spoke.

"Raise your right hands and repeat after me..." A forest of hands shot up, and they repeated, word for word, the solemn oath of allegiance to the British Army.

"...*I hereby swear by Almighty God that I will bear faithful and true allegiance to His Majesty King George V, his heirs and successors, and will obey as in duty-bound commands of all officers set over me, so help me God.*"

"Now kiss the Book," he said, and they each kissed the tatty volume with various degrees of fervour and commitment. Bernie and his brothers offered no fervour or commitment but only tentatively touched their lips to the book's spine, now becoming soldiers of the British Empire. They had been duly accepted and sworn. Actually, Bernie felt rather guilty at the feeling of relief, as did his brothers. They looked no different, they felt no different, unless it was for the sense of suspense ended, though they all made sheepish glances towards each other, each wondering if they'd made a mistake; but since conscription had come they'd had no choice. They felt rather dazed, but at a pointed hint from the recruiting officer, they picked up their hats and left for the quartermaster's stores. It was now ten o'clock at night, and the order was to appear the next morning at 9am.

Six weeks later after their hasty training in England and transfer to Belgium, on their first morning, they met and passed an unending stream of khaki, some soldiers marching back from their four days in the trenches.[xxii] All steadily trudging on with the same coating of mud from head to foot, packs and rifles carried anyhow. Each lot had a tail of limping stragglers in ones, twos, and threes. Bernie talked to some of these men who said they'd had a very rough night the night before in the pouring rain, meaning water up to their knees and standing to all night expecting an attack which didn't come. Some mines had been exploded meant for their trench, but luckily, the Huns were ten yards out in their calculations, and they were only smothered in earth instead of blown to bits. He felt more shocked hearing this and the feeling of difference, of the reality that they were at war, struck him now with a fierce grip. He went to follow the others but their commanding officer split the battalion up and some were marched further on to another battlefield. He looked back to wave to his brother Frank, seeing only their kit bags and the top of the company's helmets. He would never see Frank again.

Now it was Bernie's battalions' turn to spend at least four days in the trenches, which appeared to lead from one to another, to another and another in a depressing muddy maze. As they clambered in, they realised in sudden shock that the feet, arms, and faces sticking out from the sides were the dead of previous battles, unburied beyond their fate as trench supports. Some soldiers in front of him gagged and Bernie felt a tremble start up in his limbs. As they encountered the seemingly countless bodies one after another and another and another, they would eventually come to casually mumble "One of our fellahs," recognising one by his boots or another by his uniform, or commiserate, "A Hun— Poor fellah!" They could afford to forget animosity in the presence of the dead.

It was truly difficult sometimes to distinguish between the living and the slaughtered—they both lay so silently in their little boxes in the earthen bank. Sitting later in his dugout with shells passing over his head and the sound of ripping fabric, he got a shower of mud on his sleeping-kit each time the guns fired. Most didn't mind that particularly, especially when they knew that the earth walls kept them safe; but not fifty yards away from him a dead German lay rotting and uncovered—he'd probably been buried once, then later blown out by a shell.

~

Frank already had the new experience of firing a battery, and tomorrow he was to go up to the first line trenches.

That was the first day he took a trip into No-Man's Land. He went in the early dawn as the light slowly wakened the sky. His heart jolted when he suddenly encountered a show of the dead, frozen into immobility in the most unlikely poses. Some of them were part way out of the ground, one hand pressed to its wound, the other pointing; their heads sunken and hair plastered over their foreheads by the rain as rats scattered at his footfall. His imagination started to become more morbid than even the sight at his feet. He kept on wondering what his live companions back in the dugout would look like had they been three weeks dead while the stink of smoke, gunpowder and rotting flesh filled his nostrils.

When he had to step over the bodies to pass, it felt eerie and he couldn't help but shiver, for it seemed like they would reach out to clutch at his trench coat, begging him for help. Poor men and boys, they had been so brave and were now so silent in death. Somewhere there were people who loved each of them and would give their life for the opportunity to touch the cold clay that held them. It was like walking through the day of resurrection with their startled positions and gestures, except that they would never rise again. Then the Huns must have spotted him for shrapnel began to fall, so he quickly crouched low and ran for it.

Frank didn't realise he was in danger until he came to think about it afterwards. At the time it often seemed like playing coconut shies at a fair except you were the coconut. You had to be too concentrated on dodging to be afraid. Soon, all his apprehension that he would be scared under shellfire was gone; he came to believe that if you were going to be hit you would be. Not quite fatalistic but in acceptance rather than resignation, for he had realised a curious thing. "Have you noticed? Isn't it the men who're most afraid are those who seemed to get most easily struck?" A friend of his brother Patrick was hit the other day within thirty yards of him. It was a fleeting recognition as they were diving to the ground after a shell exploded and the man fell towards them nearby. "Wasn't that Matt O'Malley?" Frank shouted, but was hoarse from the smoke and dirt. Brooks gave a brief non-committal, "Aye," while he ducked.

Worst of all was those whistle-bangs because they didn't give anyone much of a chance; it pounced and was on them the same moment that it banged. Luckily, he seemed to be a good dodger of them. A person got kind of used to shellfire up to a point, but there definitely wasn't a man who didn't duck when he heard one coming. Besides, Frank had a superstition that there was something in the power of Lizzie's crucifix to bless him. It had been around his neck ever since she'd given it to him before he left Scotland.

Touching the cross made him think of the cottage and the sounds of home that in the field, were soon compared then became distorted, like when Henry, the coalman (had he joined up?) came with his horse and cart to deliver around the village streets. Coal or nuts, people could take their pick for two bob a bag and many times on tick before he was pouring coals down into the steel bunker; but it was more like hearing cartloads of them. That's what he was hearing while he crouched in the dug-out. In his mind now, with the constant hail of shrapnel and the ground below repeatedly jumping under and around them, the incessant roar, the bang of artillery, and the screams of men as they were hit and fell made memories of the village and green hills around Kirkston make the sight of that battlefield like an apocalypse. It was like a vast stretch of dead country, pitted with shell-holes as though it had been mutilated with chicken pox. There wasn't a leaf or a blade of grass in sight. Every house had either been razed to the ground or was in ruins. No bird sang. Nothing stirred. The only live sound was the scurry and squeak of rats in the night.

~

They had just finished with two days of penetrating rain and mist. In the trenches the mud was up to their knees, making it hard work to wade down those shell-torn tunnels. They were being drowned out of their little dens below ground with rain pooling like a river running through their beds. The mud once more got into whatever they ate. He never knew that mud could be so thick and treacly.

The wonder was that they, for the most part, remained healthy. Between them, they decided it was probably due to being in the open air. His throat never troubled him as it had before joining up and he stayed free from colds in spite of having constantly wet feet. Enough good thick socks to change into regularly would have been priceless had the amount of rain more often caused many of them degrees of 'trench foot'. Their limited supply of whale oil and being paired up to make sure checks were made three times a day to prevent it becoming gangrenous helped. Still there was the sheer terror and horror of seeing men sobbing because their feet had gradually gone numb and the skin red or blue and if not quickly dried out, would lead to the development of gangrene, leaving them knowing they would have to have toes or a leg amputated. Another main disadvantage was that they rarely got a chance to wash or change their clothes, resulting in the sour, stale smell and infuriating itch of lice that impregnated their pale rice-sized bodies in the seams of trousers and sleeves and needed burning out to prevent the soldiers becoming infected with trench fever.

When he looked round at himself and his compatriots, they all looked like disorderly drunks who had spent the night in the gutter with their ill, grey, worn faces in the dawn; unshaved and dirty because there was no clean water. The thing that wore them down the most and called out to their want of perseverance and determination was this endless physical discomfort. Not to be able to wash, not to be able to sleep, to have to be wet and cold for long periods at a stretch, to find mud on your body, in your food, to have to stand in mud, see mud, sleep in mud and to continue to smile— that was what tested their spirit.

"I think it was Lizzie's cross that accounted for my luck." Frank had been in a gun-pit when a shell landed, killing a man only a foot away from him and wounding three others—he and Brooks were the only two to get out all right.

"A few of the men who've been out here a while have a dozen stories of similar near

squeaks," shouted Brooks as he coughed from the dirt and smoke before making his way on his belly over to help out injured platoon members. Later, after they had done what they could to carry or drag the injured men back down into the trench while the Huns were still shelling and firing at them, and in the mess-dugout the oniony-flavoured drink that passed for tea was made and fags lit, Frank finished his story of yet another near miss, not his, this time.

"Talking of squeaks, it was a mouse that saved one fellah. It kept him awake to such an extent that he was determined to move to another place. Just as he got outside the dug-out, a shell fell on the roof." He sucked on the cigarette, blowing out the smoke into the night then passing it to Brooks.

"Not everyone is so lucky Frank. I'd been up forward when word came through that Private Trotter was still further forward, was wounded and been caught in a heavy enemy fire. I only had a young telephonist with me, but we found a stretcher, went forward and got him out. The earth was hopping up and down like popcorn in a hot pan. The unfortunate thing was that the poor chap died on the way out."

"Was it not only last night that we ate together and that same fellah had been telling us what he was going to do on his next leave?" Frank shook his head at the bum luck of the way the cards fell for some and not others.

A few days later, he had the weirdest experience of his life while being caught in a Hun barrage of fire. He'd had to lie on his belly for two hours in a trench with the shells bursting five

yards from him and somehow never took as much as a scratch. Now that he'd faced the worst in so many ways, he was losing his fear and arriving at a kind of peace. For all the horror and destruction, the spirits of the men around him seemed to rise above the carnage, as if they knew they had to in order to survive and fight another day. When he saw how disposable, how easily broken and maimed men's bodies were, he realised how the physical body was the least important part of a person. He and the other soldiers now and then asked strange questions when they saw what men were doing to one another. The chaplain or Padre, as he was known there, giving his guidance was a fine thing to have. Keeping in constant touch with a committed fellah who risked his life daily to speak of the life hereafter to dying soldiers, they felt was like a gift.

They were all pretty fed up with the continuous gunfire and living so many hours in the trenches, which was fairly bad. They were so narrow and smelly with the heat in the summer months during the day and the still unburied dead bodies as trench walls or lying about. There were so many flies and they were all over everything, but despite it all there was always a wonder to relate. In the winter months, it was the frozen land and the incessant rain in between. "Did you see that fellah go over the parapet in that attack the other day?"

"Aye, he went charging the Huns with a bar of chocolate in one hand and a revolver in the other didn't he?" The fellahs around all chuckled or shook their heads at the man's madness or courage or stupidity; they could take their pick.

"It seems like he'll be setting a fashion that'll surely be imitated."

"I doubt it, unless you've got plans for following in his footsteps, Maguire."

~

Three times in his experience so far, he'd been with the infantry as they jumped out of the trenches and went across the front line. It was a sight never to be forgotten. One time there were machine guns behind him and the officers sent a message asking him to lie down and take cover. But that was impossible, so he lay on the parapet until the bullets began to fall too close for comfort, then he dodged out into a shell-hole with the German barrage bursting all around.

He'd seen his first modern battlefield and was quite disillusioned about the so-called glories of war. The glory was in the souls of all the men who crept through the squalor like vermin, not in anything external. There was a fellah there another day who deserved the V. C. four times over by running back through the Hun shell fire to bring news that the infantry wanted more artillery support. How he managed to live through the ordeal nobody knew. Frank thought there was no "To Glory" about what they were doing out there; there was no flash of swords or splendour of uniforms. There were only very tired men determined to keep going. The war would be won by exhausted men who could never again pass a health check; a mob of broken travelling salesmen, jaded ex-plumbers and quite unheroic people. They were civilians in uniform, but because of the ideals for which they fought, they'd managed to grow soldiers' hearts.

Mathews caught him before he started emptying his canister, "Thank goodness it's stopped raining and we'll be able to get dry." He'd come into the dugout plastered from head to foot in mud from lying in the rain on his belly and peering over the top of a trench.

"By the way, have some rum. Have I mentioned rum to you before? As far as I know, I never tasted it until I came out here."

"Aye, we get it served to us whenever we're wet. It's the one thing that keeps a man alive in the winter. You can sleep when you're drenched through and never get a cold if you take it."

They lived for the most part on tinned food, but their appetites made anything taste palatable. Living and sleeping in the open air kept them ravenous, but he never wanted to see tinned food again after the war ended. At night, by the fire, eight feet underground, they sang all the old songs: Clementina, The Long, Long Trail, Three Blind Mice, Long, Long Ago and Rock of Ages. Hymns were mostly the favourites.

But it wasn't a singing matter to go on firing a gun when gun-pits were going up in smoke within sight of you. What a terrible desecration war was. They'd go out one week and look through their glasses at a green, contented country—little churches, villages nestling among woods, next week they saw nothing but ruins and a country-side pitted with shell-holes. All night the machine guns tapped like riveting machines when a building was going up. Then suddenly in the night, a bombing attack would start and the sky would grow white with signal rockets. Orders came in for artillery retaliation, and their guns began to stamp the ground like stallions. In the darkness on every side they could see them snorting fire. Then stillness again while Death counted its haul. Then they saw the white rockets grow fainter and become less manic. For an hour there was blackness. Their batman consoled himself with singing, "Pack up your troubles in your old kit-bag/And smile, smile, smile." It seemed best to go on smiling even when someone who was once your pal now lay forever silent in his blanket on a stretcher.

All that day he'd been having a chilly, but strangely amusing time at the Forward Observation Post. It seemed brutal to say it, but taking pot shots at the enemy when they showed themselves felt like fun. While he watched them scattering like ants before the shell whose direction he had ordered, he would somehow forget to think of them as people or men like him and his platoon, any more than the hunter thought of the young that were left motherless. He watched his victims through his glasses as God might watch his universe from above. He realised his skill and accuracy in killing made him what outside of war, would be called murder. He wondered at his main sensation of curiosity rather than horror at the loss of life he was causing. There was definitely a feeling of satisfaction, yet at close quarters only in defense would he have hurt any man. If it wasn't for the rattling of the machine guns in the distance, he might have been here for entertainment. (Those coconut shies again.) And still they learned to sleep the sleep of the just, despite the roaring of the guns and the atrocities they committed.

War was not at all, what their civilian minds had imagined. It was much more horrible and far less exciting.

The horrors that the civilian mind dreaded most were mutilation and death. Out here they rarely thought about those until they happened, then they did what they could for the poor fellah or since death happened constantly, just got on with it. They had to crouch and move warily then Zing! A bullet from a German sniper. They'd laugh and whisper to each other, "A near one, that." Then the questioning of themselves, of each other. "Are we really killing men every day? Are we really at risk ourselves?" A sense of disbelief began to take hold of him.

During the battle at Arras, Frank briefly saw his brother, whose platoon had been redeployed back with the battalion, killed on one side of him and another fellah on the other. He went on shooting over the parapet; then the parapet was knocked about, and still he wasn't hit. He seized his brother's body, then the other man's and built them up into the parapet with sandbags, and went on shooting. When the stress was over and he could leave off, he looked round and saw what he was leaning against.

"Who did that?" he asked. And they told him. Soon after that others started to notice that he was muttering strange phrases to himself. "He's just 'Gone West', that's what we call dying out here. We don't say that a man is dead. Bernie's just 'Gone West.'" Or other hard to fathom declarations like: "You can't send steel bullets to the Huns and love letters to your wife in the post on the same day," he'd say to no one in particular for no reason in particular.

It had been hard to get to know Bernie back home for the short few years they had been around each other after he'd come back from Fermanagh just before their mother died. Only five years later, the war started and when conscription came, they and their two younger brothers (who were deployed in a different battalion) had all signed up. Bernie had seemed overly enthusiastic to do so, couldn't wait to finish his training and start fighting. That was a surprising act since he'd spent so many years with their Republican supporting grandfather in Fermanagh, who'd more than likely give out a stink and be full of begrudgery about their slight on, no their betrayal of Ireland, but what else could they have done?

Frank got to know Bernie better in the short months at war together than those previous five years. Their true family turned out to be their comrades in arms, fighting and suffering and getting up to fight again after another attack. The ache of the loss felt like a cold reflection of the frozen forms around him; an icy emptiness that kept him estranged from his beating heart and left him shivering.

The country was strikingly white under the light of the moon. Every yard was an old battlefield as far as the eye could see; beneath the soft white down of snow lay unburied bodies like sleeping snowmen, their rotting bones singing their frozen goodbyes into the sky. All across the night, German lights were shooting up and drifting across their field of vision.

"Do you hear that? Tappity-tap go the machine-guns! Whoo-oo woo go the big guns, stamping like angry bairns." He was shouting at the empty night. He had to return by himself across the slippery drifts covering the mounds of deathly shapes. All the way, he asked himself how could he not be frightened. "What has happened to me? Ghosts should walk here if anywhere. For sure, I'm definitely going to be frightened again before this war has ended." He began to shake uncontrollably. His mind was running on without him. "Phone up the password, 'Slaves of Freedom'. We all understand what that means don't we? Isn't it a funny change from comfortable breakfasts?"

After an attack some weeks later, an officer met a solitary Private wandering across a shell-torn field. While he'd watched him he thought something was wrong by his staggering gait and the muttered sounds, as if he was talking to himself. "Hey soldier, are you alright? Where's your battalion?"

When Private Frank Maguire eventually turned his head in the officer's direction, he looked at him with confusion and said only, "Dead faces. Muddy road." He kept on repeating the phrase, and it was all that anyone could get out of him. Probably the dead faces and the muddy road were the last sights he had seen before he'd finally lost sense of himself. They got Frank to a field hospital where the place was close to unrecognisable; every corner of every floor covered with wounded soldiers. Some sitting up and some wounded all over, several appeared to be dying and others critically wounded; and they still kept coming in. They were all strewn about the floor, some soaked to the skin from wet shell holes; on their stretchers, waiting to be put to bed but by then all Frank could do was shake and jerk at the bark of artillery fire and the sound of shells exploding outside.

They sent him home to recuperate but it was unlikely he'd ever return to battle. His last question to his commanding officer was, "Do you think the soul of courage dies out of humans any more than love does?" The officer's eyes widened at the question as Frank was taken away, remarking to those around him that maybe Private Maguire wasn't so mad after all.

Chapter 20 - Spanish Influenza – Nora/ Jeannie

For all the deaths of the men from the fighting in the war up to 1918, the Spanish flu epidemic must have been at least as deadly. There were bright red fiendish looking posters all over the walls of the mill and ones on the street walls that shouted:

> THE   GOVERNMENT   HAS   THE SITUATION WELL IN HAND.

> THE EPIDEMIC IS ACTUALLY IN DECLINE THERE IS NO REAL RISK
> EXCEPT TO THE RECKLESS WHO TRY TO FIGHT THE FLU ON THEIR FEET.
> IF   YOU   FEEL   YOURSELF   SUCCUMBING REPORT YOURSELF AND
> LIE DOWN FOR A FORTNIGHT.
> WOULD THEY BE DEAD IF THEY'D STAYED IN BED?

That hadn't been true for Jeannie, the staying in bed bit. She had stayed in bed and didn't get out again. She had been aged just twenty and Mary recently turned sixteen. Nora was there as always; the one who took over from their mammy at the same age as Mary was now, when she'd passed on seven years before. Not an entirely new responsibility for Nora, but the having to nurse her younger sister Jeannie at home as she went every shade of colour from red to blue to black was an horrific role she'd had no choice but to play. Caity was married by then and living in Paisley with her new husband and their first baby, but Jack was still at the front so Mary was the only other one around. At least of those who lived at home. Patrick and Seamus hadn't yet returned from the war either and while, according to the newspapers, apparently there was an end in sight, nobody wanted to rely on just their word for it. It was too much to hope for.

With Jeannie, it had started with flushed cheeks that she quite suited, except it was June and not the kind of weather to produce that at this time of year. Jeannie was one of those dreamy sorts of girls. Mary loved her strawberry-blonde curls, elfin face and her slim figure. She had a very sophisticated look for one so young, as opposed to the big and broad motherly look of Nora.

"Are you alright, wee sis? There's a large order in at the mill and it's all hands-on board." Nora had been working at the mill for almost ten years now, so knew the goings on and was kind of a supervisor (not of course, paid as such) down to the stories about her role in the 1910 strike that Mary had heard about. Nora moved forward to cup Jennie's cheek but felt the heat radiating before she actually touched her. Ten days before, she had had some strange symptoms herself: with weakness, limp limbs, chills, fever, headache with double vision, and heavy, drooping eyelids. Surprisingly, she had a lack of thirst, even during her fever and the children seemed to share her symptoms. Doctor Paterson came round within a day or two, leaving enough *Gelsemium* tablets for her and the children.[xxiii] Mary became similarly ill after a week but she became more irritable and didn't want to move for fear she would feel much worse and kept moaning about wanting to go home. "You are home Mary. What can I help you with?" Her sister Caity asked in puzzlement as she gave Mary the remedy *Bryonia* left by Doctor Paterson after his brief consultation with her.

Nora could see a sheen of sweat on Jeannie's forehead and tutted loudly; gesturing to Mary to take Jeannie's other arm. Between them, they quickly caught their sister as she swayed forward. "Into bed with you now." They helped undress her, piling on blankets to help break Jeannie's fever to no avail as she mumbled in delirium for several days before her face turned reddish-brown then darkening still further as her breathing laboured and became negligible wisps of air. Her ears and fingertips, never mind her lips, started to become blue for the lack of air in her tortured breathing.

"What can we do?" They couldn't understand why she had become so bad when they and the children had had a dose of the flu with similar symptoms too but the remedies that Doctor Paterson had given them had helped them to recover, though there was no tablets left by the time Jeannie was infected. Mary knelt by the side of her sister' bed as she mumbled and sweated, occasionally starting. "It's okay Jeannie, I'm here," she whispered as she took the damp cloth to Jeannie's forehead, but it was no use. The cloth dried out with her body heat before providing a drop of relief. Mary had to stifle sobs as she realised her sister's life was ebbing away. By then, Doctor Paterson had succumbed and had to isolate, so another non-homeopathic doctor was sent round, who diagnosed bronchitis. When they mentioned the remedies he scoffed at them, remarking, "Homeopathy! That sham of a system?! What on earth would I use that for, even if I knew how."

"But the rest of our family, including the children, have become better. It must be helping in some way. Can't you see that we've all recovered?" Nora implored. However, he just pushed past to bend over Jeannie's now, after ten days, emaciated frame declaring it was influenza. After another eight days, he said it was pneumonia and gave Jeannie aspirin. From that moment on her deterioration speeded up. "Essentially, it's the Spanish flu. There's not much more I can do for her. Sadly, you should say your goodbyes to your sister now, ladies." They called the priest and crying softly but continuously waited with Jeannie as she slipped away. They washed and wrapped her body before the undertakers, and swathed in masks and body coverings, almost as if shrouded themselves, came to lift her into and seal the coffin. No wakes were allowed now for fear of further spread of the illness and just those in the cottage at Threadmill were allowed to accompany the coffin to Moorhead cemetery. Like others affected, a bereaved home was easy to find, lying behind a customary white blind. It was a common sight, a grieving family behind ghostly sheets with pictures and mirrors all turned to the wall since no reflection was allowed to be seen. Their house of death kept an open door for a wake at home the night before but most were too scared to attend or were advised to stay clear. There was no chapel of rest and the only possessions she'd take to her grave was a favourite rosary and her First Communion bible. On behalf of God, the robed parish priest was there to welcome her back, even if making sure to keep an appropriate wide berth.

Jeannie was far from the only one succumbing to the dreaded flu, which was being called, 'The Great White Plague'. Many at home and soldiers on the battlefields in France and Belgium were dying of the illness in numbers as many or more than those killed by the fighting. People who lived through it sometimes reported that someone who appeared well in the morning could be dead by evening. It had been a longer and more drawn-out deterioration for Jeannie, who'd only worsened after the aspirin prescription, which made them wonder just how many more had been affected in a similar way.

When Dr Paterson managed to call in after his own recovery, he said, "I'm so sorry that there was no other replacement for my services to help Jeannie. It's a terrible shame that there have been so many unnecessary deaths, including your sister, because the guidance to not give the one drug which directly or indirectly has probably been the cause of the loss of more lives than influenza itself, has been so often ignored. Aspirin is the most pernicious drug of all. It beguiles by its quick action in the relief of pain; a relief that is deceiving. In some cases, aspirin weakens the heart, depresses the vital forces; increases mortality in mild cases and makes convalescence slower. [xxiv]

In all cases, it masks the symptoms and makes the selection of the curative remedy much more difficult. We'd be as well communing with the astrologers for all the help that approach provided."

"Astrologers?" Mary puzzled.

"Yes, for all their harping on about scientific theories of medicine, the name 'influenza' comes from the Italian and Latin, *influenza delle stele* meaning 'the influence of the stars' from an epidemic originating in 15th century Italy, when people believed our fates to be decided only by the movements of the celestial bodies of stars and planets." Scepticism raised his rather bushy eyebrows. Neither Mary nor Nora were familiar with this 'Astrology' as described by Dr Paterson but took heed of his concerns about the use of aspirin, but they were still more concerned about how they would break the news of their sister's death to their brothers on their imminent return.

Neither Nora nor Mary managed to return to the mill until a month later, having allowed time for the intensity of their grief and the pain of their sister's absence to subside and even then, they only returned because they had to. Their sister Caity, and their neighbours had been kind enough to see them through so far but there was little food in the house and they needed to earn money to be able to stock up on groceries.

Chapter 21 - Shell Shock – Nora/Frank

Seamus Maguire, now a man at heart and the manlier age of nineteen, returned home from the war with his older brother Patrick. On arriving at the cottage, they discovered they had not only lost their barely-known brother Bernie, but that the Spanish Flu had taken Seamus older and Patrick's younger sister Jeannie. Frank was also conspicuous by his absence.

Notification of Bernie being missing in action had come some weeks after the event in April 1917 and then some months later the final envelope declaring his death and no body to be brought home, just his tag and the cold formality of the telegram. Nora had been the one to open it and felt herself blanch as she read the words, dropping the telegram to the floor.

"What?" Mary asked as she came up behind making Nora jump before stooping to retrieve the telegram.

"It's about B..B..Bernie." Nora forced out his name as her throat tried to swallow down the ball of tears for the big brother she had known so little. Frank had warned them that they would hear soon after that first notice when he'd returned between the MIA letter and the official notice of Bernie's death. At the time, he'd seemed so confused; seemed to be uttering gibberish, talking about burying Bernie and propping up trenches; how it was all his fault. Jeannie's delirium a year later had given her the shivers, since it had reminded her in some ways of how Frank had been.

On his return, Frank had been admitted to Cowden Hall on the estate in Kirkston, which had been converted into a convalescent home for British and Belgian soldiers in 1916.[xxv] There he had to stay until he was considered fit enough to be discharged. Not even the nurses there seemed to understand what was wrong with him. When they'd eventually been allowed to visit after Lizzie, his very relieved and anxious wife had done so, he was hardly recognisable with his glassy, staring eyes and the strange words he spurted out while trembling and stuttering. There were nurses chatting in loud whispers in the entrance hallway when they were leaving after their once a week visit to Frank and somehow, they seemed to think being partially hidden by a large fern meant their voices couldn't be heard.

"I just admitted a gunner suffering from shock alone, no wound, completely knocked out. He couldn't tell you his name, or stand, or even sit up, but just shivered and shuddered. Now he's

warm in bed and can say 'Thank you.' He's like that other Private who came in a month ago. I wonder what exactly did it to both of them?" The other nurse just shook her head adding,

"When they arrive, the wounded ones are generally in "the excitable stage"; some are surprised and resentful, some seem relieved that it's no worse, and some very quiet and collapsed. There is a chance he and those like him might just be malingering and not too keen to get back to the trenches in Belgium." On noticing the raised eyebrows and brief look of disgust as the nurse concluded her opinion, Nora and Mary blushed on Frank's behalf at her cruel words.

She wasn't the last to offer even more damning or ignorant opinions about Frank's early homecoming minus a visible wound.

The resident doctor at Cowden Hall confirmed Frank's diagnosis as 'shell-shock', but in soldiers it was often value-loaded and associated with negative judgements like being 'unmanly', 'effeminate', 'childish' or physically and psychologically 'degenerate'. Even while ill in hospital, Frank wasn't free of it and it was likely to be even worse whenever he was discharged back to his new home with his wife Lizzie.

Nora wondered what help, if any, he'd been receiving and hoped the doctors knew more than the nurses seemed to. She remembered then the man who'd helped the family over the years before with his unconventional remedies. Since he'd always emphasised the importance of a

person's mental and emotional symptoms, he could be just the man to pay Frank a visit.

The first Homeopathic Hospital, at 5 Lynedoch Crescent, Glasgow was called the Houldsworth Hospital, grown from the 1909 Dispensary and opened in 1914 under the guidance of its first honorary physician, Dr Gibson Miller. Unfortunately, like his mentor, Gibson Miller who died in 1916 after losing his son in the war, James Paterson also lost a son in the Great War in 1918 and never recovered from his loss. He had eventually reduced his hours at the Glasgow Homeopathic hospital and when the war ended passed on some of his patients to a relatively newly-qualified female doctor named Agnes Moore. An occurrence Nora, Caity and Mary were all surprised and heartened by, given the mostly ignored and limited impact woman gaining the vote in 1918 had had on how they lived their lives. It was very early days but she felt the challenges this and many other women undertook on a daily basis to have their efforts acknowledged was a slow and thankless process.

She had high expectations of Dr Moore when she made the appointment to ask her about carrying out a consultation with Frank. She was led into a small room in the new premises, a little shaken up by her journey all the way from Kirkston, having had to change trams several times. She patted down her frizz of hair and smoothed the damp creases in her skirt just before Dr Moore strode into sit opposite her with an expectant look on her face. Nora explained the situation as best she could but Doctor Moore soon halted her.

"Thank-you for your information, Mrs. Simpson but it is clear I must visit the patient, your brother, myself in person. I'm sorry you've come all this way to not much effect but I will contact Cowden Hall and make arrangements. You will be notified so that should he wish it, you can be present with your brother when I speak with him to properly take his case." The doctor tidied her notes and dried her quill as Nora buttoned up her coat, readying herself for the return journey to Kirkston.

"Thank-you for considering it important enough for your attention Doctor. The journey was worth it to know Frank will be looked after, dare I say, by someone who is unlikely to dismiss his health problems of the mind as seems to have been happening so far." Nora offered the doctor her hand and was relieved it was taken in friendship, sealing it with a firm shake. It was a week before the letter arrived informing Nora of the consultation at the Hall and on her last visit, she had previously secured Frank's permission to be there. Nora bundled herself in hat and scarf to keep out the cold wind as she made her way to the Hall, so very changed since the start of the war with any previous social events in the grounds having long ceased. Now the Hall was a home for recuperating British and Belgian soldiers. The home contained workshops offering the patients, not returned to duty, regular employment as well as "curative treatment" and the opportunity to learn a trade, such as carpentry, woodwork, basket making, boot making or electrical engineering. Efforts were made to find employment for those patients discharged from the army and close to 80% were regularly sent out to work or train in special trades. All treatment provided was free and patients could not be nursed against their will.

Notwithstanding her brother's erratic behaviour and that terrible habit, he'd developed of swearing at every second word or that time Mary and her had taken him out for a walk in the grounds and he' been so fearful of walking outside or of any other patients approaching him and had soon begun imagining he was surrounded by enemies; behaving as if he was being pursued by some unknown enemy. He even tried to hide in the bushes. He became very low-spirited and disheartened though relieved after they convinced him to follow them back to the ward. The scene that occurred some thirty minutes into the consultation the next day still threw Nora.

Frank was sitting in uniform in a sunny ward, where he was discussing his symptoms with the homeopathic doctor, who would assess any phobias and conflicts and formulate them into a prescription to help treat those symptoms. His usual tremor since being there was present and his words sounded hesitant and stilted whether cursing or not. When Dr Moore began to directly address his time in the still ongoing war, he jumped off the bed and crawled underneath in fear when the words 'bombs' and 'soldiers' were mentioned. He eventually, after much cajoling, emerged looking up and around the room in anticipatory fear. When he tried to stand, he could barely walk; was simply shaking and staggering. At one point he fell to the floor and bent into what seemed such unnatural positions it almost looked as if he was having some kind of fit, which lasted some minutes before he managed to lie down at rest while his tremor continued. Nora was quite frightened and alarmed by seeing what she had never witnessed in Frank until that day. Doctor Moore was good at calming him while closely observing his actions and responses and noted down as much as possible when he'd calmed, including Frank's comments about his nightmares. Dr Moore slowly wrote down his significant dreams, saying that she would be trying to find a remedy that would alleviate any suppressed traumas of battle. By night this man, her brother, described being back with his doomed section in the horror-stricken trenches, where the panic and the rush of some of his terrifying experiences were repeatedly re-enacted among the livid faces of the dead. He appealed to the doctor, saying, "It is like becoming the bloody victim of my trench disasters and feckin delusions. No feckin doctor can save me when the devil has a hold of me and that angel won't feckin help me out!" he exclaimed while jerking and twisting the sleeve of his pyjamas round and round between his fingers.

"I understand that it is hard but please don't give up Mr. Maguire. Let's see what I can find to try to help you first." The doctor was taking her time to explain as much to Nora, as to her brother, that the diagnosis of 'shell-shock' was entered almost routinely in the logbooks yet often marginalised compared to any physical complaint in the patient; however apparently insignificant. There were patients to be found admitted with 'migraine', 'glycosuria', 'gas poisoning', 'compound fractures', and even 'haemorrhoids' when their most significant mental and emotional symptoms were omitted to the extent that they became next to invisible in their medical notes.

"These are not relevant reasons to be sent to a 'shell-shock' soldier home and granted, they may be part of the total symptom picture but the lack of focus on them as a main complaint surely reflects an unwillingness to ascribe sick leave to crucial mental or emotional factors," she remarked, clicking her tongue while shaking her head.

Just then, a uniformed barrel of a man with square shoulders and a protruding chest marched into the small sitting area of the ward, the air being immediately sucked out as he strode in demanding, "What is going on in my wards, might I ask?" He flipped Dr Moore's writing pad from her hand and it flew to the floor, its pages fluttering as it landed. She quickly stood to face the obnoxious man who continued to bluster at her.

"We don't allow women to treat our men here and especially not with the quackery I've been informed that you are foisting on my patient!"

"I'll have you know that I am a qualified medical doctor and well within mine and the patient's rights to carry out a private consultation if that is what he so desires! I would respectfully ask you to allow me to finish my consultation with Mr Maguire and I will thereafter meet with you in your office should you require some instruction on the art and science of Homeopathy, sir. Otherwise, it's to the Registrar I go to make it known how you very rudely interrupted a confidential consultation." At that moment Frank gave a loud guffaw and Nora tried to quietly ask him to please stop laughing. She knew this was a serious situation. She received a rapid litany of cursing but he did stop laughing for a moment. "Where's those strange smells coming from?" he said loudly then. Nora shook her head and leant in to try quieting him.

"Smells like burning wood and there's a whiff of feckin pigeon's dung. This is supposed to be a blasted clean place; it's a hospital and they're burning us down and stinking us out for the love of God! Are the doctors in here eejits or something? Who's that anyway, standing there like a toy soldier in a huff?" Nora and Dr Moore tried to restrain themselves from laughing at Frank's appropriate description as the medical officer quickly straightened up, puffing out his chest even more.

With a surprised expression that quickly became a sneer, the stout uniformed doctor completely ignored Frank, choosing rather to respond to Dr Moore. "You, madam, neglected to come to my office to secure my permission to carry out such a thing in the first place. In here, patients do not decide what treatment they will have." His loud belligerent voice was having an effect, as a jolt of shock lit Frank's rigid wide-eyed face.

"Is he the doctor?" Frank said looking around the room then, his expression quickly

changing to one of confusion. "He's not the one that was here this morning. Where's my feckin

doctor gone; he was here a minute ago? You? What's your name again? Caity, Mary, Jeannie ...no, she's dead now isn't she, just like Bernie. Did you know I killed him; I did. The shells were

exploding and in he came dropping down with the bullets and boulders and clods of mud and

showers of blood that landed right on top of me, no, in front of me, right there! His poor face was

half gone and his eyes not ready for sleep. The devil got him, you know. That feckin gobshite of a hoormaister making me do horrible things. I needed something to protect me, I was hoping for an angel but it was too dark. Those bastard shells, those whizz-bangs breaking up bodies, slaughtering friends and there it was, that angel sitting watching that devil do his worst. They told me I was pushing and pulling Bernie's floppy body on top of the trench sandbags but I couldn't stop crying and crying; those wee jessie tears for ma big brother. He feckin helped me a lot. Maybe he was swapping my life for his. D'ye think that's what it was?" Dr Moore was watching and listening intently to Frank, nodding at him in reassurance at these important insights, despite or perhaps because of the overbearing but unfeeling presence of the medical officer who stopped only until Frank drew breath, threw a brief dismissive glance in his direction before continuing on with his own diatribe.

"Their doctors decide because they know best. Not some flibbertigibbet woman posturing as a medic while practicing one of the most unscientific systems of charlatanism I have ever come across. Please take your scribblings somewhere else. I am the chief medical officer of this facility and *my* wishes will be obeyed, or would you rather I had Mr Maguire removed instead and you can both carry on as you like elsewhere?" Frank's face completely leeched of any colour when hearing and somehow understanding the import of this exchange. His breathing became rapid and his tremor intensified as his panic increased. Nora had been transfixed between Frank's story and the arrogance of the doctor, but now moved swiftly to his side putting her arm around him and speaking softly at his ear to allay his fears but had to shake her head at Doctor Moore and plead with her eyes at her not to argue further with this horrible man. Frank needed to feel secure at least here even if nowhere else. Dr Moore gave a brief nod of understanding, but her flaming face belied the apparent calmness of her movements as she slowly gathered her notebook, picking it from the floor. She looked directly up into the florid face of the overbearing medic saying, "The director of the Homeopathic Hospital in Glasgow will be in touch over your abysmally unprofessional behaviour, sir," then lifted her Mackintosh to go, head held high, past the matron who'd hurried in at the sound of the monstrous Commander Walsh's barking voice, which unfortunately was imitating the sound of gunfire and disturbing other neurasthenic patients. Dr. Moore made her way back down the stairs and out into the wind and rain.

The next day Nora again made the long trip up to the Dispensary at Charing Cross in Glasgow in order to apologise on her and Frank's behalf.

"Doctor, he really does want to try your treatment despite that bully. Homeopathy has been a great help to him and other family members under Dr Paterson's care for at least the last decade. If you have enough details, couldn't you find a remedy for him to try? I can slip it to him at my next visit. Just give me your instructions and I promise to do as you ask."

"I can try, but it may depend on what kind of medicine that obnoxious man has or will be giving Francis. Homeopathic remedies are very subtle and can be antidoted by strong substances and practices, especially those like ether or chloroform and electrotherapy which have been commonly overused in cases such as your brother's," [xxvi] the Doctor explained.

"That does sound distressing and we haven't been given any information on what treatment Francis has had. 'Doctor knows best' as that unpleasant man pointed out," Nora commented in a sarcastic tone with a rueful smile on her face before continuing. "I will ask Elizabeth, Frank's wife if she knows anymore and if not, ask her to try finding out which medications are being given to Frank. Please do still try to find a remedy if you can." Agnes Moore let out a long, troubled breath before asking Nora to return the next day. Nora had already had to take a few days off from work, which she now remembered had not been very well received by her supervisor, so had to change the arrangements. Now she would have to ask Lizzie, who wasn't as convinced about homeopathy being only recently introduced to the details of the alternative system of medicine.

"Sorry, I've realised I'll also have to ask Lizzie, my sister-in law, to collect whatever you prescribe with instructions for how Frank is to take it, which she will hopefully carry to the Hall. Now that the commander has met me face to face (and not before time I'd say), but I am only his sister and just a woman after all." There was that wry grin again. "I think she will be less conspicuous than myself."

When Nora broached the subject that evening Lizzie remarked, a light tremble in her tone, "I'm not even sure about this homeowhatsit medicine?"

"Lizzie, you know our family have used it for years. Did you not take some when the flu was around? Besides even the King uses it and his homeopath is Scottish too. Dr John Weir was born in Paisley, where Caity lives. He trained at the University of Glasgow, the same as old Dr Paterson and Dr Agnes Moore who's trying to help Frank just now. He looked after the last King Edward VI at the end of his life and has just been appointed Physician Royal to King Edward VII. [xxvii]In the papers the article about his appointment said Weir first learned of homeopathy through his contact with old Gibson Miller, who's head of the Glasgow Homeopathic Hospital where both the doctors who've helped us work. Dr Gibson-Miller treated Dr Weir for boils and converted him to homeopathy, can you believe it? Now he's treating royalty. It cannae be all that bad, so?"

"But what if the Commander should discover our plan? Will Frank be able to deal with the possible consequences; perhaps being thrown out of Cowden Hall? Where would he go then? I'm not sure this is a good idea Nora."

"Please let's try Lizzie. You do want him to be able to come home to you don't you?" However reluctant she felt, Lizzie eventually nodded in agreement. She did miss Frank being at home and resolved not to allow herself to become overly anxious.

With her own similar reluctance, Agnes Moore spent some hours the next day trawling through the Dispensary's copy of Kent's Repertory and Materia Medica. She had now seen several patients, officers as well as privates, suffering from neurasthenia; this more often occurring in officers. Then there was the state that had become known, for better or worse, as 'Shellshock', which seemed to predominate in privates, those soldiers by far the majority on the front lines. Then she'd heard that the Army Council had issued a writ, commanding that cases, be labelled either wounded ('shell-shock W') or sick ('shell-shock S') with the distinction made on the basis of whether the symptoms were a result of `enemy action'. It decreed that only the former class would be entitled to wound stripes and military pensions. With this ruling, the military officially and effectively recognised that there was a grey area between cowardice and madness for the first time, but then immediately withdrew from this acknowledgement by imposing the traditional military distinction between `battle-casualties' and `sickness' on shell-shock.

Agnes Moore, in addition to her professional interest, had the personal motive of her own fiancé's situation for finding out various aspects of the way the army was dealing with casualties, therefore spending time researching the process of diagnosis in the military. She found that typically soldiers were first sent to Not Yet Diagnosed Nervous centres with this NYDN label, and then enquiries were made of their units to check whether they should be classified as 'shell-shock W' or 'shell-shock S' and those who failed to recover but had no visible cerebral injury were then classified as "neurasthenic."[xxviii]

Cowden Hall in Kirkston was one of the special centres and she wished that they had thought to appoint a trained homeopath to the board. Unfortunately, she'd been informed by her frustrated and angry fiancé Andrew, who described the instigation of an unsympathetic and disciplinarian regime under the control of Colonel Balfour Graham, a cruel man who ran Craiglockhart in Edinburgh on strict disciplinarian lines and who called his approach 'homeopathic' because exposing soldiers to additional traumas, which of course didn't work and in fact, were more in the nature of aversion therapy, consisting of finding out the main likes and dislikes of each patient, and then ordering them to avoid from the former and apply themselves to the latter. Andrew had explained saying, "The patients who disliked noise were allotted rooms on the noisy main road. Those who had been parsons, school masters, journalists, and poets, were forbidden to use the library and driven off in groups to physical drill, lawn tennis, golf, and badminton."[xxix]

This regime had remained in place from November 1917 until around March 1918 when, perhaps because of decreasing therapeutic success, another inspection was prompted. By that time Andrew had been about himself enough to be discharged back to duty for the foreseeable future at least.

This debacle resulted in the actual therapeutic value of homeopathy only being ridiculed and left ignored as a valid form of treatment beyond the means of those who later sought it through doctors in private practice. This meant mainly the officer classes who, more often, had recourse to knowledge of it and funds to pay for consultations.

Despite this unfair restriction on access for the majority of those requiring and able to be helped, she was glad Andrew, as an officer, would have the advantage of receiving appropriate treatment when next home again. Her personal experience had given her an edge when treating other men but which did not compromise, as with any other homeopath, her practitioner role as an impartial observer, but it did make her keener to find the most accurate and beneficial medicine in each case and madder than she had words to describe about the condescending attitude of the obnoxious medical officer at the Hall, who was apparently willing to deny someone, possibly anyone, the opportunity of additional help since in his arrogance and faulty interpretations if, in fact, he'd even heard about Craiglockhart, decided the conventional way was the only way.

Generally, the failure of acknowledgement of the severity of a soldiers' actual state of mind also had immediate consequences for the individual men, who could be left facing years of

wrangling with the Ministry of Pensions because of the label they had been given.

In practice, shellshock was being described or identified in various ways such as: the flight from an intolerable destructive reality through illness. Men were sometimes being labelled as being psychologically wounded soldiers or described as those whose bodies were tortured by their minds. It seemed there was also much fear about the effect on 'manhood` with even more surprise and disapproval of the unexpected phenomenon of wholesale mental breakdown among men, which by some was also considered an early twentieth-century epidemic of hysteria. Despite these misgivings, the debate about the mental and emotional effects of combat did, to some degree, advance the understanding of psychological disorders. Agnes thought it was high time the mental state of mind was given its proper importance in the human being, but only by such a tragedy it had and was, still claiming millions of lives and much sanity as the heavy price for this realisation.

Not all soldiers' cases were regarded as serious enough to reach the final stage. As Andrew had tried to explain on his last too short leave, initially there would be contact with their Regimental Medical Officer (RMO). [xxx]

It interested Dr Moore that as the war had gone on, it also became clear to those observing the systems of dealing with soldiers affected, that removing a man from the military environment tended to fix his pathological symptoms and make them harder to cure and not surprisingly, made it particularly hard to send them back on duty in the trenches where most of their trauma and disturbances had occurred. Charles S. Myers, consultant psychologist to the British Expeditionary Force, had come up with the new diagnosis and title of 'shellshock' in 1915, but in November 1917 was denied permission to submit a paper on shellshock to the British Medical Journal because orders had been issued to the press bureau that nothing regarding the disorder should be released to newspapers.

But by the time a man reached the hands of the doctor at home, the soldier had already been diagnosed at least twice and was now definitively a patient. The primary objective was also, unlike the other doctors they'd seen previously, to treat these cases. Agnes had had much discussion with her colleagues at the homeopathic hospital about their mainly thwarted desire to help, especially since conditions presented being of mainly mental and emotional origin, would be so amenable to homeopathic treatment.

She considered the fact that there were no characteristic pathological changes in this disease, and about all that could be said was that the symptoms were so varied and complex that it simplified the presentation to study the grouping of cases according to the predominance of certain symptoms, similar in some ways to finding the 'genus epidemicus.' She checked and weighted the predominance and intensity of Frank's symptoms where they appeared significant and particularly were appearing strange, rare or peculiar.

The medicines she worked out to be most similar came down to a choice between three that indicated therapeutic affinity but it was not yet a complete and definite choice for the treatment of his particular presentation. She moved then to study the Materia Medicas of Kent, Boericke and Clark for further comparison in an attempt to come as close to the simillimum as it was possible to do based on the information she had. So far her choice was between: *Aconite, Kali Phos* and *Anacardium*. The *Anacardium* picture struck her as being highly plausible and perhaps Frank wasn't as far gone as this state just yet, for his mind was not so feeble and appeared more excitable than dull and sluggish. Francis did though, talk of a conflict between the devil and an angel and all that cursing and swearing was very prominent. Choosing this remedy may prevent his final tipping into insanity.

She continued checking her differential diagnosis in the Materia Medicas before making up the remedy in readiness for Lizzie's arrival in advance of visiting her husband later that afternoon at Cowden Hall.

After much deliberation and a necessarily stealthy approach, homeopathic treatment began. Nora was instructed to return a report of any changes in his symptoms to the dispensary office on a weekly basis and to check in regularly by phone, which was only possible because of the availability of one fitted in the Kirkston Mill offices. As Frank began to show signs of improvement, he very slowly asked to reduce some of the heavy doses of the ether that he'd been on. Nora's first observation was that he wasn't swearing quite so much and that Frank had remarked that he knew he was feeling better because he felt less paranoid and had begun to help around Cowden Hall and not too much later, became more able to spend time in other people's company. After five weeks the nightmares and stomach pains hadn't changed much but he was no longer seeing devils and angels. This resulted in his being allowed home for a day or two where he was able to help with some chores to the delight of his wife, Lizzie. At the two-month mark he had completely barred himself from using ether with the result that the nightmares had subsided dramatically. He had less stomach pain, stated that his "paranoia" was "pretty much gone" and, amazingly, had begun to put in a few hours of work at his former job as a steel moulder[xxxi]. All the while he continued with support services at the Hall, which included weekly meetings.

After three months, Frank was no longer having flashbacks, and when Nora had the opportunity to speak personally with him, he remarked, "My mind is starting to come back to me." He declared himself "definitely motivated" and ready to enter a program of further rehabilitation.

After successfully completing the program, he began to sleep in four to eight hourly stretches at night. Over the ensuing months Frank continued to have small bouts of various symptoms but they would always settle down relatively quickly. His overall health steadily improved. He even began to cut down on his cigarette smoking. Seven months after beginning homeopathic treatment he enrolled in night classes. He was also beginning to identify long-buried emotions. "I'm trying not to feel so guilty about Bernie's death. Before I didn't know what reality was when it came to how he died." He expressed having difficulty because it was hard to accept God's existence, given all the horrible things that he had experienced.

One full year from when Dr Moore had first met Frank, he had been discharged from the army and moved with his wife into a new two-bedroom apartment where his first and only son Robert, was born. The changes were remarkable and the medical officer at Cowden Hall had predictably claimed all the credit for his recovery, despite Frank's being the only soldier to have had such dramatic improvements compared to the other resident patients at that time. He was no longer paranoid or aggressive or dwelling on thoughts about salvation and had managed to accompany his wife to Mass once or twice. There'd been fewer sensations of the mental state that had driven him close to madness; of strange forms accompanying him, one to his right side and one to his left and importantly he remained able to have an acceptable amount of sleep. Dr Moore felt deeply privileged to be witness to his and other men's courageous journeys to reclaim their souls and gather together the shattered fragments of their lives.

While several different homeopathic medicines had been prescribed for Frank at different points in his treatment, *Anacardium* had been particularly helpful in his case. It was indicated, among other reasons, because it matched the episodes of delusions and the intense struggle, he had to be at peace with the actions he had carried out, albeit in time of war, with his brother Bernie's body and his perceived culpability in his death for which the enormous amount of guilt had come close to splitting his personality. *Aconite* and *Kali Phos* had also been helpful, but to lesser degrees.

~

Nora, while trying to keep on top of the situation with Frank, had not forgotten her concerns about her sister's involvement in Cumann Na mBan. Mary thought no-one else knew, but all the family including her brothers, were aware. They'd long kept in touch with their Fermanagh relatives and honoured their Da's sentiments about an independent Ireland. That was, for the most part, through donations in support for the local branches of the IRA.

Frank, who was still reluctant to be involved in warlike activities kept his distance though gradually less so since his homeopathic treatment. Patrick and Seamus had their own levels of involvement as Volunteers. Seamus found the meetings in Glasgow challenging, both because he found it difficult to watch his sister be with a man fourteen years her elder and despite being related, he didn't really like the man. He was a boaster, full of his own importance.

Mary, when she wasn't keeping company with cousin Paddy, was also spending most of her time in Govanhill on the Southside of Glasgow. That was a pairing Nora wasn't too keen on either considering the age difference between them. True, she herself, was unusually older than her new husband Victor but by much less, at a difference of only five years. They had each taken a slagging in their own social circles, for Nora including and probably some of the worst from her sisters. Theirs was often sprinkled with humour despite its barbs, whereas some of her old school friends and a couple of those from the Mill had turned their backs on her. She hated that kind of discord, wished they could all be friends, but she couldn't make that happen and maybe they hadn't really been friends after all. When Christmas came around again she hoped to try meeting with Janet, who'd been one of her oldest friends and unfortunately was one of those shunning her.

Victor had obviously taken a dubbing from her brothers but it was their Patrick's responsibility. He'd been the one to introduce them. Victor being in Kirkston with none of his family being present at the wedding, never had to deal with it from that perspective. Nora'd felt sad for him when there had been none of them there the day, they'd got married in St. Michael's, but his conversion to Catholicism may have been a major reason why.

Chapter 22 - Irish Women's Council - Mary

What did she have to complain about really? She was young and alive and often seemed more worried about being able to buy a fancy new dress than the fact she was pregnant. But she was hiding. It was like playing a game or at least that was how she thought about the events that had led to her what...condition? situation?

The attack at the 'Kissing tree' hadn't, at the time, been her only concern. She guessed it was the fellah from the mill but obviously the darkness and sheets of rain, besides the cowardly attack happening from behind her, all led to the impossibility of being able to identify whoever had used her so. Because of her severe loss of confidence after that, she hadn't even been close to being brave enough to confront him and why would he have been so obvious about it? She still nevertheless, hadn't seen or heard from him since.

She'd slowly dragged herself home very early that morning, the heavy pain in her lower belly weighing her down. The trickle of blood that ran between her legs made her worry more but after sneaking in the back door of the cottage and briefly cleaning herself with cold water, she got under the covers of her solitary bed, the others out to work, managing to eventually stop shaking and rest fitfully as her body healed over a number of days before returning to work. Mary deflected questions with the 'curse' excuse of 'ladies' problems'; though for some reason her sisters seemed to be solicitous without prying too much, which, although left feeling alone in it all, she was ridiculously glad about not having to divulge her humiliation. Hadn't she asked for it by agreeing to meet so late at night? What had possessed her to do such a thing; had she been that desperate for a kiss?

Her next older sister Caity was, like Nora, married with her own kids now so had little time for her younger sister, or was it to do with the fights between Caity and Jack she'd heard her sisters discussing in hushed voices? That reminded her then, about that day outside in the garden when she'd seen the purple bruising on Caity's arms when her sleeves slipped down her arms as she helped Mary hang up the washing. "What's happened to you Caity? Your arms look sore. Are you all right? Did you fall or something?"

"Don't be daft Mary. I just banged it. And don't be so nosy anyway. Some things you're just too young to know."

"I'm only asking. No need to be so crotchety Cait." She stifled the burning anger in her gut and the heavy feelings of unfairness at her sister's dismissal. She hated being the youngest sometimes. She did, when younger, get to have a few of them looking out for her or helping her if she needed it and annoyingly even when she didn't, which felt like always being treated as a baby, as if she couldn't do anything for herself or by herself. It had been difficult too to get her mammy's attention sometimes with so many of them and her mammy assuming one of the others would be looking after her and she missed her even more now. She had actually liked being the baby when she remembered her mammy needing to feed her and so spend some time only with her, but having so many big sisters meant her mammy got and needed time off from being her mammy, and as time went on there was more distance between them and she'd had to learn to be of two kinds of person. One side kept trying to please her mammy and all the sisters and the other trying to be a good girl to get approval from her brothers. As a result of this confusion about what whoever she turned to would think of her, she hadn't confided in Jeannie, Caity or anyone else and that seemed to add to the growing anger blossoming unchecked.

She had been grateful to Seamus for his introduction to their cousin, also called Patrick like her brother, but known as Paddy. She had at first thought of him like another big brother but he seemed a bit older and more knowledgeable in his ways. His self-assurance both attracted and sometimes overwhelmed her.

"What's up with ye Mary? I'm only wanting to take care of ye, acushla." he'd say with a disappointed look as she was wriggling out of his arms. It was just those kinds of times when he said he wanted to look after her as if it was for her own good, that she would stiffen and feel wary, struggling to remain calm during his attempts to embrace her. But, over time, he wore down her resistance, her fear of closeness with warm words, tickles that became touches and helpful holds that became the embraces she had at first wanted to flee from. Despite the similar, familiar accent, she had to tell herself he wasn't the clergyman of her childhood; a childhood that wasn't so far behind her.

Around her, the Representation of the People Act was passed and she continued to be impressed and motivated after that, even in 1918, when the vote was only given to women over the age of thirty who met a property qualification. It was definitely an encouraging beginning since now being enshrined in law. The same Act abolished property and other restrictions for men, and extended the vote to virtually all men over the age of twenty-one. Additionally, men in the armed forces could vote from the age of nineteen. That part did not douse her sense of injustice and anger. Especially since as women weren't allowed to fight, they lost out on several counts. However, she'd learned from Paddy about an organisation that did let women fight and treated them as equals.

Cumann na mBan was re-organised in 1917 and school teacher, Sara O'Kane was the Officer in Command. Its ranks were swelled by experienced women like Alice and Kate Byrne who had been members of Cumann na mBan in Dublin.

From 1918 onwards, the Republican Movement in Scotland mushroomed in strength. Paddy asserted that, "Both the Irish Volunteers and Cumann na mBan are experiencing a period of fast growth, especially after guerrilla warfare broke out in Ireland in January 1919 and acquiring explosives, guns and munitions became much more urgent." Her and Paddy had become closer in these last couple of years, the cuddles gravitating to sexual relations. That was a shocker for Mary. Having been initially so wary of just kisses, she, with Paddy's help managed to actually enjoy what they did together and she came to feel that it was one of her favourite things to do and of course, Paddy didn't mind her enthusiastiasm. As much as she'd have liked to talk about it with her sisters, she just couldn't face the expressions of disapproval and judgements about their age difference or her being the baby of the family and too young for anything like that, especially while still unmarried.

Meanwhile, by 1920, Mary had kept informed that there were now fourteen branches of Cumann na mBan in Scotland. From July 1918 to March 1919 Margaret Skinnider was Captain of the Anne Devlin branch of Cumann na mBan in Glasgow. She gave instructions to the members in first aid, drill and the use of small arms and signalling. This branch had between 30 and 40 members. Mary had managed to join and be introduced to Margaret, "You're too young to be getting involved," she'd said on meeting Mary. Though she didn't appreciate her opinion, Mary was careful not to become overly defensive and ruin any chance she might have to participate at all. "I'm a quick learner and not easily frightened ma'am."

Members with whom she took part in armed raids, stored and transferred ammunition, supported prisoners and dependents and participated in drilling and training were Hannah 'Pidge' Duggan, Annie Mooney, Christina Caffrey Keeley and Leanne McDonald. Other women such as Rose and Bridget Hilley, Chrissie Little and Jean Quinn, to name a few, were arrested and ended up being jailed for their activities, but that never stopped any of them. It was thrilling and scary and just the very best thing for her to be doing.

Mary became excited, now that it was all over, when later describing the women's capture after they got back to Glasgow and were having their debriefing. "After Collins made the treaty with the Brits, Pidge Duggan, Lizzie Morrin and me arrived from Glasgow to a safe house in Dublin. We were detained by Free State soldiers this time rather than the Auxies or Black and Tans. Usually, men who used to be fighting on the same side as us now had to be avoided at all costs, but this time we women had had no warning.

"The military were looking for Seamus Robinson, the head of the IRA in Scotland, and they knew that he was Pidge's fiancé. They tried all kinds of tactics to find out information on Joe's movements, including bringing us up to the Dublin mountains and threatening to shoot us. As terrifying as it felt and bejaysus, was I shaking, but none of us gave them any intel. Three times they stopped the lorry, got out their guns, made us kneel on sodden turf, and advised us to say our prayers, telling us they would shoot us on the count of ten. I was close to wetting myself at least once. Eventually they dragged each of us to our feet and threw us one by one back up onto the lorry." Mary said that the women were imprisoned for a couple of hours and then brought to a boat that was sailing for Glasgow that night. Someone asked her,

"What happened when you got back to Glasgow? Did you get arrested again?" Mary felt tense as she remembered when they were disembarking from the boat. They were all waiting, expecting hands on shoulders to take them off to jail but nothing happened. Their audible sighs of relief made them glance nervously at each other, hoping no-one else had heard or made anything of them.

"We were warned not to return to Ireland, under pain of death. But us three women arrived home, slept for a few hours, got up, packed our waistcoats with guns and were back again in Dublin the following evening." Mary was laughing as she related this, relieved to have survived the entire scary escapade.

"Jesus, Mary and Joseph! Were yis mad?" the woman's eyes were wide with both astonishment and admiration.

The Cumann na mBan went on to play a key role in the 'Smashing of the Van' incident, when Republicans attempted to free Brigadier Frank Carty from a police van on its way to Duke Street Prison in Glasgow, on May 4, 1921. In an atmosphere of urgency, given that Carty was under sentence of death, together with the need for on-the-spot decisions, they realised later this might have added to the confusion. They all knew, Carty's record had endeared him to his fellow soldiers of the IRA, so those on the spot decided the best thing to do was make an effort to ensure his release. When the inevitable objections arose, Commandant D.P. Welsh was probably right when he responded urgently, "Calling off the Glasgow plan will shatter the whole Republican movement here." They were all feeling shaky at the prospect of the entire plan and despite Mary's growing belly she was too fired up to stop now. And Paddy seemed not too enthusiastic about the prospect of an actual baby as opposed to the making of one. Marriage was never mentioned as they each got on with their military exploits with the Irish Republican Army.

Frank Carty stayed in the home of Anne Graham following his arrival in Glasgow on 29th of April but was arrested at the home of Frank O'Hagan, in the Gorbals. Carty had intended to leave for Dublin the following

Monday, 2nd of May. Following Carty's arrest, plans were immediately put in place to rescue him.

On the night before the rescue attempt Lieutenant Sean O'Daire of 'A' Company called in at Pidge Duggan's for several revolvers from her, which he needed for the men who would take part in the ambush. Alice Byrne conveyed two revolvers from and to dumps, some of which were used in the armed attack on the van and carefully concealed afterwards. Mary, because of her now visible condition, only carried dispatches in connection with the rescue attempt. That night she was given instructions about her part along with the other members involved. Commandant D P Welsh instructed another Cumann na mBan member Annie Murray, how she would cycle ahead of Carty's van,

"You'll be tipped off by an old woman who's a cleaner in the Central Police Station." Welsh said he would give her a description of Carty. "She's been instructed to throw out her bucket and mop, just as Carty's van is about to leave. That's the signal for you Annie, to start peddling up the hill and alert the Volunteers who will be waiting in readiness to ambush the van and attempt to free our comrade."

Carty was handcuffed in a small cell in the front of the van guarded by six police officers in the rear of the vehicle. They attacked the van before it reached Cathedral Square. Edward Walsh signalled by raising his cap when he saw the prison van coming up High Street. While it was travelling up the hill it was forced to change gear and the attacking party stepped into the path of the vehicle forcing it to stop. Eamonn Mooney, who was in command of a section of the attacking party, later reported that, "The van was very different from any I'd ever seen. There were no handles on the back of the door. I couldn't get a hold of anything. The front portion was steel plated with a glass windscreen".

One of the attackers jumped on board the van in an effort to blow off the lock by emptying his revolver into it, but the lock held fast. Crowbars and pickaxes were now brought out in a last desperate effort to smash the van. Having failed to break open the lock, they were forced to retreat after just a few minutes. While the police were quickly approaching, Seán Mooney got on the running board of the vehicle and told the advancing Inspector to put his hands up. Then someone fired from behind Mooney and hit the Inspector who then fell on top of him. Frederick Quinn was to cover the man attempting to open the back of the van when he saw a police Sergeant step out from the front of the van brandishing his revolver, so Quinn fired. Michael O'Carroll who was posted at Rottenrow armed with a revolver, also fired three shots at Detective Stirton. In the confusion, Inspector Robert Johnston had been shot dead and Detective Sergeant George Stirton wounded.

This turned out to be Mary's last involvement with the Women's Council activities. She'd seen less and less of Paddy since he'd been incarcerated and she'd become increasingly impassioned with the cause of those from the old country, which despite her birth as a Scot, had slowly moved her thoughts and sentiments backwards in time and often made her wonder what her father, Francis would think of what she was doing. He was a believer in equality and fairness, according to what she'd been told, so wouldn't he have approved? She liked to think of him at her most fearful bone-rattling moments, smiling down encouragingly at her even after a failure like this, for at least she'd tried.

In the aftermath of the rescue bid, the IRA ambush was just one step further down that line, and the police were desperate to stamp their authority and nab the culprits. In doing so, they arrested as many people as they could, until the mob sussed out what they were up to.

The arrest of a priest is thought to have triggered the violence. When the cops came out of a house in the Gallowgate they were met by a screaming mob, looking for blood. Later that day, an even larger crowd chased a team of policemen who'd tried to arrest five well known young men.

By evening, an estimated 2000 rioters milled around the Gallowgate, making it a no-go area for the police. The mob chanted, threw stones, smashed up shops and attacked trams. That night, they lit bonfires and continued the rampage, looting and robbing. They assaulted everyone in a uniform, and anyone they suspected to be on the side of the police.

Glasgow seemed to have turned in to a lawless city. Detective Superintendent Johnstone had died and DS Stirton was in a critical state. The police were armed and moved through the streets in convoy, determined to catch the suspects. The Army moved to a central location in the city and waited for orders to act.

In the houses the cops hit, they didn't just find suspects. They found more than fifty handguns, dozens of rifles, boxes of ammo, gelignite and blades. The weapon finds in the Calton in the east end of Glasgow were the biggest ever in Scotland. Glasgow had become like a sectarian tinderbox.

It turned out that the IRA had incorrectly believed that one of the guards on board the van would have had a key. However, the vehicle was locked at the Central Police Station and could not be opened until it reached Duke Street and this is what had doomed the attempt to failure.

Frank Carty suffered a beating by the police in retaliation for the tragic and unintentional death of Inspector Johnston. Following the unsuccessful operation there were sweeping arrests with up to a hundred individuals being rounded up, including Father Patrick MacRory, a popular young curate at St Mary's, Abercromby Street, Calton. Thirteen were sent for trial in the High Court of Justice in Edinburgh. The press remarked '*This was the first trial in which a capital charge was involved, at which there were ladies in the jury.*' The trial ended in August with the acquittal of all the accused. The fact that the friends and families of the arrested men were willing to perjure themselves in a Scottish court showed their immense loyalty to Ireland and her government in her hour of need.

Mary was fierce proud as if it had been her own Da who'd said the words when she heard Michael O'Carroll give his opinion of the Glasgow Irish: "The people of Glasgow and the west of Scotland —the first, second and third generations of the Irish —I will always remember them, their loyalty, their sincerity and the ideals which were in their minds. They were wonderful."

Frank Carty, meanwhile, was returned to Ireland, court-martialled and sentenced to ten years' penal servitude. In June 1921 he was elected a member of Dáil Éireann for the Sligo and East Mayo constituency. As a result, he was released from Mountjoy Prison, Dublin on 8th of August 1921 to attend a meeting of the Dáil.

Negotiations followed with British and Irish representatives over the future of the

country, which resulted in only a Treaty allowing for a self-governing dominion of two countries within the British Empire. The new Irish Free State would be permitted its own, but limited, army. Also autonomy in internal affairs and, in theory, control over its revenues. It would not be a republic yet. Members of the Free State parliament would have to take oaths to the British monarch. The monarch would appoint a governor-general to reside in Dublin and among other tangible restrictions British forces would keep strategic harbours and no Irish navy would be permitted, for 'security reasons.'

The debate over the Treaty rumbled on even after it was signed in December 1921. The leadership of Sinn Féin and the army was divided, bitter arguments ensued and the Republican Movement was split. Cumann na mBan was one of the first Republican organisations to reject the Treaty. On February 5th, 1922 in an emergency convention, it reaffirmed allegiance to the Republic and called on the women of Ireland to support at the polls only "candidates who stood true to the existing Republic." The resolution was carried by 419 votes to 63 and the dissenters left to form a pro Free State group called Cumann na Saoirse.

Paddy, having been promoted after his last mission to Commander of the 3rd Battalion, 2nd Northern Division of the IRA, also found himself imprisoned again. He had made a decision to return to what was now Northern Ireland since the treaty, but was as determined about still fighting for the creation of a Republic rather than continue with having to kowtow to the British Monarchy and he wanted to see his remaining family there. Mary wondered if his leaving then had anything to do with her present condition and the imminent, to his mind at that time in the middle of September in 1921, 'complication' due to appear in a couple of months? Mary travelled alone to have her baby at the end of 1921 and either way by the end of May 1922, Paddy had been arrested. This time he was imprisoned in Belfast itself and of all places, on a ship.

Under the 1922 Special Powers Act the British were detaining 263 men on the ship *Argenta*, which was moored in Belfast Lough. This was supplemented with internment at other land-based sites, such as Larne workhouse, Belfast Prison and Derry Gaol. Together, both the ship and the workhouse alone held 542 men without trial.[xxxii]

Paddy described conditions on the prison ship *Argenta* as "unbelievable" in his letters but could say little else and she would receive only cut out gaps in place of any banned comments. After he went on a Hunger Strike involving upwards of 150 men in the winter of 1923 over their living conditions, he was released due to subsequent illness in December 1924. He later told her in a letter that the prisoners had been forced to use broken toilets, which overflowed frequently into their communal area. They were cloistered below decks in cages which held 50 internees to each cage. Being deprived of tables, the already weakened men had to eat off the floor, frequently succumbing to disease and illness as a result.

Meanwhile, Mary had distanced herself from the ongoing events and was by now halfway across the world but Paddy came back to Glasgow hoping to meet his by now, four-year-old child. Mary had gone incommunicado and he hadn't known if it was a son or a daughter. He'd decided to make his way to Kirkston to find out.

In 1923, Cumann na mBan was banned and 645 women were incarcerated. Prior to the close of the Civil War in March 1923, British authorities arrested 110 Republican activists in Scotland and England in an attempt to shut down their activities. They were deported to Ireland and interned in Mountjoy Gaol in Dublin.[xxxiii]

Mary had been glad to hear that her former commander was able to carry out her sentence without having to die of starvation, after ending her hunger strike. Mary had had little contact with anyone from the organisation since leaving with their blessing and condolences for her enforced journey to and confinement in, London in December 1921. She wasn't the first or the last to be in that situation.

Chapter 23 - A Lost Cause? – Paddy

No-one answered the door on his first knock, so he knocked again with the same lack of response. He went to look in the window at the front of the cottage and stepped quickly back on glimpsing the scene in the living room between a small gap in the curtains, tripping over a stone in the grass behind him. Then he heard the front door open and hurried footsteps crunch on the gravel footpath before becoming silent on grass as the man stomped towards him. "Hey you! What do you think you're doing, peering in people's windows like that?

"I knocked the door but no-one answered, so I came round to see if anyone was at home. I'm sorry for ehm...disturbing you." The man looked vaguely familiar, but he wasn't one of the brothers that he knew. As far as Paddy could gather in the brief glimpse he'd had, he wondered at the scene of a half-dressed woman lying on a couch with this man's hands all over her.

"Who are you? What do you want?" The man glared at him while waiting for an explanation.

"I'm looking for Mary. I'm Paddy. You might not remember me; it's been a few years." Paddy offered his hand to the frowning wiry man and wondered out loud, "Sure aren't you Nora's man? It took me a while to place you. I'm the Irish cousin from Belfast."

"Yes, I'm Victor and same here, you did seem familiar but I don't think we can help all the same. Mary lives in America now as far as I know. Ah, here's Nora," he said while tentatively shaking Paddy's outstretched hand. Just at that moment a slightly dishevelled Nora came to the door while shushing young ones at her back, "What is it? Paddy? Is that you?" Nora said while squinting at him in surprise, her eyeballs magnified behind thick-lensed glasses, a new feature he didn't remember.

"Aye, what are ye about Nora? I'll be looking for Mary. Your man here says she's in America. Is that so?"

"Come away in, Paddy. Did ye not know? I thought she'd have written to tell you."

They followed Nora inside and the young children scattered into a bedroom, leaving the adults in awkward silence until Victor offered to make them a brew.

"Sit yourself down till the tea comes, Paddy. Where have you come from? Last I heard you were in jail over there and ill too, isn't that right?"

"Aye, that's the truth and I wasn't released until 1924. Feels like I've missed a lot. What happened with the baby?" Nora's face reddened as she avoided looking him in the eye. While watching his shoes she blustered out excuses about family reputation and the church and Mary being too young to manage a baby with no husband and how they'd done what they thought was best.

"She might not have had a husband at the time, but the baby had a daddy and I can't say how we could have got wed with me in the jail across the water, can you?

"Well, that's just it, Paddy. She was left here pregnant with no idea that there were any plans for marriage that she told us. Did she even know you were interested in wedding her?"

"Well, not in so many words and I was up to my ears in the fighting when not in a cell, so I can't say we had time or opportunity to plan a wedding." Nora's head shot up as she bristled.

"But the baby was coming. You knew she was pregnant. Couldn't you have at least got engaged?" Up till then Paddy had waited to hear the explanation but now he could hear that the judgement on him and worse, on Mary had been made long before they'd thought much about wedding plans. Now his anger flared.

"So where is my child? Did it survive the birth? Is it in America with Mary?" Nora's eyes slipped away once more and his shoes got more attention as she stuttered out the truth.

"We...we...did what the priest advised. He was as worried as we were about how Mary had sinned getting pregnant outside of marriage and how she just couldn't keep a child in those circumstances so..."

"What?! So, the local priest suggested what?" He knew what was coming and the full horror was in his eyes as he waited to hear it from Nora's mouth.

"Well, he thought it best to...

"Best to?" Paddy demanded; eyes boring into the top of her still lowered head.

"Yes! Best to have the child adopted by a married couple. Give her a proper home with parents married under the eyes of God," she rapidly spat out before her courage failed her, then shuffled backwards as if expecting more than his angry words being propelled towards her.

"So, let me understand. My daughter was taken from her mother and given to another couple without me seeing her even once?!"

"Mary didn't get to see her after the birth either!"

"And that makes it alright? That just makes it worse! I thought over here you could use the lighter grip of the church to make your own decisions rather than those based on the cruel commandments of the church. No wonder Mary didn't tell me. She must have been distraught. You let them take her wee lassie away from her? And where did all this take place, might I ask, so? Were you at least with her at the birth?" Nora's face reddened deeper as she mumbled.

"No, she went to London to have the baby."

"On her own?! Jesus wept! So where is the child?" Victor had come through with the tea while this was ongoing and intervened seeing his own wife's distress.

"Hold on there, mister. Nora did her best for Mary. The fault is in you getting her pregnant and disappearing, not Nora finding a good home for the baby!" He ignored the jibe, stuck in the shock of the disappeared child.

"My baby...my daughter. Mary's daughter. Did she have a name?"

"Yes, Mary called her Therese." That had been the only easy question so far. "But she won't be called that now, her new parents will have changed it." Paddy slumped into the nearest chair and loaded some sugar into the hot cup of tea in his trembling hand, then placed it very carefully back on the table beside him lest he fire it across the room and saying, "Feck this, I need something stronger," before abruptly striding out the front door, slamming it behind him.

He went back after a couple of whiskeys in the nearest pub, a talking to from himself and lots of deep breaths. He received a nervous version of the sordid tale from a very contrite, yet indignant Nora, with the result being he was going to have to travel to London and make enquiries at that workhouse. He'd been even more disbelieving of that outcome - a workhouse?! What century was this? How could her older sister have treated Mary that way? Those damn priests! He sometimes thought they more did the work of the devil rather than that of Christ, based on the misery their 'good works' often inevitably caused. If he hadn't been so caught up in the civil war after the initial fighting, he may have been able to prevent this from happening, but Mary being her stubborn independent self, had chosen not to tell him of her family's plans and manipulations concerning her pregnancy. Knowing how it most often was in Ireland with unwed mothers, he shouldn't be surprised. He had thought, if he'd thought at all, that in Scotland it might be easier but he'd been dead wrong there. Nora was a strong practicing Catholic from generations of Irish. It took more than a change of location to create a shift.

"It is not how many times you fall down, but how often you get up again."
Vince Lombardi

FINALE
1921-1935

Chapter 24 - The Lost Child - Mary

Mary was extremely disorientated when she arrived after the long journey and became further confused when she saw the signs for the hospital. Why had she been booked in here? By 1920 it had been adapted for use as a hospital for women suffering from Venereal Disease. Had Nora and her brother made a mistake? Was this just another attempt to make her feel even more humiliated?

She had made her way alone on an extended train ride to London where it was apparently arranged by Nora, she could only assume, that she would bear her child at the previously named Strand Union Workhouse. The larger south block, Sheffield House, contained the administrative offices and staff accommodation. The treatment rooms and wards were in the north block, together with the kitchen and the patients' dining room.

Although the hospital had not been intended for prostitutes or for people convicted in police courts for soliciting or other offences, but for "girls who had followed soldiers from the country or who been infected as a result of an occasional lapse into immorality,"[xxxiv] nevertheless, a large number of patients came under those former categories. Many of them were described as being a "very depraved class" and who refused to stay more than two or three weeks. They had often been heard using the most offensive language and apparently having the coarsest manners. Patients of the class originally expected were frequently directed elsewhere but for some reason, not Mary.

What class exactly, did she fall under then? Perhaps she was considered as one of those "girls who'd followed soldiers from the country."[xxxv]

Inside the two-storey building at the north end of the Infirmary allocated to maternity cases, it contained two labour wards and two general wards of five beds each and which looked as if they were supervised by a trained, registered midwife. The facilities appeared quite clean and orderly as she was led nervously to a bed and asked to disrobe and get into her nightdress so they could settle her before her labour began. Then the nurse came with a black trumpet-like item, saying, "We need to have a listen to hear the baby's heartbeat," and the cold touch on her by now, hugely swollen belly, of whatever the thing was made from as the nurse put the other end to her ear, made her gasp and startle a little.

While lying there a fear crept up on her as she thought of all the angry words and disapproval from her family over the last nine months, the absence of and silence from Paddy and the long, lonely journey on the train all the way there. Despite feeling this way, she was reluctant to be among strangers at such a time. Her aversion to a hospitalised birth was more than just a reaction to alien surroundings and the loss of family contact, it was also in defiance against the stringent, almost regimental attitude to her pregnancy that was adopted by an overwhelming majority of people and organisations and no doubt by hospitals, and as she was to discover, the overbearing and condescending manner of the doctors. It reminded her of the same attitude she had experienced long ago with the priest. The additional stigma of pauperism was apparent because it was a Poor Law

Institution, but nonetheless, she definitely felt a general fear of entering any institution whatever its affiliation, having always, like most others, been used to being treated at home. Her only small source of reassurance was the remedies Dr Moore had equipped her with, having been prepared for her before she left home.

As she looked around, she thought of her mother who'd had no choice but to bear her children at home but who would likely be the first to say, "I'd like to be with ye hen, but I cannae leave hame, wae all these bairns about and not a soul to keep order." She did wish her mother, whom she would dearly love to be able to talk to right now, at least had had the opportunity to be better cared for, though she was sure Granny O'Connell (when she was still here) and her mammy's sisters would have argued about how hard they'd always tried to help and that wasn't being around family at home the very best way to bring a new baby into the world? Because Mary was so far from home and, despite the fierce disapproval she'd experienced with Nora and Caity, she was really missing them now. Not to mention her guilt and doubts about the part Victor may have played in things turning out as they had.

Her contractions had started a couple of days into her confinement. At first they were weak and had much time between them. The worst pain at that point was the ache in her lower back with a need to get out of bed to pace the floor. The nurses were not so keen on all this movement and repeatedly shooed her back into bed, but it was no good; she was too restless with the pain and up she would get again, jamming her feet into her tatty slippers and pacing once more. The next day the contractions had become stronger and she held, what seemed like, her huge belly, feeling the child twist and turn, its heels and elbows digging into her insides, intensifying the pain of the cramps, which frightened her into shivering.

By the third day of this, while walking, the contractions that afternoon heralded the flood of water that cascaded down her legs and she had to take care not to slip in the puddle at her feet. Her waters breaking got the midwife into an initial flurry of anxious fluttering around her before

becoming all efficient and ordering her back into bed. But for all their being at battle-ready stations, the baby still wasn't born until about two o'clock the next morning. Once in the labour suite and laid flat with her legs wing-like in the air, the contractions intensified further and now as they came quicker, she breathlessly asked the nurse, "Can I have some water?" The midwife only dampened her lips but would not give her the big long drink she craved. As she tried to breathe into the waves of pain, her groaning and screams filled the small room.

"Push the pain away!" demanded the midwife. Eventually, after some more frustrated pushing and hollering over a number of hours, the midwife commented in a concerned tone, "This baby should have been born by now." Mary continued to push, the sweat dripping from her as the contractions became weaker again. Then the nurse, looking worried said, "I don't know why it's not coming forth."

Then Mary asked her, "What does it say in my notes?" She remembered then the pouch from Dr Moore and added, "I have some medicines for the birth from my own doctor to take. I think she said if I had a backache and was becoming irritable to use the *Kali Carb* one." The nurse responded with a relieved sigh,

"Oh, thank you for telling me, now I know what to do," and of course after taking the remedy, as Mary started pushing again with the next big contraction, the blockage dissolved, helping the baby to move into her birth canal and was born much more smoothly soon after. She could honestly say she had definitely brought her baby into the world through a natural and painful birth. "What a big baby she is, for a girl!" exclaimed the nurse on catching the child as she slid out, removing her from Mary's sight directly as soon as she was in her hands and the cord was clamped and cut before the baby was cleaned and bundled up in a blanket all the while crying and crying. Mary had held out her arms to take the bundle but the nurse quickly left the labour suite as Mary gasped in shock at the sudden and heartless removal of her daughter. The nurse then returned empty-handed making apologies; placating her with, "It's for the best. Really, it is Mary," as she dissolved into tears of disbelief, panting in panic at the surprise thump of grief in her chest; caving, crumbling, breaking her down. Because of all the pushing and not getting anywhere, the nurse noticed the stream of blood streaming from beneath Mary, urgently declaring, "You're haemorrhaging." Feeling weaker and angry now Mary tried to stifle her tears, demanding,

"Well, what are you going to do about it? Can't you give me some of the *Arnica* from the pouch that Dr Moore said was for bleeding?"

"It's now four o'clock in the morning. I'll give you a couple of the tablets." the nurse said, adding, "If you stay lying down in the bed with your legs tightly crossed and don't move, I'll get the doctor to come and see you as soon as he can." Mary was frightened to death in case the haemorrhage continued flowing, but fortunately the remedy the nurse had tipped under her tongue helped slow and eventually stop the bleeding before she fell into an exhausted slumber. From what she could remember the doctor didn't come around until six or seven o'clock in the morning, waking her from a short restless sleep caused by general body and heart-ache of constant tears from missing the baby; the baby in whose absence, she'd decided to name, Therese. When the doctor eventually examined her, all he said was, "Oh, they said you were haemorrhaging, but it looks like it's stopped for some darn reason." He took his annoyed and puzzled expression out of the room with an irritated flounce with not another word to Mary who had tremulously tried to stifle her tears and sit up straight, but he'd gone before she managed it and that set her off once more.

At the age of nineteen and barely attended by a doctor, she'd given birth for the first time and left the labour room tired, weak and in constant pain, only to be told it was just nerves and that she would soon recuperate. Mary was ashamed of what she thought was her lack of character, and tried to do everything in her power to overcome the pain and weakness. Before her discharge a month later, she was told by the matron, in a very arch tone that, "You should think yourself lucky not to have become infected like many other women who've got themselves into trouble do, and who never make it out of here alive." The nurse watched Mary leave empty-handed bar her small bag with her nightclothes, feeling slightly remorseful for her harshness as she pictured the young woman's pale, wan face that reminded her so much of their charges in the previously named St Philip's Building when it was used only a couple of years before during the war as an observation hospital for war refugees.

Mary was to struggle for several months as other mothers must have done; with washing, scrubbing, cooking and nursing their child, except she didn't even have the nursing of a baby to do. Not the tiring parts of having to get up during the night to feed her or feeling the joyful bonding and getting to know her own flesh and blood. She mostly spent the time for several months, nursing her own grief as well as her slowly recovering health, often unable to rise from her bed at the thought of the empty days, the empty crib and the emptiness in her heart that was like a sharp blade when she leant into it. With the trials and disappointments of the birth and now ill health, any plans she'd had to continue being part of Cumann Na mBan dissolved into a dream-like memory.

Her experience at the hospital never left her, despite its mild comparison to other women she'd since spoken to and read about. And starting from the First World War period, reports from government officials, such as those presented by Doctor Arthur Newsholme and Doctor Janet Campbell and others, were questioning infection and excessive obstetric intervention that were prominent features of many hospitals and a major factor in high maternal mortality rates. [xxxvi]

By the mid-1920s, the lay as well as the medical press were also drawn into the debates about maternal mortality, giving it a prominence never before accorded to any medical question; namely, death in childbed.

A surprising outcome was that voluntary maternity hospitals became recognised as being able to drastically reduce sepsis rates and greatly improve service only if they ran on the same lines as Workhouses, which, after inspection, had come out as having significantly fewer maternal deaths. This meant in practice the withdrawal of clinical instruction, minimum communication with other hospital departments, regular inspection, ample cubic space for each patient and a much smaller caseload. This was based on the impressive findings of the consequently admirable work done in maternity wards of the large city infirmaries. In nearly all cases, the wards became models of comfort and cleanliness, the nurses well trained, the instruments and appliances beyond criticism, and where medical assistance was available whenever required.

The interwar years were a time of great change in Scotland, economically, socially and culturally. While the 1920s and 1930s were traditionally portrayed as a time when women experienced a 'backlash' and a 'return to domesticity' following the First World War, in fact women were entering public life in greater numbers than before. Many women's organisations encouraged 'active citizenship' among their members after some women over thirty gained the vote in 1918. The demands of women's organisations in interwar Scotland were varied and not all were feminist, but this didn't mean they weren't political. There was a wide range of them active in Scotland then and a thriving associational culture. Not all groups agreed on or supported the same issues and often disagreed. But sometimes they were able to put aside their differences s in order to work together for a common goal.

Mary discovered much of this after her renewed interest in the plight of women, which gave her a new interest, a cause to commit herself to, that helped fill the gap inside. More importantly then and after, it broadened her social life.

At the end of the year just before Hogmanay in 1921, she gave her new house in Govanhill an, 'out with the old and in with the new' clean from top to bottom, making sure it was free from dust: cleaning the fire, clearing the flue, washing the windows and polishing the grate. This was the norm in every Scottish house at this time of year, every year. She hurried out to get the messages before it was too late since it was early closing that day. When she got home, she looked around and gave a big satisfied smile. The house was cleaned like a brand-new pin and she had the annual treat for this time of cordial and ginger wine, ready for the 'Bells' and to welcome in her first footer to bring in the New Year with their piece of coal and bit of black bun.

Chapter 25 - New Beginnings - Mary

She hoped her lost daughter had survived and flourished with her own new beginning in life. That letter about, yes, just a simple donation, was the last external reminder she'd had and now she needed a change of location to at least try to subdue her everyday yearning.

She'd had thoughts of sailing off and decamping to America several times over the years, for her Aunts Rose and Rebecca had made their homes in Boston quite some decades before and particularly aunt Rebecca, who while on her most recent visit back to Britain had tempted her not long before Therese was born, but she'd been in no mind - no state to consider the offer with a clear head. Though it could have been an escape from her surroundings, of the reminders of her time with Paddy as the, at least, perhaps substitute father. But it just seemed, at the time, to be more exile, further widening of the too recent yawning gap of distance and loss.

Aunt Rebecca was on an extended vacation to visit with some of her grown-up children and remaining family in Ireland the last two years and occasionally, as when last coming across to Glasgow before that fateful journey to London, tried to sway Mary into joining her when she would be making her way back to Boston later in 1922.

Looking out on another grey day and threatening rain, she reflected on Aunt Rebecca's last visit spent describing all the advantages: like warm weather, support from her cousins, work in the garment factories there. Now at the thought excitement fizzed happily throughout her body. Why not now? The sound of her heart thumping in her ears reminded her of the fear of not being easily found just in case someone was looking for her. Mary shook herself and in defiance of her anxious forebodings decided it was time, it was time before the chance passed her by. Before the sense of beginning again slipped away. She picked up a pen to write to her aunt Rebecca whom she knew was currently making plans to set sail back to Boston on the other side of the ocean.

~

Rebecca had written to arrange meeting her at the Broomielaw. This was only their second meeting and Mary smoothed her recently curled hair again, feeling her stomach tumbling as she stood with her over-packed suitcase on the quayside among all the other travelers dressed in their finest, which didn't disguise their frowns of concern at the sight of the roiling waves; thick, heavy and breaking loudly against the sides of the ship '*Londonderry*', which was waiting for all the cackling, sniffling and last-minute huggers to embark for the journey. Rebecca's lateness added to Mary's anxiety as she strained to see between and over the heads of the milling crowds, trying to catch a glimpse of her, so far, elusive aunt. Their first meeting had been just before that train journey in late September 1921. Mary had been surprised by her aunt's visit, especially since there had been no warning of her arrival in Glasgow. Her height had been the first surprise and the booming voice another. That she was unusually tall for folk in their family made her feel dwarfed again as, at that moment, the sleeve of her mackintosh was unexpectedly grabbed. Mary, who glanced up sharply ready to castigate the offending person for their rudeness, then exclaimed, "Aunt Rebecca! There you are. I was becoming anxious. The ship is almost ready to sail."

Aunt Rebecca boomed and those around them turned on hearing her loud response. "We're grand, colleen. There's plenty of time, so. Tis not my first time on this journey and ye won't be quite so keen once we set sail, I can tell ye, niece." She then pulled Mary in the direction of the gangplank to embark on their adventure. Mary had to quickly grasp her case feeling a sudden sense of finality about leaving Scotland after all the worrying and planning these last few months. Now it was happening and the gangplank was being pulled up and the people waving on the quay were becoming smaller and smaller and her sight seemed to collapse to a point of everything in her vision disappearing as she swayed with the movement of the boat riding the waves as they headed away down the Clyde River to the sea mouth and out to the expanse of swelling greenish ocean that would carry her to the new world. Her Aunt Rebecca chuckled as the colour of Mary's face turned puce and greenish like the frothing water below them. The sea swells definitely did curb her enthusiasm. Mary vomited for several days until she became acclimatised to the rolls and dips of the onward voyage, eventually finding her sea legs.

~

The last on the list of her prospective new homes and by far the cheapest was the Franklin Square House. Mary wasn't that good with numbers, but how could she ever forget paying only $5 a week, two meals a day included? Two large meals that was; large enough to make three. She came to live at the Franklin Square House in September 1922. She was almost twenty-three now and not yet collecting things. As a result, she'd never kept the brochure, circa 1920, claiming the Franklin Square House was located "close to the heart of Boston." It showed a smiling driver on the Copley Square bus welcoming aboard thoroughly respectable young ladies from the thoroughly respectable Franklin Square House. Her aunt Rebecca had suggested it with all good intentions. She herself was fifty-five years old now and having been in America these last fifteen years had opened her mind to much more than her very restrictive Catholic upbringing and previous life in Co. Fermanagh, until it came to Negros. Many Irish immigrants believed that abolitionists of the past had cared more about slaves and free blacks than about the problems facing the new Irish immigrants. Historically, the intersection of these issues had made Boston's black and Irish communities suspicious and hostile towards each other from the beginning. That for centuries the church had accepted slavery's existence as part of the natural order didn't help matters. The church accepted a form of slavery which recognized the right to own the work and production of another, but not recognising ownership of the person's soul.

The church separated the question of a slave's intrinsic moral worth and dignity from the institution of slavery and the slave-trade. It had instructed its members to care for the spiritual well-being of their slaves while preaching that slavery was not contrary to the rule of God. Many early Catholic historians excused this double standard and "hailed the church's neutrality" on slavery. The hierarchy had had a choice to make between condemning slavery and remaining silent. They chose silence over confrontation.[xxxvii]

Aunt Rebecca, even if she never made the same allowances for other human beings because of the colour of their skin, did seem to recognise Mary's desire for freedom and independence, encouraging the distance of her living accommodation but acknowledging the need for safety in new surroundings especially since there was a high population of African-Americans in the area. Of course, that meant she wasn't at all impressed by Mary's eventual relationship with Pete.

How was Mary to know that the Franklin Square House was not only not close to the heart of Boston, but in an area considered by the white lower and middle-classes as completely off limits, to be avoided at all costs? No doubt because of the high number of Negros and immigrants who lived in the area. For her, it *was* right in the heart of Boston. How else could she explain spending the next fifteen years within it? Her cousins were horrified; why couldn't she live in the terraced brownstone with them? Her aunt joked that Franklin Square itself looked like the final act from a horror show but did nothing to dissuade Mary, knowing her nieces' previous attempts at gaining accommodation had been much more horrific and much less safe. It did have a desolation about it: yesterday's newspapers blowing across the park, drunks sleeping on benches, and a yellow brick housing block looming up on the other side. Mary liked it immediately.

Her first room at the Franklin Square House didn't face the park. Those rooms cost extra. Her room faced a stairwell, dubbed "The Pit," down which residents liked to fling objects like intimate underthings. In her second and last decade, she nurtured herself by renting a tiny room at the front. Both rooms were in the "new building." She could never have afforded the big rooms in the "old building."

You had to be at least eighteen to get into the Franklin Square House. Although the upper age limit was forty, they didn't throw you out on your fortieth birthday, and many elderly women lived there. Early each morning, maids went down the halls, unlocking doors and calling out, "Just checking." She could never sleep in on mornings when she didn't have to start work early because they woke her up, rattling their keys, poking their heads in every room. "Just checking, just checking." "Checking what?" she wanted to scream from her bed. The checking paid off, though, because every once in a while, a body was found. The maids also checked for forbidden electrical devices, such as coils for boiling water for tea. Mary kept hers in a drawer under her underwear.

Each room had a phone with a bell on top. When an outside call came in, the front desk rang them in their room and they went out into the hall to talk. During her first years at Franklin, there was a hall phone right outside her door, and she sometimes had to step over scantily-clad female students in relaxed postures holding intimate conversations with their boyfriends, especially as the 11:00 p.m. curfew approached.

Porters made their rounds every night. They seemed like such ancient, sexless dummies, looking neither to the right nor the left as they marched past the rooms. They occasionally requested someone turn her radio down, but their eyes never strayed from their face no matter what they were or weren't wearing. In contrast, they would look everywhere but at Pete's face as they remonstrated with him every time he walked her to the Franklin House entrance and he never did get any further than that.

Some of the rules were easy to break. Students had to be in earlier than "business girls" and the over-40 crowd. When "business girls" as opposed the more suspect 'working girls' like Mary came in after a late shift or an evening out, she signed 'B' for Business after her name in the ledger. Mary could officially stay out all night if she applied for permission to stay with a relative. Quite a few boyfriends were listed as uncles for this purpose and Petey Palmer was eventually designated as an 'uncle' on more than one occasion.

She walked to Boston Maid and back every day, taking different routes through the South End after her early shifts gave her a finish during daylight. That in itself was an education. Seeing the Victorian-style terraced houses like her Aunt Rebecca's and the many parks in and around the area. The South End was the largest intact Victorian row house district in the country, made up of over 300 acres. Eleven residential parks were contained within the South

End and took her some years to visit and enjoy them all. Her best find was the Massachusetts Homeopathic Hospital, housed in the Talbot Building, at 715 Albany Street two blocks from the Boston Maid factory on Harrison Avenue.[xxxviii]

The South End was real in a way she'd never experienced before, having grown up mostly in rural Kirkston where, now she thought about it, had never seen a black person—not even in Glasgow. She liked it when the Negro people talked to her, finding what they said witty, unpredictable, offbeat, profound or poetic; at least some of the time, especially compared to the silliness of some of the Franklin House female residents. They just had that sense of rhythm that was expressed in their talk, dance, food and always being together with each other. She felt like the outsider she would always be with her pale white skin, even after her and Pete had been dating for years.

There was so much more diversity in Boston, racial tensions notwithstanding, between immigrants like her starting out in a new country and those residents disenfranchised despite being born here. Also, when she arrived, women were often deep in debate in the dining hall, caught up in the push for the vote for women from the election the previous year and some of those discussions suited her own mind well after her first episode of extreme independence with Cumann na mBan and subsequent introduction to women's suffrage. Yet there were still many, even young women, who didn't quite get the point of it all. Usually those determined to marry a, preferably rich, man who would look after them.

Up the top of Massachusetts Avenue was where prostitutes (as informed by her fellow residents and house neighbours) in outlandish outfits paraded round corners even in the early morning. A group of hangers-on also loitered about there every day when she passed. Sometimes they said "good morning," and she said "good morning" back. One day, one of them stepped into her path and asked if he could ask her a question:

"Do you walk that fast because you're in a hurry or is it from nervous tension?" Pretty soon Pete Palmer was walking alongside her giving her daily insights into her life, predicting her future, and warning her against involvement with a "bad-foot boy." Despite the slurs and whispers after she was seen talking to him, she began to look for Pete every morning—he was a crazy guy in a kind of zoot suit who made her laugh, which was a welcome antidote to the sometimes-lonely stretches of unfilled time when not working in the factory and feeling holed-up alone in her small room or having an occasional noisy and chaotic Sunday dinner at her aunt's house.

On Friday and Saturday nights, she used to come home on the last Forest Hills elevated train or the last Harvard-Dudley bus, get off at Northampton Station, and walk the five blocks to the Franklin Square House. That stretch of Washington Street flaunted two pool rooms, two stores, several vacant buildings and a cemetery. She would walk past the corner guys, speaking politely when spoken to. Many times, Petey accompanied her the rest of the way—insurance that nothing worse would happen. She thought that, if she ever met someone, she'd title it like a book: "It Happened on East Newton Street!" It was a while before she realised that that someone turned out to be Pete Palmer. Not an easy decision re his race in such a segregated city such as Boston was, but his light skin sometimes made him able to pass, until he spoke. Then there was only one culture he'd fit with that cool chat and rhythmical slang. But all that stramash was still to come.

Franklin Square House was a big place with more than 700 guest rooms and a lot of interesting nooks and crannies. Jane Champing, ran the house's coffee shop called the Grey Gander Gift Shop and Tea Room, Mabel S. Worcester, was the "hostess" or head manager of the house and was a kindly yet firm woman. There was also a fudge room, bowling alley, interfaith chapel and a dark-panelled library run by a librarian in her late fifties. The librarian liked Mozart and asked Mary to leave her a note whenever WHRB[xxxix] held its 24- hour Mozart recitals.

Grandin Hall, the ballroom, had tiny alcoves around its edges, in which residents could entertain male guests (men and Negros were NEVER allowed upstairs). These "beau parlors" were furnished with two straight-backed chairs, a table, a lamp and a curtain that didn't quite make it across the door opening. Despite strict supervision, there were rumours that couples "did it" on top of the beau parlor radiators, but not her of course. Palmer was lucky to have his own room across the square where she could visit him overnight. On Saturday afternoons, they would walk a mile or two downtown on Washington Street, checking out anything that looked interesting along the way. And to Mary, everything did. She loved the names of the businesses: Uncle

Ned's Money to Loan, Baby Tiger's School of Boxing, Checker Smoker, Turf Tavern, and "The Drs. Grover, Dentists."

At the grocery, people pushed shopping carts down narrow aisles of shelves piled high with bashed-in cans and boxes. Bullen's Bakery did a brisk business in big round cans of Boston brown bread, and she loved to watch the big puffs of Syrian bread roll to the end of the bakery's conveyor belt, deflating on the way. Mary always made a stop at the Old French Trader with its three rooms of fascinating junk. She bought an art deco ashtray, having taken up smoking since her arrival, and a bizarre portrait of a goat that she kept for a long time on her shelf.

Franklin House sometimes held socials on Wednesday evenings, hiring the new swing bands. Chairs were lined up against the walls, "business girls" like her and older residents were on one side, sailors and students from the technical schools on the other. The university students wouldn't have been caught dead in there. Instead, she would spy them creeping down the back stairs to beg fruit punch and cookies from the porters and, throughout the evening, annoyingly phoning the front desk to complain that they couldn't concentrate on their studies because of the noise in the ballroom. She, on the other hand, started to enjoy those Wednesday nights for a wee dance and Pete coming along would have made it all the better. After those walks home, he was adamantly refused entry to the 'Beau parlour' despite subjecting himself to the critical gaze of the house manager Miss Worcester, who even refused him the predictable once over from the home supervisor so that he could come along on Swing Nights. His presence became a regular part of Mary's life, though she didn't ever move out of the home to a place of her (and Pete's) own. He hadn't had regular work since the Depression hit and she was still reticent about any further commitment.

The Franklin Square House had its own chef, and everyone ate well. Tired from the all-be-it, relatively short trek to Boston Maid on Harrison Avenue and back and starved from a lunch of bread and a hard-boiled egg filched from an-only-just-made-it-to breakfast, she'd always eat the maximum amount allowed.

Mary learned that from the 1820s on, the Irish had been the neighborhood's dominant immigrant group and the remaining resonating accents from other newcomers kept a feeling of familiarity going for her. Aunt Rebecca had known this would be a help, since it had also helped her with the bouts of homesickness at the time, all those years ago after first emigrating herself. Aunt Rose had also done the crossing even earlier, way back some decades before. Many of the early settlers then had been skilled craftsmen and business owners, but with the onset of the potato famine in the 1840s, the Irish population had surged. Impoverished newcomers like aunt Rose, settled mainly in the Lower End, where they worked as seamstresses, labourers and dockworkers. The Irish population grew rapidly again after the Great Fire of 1872 swept through Boston's Fort Hill neighbourhood, driving some of the city's poorest immigrant residents into South Boston.

The 1872 Fire also destroyed the earlier garment and leather factories. The industry then revived before further expanding in the late 19th century south towards Essex St. At the same time, Chinatown was establishing itself on Harrison Avenue between Essex and Beach Streets not far from the Boston Maid Factory.

Mary's aunt Rose had arrived in 1880, at around the same age as Mary, not that long after the fire and had had a husband or such-like that produced a young girl, Agatha, but again the birth was like Mary's experience; taking place in an Alms house due to poverty or the inferred abandonment by the elusive Joseph Watson, father of the child. Mary Agatha was now a 27year old woman who had an excellent sense of humour and promised to be good company for Mary and her mother Rose, elderly at age sixty-five years old now but to live almost two decades more.

Aunt Rebecca had arrived almost thirty years later in 1907, bringing some of her five grown children previously born in Fermanagh, Ireland. This completed Mary's family circle and lucky she was too, having so many first and second cousins around her own age that she could interact with every day if she wished, though, other than with Agatha, she mostly didn't wish, since there were always a few remarks about her association with Petey and interest because of her known involvement back in Scotland with Cumann na mBan. People here, since they'd started that celebration for Evacuation Day parade in South Boston to celebrate the British retreat from the area on March 17, 1776 became a yearly St. Patrick's Day parade, were fiercely supportive of all things Irish, good or bad. As exciting as the experience had been, she didn't like to talk about that and its association with her lost daughter and the revelations that had further impacted on her relationship with her family, or rather with Nora.

She remembered just managing to get away from Victor's grasp and breathlessly attempting to straighten the disarray of her clothes created while trying to fend him off, when he pulled her to him again from behind and she froze as his hands grabbed and kneaded as she winced under his enforced touch. They were in the small hallway in the Threadmill Street cottage and had thought he would quickly move past her. "You just can't accept I'm not interested in your incessant demands!" He had become bolder over the last few months.

"I'll convince you Mary. I know you love those massages, don't you? You wouldn't want me to tell your big sister how much, would you?" She'd been unlucky to get caught alone with him since having thought Nora being in the house, would deter him. She was just averting her face as he leant forward while clutching her to his chest, when she noticed Nora step into the hall, immediate shock registering on her face at the sight of the supposed embrace.

"Mary, I can't believe you're cheating on me with Victor, my *husband*!

"I'm sorry Nora, I didn't mean to hurt you."

"How could you do this to me?"

"I don't know. I just couldn't stop him; he won't leave me alone!"

"You're a slut!" She wasn't even looking at Victor who had a sly smile sliding off the side of his face turned away from Nora. Then he turned to her with a repentant look.

"I'm sorry Nora, I don't know what got into her. It was just a harmless wee rub I offered after she complained of aching shoulders and she seems to have got the wrong idea?" He held out his hands in supplication to his now crying wife.

"You're lucky I don't kill you, Mary!"

"I'm sorry, I don't know what to say. I didn't do anything Nora; you must believe me. I wouldn't do that to you." But Nora abruptly turned and stomped back into the kitchen. Having no other options, it was to her sister she'd had to admit her eventual problem and take the consequences of the bitterness her sister never minded to sweeten over the years. There were few exchanges between them after that and absolutely no acknowledgement of the possibility Victor was a candidate for the father of her lost child. The memories of the break with her sister were coupled with the situation of her abandonment of Therese and she felt helpless to shake off the overwhelming gloom that often enveloped her, deciding to seek the help of a homeopath in the Talbot Building at the hospital on Albany Street, which even on a hectic day was hard to pass by without admiring its commanding presence. The original structure—the central wing of the building—was designed by William R. Emerson, the great-nephew of writer Ralph Waldo Emerson, a keen supporter of Homeopathy. It served as the home of the Massachusetts Homeopathic Hospital (MHH), which was founded in an act of defiance by homeopathic physician Israel Talbot (who also concurrently served as the first dean of the School of Medicine, established in 1873) after he and six other physicians were expelled from the Massachusetts Medical Society for their embrace of homeopathy.

"Yes, there is guilt. And not just because I'm Catholic but because I abandoned my daughter. I let my big sister down by betraying her though she turned out to be not so bad at the betraying herself." The tears that had begun when the homeopath with the soft face and large head of reddish hair started to ask why she had come, continued to stream down her cheeks. "I don't think there's any way to forgive myself for those things even though much of it has been forced on me,"

"Aren't you feeling angry at all Miss Maguire? He encouraged.

"Angry, that's a tame word for the fire that scalds my heart and scours my guts, yes, just a little, I'd say." He didn't delay for more questions and duly prescribed some *Staphisagria* for Mary to take at home that night.

Mary felt lucky for the years she was able to benefit from the hospital's presence and those doctors committed to the science and art of the subtle and direct system of medicine that had long been a beneficial support to generations of her family. Due to practitioners being hounded by allopaths and despite or because of their many medical successes, many famous great writers, politicians and businessmen including great writers like Mark Twain, William James, Louisa May Alcott, Harriett Beecher Stowe, Henry David Thoreau etc. played an important role in supporting Homeopathy in the late 19th century. But the unorthodox practice of homeopathy still began to lose popularity[xl] and MHH was eventually renamed as Massachusetts Memorial Hospital (MMH) in 1929.

~

The Archdiocese of Boston had previously opened a spate of new Catholic churches to serve Southie's burgeoning Irish communities. By the time Mary arrived in 1922, there was a plentiful choice of chapels but ironically, she chose Immaculate Conception for any occasional visits that she herself made.

Some years after settling in Southie there been a few letters (from Paddy on the *Argenta*) and some news from Glasgow. Cousin Michael came to Franklin House's reception in August of 1929. He wore a hangdog look on his big freckled face as he mumbled out the news. "The son that your brother Seamus had with his wife Ann earlier this year in June, didn't live past two days old."

"What could be crueller?" Mary gasped but then she knew exactly what. Not her loss; for her child most likely still lived and lived well, though she could never be sure. Michael shuffled his feet and was unable to look at her as he relayed the rest of the message

"Well...Seamus' suffered further when his Ann died four days later, leaving him all alone." Her legs almost buckled with shock then and Michael grabbed her arm to hold her up. It seemed Seamus never quite recovered after that to be able to think of marrying and having children again, for she was never to hear any more news of him. This compounded her grief after the news that had arrived earlier in the year in a letter from Caity.

Kirkston 14th Feb 1929

Renfrewshire
Scotland
Dear Mary,
I hope all is well out there in America. Sad news comes with the death of Frankie. He passed in January this year. Despite the great improvements to his illness, he'd experienced all those years ago, he had a major relapse and took his own life at only 41 years old; the same age Dada was when he died. We know to take your own life is a grievous sin against God and meant we couldn't bury him with dada and mammy. Poor Liz is still recovering from finding him and is trying to comfort Robert, their son who's 9-year-old now. My heart also still pines for your namesake niece - wee Mary who passed from fever in '24 at only five, when God took her to be with the Angels. We pray for them both and you so far away,
Your sister Caity

Now Frankie had joined those, like herself, consigned to the fires of hell; but maybe his life had already felt like hell and was why he'd made the choice he did?

The Maguires surely were not the only family to experience losses like these, for reductions in infant mortality took some decades, as did further advances in medical and hygiene practices to reduce mother and infant deaths come too soon, which was the same in the poorer areas like Southie and across America, especially in 1929. She also reckoned there were more than a few American servicemen who had had similar shell-shocked conditions as Frank to deal with after WWI.

She learned while living there that while Irish immigrants fuelled most of South Boston's growth in the nineteenth century, the neighbourhood had also attracted a large number of Canadians, German immigrants and other northern European groups. There was too a sizeable community of Polish and Lithuanian immigrants also settled in the Lower End, where they also built a Catholic parish, St. Peter's. Further east, a small Italian settlement had grown along Third Street. Although its population had diversified by the early twentieth century, the neighbourhood maintained its Irish identity and continued to attract newcomers from Ireland and Scotland. Alongside its churches, dozens of Irish social and charitable organizations also flourished in Southie.

A drop in property prices coincided with the expansion of the garment industry in the early 20th century. The noise of the elevated trains was no hindrance for manufacturing but daylight was still necessary to supplement electric lights for the workers. As a result, the first wave of buildings were about nine stories tall, steel framed with large windows. Corner locations with two outside walls were favoured. Most notable was the intersection of Beach St. and Harrison Ave. – where the station entrance for the El and five garment buildings were. Looking north on Harrison Ave. intersection with Beach St. showed that all four corners were dominated by garment buildings with large windows on two sides. The street level stores were those that served the industry – sewing machines, buttons, textiles, embroidery, lace etc. The industry reached its peak in the late 20s.

Prohibition was initiated across the country in 1920 about a year before Mary had arrived. This "noble experiment"—was declared to have been undertaken to reduce crime and corruption, solve social problems, reduce the tax burden created by prisons and poorhouses, and improve health and hygiene across America. At the beginning of Prohibition, the Reverend Billy Sunday stirred audiences with his optimistic prediction: "*The reign of tears is over. The slums will soon be a memory. We will turn our prisons into factories and our jails into storehouses and corncribs. Men will walk upright now, women will smile and children will laugh. Hell will be forever for rent.*"[xli] Mary having arrived just when this had been implemented, hadn't known it any other way until they stopped it in 1933, but she, in all those years, hadn't ever noticed the slums being cleaned up by sober residents and hollow-eyed children still begged a cent or two; even more often after the Depression hit in 1929. There were still plenty of drunks on the streets too. People seemed more determined to drink as much as they could whenever and wherever they could get their hands on any liquor and damn the police and the prohibitionists, especially during the Depression. What else was there to do? Unfortunately, at the same time the clothing industry was suffering from the dominance of New York and competition from other centres like Chicago, like most other businesses it was also hard hit by the Depression.

Chapter 26 – Down in the Docklands-Paddy

Paddy made preparations to travel down to London without stopping to see the Maguire brothers, who'd all been out working or in their own homes when he'd appeared at the cottage on Threadmill Street. He'd not been keen on the assumed hostility they might subject him to, if the previous visit was anything to go by. Scottish involvement in the Easter Rising was hardly surprising given the level of Republican organisation there, particularly in the Glasgow area. Mary had her introduction through cousin Paddy who'd come over to Scotland in 1912 when she was just ten years old and he aged twenty-four. They didn't actually meet in person until several years later when he was introduced to her by her brothers. They were all kind of at odds though.

"Hey fellahs, are yis mad. Wanting to fight for those eejits that did and are still doing so much damage to Ireland, the old country. Tis just as well yir Da's no around anymore to see it."

"Who are you to be speaking for ma da? Did ye even know him?" Seamus said with anger in his voice. He had helped cousin Paddy to find somewhere to stay in Glasgow four years before the 1916 rising but the brothers' distance from happenings in Ireland beyond the occasional holiday in Fermanagh left them adrift of the most recent fast-moving events. After that Paddy minded what he said around them and Mary being their sister and all, well...

He huddled into a corner of the busy train reading his paper before once outside the city, the passing greenery soothed his flickering thoughts, as the rocking of the carriage further lulled him into sleep. He only came to when roused with a shake by the conductor as the train pulled into Euston some eight hours later.

He wasn't sure what he hoped to find. With Mary across the ocean in America, another piece of information she'd neglected to tell him, and the child said to be adopted by some other family, he hadn't much to go on. Maybe he could convince one of the Sheffield House staff to give him some details. He chose not to confront anyone at the hospital's surprisingly bright clinic building where the maternity rooms were. He did notice that awful sign about venereal diseases and his heart went out in sympathy with how Mary must have felt having to come here and be subjected to the judgements and assumptions inherent in an enforced confinement here. He remembered his own not-so-long-ago confinement on the ship *Argenta*, which was though, probably much worse than conditions here. It was the lack of choice, the compulsion to do as others decided with no autonomy which had been what got to him and many of the men incarcerated with him.

Particularly, the young ones unused to the military regimes and regulations with which he had been previously trained. He realised that was what pained him so, Mary had only been nineteen, a young lass here on her own, pregnant and lonely without her family or her baby's father. He should have done more.

"Good morning, Miss, d'ye think I could have a word, now?" Paddy was in the teashop round the corner which he'd realised was a gathering place for Sheffield House hospital staff when he saw uniformed nurses come and go while he watched from across the road for an hour or so before joining them to have a much-needed cuppa and sandwich after the long overnight journey down. The fresh-faced nurse had a wary look as he leaned in to speak quietly to her. "I don't mean you any harm, colleen. I just wondered if there were any jobs going there at the hospital, d'ye know?" Her nose crinkled before she shook her head and moved quickly away from him. It wasn't till the fourth try he had any luck. "Best ask for the maintenance supervisor for that, mister."

Paddy trudged back to the hospital and approached the security man in the cubicle near the gate and was directed to the basement to ask for Mr. Goodbody, who was as helpful as he could be, looking surprisingly glad to hear he was looking for work.

"Now a porter's job is very important, so you'd best be about yourself. You're a godsend. We just had a lad finish yesterday. He didn't have the strength or the stomach for the job. I hope you won't go vomiting rings around yourself, with people having to clean up after you, like he did?"

"No sir, sure having been in the wars, I've dealt with some horrors myself before now, so." The job was handy for keeping him afloat while he snooped around the maternity wards as unobtrusively as possible. He mostly wanted to link up with the nurses there to try getting any information about adoptions but for the most part they were very close-lipped.

He turned on the charm and spent some of his actually pretty hard-earned cash on taking various nurses for tea and cake or what in those hard times passed as cake. Surrounded by all the English accents galled him some, a reminder of the difficult times in Ireland the last few years. It wasn't all resolved by any means and the IRA still fought for Irelands' independence despite the uneasy treaty that existed between the English government and the divided country of Eire and North Ireland. He'd had the misfortune to have been born and bred in the North and hadn't the stomach to move to Eire; rather Scotland than there, or at least that's what he told himself these days, while, in the back of his mind knowing that if he found the child it was home he'd prefer to be.

It took some weeks, longer than he'd expected, but eventually a sweet young nurse, who struck a paternal chord in him, let slip the name of the organisation 'City Foundlings', that arranged adoptions. His next stop was their offices in Piccadilly and where he was summarily tossed out on his ear, regulations and confidentialities and what not, thrown at him for even just daring to ask the whereabouts of an adopted child, *his* adopted child, he'd bellowed at them as he tried to maintain his balance when they barrelled him out the door. He received a similar rebuke from the receptionist as that previously dished out by Nora and Victor about why hadn't he thought of what might happen before, and how he'd missed his chance to care for the daughter he clearly had already abandoned. So, criminality was the next and only option left to him and therefore a touch of breaking and entering was in order.

He was once again glad for his paramilitary training with all these stakeouts he was having to undertake, all be it in less threatening circumstances. He watched again from the side-lines, hidden by people coming and going along the street, then sloped down the lane at the back of the shop to check out alarms and other exits, before managing to slip in the back entrance by catching the open door as someone left the building. Paddy tiptoed up the two flights of stairs, staying close to the wall, listening for any footsteps moving in his direction and just as he was stepping into the corridor on the second floor, a door creaked as it opened and he jouked back into the stairwell, breathing fast, waiting for either the sounds to subside or to have to confront someone if they came through that door.

He breathed a sigh of relief as the footsteps moved on past, then waited a few more minutes before going through the door into a dimly lit corridor, its walls looking rather grotty and unkempt, the lino under his feet ripped in places. Not the most salubrious set-up he'd seen, which made more doubts about his daughter's adoption flare up. He gently turned the handle of the nearest door hoping to find filing cabinets where the information he needed might be kept. He held his breath as the handle turned and the door cracked open. When there was no sound of a reaction from inside, he pushed the door open further and took a sharp intake of breath on seeing that there was in fact someone bent over a desk studying some papers, seemingly oblivious to his entry. He glanced swiftly around noticing more empty desks but no filing cabinets or drawers and even more gently closing the door on stepping back outside the room before moving on to the next door to try again. This time the room was empty and to his relief, there were cabinets lining the walls. He hurried inside, checking the corridor before closing the door and scanned for the cabinet holding the 'M' files. He was in luck, these old cabinets were not lockable and he flicked through numerous files before he found 'Maguire, Mary.' It made a quick study of Mary's situation at the time of giving birth, mentioning again the name 'Therese' having been given by Mary and to his surprise retained rather than changed by the new adopting couple, a man and wife by the name of Smith, who lived in in London's East end. He grabbed a scrap of paper scribbling the address onto it and retreated as soon as he was able, down the stairs and out the way he'd come in.

On the next Sunday, he discovered Rotherhithe was close to the docks and its run-down state further worried him about what kind of situation he'd find his daughter living in. Despite an ongoing prejudice against Catholics, Sam Smith and his wife Eileen attended one of two Roman Catholic churches on the street, namely Our Lady of the Immaculate Conception, which he discovered when watching their house, a shambolic wood-fronted two-storey house already filled with dirty, ragged children where he saw Therese trip over her feet trying to keep up with the pack gambolling down the stairs.

Rotherhithe had a long history as a port, with shipyards and working docks. He watched Sam Smith leave and return at odd hours to and from there, at times with some dubious–looking cronies. Eileen Smith looked worn down with looking after their, by birth or adoption, brood of children and the sense Therese was lost and neglected among them strengthened Paddy's resolve to take her away from there. It was unlikely they'd miss her, probably they'd more likely miss the Poor Law money they'd been promised to feed and clothe her.

Leaning out precariously on the Thames' bank close by was an old tavern known as *The Spread Eagle*, close to the docking bay of The Mayflower, from which the Pilgrims sailed to Southampton in 1620, on the first leg of their journey to New England. Mary might be interested in that living in the USA these days as she was and he wondered again, beyond running away from the loss of her child, what had brought her to that decision.

Facing it across the other side of Rotherhithe St. towered John James' St Mary's, Rotherhithe. The pub, the church and the nearby schoolhouse defined the centre of Rotherhithe with a line of warehouses extending along the river frontage for a just couple of hundred yards in either direction and then beyond this the vast complex of wharfs, quays and stores that filled the entire peninsular.

The soot-blackened houses, the clogged gutters, stray feral dogs and children running barefoot amongst it all, reminded Paddy of the state of inner-city Belfast or even Dublin. Despite this, he still considered taking Therese back to Ireland but instead to Enniskillen in Fermanagh away from the smoke-laden tubercular cities here or there, to the green hills and craggy mountains with pure air, nature and real family all around. He planned his next move carefully because he'd only get one chance and really didn't want to end up being incarcerated once more, he was getting too old for that.

Chapter 27-Life in America - Mary

The word "shopping" in the early days was used almost exclusively to designate a trip to Boston to the big stores for clothing, furniture, etc. but Mary just went to the nearby shops. Mary imagined mothers would do their shopping early in the day, wheeling their baby carriages to the market and that was therefore the time she purposely most often avoided. She noticed that there were some enterprising young boys who took orders for meats and groceries and delivered them to the folk living in the nearby houses. From her window she watched the boys loading the truck that carried the supplies and for $3.00 or $3.50 a week made deliveries after school and on Saturdays. After she became friendly with freckle-faced 12-year-old Sam, he would drop off a parcel of her favourites that Franklin House didn't provide to her.

The residents of Southie were served by many businesses on nearby streets in the 1920's. There was also a Music Teacher, a Tea and Coffee Shop, Drug Store, Meat Markets, Delicatessens, two Fruit Stores & Ice Cream Parlors, the Hardware & Dry Goods Store, the Fish Market and of course, the Boston Maid Dress Manufacturer.

It was fun for Mary to do her errands as if with the eyes of a child until she got to know the neighbourhood, eventually becoming friendly with the shopkeepers and could then call them by their first names. Soon, from speaking with those customers whose faces appeared regularly when she was trying to find her way around before starting work at the Boston Maid factory, she knew which of them had a reputation for quality products. She came to know that Mr. McNulty worked in his store sitting in his wheelchair at no.85, and had the best beans and brown bread in the area. Mrs. Osmond at no.179 ran the delicatessen and catered to the German trade. Her potato salad was undeniably her own recipe and so good she bemoaned how she couldn't keep up with the demand.

The A&P at no. 115 did a flourishing business, due in large part to 'Bernie,' the manager. He had an outgoing manner, and quick and efficient to boot., "Now YOU are next, so," he would say pleasantly with an Irish lilt, which helped endear him to her too.

"Thank you." Mary would respond, feeling the flush of the chosen customer. Then she'd give him the first three or four items of the order. While the coffee was grinding Bernie quickly gathered the items from other parts of the store. She watched him sometimes managing to retrieve items from shelves eight feet high that could only be lowered with the use of a long-handled hook, which deposited the item directly onto his hand. After the order was assembled, he put them in a brown bag with the cost of each item listed on it. He could add faster than any person Mary had ever met in her life. Other customers watching stood in awe, like her, at his speed and accuracy.

Early on Saturday morning, rabbits, fur still attached, were on display at the Market at no. 122. Henry, the handsome young butcher, would appear wearing a straw hat and long white coat, his outfit for the whole year round. He carried a pail of water with flour mixed in it and a brush.

The specials of the day would be listed on the window of the market in his beautiful script. Some of those watching were interested in the price of the specials but many of them gawped in the window marveling at his talent, and at the attractive appearance of the window when he was finished.

Immigrants who opened businesses became of tremendous interest to the now many Irish and African American residents. Karl Bowen, from Bohemia, then named Czechoslovakia, opened a shoe repair shop at no.120 and it looked to her like they were doing very well. She heard that Karl was joined a little later by his fellow countryman, Peter Sivacheck, who opened a tailor shop at no.116A. Both, that she knew of, spent their entire working lives in the area.

Men wore those stiff collars and shirts that had to be washed, starched and ironed at the Chinese laundry. Yee Sun at no.125 knew only a few words of English, but being a good businessman, when shirts and collars were left with him, he gave out a slip with Chinese characters on it. He appeared to make a similar slip for himself and when anyone called for their laundry, he would match the slips. Looking back on it Mary realised Yee Sun had it all organised. There were never any mix ups. From what she heard, at least the men always got their own collars back.

Albert Hessel had a tea & coffee shop at no.95 and also made deliveries of fresh eggs and butter to customers. Ethel, his daughter, opened a music studio at the same address and brought her musical talents and culture to the community.

Mayo advertised their hardware store at no. 149, which served the needs of the carriage industry, blacksmiths, builders, homeowners and everyday citizens. It also had everything to keep children happy i.e. sleds, skates, hockey sticks, bikes, express wagons, etc. It had served the community longer than any other retail store in the neighborhood.

Mrs. Duff's dry goods store was at no.160, at the corner of Brooks Avenue. Children's clothing and adult's clothing were also available. Lots of the small gifts given by children at Christmas were bought there. Since they were no longer in vogue, gone were arm garters to buy for fathers, grandfathers and uncles to keep their shirtsleeves in place.

The delicatessen at no.201 was owned by Mr. William Galston. The great attraction for children in this store was the 25 or 30 lb. pig, head and all, that was displayed in the window each week. It was a puzzle to any children without a German background why the pig who was not alive had an apple in its mouth, which it could not eat. The passage of the Prohibition Act from 1920 to 1933 took its toll on some businesses. Liquor shops and bars, of course, became the immediate victims.

From 1922, after her arrival and a speedy job-hunt, Mary had managed to gain employment at the Boston Maid ladies' clothes factory on Harrison Avenue in the South-end of Boston, eventually working in quality control there. She also had a particular friend from Franklin House, Rena Hamilton, who worked as an over-locker beside her. She enjoyed the good atmosphere and camaraderie between the women; well, most of the women. Most of the lassies in the factory were sewing machinists. There were over a hundred of them at their machines all singing away to the wireless, but as soon as a fellah entered their domain, it would go dead quiet, then they would slowly start banging their scissors on their work benches, then came the cat calls.

"You want tae talk about a riddie for a young lad?" Rena would say. It happened as often as the youngest apprentice tailor's cutters were sent up the spiral staircase with the freshly cut bundles for the machinists, by the other three senior cutters, knowing what the youngster was in for.

Nevertheless, for the fellahs at that age, it must have been a wonderful, if scary, introduction into the world of women. The lassies meant no harm but rather enjoyed being in the position to safely heckle and tease the fellahs for a change.

She had started out in the cutting room and moved on to the sewing section. Mary didn't much care for sewing for piecework though. If she remembered rightly, you were paid something like one dollar and two cents for a dozen sleeves. This was a dozen pairs. Forty-eight seams in the sleeves, another forty-eight in the lining and twenty-four seams to join the sleeve and lining together. She stuck that out for a few years until another young girl on her machine line lost her fingers trying to put her machine belt on without turning the power off.

"I can't get this damn thing on! It's slipped off again damn it, damn belt, damn machine!" The surrounding women all raised their eyebrows at her cursing and some sniggered and then there was a piercing scream and the woman beside her jumped away, suddenly vomiting on the floor at the sight of the girl who'd had the belt problems, as blood gushed from the hand she held up, while staring at it looking horrified and still screaming. When Mary quickly crossed the factory floor to help, she saw the girl's little pinkie lying in a pool of blood among tartan-patterned scraps of cloth. She pulled out a handkerchief, offering to staunch the blood and wishing she had brought a couple of first-aid homeopathic remedies with her to work, for *Arnica* would have helped with shock and staunching the flow of blood. The screaming girl wouldn't even let her near and didn't stop screaming for the longest time. Everyone around had either backed off or crowded in but there was a jittery sense of chaos and many of their drawn faces indicated feelings of relief; feeling lucky it wasn't their finger lying there. They all knew it was a risk you took and had known all the old hands did it regularly because they didn't want to lose the time to wait for a mechanic to change the belt for them. Time was money. The poor girl didn't get a penny in compensation because it was considered her own fault.

Mary worked in Boston Maid for thirteen years, leaving partly because all the women seemed to be constantly having babies, and who would then leave soon after and she'd never see them again. Even the supervisor had, more than once, jokingly commented: "You girls are not to drink from the same tap in the toilets; I can't have anyone else leave my line." She did regularly have to come and chase Mary out of those toilets since she always seemed to take ages. Mary wouldn't say so, but she was in there mostly because of being reduced to tears from all the talk of babies this and babies that. After managing for ten years, she had begun to strangely dissolve into tears, not just sometimes, but every time another woman started up on the subject of babies again or when yet another declared herself pregnant. In fact, what had made her give notice the same week was when seven of the women on the same line on the same day, all declared that they were pregnant. That she had not only lost her child but could no longer have any more since then, was brought home to her repeatedly here amongst all these fertile women. It had happened not long after having moved on to the quality control side of things and where the assembled dresses were hung on overhead trollies by their wheels on a uni-rail-like mechanism that ran to and from across the factory by switch-tracks to specific work stations. Her job was to inspect the garments, mostly women's dresses, before they were sent out to independent retailers after being made in the massive factory.

Workers like her used to be able to get everything cheap. Everyone Mary knew on her floor at Franklin Square was dressed in Boston Maid clothing goodies because she and other employees staying there could sell on reduced or items considered as 'seconds' with a wee profit in it for themselves and so, after leaving Boston Maid, she missed that bit of extra money too, even though it had dwindled over the years when more gossip compounded their opinion of her each time as that untrustworthy NLW.

Mary could neither agree with what she thought as the factory's callous treatment of anyone injured while in their employ or since by then she'd had more than enough of the other women's baby talk. She'd also had enough of both the snide remarks and open prejudice about her supposed-to-be hidden relationship with Petey. "Nigger loving whore!" was a common insult usually accompanied with being spat in the face by women and men alike. The continual vicious whispers and sharp looks were meant to cut her down to size.

The estimation they had already decided Petey merited for no other reason than that he was coloured, wore her down. If it had only been words their life might have been more bearable, but some people didn't stop there. Petey had told her of the attack in Maine a couple of years before in 1919 on two boys at the University there. He couldn't help becoming agitated when telling her the story.

"One cold April night in 1919, at around 2 a.m., a mob of sixty rowdy white students at the University of Maine surrounded the dorm room of Samuel and Roger Courtney. They planned to attack the two Black brothers from Boston in retaliation for what they thought as their 'domineering manner and ill temper.' They were just two among only a dozen black University of Maine students at the time."

Even though they were outnumbered, the Courtney brothers managed to escape and knock three freshmen attackers out cold in the process! Soon after, a mob of hundreds of students and community members gathered to finish what the freshmen had started. They captured the brothers and led them about four miles back to campus like animals with horse halters around their necks.

Before a growing crowd at the livestock-viewing pavilion, members of the mob held down Samuel and Roger while their heads were shaved and bodies stripped naked in the near-freezing weather. They were forced to slop each other with hot molasses. Then the mob covered them with feathers from their dorm room pillows. The victims and bystanders were crying out for the mob to stop but they took no notice. Local police, who'd been called alerted hours earlier, only arrived after it was all over. No arrests were made.[xlii]

"Nothing like that has ever happened to you has it, Petey?"

"Not the tarring and feathering, but I've had a few kickings when told, or shown in no uncertain terms more like, that I've been in the wrong place at the wrong time and that's been a lot of places and times over the years, Mary. You know, incidents of tarring and feathering as a form of public torture has been happening since colonial times. Even nearby in Ellsworth, Maine again, a Know Nothing mob, a forerunner to the KKK, tarred and feathered Jesuit priest Father John Bapst back some seventy years before in the 1850's.

"After World War I, this vigilantism was regularly used by the KKK and other groups against not only Black Americans, but immigrants and labour organisers, especially in the South and West. Labour and housing tension spurred the first wave of the Great Migration, that is, not only Irish folk like yourself arrived, but haven't you noticed more and more black faces around? Then the Depression came, so everyone's fighting for jobs and houses and back in 1919 when all the soldiers came home from war, it ended up increasing the number of attacks even against Black soldiers. That was all the thanks they got for fighting for their country."

Dealing with the racism here, to Mary, was all too reminiscent of the regard for the Irish from the English but here both Irish civil war and colour prejudice sentiments were empathised with. Despite their shared nationality and awful treatment in first or further generations back, people didn't hesitate to force their opinion on her about their regard or lack thereof negro people, who had in fact been in the States much longer than many of the Irish families. Always the disenfranchised protecting and pitting themselves against other disenfranchisees out of fear.

~

Hearing the news of Caity's death in 1931, once again a result of the poverty trap and the ailing lungs of those predisposed to the malady of the times: T.B. had added to the emotional difficulties she'd been experiencing the last year or so. She often thought of those homeopaths that had helped her family all those years ago and since the take-over of the Talbot Building by the allopaths in 1929, she had little knowledge of where any homeopathic doctors were consulting in Massachusetts now, but she could have sure used their help.

Before her first consultation, the one homeopathic physician she'd eventually discovered, explained that she was about twenty years too late, for in 1910, the Carnegie Foundation issued the infamous Flexner Report. While pretending to be objective, the Report actually established guidelines meant to sanction orthodox medical schools and condemn homeopathic ones.[xliii] That was the beginning of the end for wide-spread homeopathic education through medical schools and subsequently homeopathic hospitals all across America.

~

Despite enjoying moments of flirtatious behaviour, for one reason or another, Mary had been unable to form any more of a committed relationship other than what she'd shared, in semi-secret, with Petey over the years; apart from that car wreck of whatever it was she'd experienced with cousin Paddy; yes, cousin: first cousin - so another sin on top of the pregnancy. It was definitely going to be the bad fire for her for sure, though in truth she'd given up worrying about what God thought quite some time ago, but old habits and cares did seem to linger on. She hadn't seen Paddy in a long time, not since he'd been carted off to jail again by the Ulster Constabulary. Other than meeting Petey not long after her arrival, for the next thirteen years she could only handle an on/off relationship. He didn't want to be tied down and she was too scared for any deeper commitment anyway. Their coupling was a major incident because of the colour divide, the colour difference in the severely segregated city that was Boston. It was his generosity of spirit and wish to take care of her that attracted Mary to Pete from the get go but most others weren't interested in anything but the fact he was a negro. Her friendship with Rita, one of the very few she'd confided in about being with Petey, went by the wayside. "How can you want to be with the likes of him, Mary? Those people are savages!"

"You know this how?" Mary said through gritted teeth, struggling to maintain her calm.

"I've heard stories. I mean they're from Africa; a dirty backward country. They just come here to take jobs from Irish folk, never mind Americans!" Mary threw her hands up and walked away in disgust tossing back just one last remark.

"Petey was born in Boston." There was no talking to her or some members of her Boston family for that matter. The irrational hostility constantly reminded her of the stories and conflicts in the north of Ireland all those years ago and the snipes from the other women at the mill then, in Kirkston before she'd left. Disgraced for being a known 'Fenian' and appearing proud of it; disgraced for sleeping with her sister's husband and at the last, disgraced for being a Catholic girl who couldn't keep her legs crossed never mind cross herself and then ending up in the family way. Ha! What family?!

Apart from the palpable daily tension over her thing with Pete, and he ever wary of another kicking, life had trundled on for her sisters and brothers across the pond succumbing to various illnesses, usually of the respiratory kind, which seemed like a sticky predisposition that also ran in the family way. Still, she constantly hankered after her missing daughter.

"Are ye alright, lass?" The elderly man's concerned crinkled face appealed to her gasping frame as she bent into the ache of emptiness inside that had made her legs buckle beneath her. It would catch her unawares at the sound of a child crying or even laughing that deep chuckle that would hit her heart as if with a hammer, reverberating all the way through her body and down her now buckled legs. The man, his glasses misted by his short warm breaths in the cold air, reached out to help Mary back to her feet. Now the tears were streaming down her face and she struggled to quell her sobs as the hankerchy he went on to hand her quickly became sodden.

"I'm sorry mister... your hanky...I..." Mary held it out by its corner.

"It's okay lass, you keep it. You can wash or toss it, as you like. Where are you going? Can I hail you a taxi?" Embarrassingly, they were on a main street with traffic going in both directions in the middle of the day, so many more passers-by were pretending not to stare at her in emotional fall-out while sneaking glances anyway. She dipped her head again as her skin flared in shame. The child's cry sounded again and her head swerved towards the sound, seeing then the pram parked outside a nearby butcher's shop. How could they just leave the child on its own like that? She made to move to comfort the child just as the head-scarfed mother rushed from the shop onto the street and bent to the pram. The man detained Mary with his arm.

"It's alright," he said again and gave a tug on her arm as he waved down the taxi. It pulled into the kerbside and she allowed him to guide her in and slam the door, waving her off with a sad grimace at the sight of the disappearing cab. Mary mumbled her address to the driver and was relieved when she finally got inside her room at Franklin Square House, though annoyed at herself for not thanking the man properly. She was still clutching the sticky cotton fabric as the tears erupted again. She fell onto her bed, burying herself under the eiderdown quilt and helpless to prevent the suffocating yearning in that space; in that place that had for so long surrounded her own absent child.

Chapter 28 – Faith of our Fathers - Paddy

Through the murk and lattice-work roof, a pyramid of light shafts surrounded the London & North Western Railway train as it started its northbound express out of Euston station with Paddy on-board and a little five-year-old snuggled in beside him under his heavy winter coat. His heartbeat was still accelerated with that last dash before clambering onto the train when the inspector was looking a bit too suspiciously at him carrying Therese and no woman around. That wasn't a common sight but he'd had no choice and moved quickly past, making for the waiting train on the platform.

The rest of his plan had been easier than expected, such was the level of neglect for Therese and the lack of minding of the Smith brood. Therese had been left behind again as the older, faster children had carried on chasing and hiding as she slumped on the street looking tearful and tired out from trying to keep up. Paddy had with him his bag and tickets booked for the train and took advantage of that lucky moment, offering his hand.

"Are ye lost wee girl?" Her upturned face was a picture of grubby innocence and tear-stained disappointment.

"Me bruvvers an sisties have all gone away. Did you see where they went, mister?" She took his hand and rose with a wobble, to her feet.

"Let's you and me go and find them, will we?" Therese nodded enthusiastically, a glimmer of happy in her expression as they walked out of that dockland warren, through the Rotherhithe tunnel towards the city centre. He had to carry her in the end up as, not surprisingly, her short legs couldn't keep up with him either, with his long strides on legs three times her height. An omnibus trundled by and they got on it to get out of the East end before Therese's brothers and sisters realised how long she'd been gone, though he suspected this wasn't the first time she'd been left on her own and god knows what other more dubious gents had previously taken her for a wee walk, but he shook that thought away, chatting to her, trying keep her awake while she was still trusting of him, planning to let her sleep on the train.

It was a long journey for both of them, but while he'd done it before, she looked wide-eyed in fear of the huge metal engine clanking and puffing noisily, the clamour of people in the station and the push and tussle to board and find their seats. He noticed the looks he was getting being a man alone with a child but kept his head down and his feet moving one in front of the other till the door of the carriage was closed behind them, the whistle blown and the 'chug, chug' of the train moving was a song in his ear as they started on the first stage of their journey home.

~

It was as well his mammy was still around and not such a devil as to disallow the wee one into her sight. In fact, she was the opposite after learning this was her granddaughter.

"Bejesus, she's the spit of you Patrick! How did you know? How did you find her? Where's her mammy?", she exclaimed, lifting a sleepy Therese from his cramped arms.

They'd just got in the door off the bus from Belfast and before that the crowded Derry boat from Glasgow. Much of the trip was a blur squashed up among so many others, since he hadn't wanted to hang around anywhere in case they were caught up with or noticed by the bobbies hanging around the Broomielaw Quay and especially the URC at the Lough in Belfast, his being a familiar face there for all the wrong reasons.

"Mammy, will ye give me a minute to get my coat off, so?" He was glad to be bringing good, if controversial, news for a change, since he'd put his mammy and daddy through the ringer those last years with all the IRA and prison debacles, he gotten himself into.

~

Paddy had joined his fellow IRA members in early 1916 after he crossed from Glasgow to Dublin to join the Kimmage Garrison on the outskirts of Dublin. As well as route marching and drills in the camp, the men made hand grenades and cartridges for shotguns. Paddy remembered removing the pellets in the cartridges and replacing them with lead balls. He also helped fellow Glasgow Volunteer Séumas Robinson, to heat the pike heads in a rivet fire and beat them to a sharp point. On Easter Sunday and every Volunteer in Kimmage carried a pike along with his rifle.

He remembered a feeling of pride about that. Some of the Volunteers had obtained work in local quarries where they obtained dynamite to make hand grenades and bombs, not to mention those being transported from Glasgow by women Volunteers from Cumann Na mBan.

It was recognised that of the ninety men at Kimmage, eighteen were from Glasgow. Paddy had recalled to Mary soon after that, "There was a general impression in our garrison from the time we left Scotland, that a fight was bound to come."

On Easter Monday, when the Rising began, he was part of a force that took over the GPO in Dublin's O'Connell Street. A number of the Glasgow and Liverpool Irish manned the bottom of Sackville Street at the bridge once the Rising had begun. He thought it would definitely have been a strange experience for native Dubliners to be chased off the bridge and quays by men with Glaswegian, Liverpudlian and Cockney accents.

On Easter Monday morning, the members of the Kimmage Garrison boarded a tram at Harold's Cross. At O'Connell Bridge, where they got off and marched to Liberty Hall then marched via Abbey Street into O'Connell Street accompanied by all of the General Headquarters Staff. No. 1 Company marched past the GPO, Nos 2 & 3 faced the GPO and No. 4 Company had taken up the rear. Those Volunteers were the first to enter the GPO building before Pádraig Pearse read the Proclamation of Independence at 12 noon and the Republic was proudly declared. Paddy had remained in the GPO throughout the week. By Friday, the building had caught fire and it became so hot that they were forced to evacuate. By Saturday April 29, much of central Dublin was in flames from attacks by British artillery. Forced to evacuate the GPO, Pádraig Pearse ordered a surrender. The first three Republican prisoners Pádraig Pearse, Thomas MacDonagh and Tom Clarke, were executed by the British government—being shot in the prison yard at Kilmainham Gaol on May 3rd.

After the surrender Paddy and his comrades were transported to Stafford Jail in England and then to Wormwood Scrubs where they were taken before an interrogation commission before being moved to Frongoch Camp in Wales. This internment, which resulted in its occupation by Irishmen, was very much a British own goal, just like those executions that immediately followed the 1916 Rising, because at Frongoch there were classes in everything including the new style of guerrilla warfare that ended up becoming the core tactic of the War of Independence. While many of the other internees had not participated in the 1916 Rising, or were not actively involved in the revolutionary movement, Paddy described a lot of their number in the Camp as either becoming political or being reinforced in their previous politics.

Paddy emphasised, "Discipline was strict and loyalty almost absolute." This was further confirmed when their captors began trying to isolate those internees who had previously lived in England with a view to conscripting them into the British Army. Paddy described the conditions there being tough and very insanitary, and the internees having a hard time of it from some of their captors. Paddy said he himself was released from Frongoch Internment Camp at

Christmas 1916 and he'd made his way back to Glasgow, and then living in the Springburn district. Patrick took the anti-treaty or Republican side in the Civil War.

His daddy had passed away while he was stuck on the *Argenta* and Paddy, having been promoted after his last mission to Commander of the 3rd Battalion, 2nd Northern Division of the IRA, had found himself imprisoned again.

He'd made a decision to return to what was now Northern Ireland since the treaty, but he'd been as determined about still fighting for the creation of a Republic rather than continue with having to kowtow to the British Monarchy plus he wanted to see his remaining family there. He knew Mary must have wondered if his leaving then had anything to do with her condition and the imminent, to his mind at that time in the middle of September in 1921, 'complication' due to appear in a couple of months? Either way by the end of May 1922 he'd been arrested. This time he was imprisoned in Belfast itself and on a ship. Under the 1922 Special Powers Act the British were detaining 263 men on the ship *Argenta*, which was moored in Belfast Lough. This was supplemented with internment at other land-based sites, such as Larne workhouse, Belfast Prison and Derry Gaol. Together, both the ship and the workhouse alone held 542 men without trial.[xliv]

Paddy had described conditions on the prison ship *Argenta* as "unbelievable" in his letters to Mary but could say little else until his return to Glasgow. After he went on a Hunger Strike involving upwards of 150 men in the winter of 1923 over their living conditions, he was released due to subsequent illness in December 1924, glad to no longer have to use broken toilets that overflowed frequently into communal areas. They'd been cloistered below decks in cages which held fifty internees to each cage. Being deprived of tables, already weakened men had to eat off the floor, frequently succumbing to disease and illness as a result.

He nevertheless, regretted not being able to share the arrival of his new daughter (even if five years late) with his father. He gulped down the rising lump as he retrieved Therese from his mammy. She had awakened more now and her wee face was white with the puzzlement of strange faces and different voices. During her first five years she'd have been surrounded by English Cockney accents. How much was she really able to understand them?

"Where's Ma Leeny, I want Ma Leeny!" She'd only done this once before on the boat halfway through their voyage but it had lasted a good twenty minutes and that really had him worried they'd get huckled on landing, but Therese had at last cried herself to sleep. Now she was wailing like a banshee once again and he let his mammy feed her a cup of warm milk not long out of the cow's udder, so creamy and comforting. Gladly, the surprise of the healthy beverage quietened her quicker than he'd managed on his own before.

The last twenty-four hours had made him wonder why he'd felt so indifferent when Mary had told him about the pregnancy. It wasn't that he hadn't wanted a family but with the dangerous activities that he'd committed to, it didn't feel fair to impose that life on Mary, though she'd have ben incensed at his presumption having been so fired up herself when involved with the Irish Women's Council.

Paddy set out to see the priest, very much with his mammy's encouragement, to have Therese baptised and though after some years living with his mammy (she loved the company after waiting so long for him to come back) He found a small cottage for them both and had her enrolled in the local school. He thought often about Mary but didn't hurry to write to her that he had Therese. Somehow, he had an unshakeable feeling they would see her again. He still felt guilty for leaving her in that predicament and didn't have any explanation other than his IRA involvement but now, taking care of and the love that had grown in him for Therese, he couldn't quite forgive himself and that guilt kept him quiet from across the ocean until years went by and Therese was before too long, too soon becoming a young woman who loved to dance and a regular participant and winner at the crossroad dances and, to his enormous chagrin, a favourite with the young bouchaleens.

Chapter 29-Homeward Bound - Mary

Mary had been experiencing the pull of home more strongly ever since that day she'd practically collapsed on the street. She was having to admit that moving across the ocean hadn't had the effect she 'd wanted or needed. Thoughts of Therese now never left her mind for a moment and resulted in her becoming too distracted to even contemplate how she would find work after she'd given up her job at Boston Maid. She soon left Franklin Square House too, a wrench after the many years there but her Aunt Rebecca had since passed away and she moved into the family home to help with funeral arrangements and look-out for the surviving family members after a request from Agatha, her cousin, who had over the years become a firm friend. She was one of the few who hadn't turned their back on Mary over her relationship with Petey and now she could use some help clearing the family home. Aunt Rebecca, despite her prejudice, had still thought to leave Mary a small inheritance of one hundred pounds and that there made all her excuses about ignoring the homeward call disappear.

She met with Petey in his cramped room for a final time once her decision was made. They'd had some good times over the years but he could never fill that hole in her soul. No-one ever could, except her daughter, though should they ever meet sometime it was as likely Mary would be dismissed out of turn for her abandonment of the child Therese was back then. She'd be a young girl of fourteen years old now;

wouldn't be a child much longer, and who may never have been made aware of her birth mother.

"I knew this time would come," Pete said while holding her hands in his. His tight curls were more salt than pepper these days and his silvering beard scratched her cheek when he bent to kiss her, tears moistening his eyes, but not falling. He had been born here, had his life here, their distance was not, had not, been only of her making. They'd both had to find ways to deal with the backlash of their joining within the cultural divide; the colour barrier that Boston so willingly upheld, which Mary couldn't then or even now comprehend and she wanted to say sorry, sorry for not being able to commit more fully, sorry in the end, for leaving him to deal with it all on his own.

"It's always been mine to deal with Mary, honey. Thank you for having the courage to face these years by my side, sweetie."

~

It was described as the devil's decade: ten grim years that opened with the Great Depression and ended with the outbreak of World War II. Arriving half way through amidst the grimness as a thirty-three-year-old spinster of questionable means; her decision to journey to what was now known as Northern Ireland, had been an impetuous one. The lack of support she remembered in Glasgow still stung and that abandonment left her without a home to return to. Family members remaining in Scotland by that time were only her eldest sister Nora, forty-eight years old now with, at last count, six children and brothers Patrick, who was forty and who'd married in '23, now having three kids and Seamus the second last born at thirty-seven, still on his own after losing his wife and daughter in child birth. Nora, being married to Victor and, from her last communication, still as blindly loyal as ever meant there was no offer of support which Mary wasn't too unhappy about since in any event, she simply couldn't face Victor's smarmy leer or slippery fingers.

Before she thought too much about it, Mary boarded the ferry to Londonderry at the Broomielaw after landing back. The 'Derry' or 'Scotch' boat, as it was known, was completely overcrowded. It was a rough old boat and the facilities were very poor for such a long overnight sail. There was a small hatch that acted as a bar that had a very long queue and quite a few drunks staggering about with the heave of the waves and the limited food available invariably adding to the stomach upsets.

Around her on-board, mothers were opening suitcases and placing their babies on top of the clothes to sleep. Children also lay sleeping on the floor with irate mothers trying to prevent the drunks lurching about from falling on top of them. The toilet basins were blocked with vomit, which sloshed from side to side with the boat's movement. Both the drunks and those without sea legs were the contributors to that.

The seating was timber-slatted benches and passengers had either to sleep across them if lucky, or choose the only alternative, which was the floor. There was a large open area on deck with a tarpaulin stretched over it that lent shelter to sleep under in case of bad weather. It was a long weary night, broken up for a short time by everyone having a sing-song up on the deck. And of course, her re-entry into the Irish Catholic way of living was heralded with, while the boat heaved, women on their knees saying the Rosary out loud in Gaelic and English, particularly around midnight when passing Paddy's Milestone at Ailsa Craig.

Strong smells of diesel and cattle permeated every corner of the ship and was another possible reason for the vomiting. Passenger comfort appeared to have been an alien concept to Burns & Laird who crammed passengers on board just like the cattle.

As she sat nearby listening to songs she'd thought long forgotten, her daughter and the question who in the end would have turned out to be her father turned over in her mind. She'd never known having, from society's perspective, been a: jezebel, trollop, slut, whore, etc., etc., or rather, been forced into one circumstance and seduced by her own fantasising in the other, both happening around the same period. Period, ha! That was the missing event that had shocked her into these circular circumstances, taking her round the world and back again. The boomerang effect of her unresolved past landing her just to the west of her physical beginnings but truly, smack bang at the creation of the family way. Sailing up the Foyle was something she would thereafter have great memories of after seeing the small boats and the green fields running into the Lough, everything so quiet and still in the early morning light.

The partition of Ireland, passed in 1920 as a temporary measure, had become a permanent feature of the political landscape in Ireland. But the existence of Northern Ireland was not accepted by all, particularly radical Republicans, and whom as part of Cumann Na mBan she'd supported, considered partition an illegal act forced on Ireland by an imperial power. Its creation had been accompanied by violence both in defense of and against partition. During the conflict of 1920–22, the capital Belfast saw major violence, mainly between Protestant unionist and Catholic nationalist civilians.More than 500 were killed and more than 10,000 became refugees, mostly Catholics, often burned out of their homes. She'd heard about the treatment of women who had still been supporting and fighting in their own way for the republic with just in 1933 alone, Sarah Grimley and Mary Donnelly, of Belfast Cumann Na mBan, receiving two and three-month jail sentences respectively for posting Republican literature in opposition to the visit of the Prince of Wales and Hanna Sheehy-Skeffington being arrested and imprisoned in Armagh for defying an exclusion order barring her from the six counties.[xlv]

As the largest city in Ulster, Belfast became the capital of Northern Ireland, and a grand parliament building was finished at Stormont Estate in 1932. The government was dominated by upper- and middle-class unionists. Being out of touch with the working class, they allowed many of the needs of low-income families to go unaddressed. Conditions in the poorer parts of Belfast remained bad; many houses were damp, overcrowded and lacked basic amenities such as hot water and indoor toilets. Mary had bypassed the city, wary of the growling undercurrent and the pull of defiance she felt in passing through on the rickety bus on her way further south to Enaghan townland in Fermanagh.

The farmhouse was looking its age though still well kept. Of the family there, her family, there was a medley of aunts, uncles, cousins and their children, who shied away when she was allowed entry into the large cottage. She had fought to still the trembling that had erupted as she was dropped off on the other side of the barn and walked slowly not knowing what would happen on knocking the door. The women of the house pulled her in in a welcome she hadn't been expecting, not sure if they knew about her pregnancy. Nora, being so worried about what people would think had more than likely kept it all a secret. Disappearing her daughter yet again. They showed her around explaining that they were usually responsible for the care of the small livestock, the poultry, pigs and calves and she was given the chore of feeding the pigs. "As long as yer here, so, acushla?"

Mary thought it was just as well there were several women of age to help, since there was also a vegetable garden and the growing of fruit to attend to. The men's work consisted of things like ploughing or winning the hay and working on the hill at the peat, depending on the season.

There was no running water or electricity, and the outdoor lavatory was not an overly pleasant surprise to Mary, though since the family had managed all these generations, why would she turn up her nose at its use, though she couldn't help covering it at the effluviant stench, even if not turning it up. Luckily one of the men's jobs, the burying of that waste, was part of the chores involved with nurturing the crops.

As in Scotland, around the whole of Britain and elsewhere, few women still worked outside the home. All was to continue to maintain what Mary had railed against; the subjugation of women into caring only for their husbands and children's needs.

Women living in the country like her aunts Catherine and Mary did, had to drag the cold water in from outside the house. For every basin of hot water needed, they had to lift a heavy kettle on and off the fire. On washing-day, washtubs had to be filled and emptied time and again. Mary wondered what it must cost in labour to keep all their churn and milk vessels clean. It all seemed such hard work and that was with the eight of them: three women, two men and three children living there when she arrived. The hard physical work and the fresh air had her falling into bed not long after dark and asleep instantly, only to rise early with the hens at daybreak when it was often not yet light. She'd been shown how to build the open fire properly and keep it lit, which looked grand and where lovely stews and the like came out of the pot-oven, but the truth was, as her Uncle bitterly complained, "Half the feckin heat's going right up the chimney!" while his wife Bridget by his side, also complained that the old pot-oven was unwieldy and clumsy and out of date, though she'd never countenance its replacement with a shiny new one. Then, when night fell in the country, like the Wise Virgin in the gospel Bridget or her daughters had to clean out, tend and fill the lamp before lighting it or else had to depend on their halfpenny dip.

~

Being there in the place her father was born made her think more about him than she had in years. She'd heard of his love for the place and his long search for a way to get the family out of Glasgow city and into the countryside. He'd managed it despite all her mammy's trials and her daddy's sacrifices, including his life; seeing as he died just four months after the family had made the move, he'd long craved.

She came to appreciate the similarities between the Scots and Fermanagh folk or just the whole historical connection of the Ulster-Scots in language and according to her namesake, auntie Mary, the origins from Co Antrim and Co Down, that weren't included in the Plantation of Ulster of 1610. By 1610 both counties were already predominantly Scottish. Before the Plantation of Ulster, and before the Flight of the Earls, two Ayrshire Scots - James Hamilton and Hugh Montgomery both from Ayrshire - pioneered the first large-scale settlement from the Lowlands of Scotland to those counties.

Beginning in May 1606, more than 10,000 Lowland Scots made a three-hour voyage across the North Channel, transforming infertile east Ulster into an industrial success.[xlvi] The Hamilton & Montgomery project was a settlement with a now centuries-old history that still strengthened the ongoing connections between generations in the two countries that she herself had benefited from.

She discovered that in the countryside, crossroads dancing was a frequent pastime and often a platform would be erected for this purpose. Mary visited one on a Sunday hoping to see some dancing, but was to be disappointed on that occasion. What she did find there were five youths sitting on a wall by the cross-roads, but there was not one girl. One boy had a fiddle, another a concertina. A number of girls eventually appeared on the scene, but unfortunately, they passed right on by, probably because the priest was right at their heels. "Girls, don't ye be stopping off here now. Off home to help yer mammies, will ye." Disappointed, the girls trudged on by and the boys, looking glum, packed up their musical instruments and departed; now having to wait till the arranged for dance the next weekend. At Mass on Sunday morning the next weekend, she had practically hidden behind her aunties as she skulked in the entrance and hurried hat on, head down to the pew where she stood and knelt at the wrong times, proving to the rest of the somewhat disapproving congregation just how long it had been since she'd gone to Mass.

At the 11am service on the next Saturday the chapel was buzzing with expectancy. The pulpit was often used to denounce immoral carryings-on and the priest again used his sermon time to highlight an alleged episode at a previous dance.

"I feel bound to mention a dance that took place in the parish very recently, and gave great scandal to the people of the town, so." he began, explaining that he'd heard that a young girl had to be carried drunk from the dance, and lifted onto a cart to get her home. The organisers of that evening's dance, took exception to the allegation and published a statement in the local paper, denouncing the claims as nothing but rumours, but the priests were determined and continued to object to any dances.

Still, the cross-dance went ahead, since being held outdoors usually earlier in the day wasn't considered quite so bad. Mary's aunties encouraged her to go along with them to it on the next evening it took place and it was a full-blown family affair. Crossroad dances were generally for set dancing or solo dancing. They were usually held on Sunday evenings in summer when young people would gather. The music was performed by a fiddler seated on a three-legged stool with his upturned hat beside him for a collection. He began with a lively reel but had to play it several times before dancers got up the courage to join in. The young men were reluctant to begin the dance but after some encouragement from the fiddler, the sets of eight filled up the dancing area and everyone was enjoying the open air, scenery and the music while some were huddled in small groups watching out for the Catholic clergy, who had been campaigning for years claiming that dancing led to sin and corruption. Some priests had taken to patrolling the ditches keeping an eye out for any courting couples who might be having a few quiet minutes together.

As Mary looked around at the happy smiling faces feeling relieved the heavy work was done until the next morning, she noticed a familiar figure with their arm around the shoulder of a young girl dressed in her dance outfit. Mary had a strong notion she knew the person, the man with his back to her. She saw her aunts flicking glances her way then looking in the same direction she was. She was puzzled, couldn't figure out why and when she looked across to the man and girl then back to her aunt, she saw her aunt looking, no staring straight at her, nodding at Mary. She made to stand just as the man turned to face her and suddenly, she realised who it was. Paddy, looking greyer, but the soft gaze he was resting on the face of the young girl made the years drop away from his face. Mary turned her attention to the young girl who must have been no more than thirteen or fourteen and again she was struck by a sense of déjà vu. How could she know the girl and what was Paddy doing here - with her? She couldn't resist approaching them, calling Paddy's name as she crossed in front of her aunt, who nodding urgently said, "Mary, go on, go on, acushla." Mary reached them both and then she knew. Therese wasn't lost anymore.

THE END

GLOSSARY

Achora – my love (Irish)

Acushla – darling (Irish)

Ae – of (Scots)

Afeared – afraid (Irish)

Anither – another (Scots)

Ayeways – always

Bairn – child (Scots etc.)

The Barras – Barrowland Marketplace(Glasgow)

Barm – roll (Mancunian)

Blether – chat (Scots)

Bouchaleen – young boy (Irish)

Caw – turn (the rope) (Scots)

Childer – children (Irish)

Colleen – young girl (Irish)

The Craic – news/gossip (Irish)

Destroyed - worn out (Irish)

Dinnae fash yersel - Don't worry yourself (Scots/French)

Dinnae - Don't (Scots)

Dreich – Wet, gloomy (Scots)

Eejit - swear word/insult (Irish)

Feart –scared (Scots)

Fierce - very (Irish)

Fellah – fellow, man (Irish)

Fettled – fixed (Mancunian)

Gaun – going (Scots)

Glaikit – senseless (Scots)

Gobshite - swear word/insult (Irish)

Grand - great (Irish)

Hankerchy – handkerchief (Irish)

Hen – dearest (Scots)

High heid yins – the authorities/superiors (Scots)

Hivnae – haven't (Scots)

Knock your pan in – tire yourself out (Scots)

Maws – mothers (Scots)

Melted – exhausted (Irish)

Mither – make a fuss/moan (Mancunian)

Numpty – Idiot (Scots)

Oul—old (Irish)

Pit – bed (Scots)

Poteen – home-brewed whiskey (Irish)

Praties/tatties - potatoes (Irish)

'Scalp' – lean to/shelter (Irish)

yer scratcher – your bed (Scots)

Simmet - undergarment /vest (Scots)

Slinkeen – insult (Irish)

Sousider – Resident of the Southside of Glasgow (Scots)

Steamie – washhouse (Scots)

Tae – to (Scots)

Wae – with (Scots)

Wan – one (Scots)

Wee – small (Scots/Irish)

Ya – you (Irish)

Ye – you (Scots/Irish)

Ye's – yous (Scots)

Yin – one (Irish)

Yis – yous (Irish)

BIBLIOGRAPHY

1. Doing my Bit for Ireland, Margaret Skinnider, Aug 1916

2. Ireland's Unfinished Revolution: An Oral History, Kenneth Griffith/Timothy O'Grady 1999, Roberts Rinehart Pub, Colorado

3. Materia Medica of Homeopathic Remedies, Dr. S. R Phatak, B.Jain Pub, New Delhi,1982

4. Relationship of Remedies, Dr R. Gibson Miller, Homeopathic Books Co. Glasgow,1900

5. Regeneration, Pat Barker, 1991, Penguin Books Ltd, London, 2011

6. Repertory of the Homeopathic Materia Medica, J. T. Kent, Publisher: B Jain Publishers Pvt Ltd (IND) 1991

7. Republican Internment and the Prison Ship "Argenta", 1922: S.S. Argenta Legacies, Denise Kleinrichert[1], 2001, Irish Academic Press, Dublin, Ireland

8. Shellshock in France 1914-1918, Charles S. Myers 1940, Cambridge University Press, UK, 2011

---

1. https://www.abebooks.co.uk/servlet/
SearchResults?an=denise%20kleinrichert&cm_sp=det-_-plp-_-author

9. The Irish Famine, Peter Gray, Thames & Hudson Ltd, London,1997

10. The Long Weekend: A Social history of Great Britain 1918-1939, Robert Graves & Alan Hodge, Hutchinson & Co. London, 1985.

11. The Scottish Railway Strike 1891, A HISTORY AND CRITICISM by James Mayor, Professor of Political Economy & Statistics, St Mungo's College, Glasgow; Pub. William Brown 26 Princes Street Edinburgh 1891

HOMEOPATHIC REMEDIES in the book

Aconite
    Anacardium
    Arnica
    Baptisia
    Bryonia
    China
    Gelsemium
    Kali Carb
    Kali Phos
    Phosphorus
    Sepia
    Staphisagria

ENDNOTES

CHAPTER 6

---

[i] Members of the 'Invincibles', an extremist element within the 'Fenian' movement had assassinated the Irish Chief Secretary and his deputy in an attack in the Phoenix Park in Dublin 6 May 1882. Ref: https://www.theirishstory.com/2012/07/31/the-invincibles-and-the-phoenix-park-killings-2/#.Y-lghnbP2Uk

[ii] In 1885, a railway bridge had been built across the Forth to the west of Alloa that aided in moving exports and gave better access to Stirling and other parts of the country. Ref:https://en.wikipedia.org/wiki/Alloa_Swing_Bridge#:~:text=The%20Alloa%20Swing%20Bridge%20was,use%2

CHAPTER 7

[iii] They'd said 1475 men out of 2100 attended and voted at various meetings. Six hundred voted for the proposal to give a week's notice at once, and eight hundred and seventy-five to abide by the decision of the Executive not to strike until the resignations justified that kind of action. Ref: The Scottish Railway Strike 1891, A HISTORY AND CRITICISM by James Mayor, Professor of Political Economy & Statistics, St Mungo's college, Glasgow; Pub. William Brown 26 Princes Street Edinburgh 1891

[iv] By Sunday night, 21st December, throughout Scotland there were upwards of 3,000 men on strike. On Monday, 22nd, there were 4,000; on 23rd, 5,000 to 6,000; and by Christmas Day 8,500 to 9,000. Ref: Ibid. James Mayor

[v] At the works of the Singer Company at Kilbowie on the Clyde, more than 5,000 people were thrown out of work straight away, due to the North British Railway Company being unable to run the usual

special trains from Glasgow to transport them to and from work. Ref: Ibid. James Mayor

[vi] In the 1880s, proponents of British rule over Ireland were said to condescendingly attribute the Irish people's so-called depravity of character to their second helping of original sin. Ref: https://slife.org/irish-proverbs/

CHAPTER 13

[vii] http://www.homeoint.org/morrell/glasgow/foreword.htm

[viii] James Tyler Kent was an American physician best known as a forefather of modern homeopathy and who in 1897, published, with the help of his third wife and fellow homeopath, Clara Louis Tobey, his magnum opus and the first invaluable guidebook on human physical and mental disease symptoms and their associated scientific homeopathic preparations entitled *Repertory of the Homeopathic Materia Medica*

[ix] The two volume *A Treatise of the Materia Medica (1789)* written by William Cullen of Hamilton, which claim by Cullen was that Cinchona, the bark of a Peruvian tree, was effective in treating malaria because of its astringency and challenged by Hahnemann.

[x] The dose and potency chosen is based on several factor's including: the severity of the individual's condition, their constitution, their levels of energy and the remedy prescribed. https://medical-dictionary.thefreedictionary.com/law+of+minimum+dose

CHAPTER 14

[xi] Noted were over 800 hygiene defects and 207 cases of overcrowding in the streets concerned. https://royalsocietypublishing.org/doi/10.1098/rsos.181695

[xii] The identification of it would result from noting the characteristic signs among all of the symptoms after studying several cases in an epidemic. There are usually various medicines identified but often one is indicated more than the others. https://www.researchgate.net/publication/331637947_Research_Review_of_Genus_Epidemicus

[xiii] https://ivcjournal.com/homeopathy-epidemics/

CHAPTER 16

[xiv]　https://www.scotsman.com/sport/football/day-1902-first-ibrox-disaster-1452411

CHAPTER 17

[xv] Historically thought to have been introduced by Protestant plantation owners. https://tywkiwdbi.blogspot.com/2013/11/these-are-left-footed-spades.html

[xvi] Within less than a year of the German doctor's accidental discovery, a Scot, John Macintyre, had established the world's the first radiology department at the Glasgow Royal Infirmary in 1896, boasting pictures of kidney stones, and included one of a penny that was lodged in a young child's throat. https://www.gla.ac.uk/schools/medicine/mus/ourfacilities/history/20thcentury/1948-2018/radiology/

[xvii] https://www.britanniapanopticon.org/history

CHAPTER 18

[xviii] From the Greek *coma* (long hair) because the ancients likened the glowing tail to a woman's flowing hair. https://en.wikipedia.org/wiki/Comet#Etymology

[xix] https://allthatsinteresting.com/halleys-comet-1910

[xx]　https://books.openedition.org/pufc/38795?lang=en　Mill Strike

[xxi] Officially, The Prisoners (Temporary Discharge for Ill Health) Act 1913

[xxii]　　　http://www.greatwar.co.uk/ypres-salient/town-ieper-history-1418.htm

CHAPTER 20

[xxiii]　　　https://www.researchgate.net/publication/343842641_Homoeopathy_in_pandemic_Spanish_flu_1918

[xxiv]　https://www.bmj.com/rapid-response/2011/11/02/aspirin-may-be-enhancer-virulence-1918-pandemic

CHAPTER 21

[xxv] https://tour-scotland-photographs.blogspot.com/2015/11/old-photograph-cowdonhall-hospital.html

[xxvi] Torpillage or 'torpedoing' was a term previously chosen by soldiers in France who have received the electric current treatment because they likened the electric part of the therapy to being hit by a shell or 'une torpille'. https://www.researchgate.net/publication/45275317_The_torpillage_neurologists_of_World_War_I_Electric_thera

[xxvii] https://www.sueyounghistories.com/2008-06-21-john-weir-and-homeopathy/

[xxviii] Shell-shock in First World War Britain: an intellectual and medical history, c. 1860-c. 1920. Tracey Louise Loughran https://core.ac.uk/download/pdf/30695926.pdf

[xxix] 'Dottyville'—Craiglockhart War Hospital and shell-shock treatment in the First World War
https://www.ncbi.nlm.nih.gov/pmc/articles/PMC1484566/

[xxx] Ibid. Tracey Louise Loughran https://core.ac.uk/download/pdf/30695926.pdf

CHAPTER 22

[xxxii] Republican Internment and the Prison Ship "Argenta", 1922: S.S. Argenta Legacies, Denise Kleinrichert[2], 2001, Irish Academic Press, Dublin, Ireland

[xxxiii] Among those deported and interned were Pidge Duggan (164 days), Molly Duffy (200 days), Lizzie Morrin (period unknown) and Mary Nelson (208 days). https://www.theirishstory.com/the-irish-story-easter-rising-1916-archive/

[xxxiv] Ref: https://www.baus.org.uk/museum/111/st_phillips_hospital_london

[xxxv] Ibid https://www.baus.org.uk/museum/111/st_phillips_hospital_london

---

2. https://www.abebooks.co.uk/servlet/
SearchResults?an=denise%20kleinrichert&cm_sp=det-_-plp-_-author

[xxxvi] Doctor Arthur Newsholme, (Local Government Board Medical Officer for the Poor Law and during 1918 Influenza Pandemic) and Doctor (later Dame) Janet Campbell, (Chief Woman Medical Adviser to the Board of Education) and by the campaign literature of women's groups, including the Women's Co-operative Guild, the Women's Labour League and their representatives, including Margaret Llewelyn Davies, Sylvia Pankhurst and Gertrude Tuckwel1. Ref: https://en.wikipedia.org/wiki/Janet_Mary_Campbell

CHAPTER 24

[xxxvii] William Leonard, "'Black and Irish Relations in 19th Century Boston: The Interesting Case Lawyer Robert Morris" Historical Journal of Massachusetts Volume 37, No. 1 (Spring 2009)

[xxxviii] https://www.bu.edu/sph/news/articles/2019/they-dont-make-buildings-like-this-anymore/

[xxxix] Commercial FM radio station in Cambridge, Massachusetts. It broadcasts at 95.3 MHz and is operated by students at Harvard College.

[xl] Supporters also included politicians e.g. William Lloyd Garrison and Zabina Eastman (abolitionists), Susan B Anthony and Elizabeth Cady Stanton (feminists), and even presidents of the United States such as James A. Garfield and William McKinley.

[xli] Clark Warburton, The Economic Results of Prohibition (New York: Columbia University Press, 1932); Irving Fisher, Prohibition at Its Worst (New York: Alcohol Information Committee, 1927).

[xlii] https://theconversation.com/the-hidden-story-of-when-two-black-college-students-were-tarred-and-feathered-147895

CHAPTER 25

[xliii] The Flexner Report was an evaluation of American medical schools chaired by Abraham Flexner, in cooperation with leading members of the A.M.A. the Carnegies and Rockafellas. As a result of the report, only pharmaceuticals drugs were allowed to be used, and only graduates of those schools which received a high rating were allowed to take medical licensing exams. There were 22 homeopathic colleges in 1900, but only two remained in 1923. These schools were not the only

ones hurt by the Flexner Report. Of the seven black medical schools, only two survived. The Report also contributed to a 33% reduction in women being graduated from medical schools. https://www.ncbi.nlm.nih.gov/pmc/articles/PMC3543812/

[xliv] Republican Internment and the Prison Ship "Argenta", 1922: S.S. Argenta Legacies, Denise Kleinrichert[3], 2001, Irish Academic Press, Dublin, Ireland

CHAPTER 26

[xlv] https://www.acenturyofwomen.com/1930s/

[xlvi] https://m.belfasttelegraph.co.uk/news/dawn-of-the-ulster-scots/28103898.html

---

3. https://www.abebooks.co.uk/servlet/
    SearchResults?an=denise%20kleinrichert&cm_sp=det-_-plp-_-author

Milton Keynes UK
Ingram Content Group UK Ltd.
UKHW010637271123
433341UK00005B/544